My Fabulous Divorce

Also by Clare Dowling

Expecting Emily
Amazing Grace

My Fabulous Divorce

Clare Dowling

headline
review

First published in 2006 by HEADLINE REVIEW
An imprint of HEADLINE BOOK PUBLISHING

1

Cataloguing in Publication Data is
available from the British Library

ISBN 0 7553 2842 6 (hardback)
ISBN 0 7553 2843 4 (trade paperback)

Typeset in Bembo by Palimpsest Book Production Limited,
Polmont, Stirlingshire

Printed and bound in Great Britain by
Clays Ltd, St Ives plc

Headline's policy is to use papers that are natural, renewable and
recyclable products and made from wood grown in sustainable
forests. The logging and manufacturing processes are expected
to conform to the environmental regulations of the country of origin.

HEADLINE BOOK PUBLISHING
A division of Hodder Headline
338 Euston Road
London NW1 3BH

www.reviewbooks.co.uk
www.hodderheadline.com

For Mum

ACKNOWLEDGEMENTS

Very special thanks to Sean, Ella and Stewart for breaking up my working day, even if I wished it hadn't been quite so often. Thanks to Clare Foss for her encouragement, guidance and tips on how to manage unruly offspring. Thanks to Darley Anderson and all at the agency. Thanks to Donal Blake for coming up with a great title, even if I didn't use it in the end. Thanks to Sarah Webb and all the Irish Girls – it's good to know you're not alone. And a big thanks to Pamela for reading almost every book published, and for liking mine the best!

Chapter One

Jackie was late to meet Dan. She had a suspicion it was their six-month anniversary too, and wished she had taken the time to check. But it had been so busy in the shop today. And Lech, the delivery guy, had mixed up the orders again, and dropped off a bouquet of red roses with a jaunty card reading 'I Love You!' to a lady who had just yesterday passed away. The wreath, meanwhile, had arrived at the lunch table of a young couple on their third date. Well, you can imagine. Jackie had had to put him on probation, which was a terrible shame but what could she do? Flower Power was only just starting to turn a profit and she couldn't afford mistakes like that.

Anyhow. She fanned her face and hurried along, or at least as fast as she could in her new red boots. Oh, she *knew* she shouldn't have; red wasn't even her colour. And the heels were far too high – a gust of wind at lunchtime had almost blown her over – but when she'd seen them in the shop window they had reminded her of something that a sassy, sexy career woman would wear. Or a streetwalker, possibly.

She looked down at them doubtfully. Still, she could be forgiven. After all, she was a beginner really, just growing into the role of businesswoman and not quite there yet. Her wardrobe would catch up eventually, she was sure. The customers didn't seem put off in any case; they knew that when they bought a bouquet they were paying for a lot more than just flowers, and she wouldn't insult them by showing up in a navy pinafore and Ecco shoes.

There was Dan! Sitting at their favourite window table in Le Bistro. She felt a little rush to her stomach. He saw her too, and his big, brown, steady face lifted, and she felt so happy that there was someone in the world whose whole evening grew better just upon seeing her that she had a ridiculous urge to burst into song. 'The Hills Are Alive With The Sound of Music', to be specific. She had never told Dan about this. She had learned that it was better not to reveal every last tiny scrap of your heart and soul to men. As if they gave you half as much back! No, Jackie had developed a small solid core inside, which was aloof and untouchable and hers alone.

She waited for a suitable break in the traffic before making a dash for it. In the window, Dan grimaced. For some reason he found it difficult to watch her crossing roads, or making fruit smoothies with her blender.

She pushed open the restaurant door, and waved across at Fabien, the owner.

'Bonsoir!' she said, as usual. 'Ça va?'

'Bien, bien,' said Fabien, very resigned. Occasionally, he tried to speak to her in English, but she was determined to do her bit for Irish–French relations and so they had been stuck on the same two sentences for a couple of years now.

Dan rose to greet her. She noted sadly that he was more dressed up than usual. There was a telltale bulge in his jacket pocket too: he had probably bought her a six-month anniversary present, which would just make her feel worse.

'Hi,' he said, bending down to kiss her. He was six foot seven and had thighs like giant chicken drumsticks. But he wasn't big in a *freaky* way, she would hastily add when describing him to her friends. None of them had met him. No, he was more like an action hero; he'd played club rugby, for goodness' sake, until a couple of compound fractures and a burst pancreas had finally driven him off the pitch. 'When can we meet him?' everyone had demanded. 'Soon,' Jackie always said, but never arranged anything.

Tonight he was all keyed up. He tapped his fingers on the menu and shifted about in his chair.

'So!' he said.

She might as well come clean. 'Dan, I forgot, OK? I'm sorry. But

2

I've had such a hectic week . . . I'll make it up to you. I swear. We'll go to Paris next weekend, how about that? Just the two of us.' Emma would go mad. She was in charge of the work roster and was always accusing Jackie of taking off just like that. And after working a seventy-hour week last week! But of course Emma didn't have any use for men at all, and hadn't been out with one since 1998, and didn't understand about romantic dinners and dirty weekends away.

Now that Jackie thought about it, she really couldn't go to Paris next weekend. They had a wedding booked and Emma insisted she just didn't have Jackie's flair.

'Unless, of course, you're busy,' she said to Dan, hopefully. Usually there was something mucky going on at the weekends involving pitches and balls.

Dan said, delicately, 'Why Paris? Not that I'm knocking it.'

'Well, to celebrate our six-month anniversary.'

'Oh,' he said.

She knew from his expression that she had made a fool of herself, or was just about to. But there was no place left to go but onwards. 'Have I got the date wrong?'

He thought for a moment before admitting, 'Technically, it was actually Wednesday.'

'I see! Well. There you go.' So much for Paris. They hadn't even gone out on Wednesday night. He had wanted to watch a TV documentary on elections in Cuba; not even on the making of a porn movie or anything like that.

'Sorry, Jackie.'

'It's fine.'

She dived into her menu, feeling presumptuous and exposed. And to think that only a moment ago she had prided herself upon learning her lessons! So pious and smug, sure that no man would ever get the better of her again. What about all those nights spent crying into her wine, raking over all the mistakes she'd made, and vowing never to repeat them again? And here she was, right back where she started. In fact, she wondered whether she was actually regressing. The thought was so depressing that she thought she might go for the broccoli and three cheeses soufflé, and to hell with the calories.

'It's not fine,' Dan fretted. Look at him now, trying to take her hand, sucking up to her. 'It's just, it's hard to believe that it's a whole six months since your back tyre blew out.'

It was hardly the most romantic start to a relationship. There she'd been, stranded on the M50 in the depths of winter with five dozen carnations on the back seat rapidly going off. Dan had jogged out of the darkness like some golden-haired hero, gleaming with sweat, and wearing the tightest, shiniest shorts she had ever seen, the kind they had stopped making back in the eighties. He had told her he was handy with a car jack. She had lied that she was too, just in case he'd thought it was a rescue-a-damsel job. Then they discovered that she didn't have a spare in the boot anyhow, and they'd waited in the dark for the tow truck to arrive, him kind of folded over in the cramped passenger seat and her twiddling nervously with the gear stick, only to realise that it was actually his knee.

He had spared her blushes by pretending to sneeze. Several times. Then his eyes had swelled up rapidly and he'd said in an odd, choking voice, 'You wouldn't happen to have flowers in the car, by any chance? It's just that I'm allergic.'

He'd asked her out in Casualty, once they'd given him a steroid shot and he could breathe again.

'Is it wise?' she'd said. 'I'm a florist.'

'So what? I'm a business banking manager,' he'd offered bravely. 'I go into client meetings and I bang the table and I say things like, "Your commercial interests grew by one hundred per cent in the last six months alone!" I bet you won't go out with me now.'

'Why wouldn't I?' she'd said, buying time. It was one of her new rules: prevaricate, instead of launching herself like a half-starved puppy at the first decent man who asked her out on a date. Sometimes it made her feel a bit false, but then she looked upon it as a necessary defensive mechanism; the toughening up of Jackie Ball.

'I don't know,' he said. 'I have a feeling I might be too boring for you.'

'I'm sure you're not,' she said, even though she had her doubts.

'No, no, you have no idea how much mileage I'll get out of this – how-I-ended-up-in-hospital-with-a-flower-allergy. I'll be telling it for *years*. That's how boring I am.'

She should have said no. What about all that time spent building up a solid core? But she could still go out with him and not let him near it, a little voice in her head whispered. And, frankly, she was sick of being good and pure and abstemious, and he had the kind of great, big, muscly arms that were meant for hugs. So she'd let her heart rule her head – again – and she had thrown a vicious look over at a staff nurse who had been inching forwards hopefully, and announced, 'I'll cook.'

And suddenly there they were, six months into the whole thing. Not that anyone was marking the date, it seemed, except her.

But Dan had had a chance to think about things, and he said now, 'You didn't remember it either. In fact, you came in here tonight and started apologising about how *you'd* forgotten it.'

'I didn't say—'

'You said your week had been too hectic. That you'd try to make it up to me, like I'm some kind of inconvenience. My God, you tried to palm me off with Paris!'

'Stop twisting the whole thing!'

'Not even Vienna!' he huffed. *'Paris.'*

Her cheeks felt hot. They'd never had a big, proper row before. In fact, they'd scarcely had a disagreement. Sometimes she thought they were a bit like a couple from a Daz commercial, all toothy smiles and hugs and romping happily through the surf. But wasn't that one of the things that had attracted her to him? The sheer comfort of the whole thing? She knew exactly where she stood with Dan; there would be no false expectations and bitter disappointments.

But tonight the gloves were off. Perhaps this was what they needed. Shake them up a bit. See what they were made of. So she counter-attacked with, 'At least I tried to make it up to you! You weren't even going to bother!'

'I was, actually,' he retaliated.

'How?' she demanded. Let him try and top Paris.

'I was going to ask you to marry me.'

For a moment she almost looked around, wondering if Fabien was having a little joke. But it was Dan all right.

'What?' she said.

'I had *planned* to go down on one knee, and do it all romantically and properly,' he said, crossly. Then he seemed to remember the occasion, and he sat up a bit straighter and cleared his throat portentously, and asked, 'Jackie Ball, will you do me the honour of marrying me?'

'Well, I . . . this is quite a surprise, Dan.' To say the very least. Getting married right now was the last thing on her mind. The very furthest thing, in fact. More remote than the idea of some day landing on the moon and opening a new branch of Flower Power.

'I suppose,' he said, obviously reconciling fast to the fact that she wasn't going to scream with joy and leap over the table at him. 'Look, I know exactly what you're thinking. You're thinking, it's way too soon. You're thinking, I hardly know this guy! He takes me out on lousy dates to rugby matches in the rain, and thinks I want to spend the rest of my life with him? He doesn't even mark our six-month anniversary, and expects a yes? And his feet stink to high heaven!' He paused for a moment. 'Hang on, this isn't going the way I planned.'

'Dan—'

'On the plus side,' he went on, 'the rugby season doesn't last all year. Barely six months, in fact. Other positives include,' and he started ticking off on his fingers, 'I have a job, a car, a house, a pension – did I send that form back? – and most of my hair, and I will promise to love, honour and obey you for as long as we both shall live. And give you possession of the TV remote control. How's that for a deal?'

'Oh, Dan.'

'I don't like the way you say that. Like you're gearing yourself up to let me down.'

'I'm not.'

'You're not going to let me down? Or you're not going to marry me? Go on, give it to me straight, I can handle it. Just there.' He pointed to a spot on the tip of his very square, very broad chin.

'Oh, Dan.'

'You're saying it again!'

She took a breath. 'It's just, marriage is a very big step, you know?' Another cheap ploy to buy herself time. Really, she was a despicable creature. Beneath contempt! But she hadn't known he was going to ask her to marry him! She had thought . . . well, what *had* she thought? It had been obvious from about two weeks in that this was going to be more than just dinner. On his side, anyhow; she was old enough to see the signs. There was very little use now bleating about solid untouchable cores when she hadn't even been honest with him.

Dan didn't notice her guilt. 'Jackie, I'm thirty-six years old. I want to settle down with the right person. I want to buy a semi-detached house in suburbia and convert the attic into a playroom. I want to trade in my BMW for a people carrier – stop sniggering – and have a boy and a girl, and if I still have the energy, maybe a dog too. I'll call him Biff, or maybe Edward.'

'You'd name your dog before you'd name your children?'

'So you've agreed to children?'

'I've agreed to nothing!' But when he laid it out like that for her, it all sounded so reasonable. So attractive and complete, like one of those 'packages' that he was forever putting together for work. And he was offering her the whole thing, no expense spared, and with a dog thrown in for good measure. How could anybody, at least of her age, resist?

But she said, 'Dan, there's something you don't know about me.'

'I'm sure there is,' he said. 'There are things you don't know about me either. We all have our dirty little secrets from the past.' And he gazed wistfully at some point above her head.

'Dan, I'm serious.'

'Monsieur? Mademoiselle?' Fabien was at their table, bearing champagne on ice. 'May I be the first to offer my congratulations.' He looked slightly embarrassed in the role of romantic host and gave a kind of a cough.

'Too soon,' Dan hissed, waving him away. Fabien retreated fast, looking at Jackie as though she were mad for not clinching the deal while she could. Even he knew nothing better was ever going to come her way.

There was a little silence after he'd gone, like the fizz had gone out of everything.

Dan said, 'Look, Jackie, I know that you've been hurt before, OK? It doesn't take a genius to work it out. The way you get all kind of prickly sometimes and cross your arms over your chest, you're doing it right now, and that's OK, you know? People get hurt. *I've* been hurt. I've been dumped on holiday, for goodness' sake. I'm not naming names but she knows who she is. Took me months to get over that.' She knew he was exaggerating a bit. He really was sweet. 'But, you know, we're together now. Whatever about the kids or the house – maybe you don't want kids, or a house, maybe you want to live on a boat, well, let's talk about that later. The point is, I love you. I've never met anyone like you. And I think we'd have a really good future together. If you want to.'

'I *do* . . .'

'So is that a yes?'

'Well, yes, I suppose.'

'You just said yes.'

'Yes. I know I did.'

'I got a yes! She said yes!'

'But Dan—'

'I don't want to hear any more buts. I officially declare all buts saved till the morning.' And he leaned over and kissed her, and Jackie felt everything in her life shift a tiny bit and slip firmly into place. Oh Lord. She was going to *settle down*. With a man called Dan. What was more, she welcomed it! Absolutely. She was through with unreliable men.

Impulsively, and to kind of put a seal on things, she declared loudly, 'I love you, Dan Lewis, and I don't care who hears me!'

Nobody did, actually; everyone was too busy forking in big plates of food to notice the little drama at the window table. Fabien had been keeping an eye on things, however, and he went scurrying off to the kitchen to retrieve the champagne.

'I hope this fits.' Dan produced a ring then, and Jackie drew in her breath. It was a serious ring, unhampered by fun or fashion, just five fat diamonds set high and proud. It would make all her other jewellery look like it had come from a lucky bag, which some of it had, but oh, she didn't care.

'Don't even start about how much it must have cost me, OK?' he said. 'Number one, it hurts to think about it, and number two, you're worth every cent.'

Now she was in tears. She'd always been able to cry with great abandon (after Dr Green's death in *ER* she had become slightly dehydrated) but not usually tears of joy. Not recently, anyhow.

'You'll set me off in a minute.' But anyone could see he was pleased as Punch.

She would do the flowers for the wedding, of course. Red and white roses everywhere, even her bouquet! Or would that be too much? She wanted to suggest passion, not a bloodbath. But she didn't think she could confine herself to plain white roses, or freesias maybe, in yellow or pink, which she often advised. 'Keep it simple and you can't go wrong,' she would assure nervous brides. As if she ever followed her own advice. She was thinking daisies now, hundreds and hundreds of them, maybe even scattered underfoot.

But Dan was allergic. Blast. She would be a florist with no flowers at her own wedding. She'd have to make some out of crêpe paper, like you see on Barney videos.

'Let's set a date,' Dan said.

'A date?'

'That's the usual procedure, Jackie.'

'No, I know, it's just . . . I thought we were going to enjoy the moment first.' And she tickled the underside of his wrist in a way that usually made him giggle.

But he wasn't to be distracted. 'I don't want one of those big long engagements.'

'No.'

'One of my aunts was engaged for nineteen years.'

'Well, that's just ridiculous.'

'Then let's say three months from now,' he declared.

She did a quick calculation in her head. It was completely impossible. But she said, 'Agreed!'

The romance of the evening made them bold and they skipped dinner and rushed from Le Bistro and into bed, where Dan roundly trounced all previous records, and then flopped onto his back as happy as a puppy dog. She was unsure whether to applaud him or not.

'Next time keep those hooker boots on,' he said sleepily, snuggling into her shoulder.

She waited until he was snoring. Then she lifted his arm and scuttled out of the bed. Downstairs, she shut the living room door quietly and tiptoed to the desk in the corner. It was only then that she realised she had forgotten the telephone number. Imagine! And she could picture so clearly the telephone: a black modern cordless affair, shaped closely along the lines of a large willy, with hundreds of important-looking buttons and a built-in answering machine. When you were finished using it, you could slide it back into its base – an attractive, deep, accommodating snug cradle that gave an excited little beep upon contact.

The effect of all this testosterone-inspired technology was quite spoiled by a large, rather tacky picture of the Sacred Heart hanging over the phone table. For it had been her house too; still *was* her house, or at least half of it, even though she had stopped going to Mass years ago and found herself unable to remember the telephone number. Could it be some sly trick on the part of her subconscious, to blot him out? But no. It was unlikely her subconscious had a sense of humour, and besides, she could hardly remember her current telephone number, never mind one she had left behind eighteen months ago.

Then it came to her in a flash. It had three sixes in it: the number of the devil. He had laughed at her superstition at the time. And look how well-founded it had been! Now she would have to talk to him, to explain herself. And she always got so tongue-tied under stress! Whereas he, on the other hand, was a man whose temperature never rose above ninety, and who had an armoury of quips and put-downs for every available occasion. What would he say to her news? After he had stopped laughing, that was.

She could just hear him now. He would most likely call it an act of supreme impetuosity. Or impulsiveness. Or any of those other *i* words he had routinely used in relation to her. Well, she had a few for him too. Most of them began with an *f.* Look at her; she was all hot and bothered now. She reminded herself that she must be careful not to let herself get irritated or riled up in any way, and Lord knows that would be easy enough. She mustn't rise to any bait. Also, she should guard against getting involved in blame. Apart from anything else, it tended to send her voice, already high-pitched, off the Richter scale. All it took then was for her hair to break loose from its clip, which it nearly always did, and her metamorphosis into a squeaking, shrieking witch was complete. 'Calm *down*, Jackie,' he would say, in that infuriating way that would make her want to apply a frying pan to his head.

At least she had the advantage of surprise. She took a moment to run through a few openers in her head. 'Hi there, Henry! It's Jackie!' No. She despised him, for God's sake. Maybe something more sombre:

'I think you know what this is about. Unfinished business.' But he'd just crack up laughing at that.

In the end she lifted the telephone receiver and dialled very fast. It began to ring at the other end in the home they'd shared in London. At least, *she* had tried to make it a home, with her tea cosies and ethnic cushions and a wonderful floor rug that she had bought at the market, and that clashed wildly with Henry's colour scheme. As for Henry, he had just carried on as usual, except to complain about her clutter and mess. She had learned early on that he was self-sufficient that way. He didn't seem to need things, not the way she did.

But then why would he bother being homely? After all, in his head he had always remained gloriously free and single.

She supposed he had quickly restored the place after she had gone. It would be male, spare, stale. He wouldn't have opened a window in months and unsuspecting visitors would fall to the ground in an oxygen-deprived dead faint. The lid on the toilet seat would resume its rightful position, which was permanently up, and he would have plonked the TV back in the centre of the room. All would be well with the world.

'Hello?' It was him. He always answered the phone as if he expected it to be someone trying to sell him double-glazing.

It must have been the shock of hearing his voice after eighteen months, because her rehearsed speech immediately flew out of her head. Her tongue was so dry that she had to unpeel it from the roof of her mouth, before blurting thickly, 'Henry! Um, hi, it's Jackie here.' Then, not wanting to appear presumptuous – after all, it had been a while – she added, 'Your wife.'

But his voice just went on, smooth and unperturbed. 'I'm sorry I can't take your call at the moment but if you'd like to leave a message I'll get back to you.'

Typically, he didn't say goodbye at the end of the message. That would be too polite, too normal. Instead, there was an abrupt, rude *beep.*

She wondered why she was surprised he wasn't home. It was Friday night after all. He was most likely working. Or else hanging out at the opening of some trendy bar with the newspaper crowd from work. Or maybe even in bed with someone and didn't want to be disturbed. Carrying on like none of it had ever happened. Like Jackie had been a mere blip in his life, and normal transmission had now resumed.

Without saying a word, she quietly hung up.

Chapter Two

Jackie truly believed that there was very little that couldn't be said with flowers. Some people thought that was a cliché, of course, but then she would do a little test where she asked that person to think of something, anything, they wanted to say.

'Oh, I don't know . . . I'd like my husband to do the supermarket run. Bet you can't say *that* with flowers.'

Jackie would pounce. 'Well, did the last bouquet you sent him work?'

'I've never sent him a bouquet.'

'Shame on you! Can you imagine his face if you did? I bet he'd skip the whole way down there!'

'Maybe . . .'

Of course, people mostly wanted to say the same thing, like congratulations or commiserations or Be My Valentine. And so in Flower Power Jackie had come up with a range of 'occasional' flowers. For new babies, she did a beautiful *Welcome Tiny Tot!* arrangement in pink or blue. She did a *Sympathiser* bouquet for bereavements, their best seller. Some of her more specialist lines like *Hi New Neighbour!* and its sister bouquet, *It's Been Nice Knowing You,* were slow enough in uptake, and Emma was on at her to discontinue the lines. But Jackie, ever the optimist, was confident they'd pick up any day now.

Some mornings when she unlocked the shop door, and the aroma of fresh flowers floated forward to greet her, she almost felt that being a florist was a vocation. Well, name one other job where she would be asked to mark in floral tribute births, deaths, love affairs, anniversaries, special days for mothers, fathers, or brides-to-be. When you thought about it, the whole spectrum of human experience walked into her shop every single day and asked for her expertise.

And she could make almost anything out of flowers: headdresses, garlands, mosaics, even. Their strangest request had been a train set, but Jackie had risen to the challenge, and fashioned little individual carriages all in different coloured buds, and everybody had been impressed no end. Lech the delivery guy had declared that it was a shame there wasn't a prize for Most Original Flower Arrangement, because Jackie would win hands down.

Today she wondered whether she should start up a new line: *I'm So Sorry.* Or, *Oops! I Lied To You.* Maybe even, *Please Take Me Back.*

She had told Dan that morning, first thing. She had expected him to rant and rave. But he'd said nothing, not a word; instead he put on his runners and shiny shorts and jogged off out the front door. But that wasn't all that unusual, Jackie had consoled herself; he would often run for miles after a difficult board meeting, even in the depths of winter, looming out from dark bushes and side roads and giving people frights. But two hours had passed with no sign of him. Then a girl-friend rang from rush-hour traffic ten miles away to say that he had just overtaken her at speed and was heading for the Dublin mountains. Eventually Jackie had had to leave for work.

'I don't suppose he could survive for long in high altitude in a pair of shorts,' Emma commented now. 'Not when night comes. You'll probably find he'll be home for tea.' But she didn't really look at Jackie as she spoke, just kept working diligently away at a wreath. Where Jackie's talent lay in extravagant wedding bouquets, Emma was great at doom and gloom, and she could knock out a first-class wreath in nine minutes flat. Such was her zest for the task that Flower Power had pretty much cornered the business from the two local old folks homes.

'Do you think?' Jackie said.

'Well, I can't say for sure, of course. After all, I've never actually *met* him.'

'Oh, Emma. I didn't think he was going to propose, OK? It's all come a bit out of nowhere.'

'Kind of like the last time then.'

14

Oh. Jackie couldn't believe that Emma was still sore about that. Talk about bearing a grudge! Flower Power had only been a pipe dream back then, a fantasy. In fact, it hadn't even been called Flower Power; Emma had suggested Blooming Marvellous. Then once the bank had got involved and began looking for all kinds of documentation, Emma – the sensible one – had got into such a tizzy about the whole thing that she'd started to have palpitations and the doctor had advised that she wasn't cut out for business. But, somehow, Jackie had assumed the entire blame for the failed venture by 'going off to London to marry that fellow'.

Well, all right, so she had. But that's what people did when they were in love! Some kind of madness took over and practicalities, never Jackie's strong point anyway, went out the window. People did wild, foolish, unpredictable things, particularly when one of them lived in a different country and weekends were no longer enough. It was never really in question which of them would give up their whole life and join the other: Jackie was an aspiring flower shop owner and Henry was, well, Henry Hart.

When she thought about it now . . . All that naivety and great sense of self-sacrifice on her part. The ridiculous notion she'd had of it being a big romantic adventure that would end in cosy happiness in London. When, really, a long-distance relationship would actually have suited Henry down to the ground. All the good times, but none of the demands of everyday life. He could have shagged her all weekend and then loaded her and her neediness onto a Ryanair flight every Sunday night. They'd probably still be together now.

'Don't be cross with me, Emma,' she begged now.

Emma turned to look at her with steady brown eyes. Everything about Emma was steady and brown, from her compact bob to the tips of her flat, sensible shoes. She was the kind of person you would ring if your house went on fire, or you got a phone call from the Revenue. In an Enid Blyton novel, she would be the one fixing ginger beer and making potted meat sandwiches for tea.

'I've never even met Dan,' she said. 'Not once. But maybe you thought I wasn't *interesting* enough for him. Maybe you thought I'd only be able to make conversation about daisies and weed killer, and wouldn't be up to speed with the NASDAQ or the Dow Jones or . . . or . . . the exchange rate on the euro!' She grabbed a pair of secateurs and waved them about dangerously.

'Oh, Emma.'

'So, maybe I'm not the wildest person in the world. But I can hold my own.' Her neck was all stiff and hurt, and she went at the wreath so hard with the secateurs that bald patches began to appear.

'Until I told him that I was already married, I didn't want to put you in the position of having to lie to him.'

Emma harrumphed under her breath. But it was an I-might-be-talked-around harrumph.

'It's true. Imagine if I'd arranged a cosy night out for us all and asked you *not* to tell him?'

'Well,' she eventually conceded.

'And let's face it. You're a hopeless liar.'

Back when they'd shared a flat, Jackie had once asked Emma to pretend to a boyfriend that she wasn't home. Emma had kept insisting to him, 'She's not here, she's not here,' but her hand had slowly risen of its own accord – she described it afterwards as being like a super-natural force – and pointed straight at the bedroom door that Jackie was cowering behind.

'So. Aren't you going to congratulate me?' Jackie suggested lightly. 'Break open the champagne?'

But Emma just looked a bit worried. 'What's he like? Dan? I mean, really.'

'He's wonderful, Emma. Wait till you meet him, you'll love him.'

'It's just that he certainly doesn't sound like your type, Jackie. I mean, *rugby?*'

Honestly. But that was Emma all over for you: so set in her ways! Rigid, unbending, never considering alternatives, such as business banking managers – who could be just as exciting in their own way as hotshot London media types like Henry.

'Since when do people have to stick to types?' Jackie said with a laugh, making a mental note to ensure that Dan wasn't wearing one of his stripy rugby shirts when Emma met him, or had a bundle of keys jangling from his belt.

The bell over the shop door tinkled and Lech burst in, back from a delivery. 'The leather on my car seats is so hot that I'm sticking to it!' he declared happily. And, indeed, the armpits of his tight white vest were damp. Emma pursed her lips. She had once accused Jackie of hiring him for his looks. Just because he was Italian! It turned out that he was actually Polish, and hadn't a drop of Italian blood in his short, muscular, compact body. His mother, however, had originally hailed from Spain, and had met his father at the World Potato Growers Convention near Warsaw, and that it was love at first sight. They had settled near the border with the Ukraine and had happily grown potatoes and raised children. But life wasn't all that promising on the Ukrainian border for young Polish men who looked Italian but who had a Spanish heritage, although he did feel he could truly call himself European, and so he had come to Ireland. To earn lots of money. And meet women. He had been told by some of his Polish friends who had arrived before him that Irish women were very hot. Then he had looked from Jackie to Emma, who at that point in the lengthy interview was holding on to the sides of her chair very hard, and he had laughed and said, 'Just kidding!' He had added earnestly, 'Just about the women bit, though. Not the money. I have two other jobs, delivering pizza and leaflets. But I can fit you in.'

At least he had a sense of humour, Jackie had argued afterwards to Emma. But Emma had taken an instant dislike to him. He was too loud, too confident, too ambitious, too everything. And those awful white vests he wore. Who did he think he was, Marlon Brando? Indeed, the very sight of him seemed to offend her, and she deliberately got his name wrong until he was forced to tell her that it was pronounced, 'Lek', and not 'lecherous'.

'Hey, Jackie,' he said now. 'I've been thinking about this guy you're married to.'

'Henry?'

'I could get someone to bump him off for you,' he offered. 'I know some people. It would cost maybe five thousand euros.'

There was a shocked little silence. Then he gave a huge chuckle.

'I'm kidding!'

'I didn't actually *believe*—'

'You did! Your face!' His smile was so gleeful and wide that it was hard not to smile back.

'You never know,' she said. 'I might have taken you up on it.'

'A creep, eh?' He was all sympathy now. 'You deserve someone nice, Jackie. Someone who makes your heart sing. Someone who speaks to you *here*.' And he thumped his broad, brown chest a couple of times.

Emma cut in, 'Those orders are ready to go. Just whenever you have a minute.'

Well, that broke the party up. 'Fine,' he said, but his shoulders went kind of stiff. He picked up the deliveries. 'I hope you have written the addresses a little more clearly this time.'

The shop door swung shut after him.

'Did you hear that?' Emma said indignantly. 'Trying to blame that mix-up on me!'

'Your handwriting *is* terrible, Emma.'

'I did not make a mistake.'

'All right, but maybe you should ease up on him. He's doing his best.'

But Emma said, 'He's on probation. When the month is up, I think we should let him go.' Then, as if to get all unpleasantness over with at once, she went on, 'And what about Henry? Not that I want to bring him up or anything.'

But Jackie was prepared for Henry's intrusion as a topic of conversation, and she said, 'Bring him up away.' She was delighted that she sounded so nonchalant; careless, even, given her unsettling encounter with his voice on the answering machine last night. Time really was a marvellous thing. Why, she could probably walk past him in the street at lunchtime and give him a cheery wave!

'Well, you're still married to him, Jackie.'

'I certainly am. But I'll divorce him, of course. Straightaway.' That's what she had wanted to tell him last night. But seeing as he had never bothered phoning her even once since she'd left, why do him the courtesy? He would hear from her solicitor. 'The minute it's through, Dan and I will be free to get married.'

'Be strange,' Emma commented, 'to be divorced and remarried so quickly.'

'Henry was a mistake,' Jackie said clearly. 'I'm not going to sit around and lick my wounds for ever. I've met the right person now and there's no reason to hang around. Certainly not on Henry's account anyway.'

'Just so long as you two have finalised things between you, that's all.'

18

'I'm marrying someone else, Emma. How much more final can it get?'

'It's not the end of the world, Jackie,' Dan said.

'It's . . . not?' She looked at him closely for a reaction. He was sitting on the couch, still in his shorts from that morning. She didn't know whether he had worn them into the office or even if he'd gone to work. But the most important thing was that he was here, he was home.

He said, 'Obviously, I wish I'd known at the beginning, but now that I do, maybe you'd fill me in fully.'

'OK,' she said, very humbly. 'What would you like to know?'

'Let's start with this guy Henry,' he said, crossing his bare legs very maturely. 'Your husband.'

He really was fabulous! And not at all like Desperate Dan, which she had learned was his rugby nickname.

'He's more or less my *ex*-husband – the divorce shouldn't take long at all to come through.' She hazarded a wild guess. 'A matter of weeks, probably.' Well, there were no children involved, and hardly any joint finances worth mentioning, and no assets except for the house. It was probably just a case of signing on the bottom of a few pieces of paper and handing back spare sets of keys and things.

Dan enquired, 'And how long were you married?'

'A year. Hardly a wet weekend!' For some reason she was putting on her jolly voice, the one she saved for small children and difficult customers.

'I see.' He nodded as if it were all mildly interesting to him.

'Look, Dan, the whole thing was a mistake from the very beginning only I didn't see it at the time.' She gave a little laugh. 'Henry and I, we were the most unsuited people you could ever put together. I mean, really, you couldn't pick two more different people in the whole wide world if you tried! He didn't even like shoes!'

Dan smiled politely and said, 'What else about him? Just so I get a picture in my head.'

'Henry? Oh, he's . . . he's a writer.' It was the least insulting thing she could think of. 'He likes food. Eats enormous amounts of it. And he drinks quite heavily too.' That wasn't really true, but anyhow. 'Dan,

I'm really sorry I didn't tell you before. I suppose I was afraid of how you'd react. I didn't think you'd be so wonderful.'

But he just waved her flattery away and said, 'What does he look like?'

'What?'

'Henry.'

'You want to know what Henry looks like?'

'Just curious.' With a bit of a self-conscious laugh, he said, 'I mean, does he look like me?'

Jackie smiled. If Dan was a big, brown, cuddly bear, then Henry was, oh, something lean and mean and dark that they would put behind extra strong glass at the zoo. And throw food at from a great distance. And urge people to keep very far back from. 'I can categorically assure you that he doesn't look like you.'

'What's that supposed to mean?' Dan shot back, all traces of good humour gone.

'What?'

'Is he better looking or something?'

It was all an act, the whole thing! She saw now that a big muscle jumped up and down in his jaw the way you see bad actors doing in movies to convey their upset.

'No! I'm just saying you're very different—'

'I bet you preferred him, though.' The muscle in his jaw was now affecting his eye. He winked disconcertingly as he ranted, 'Or maybe it was his charismatic personality, was it? Or did he have a big fat bank balance? A big fat willy?'

'Dan! Stop it now.'

He flung himself back on the couch and covered his eyes. He looked like a hulking great child trying to hold in angry sobs. After a moment he muttered into his hands, 'Sorry.'

'It's OK.'

'I've been building this picture up in my mind of this guy. This guy that I didn't even know existed until today. This guy that you *married*.' He swiped a hand across his face. 'I thought if I knew more about him it'd make me feel better. But it doesn't.'

Jackie's heart twisted. 'You know, it doesn't really matter what Henry looks like, or what attracted me to him, or any of that stuff. The thing is, it's over. It was over before you and I ever met.'

But Dan wasn't to be consoled. 'Why didn't you tell me then? I told you about all of my exes.' It had taken two nights and several photo albums. And the consultation of a now defunct little black book to double-check names. 'The fact that you kept this to yourself makes me think that maybe you still have feelings for him.'

'I don't.'

'So why didn't you tell me then?'

'I told you, the timing . . .'

'Ah, don't give me that bollocks again.'

'Dan!'

'You know, I knew from day one that things weren't quite right. That you were keeping something from me. I mean, what girlfriend doesn't come with at least a dozen friends to check you over? You didn't seem to have one! I never got to meet any of your family, either. You give me this blow-by-blow account of every single thing you've done in your life since you took your first step, all the way up to about three years ago and then, nothing! Well, now I know why. Henry.' He was so worked up that he began to break into a fresh sweat.

Jackie said clearly, 'You know, Dan, maybe I didn't tell you because I wanted to move on. Is that so bad? After a whole year of a rotten marriage, maybe I wanted to start again and not keep going over and over it.' She was feeling a bit hot herself. 'Do you know how many hours I've spent talking about Henry? How many days of my life have been given over to him? How much of my entire existence was consumed by that man until it got to the point where I wondered was there ever life before him? Until one day, I just said, stop! And that was when I started to put him behind me.'

'Jackie . . .'

'And yes, I didn't tell you the truth. I was wrong. But it wasn't because I wanted to deceive you. It wasn't that I still had feelings for him. When I met you, I was just me, Jackie Ball, and not one half of a failed marriage. I liked it, Dan. And I'm not going to apologise for that!'

Dan looked a bit frightened. 'Just asking.'

That broke the ice a bit. She gave a little, 'Phew!' and sat down beside him on the sofa. 'I'm sorry I didn't tell you before. But Henry's history. I'm with you now.'

'I suppose that's the most important thing,' he said. 'And lucky for you, I don't mind taking seconds.'

For a moment she thought he was serious. Then she gave him a playful push. 'Pig.'

But surely she felt the tension lift from the air? It would just be a case of him getting used to it, she reckoned.

She promised him, 'The divorce will be through soon. Then neither of us needs to think about Henry ever again.'

Chapter Three

'Oh, no. You're talking at least four more years,' Velma Murphy, her solicitor, declared. 'That's under Irish law. And even then they don't like handing them out.'

Jackie was appalled. 'Four years? I don't believe you.'

Velma barked, 'Right. Fine. I'll prove it to you.' And she began to hunt around on the top of her chaotic desk.

Jackie said, 'Really, Velma, it's fine, I didn't mean . . .'

Velma seemed to be terribly touchy. But divorce was her speciality, or so her ad in the local paper had said underneath the words *Fast! Confidential! Free Quotation!*

Normally Jackie wouldn't have gone that route. It sounded a bit trashy or something. And Emma had urged her to go to one of the solicitors offices in town, those expensive firms in grey, serious-looking buildings. But it was the accompanying photo in the newspaper that had caught Jackie's eye. In it, Velma was a dignified woman in her late thirties or early forties. She had swept-back hair and the kind of wide, sad eyes of someone who had been there and understood the pain. Even amongst all the ads for second-hand cars and Top Psychics, Velma's photo shone out with integrity and humanity.

It was only upon arrival at Velma's cramped little office, where she was accosted by a short, very fat woman of indeterminate age, that Jackie realised that the woman in the photo was someone else.

'Oh, that's Susan,' Velma had explained. 'She types three days a week. I didn't want to put punters off.' And she had given Jackie a searing, humourless look. 'Image is so important these days, isn't it?'

Velma now found what she had been looking for, and she read aloud, very gloomily, 'Under Irish divorce law, the applicants must be living apart and separately for four out of five years before the commencement of proceedings.' She shook her head. Spare flaps of flesh under her jowls swayed from side to side. 'Inhuman. That's what it is. Now, nobody's looking for a situation like in America, where you can walk into some place and pick up a divorce in half an hour like you were ordering a Big Mac. That just isn't right. But four years?' She rattled the piece of paper contemptuously. 'What are these guys hoping? That on year four you're miraculously going to fall in love all over again with that creep who slept with your best friend? Or the slime ball who drank the contents of your joint savings account on a two-week holiday in Thailand with the lads?'

'Henry never actually—'

'I had a woman in here last week whose husband used to write down in a log book what time she left the house and what time she came back. He even used to record how long she spent on the phone to her friends!'

'That's terrible,' Jackie said. She knew she shouldn't get drawn in but she couldn't help herself. Besides, it made her own marriage look a roaring success in comparison.

Velma nodded grimly. 'You think she's suddenly going to fall in love with that little sweetheart all over again three years into their separation? You think she's going to miss that log book so much that she's going to give him another chance? Heck, no. With any luck she's going to be lying on a beach in Spain sipping a cocktail and celebrating her freedom!' She seemed on the verge of punching the air, but restrained herself. She went on more moderately, 'Course, women can be just as bad. I get husbands in here too, sitting right where you are, crying like babies over what their wives said to them at breakfast. That's the thing with women. It's mostly verbal. If you had someone telling you that you were a sad, ugly loser every day for twenty-five years . . .' She trailed off, shaking her head as if she personally felt the pain of every break-up in the world.

'I suppose,' Jackie said, starting to feel a bit depressed. And she had walked in with such enthusiasm, thinking she was going to put this chapter behind her swiftly and move on. She had promised Dan as much; he was sitting in the car across the road right now, checking hotel availability for their reception.

'Is it not a bit soon for that?' she'd asked.

'We don't want all the best places to be gone.' She saw that he was running a finger down a list of castles and country houses. For some reason she had imagined an intimate afternoon in a little hotel somewhere.

'They look kind of . . . big,' she said.

'Well, we'll probably have about two hundred,' he said.

'Two hundred!'

'Not counting overseas people.' He looked at her. 'Is that OK?'

'I didn't realise this was going to be a *society* wedding.'

She was being sarcastic, of course, but he said, 'Well, yes. Of course it is. Daddy's still big in the pharmaceutical industry.'

That would explain why his mother looked so glassy-eyed all the time.

'I'm only going to do this once, Jackie.' Then he'd reddened and said, 'Sorry.'

'There's no need to apologise, Dan.' Things were still slightly delicate on that front. Last night when a piece on divorce had flashed up on the news, both of them had lunged quickly for the remote control. It was taking a little longer than anticipated for him to get used to it.

'So how long do you reckon this divorce thing is going to take?' he'd asked. 'Just if the castle people ask.'

'Three months,' she'd said in a cavalier fashion. 'Four at the very most.'

And now here they were, looking at four *years*. Dan would be very disappointed. Still, there would be plenty of time to swing a *Hello!* deal, she thought darkly.

'What did he do?' Velma enquired kindly.

'Sorry?'

'Henry. From the look on your face I'd say it was gambling.'

'No.'

'Oh.' She looked disappointed. 'Usually I can tell. I guessed a bigamist yesterday.'

'Well, Henry didn't *do* anything as such,' Jackie hedged.

'Listen, there's no need to be embarrassed. Believe me, I've heard it all. Some of the stories I could tell you! But of course it's all confidential.' She looked very disappointed at that. 'So?' she said. And waited.

Jackie felt under great pressure to confess to some odious misdemeanour on his part, something dramatic and vaguely repulsive. Could it be that Velma operated a client vetting process, whereby only gruesome evidence of spousal abuse qualified you to get on her books? Worse, if Jackie didn't deliver, it would look like she was defending Henry, a concept so hideously awful that she was sorry that she couldn't announce that she had caught him in bed with a goat.

Velma saw her hesitation. She said kindly, 'What was it? Did he cheat on you? It's OK, there's no shame in that. Happens all the time. It's no reflection on *you*—'

'He didn't,' Jackie cut in.

'Oh. OK.'

Jackie added politely, 'At the end of the day, we just weren't suited.'

'Ah,' said Velma, knowledgeably. 'The chalk and cheese syndrome. I see quite a lot of that too. Of course, opposites *do* attract, but they can also end up inflicting grievous bodily harm on each other. Honestly, you look at some couples and you wonder how on earth they ever believed they were going to be happy together. I'm talking about the ones who can't even agree on a venue for the *wedding*, can you imagine?'

'Could we move on?' Jackie interjected. 'It's just that I've left my fiancé over in the car. It's such a hot day and I don't think I left a window open for him.'

Velma was apologetic. 'Sorry. Sometimes my bitterness runs away with me.' She busily consulted her notes. 'Now that you've mentioned a new fiancé – you go, girl! – I take it you don't want to wait four years for a divorce?'

'I don't have any choice, do I?'

'There are ways around it. None of my clients has ever waited four years,' said Velma bossily. 'My quickest divorce ever was three weeks.'

'Three weeks!'

'Before you get excited, it was one of those hippy weddings on a beach in Haiti that wasn't registered properly.' She asked hopefully, 'Any chance you didn't register your marriage properly?'

'I'm afraid everything is legal,' Jackie said regretfully.

'Right.' She began ticking off a list. 'And neither of you was married to anybody else at the time but overlooked that fact?'

'No.'

She cleared her throat. 'And the marriage was consummated, I take it?'

'Um, yes. Several times.' To put it conservatively.

'Just checking, there's no need for detail.' Another box was ticked. She lifted her pen and tapped it against her uneven teeth. 'Our options are narrowing slightly.' She moved to the next question on her list, and paused before asking delicately, 'And you're absolutely sure he's alive? Henry?'

'What?'

'I mean, obviously we hope he *is*, but it would greatly speed things up if, for example, he . . . wasn't.'

'I got his answering machine two days ago in London.'

'Ah.' A final box was ticked, and then Velma seemed to run out of steam. Possibly she was reconsidering the word *Fast!* on her newspaper ad. She sat with a fist propping up her fleshy jaw, and stared at a framed certificate on the wall by Jackie's head as if awaiting inspiration. Jackie looked too, expecting to see a fancy law degree. Instead, it was verification that Velma had participated in the local readathon. There seemed to be no evidence at all of any proper qualifications.

'London,' Velma said suddenly. 'You met him in London?'

'No, I got his answering machine.'

'Who was in London? You, or his answering machine?'

'His machine. He lives there. He's English.'

'Well, why didn't you mention that!' Velma grabbed a pad.

'You didn't ask.'

'How long has he lived in England?'

'All his life. I moved over when we married.'

'So he's been living there since you deserted him eighteen months ago?' Velma was nearly bursting now, like a detective down to the last clue.

'I didn't desert him. I left because—'

'Yes, yes, let's not worry about the technicalities. The point is that we're eligible to apply for an English divorce!' Velma declared. 'They're much more sensible over there.' She suddenly lurched across the desk and took Jackie's hand in her own warm, surprisingly soft hand. 'Don't worry your head. I'll have that son-of-a-bitch out of your hair before you can say "quickie divorce".'

Henry hated first dates. But anyhow, here he was, on one, with a girl called Charlie. Normally that would have been enough to put him off. But Dave from the sports desk had said she was really nice – 'a breath of fresh air', which had put him off more – and then she'd turned up tonight in a low-cut top that was quite an eyeful. He wished she hadn't, because he wasn't used to the sight of breasts, not recently in any case, and he was very worried that he would keep staring at them or, worse, lunge across the table at them.

She wasn't saying much. In another minute she would sneak a glance at her watch. Already they'd covered movies, books, family and, at her instigation, their most embarrassing moment ever. Right now this date was turning into Henry's.

'How's your meal?' he asked. Oh, brilliant!

'OK, thanks.'

She shifted in her chair, and he knew she was feeling short-changed. Dave had probably talked him up, and he had turned out to be a damp squib. As if he'd asked Dave to interfere in his love life anyway! But of course it wouldn't do to let down the side by being *too* miserable. It tended to spoil the loutish office atmosphere when people broke down crying the whole time. So everybody drank too much and shagged each other and pretended that they didn't care.

But he tried again, a little harder this time. 'I can't put that down in my review. "OK."'

She looked up, wary. 'You're reviewing this place? Dave never said. I thought we were just out for a meal.'

'Oh, I'm always on the job,' he said. Did that sound crude? And why was he even worrying? 'So tell me again, how's your meal?'

'I don't want to be in your review . . .'

'Why not? Your opinion is as good as mine.' That wasn't strictly true. People didn't want to read food reviews written by lay people like Charlie. They didn't even want to read food reviews by qualified experts. Over the years Henry had come to the depressing conclusion that they didn't want to read about food at all. In fact, food was the very last thing anybody read his column for. Vitriolic put-downs, yes; the consistency of crème caramel, no.

He was proved right when his editor told him last year that he was giving over too much space to the food. 'Just describe the stuff in a paragraph at the end and give it a few stars.' But not too many, mind. Henry had been told that that tended to reduce his 'bite'. So really, Henry had said sarcastically, you want me to keep things short and nasty. 'Exactly!' said his editor.

The really appalling thing was that it had worked. Henry's reputation as a critic who was impossible to please became more ingrained. His readership had soared as he'd consolidated his position as the enfant terrible of the dining out experience. He hadn't an ounce of respect amongst his peers, of course; one of them had publicly called him a twat, and Henry would have to agree. But that scarcely mattered when Henry proceeded to take half her readership. He had power, and there wasn't one restaurant in this whole city that wouldn't roll out the red carpet should he lower himself to visit.

'Be mean,' he told Charlie now. 'Be brutal. The readers will love it.' Give them their money's worth.

She laughed. 'All right.' But she lowered her voice anyway, afraid of offending. 'If I'm being honest, my beef was kind of chewy.'

'Um hum.' With a pencil, he made a discreet note on a tiny white pad.

She peeked. 'What did you write down?

'*Beef eligible for bus pass.*' It was bad enough written down. But she laughed; she thought it was funny. Hilarious, even. She had lovely teeth.

'Go on,' he encouraged her. He felt himself relax a bit.

She said, 'I could have lived with the beef if it hadn't been for that piece of pasta on top of it.'

'The raviolo of bacon and cabbage.'

'I mean, what was *that*? OK, I'm no food expert – to be perfectly honest, I don't eat out much, I prefer to go to the pub, have a few drinks and a bit of a laugh, and when I do book somewhere, I like pizza – but pasta on top of beef? To me, that's just having a laugh!'

'I completely agree with you.'

'You do?'

'I do. And if you don't mind, I'm going to title my review, "Taking the Pasta".'

Pause. Then she laughed. 'I just got it.'

'OK, so it's pretty cheap and nasty.'

'I like it.'

'It's terrible! The sub-editor will probably change it. Or worse, he probably *won't* change it.'

She laughed again. The date had picked up greatly. He must remember to thank Dave for going to all the effort to set him up. Dave had been right, he just needed to get back into the saddle again. What was the point in letting everything get to him so much? He had a lovely house, a fantastic job, depending on how you looked at it, and women queuing up if only he would bother to click his fingers (this was the pep talk Dave had given him last night over a beer) and really, it was about time that he started to appreciate what he had. Because you can be sure *she's* not hanging around feeling sorry for herself since she left eighteen months ago. She'd set up that flower shop in the end. Dave had heard about it through his wife Dawn's cousin's sister-in-law's best friend who apparently had some hot connections in the Irish flower trade.

So she had done it in the end. Henry was surprised. She was one of those people who developed a great passion for things, usually over the course of a bottle of wine, but the following morning lacked the necessary zest to get out of bed and actually make them happen.

Let her open what she wanted. He didn't care. He was having the most refreshing evening in months, sitting opposite Charlie, with her yellow hair and her tight, tight top.

'You should use a dictaphone,' she said knowledgeably now, as he closed the little notebook and pocketed it discreetly. 'My entire office would disintegrate without dictaphones. I could order you one at discount if you want.'

'Thanks anyway. But I don't want to draw attention to myself,' he said to Charlie.

She looked a bit puzzled.

'They don't know I'm here tonight, you see,' he added in a stage whisper. See? He could be playful again.

'Oh,' Charlie whispered back. She had plump, pink lips that he had a sudden urge to kiss. 'Is it because you're famous?'

'I'm not famous,' he said modestly.

'Dave says you are. I've never heard of you, mind.' She added hurriedly, 'I hope I haven't offended you.'

His smile slipped only a little; he still had pride, for God's sake. 'Not at all.'

She said, 'Dave says you've got this really fierce reputation.'

'Don't mind Dave.'

'That you can close restaurants by giving them a bad review. He says you're called the Butcher of Notting Hill. After some bloke in Broadway who axes theatre shows with just one bad review.'

'That's rubbish,' Henry said, trying not to sound impatient, although God knows it'd be a public service if some restaurants *did* close. 'The reason I don't announce I'm here is because if they know a critic is coming the whole place is spring-cleaned, the kitchen goes to code red, and I get served up the best meal I've ever had in my life.'

'So the review isn't really a proper review?' She was agog, or pretending to be.

'Absolutely. It's a rule of mine. I never, ever let them know who I am.'

'So what do you do? Like, book under a false name?'

'Absolutely. Tonight it was Don Corleone.'

She giggled. 'I hope that doesn't make me your moll.'

'I don't know. I don't usually have a date with me.'

'You eat on your own?'

'That way I can concentrate on the food better.'

'Why, am I distracting you?' she asked, head cocked to one side.

'A little.'

'You know,' she said, 'I don't believe you're the butcher of anywhere.'

'No?'

'I think you're a sweetie underneath it all. I can always tell.'

'A psychic. Oh God.' He rolled his eyes and she laughed again.

Suddenly he had a very good feeling about this. Charlie was exactly the type of woman he needed: fun, confident, out to have a good time. Uncomplicated. Because his life sometimes seemed terribly complicated. Or maybe he just made it complicated. But he had feeling that with Charlie, he wouldn't be made to feel inadequate all the time.

He blurted, 'Charlie, I'm married.'

Jesus. At least he should have waited till *dessert*! Seen if this thing

31

had any legs at all. Who knows, maybe she'd been planning to make up some lame excuse in five minutes and get up and leave, and now he'd gone and told her he was married . . .

'I know,' she said, unconcerned.

Dave had said, for God's sake, don't tell her, there's no need to go telling her on a first date. But that would be adding another layer of deception to his life, and he had a feeling that he was reaching some kind of boiling point and that one more thing might just be enough to tip him over the edge, and he would run screaming through the office with no clothes on or something and *that* would certainly surprise them all.

Anyhow, Dave had been wrong. Charlie didn't care if he was married or not. And why should she? It wasn't a big deal. Not to anybody but himself.

Charlie's friendliness, and three glasses of wine, made him expansive, and he said, 'I don't intend to get married again. Ever.'

She looked at him. 'Phew! That's a pretty big statement.'

'I know. But, you know, I just don't agree with it.'

'You don't *agree* with it?'

'Marriage.' He was on his little soapbox now, and he relaxed even more and gave his trademark sardonic grin. 'I'm not going to bore you here, but it's fundamentally flawed on at least seven different levels. I have a chart done out if you want to see it. For starters, emotionally it's a form of entrapment. And it's not tax efficient.' He had meant it to be funny, but at the same time making a point.

Charlie didn't get it. 'OK, but I guess I'm not here tonight because I'm thinking of my tax status.'

'No, I know that. I wasn't suggesting that, I was just using it as an example of how marriage might not work. Doesn't work.' He could see he was digging a hole for himself here. 'Look, I just wanted to make my position clear upfront, OK? So that's why I'm saying it to you now.'

'In case I was sitting here hoping and praying that you'd ask me?' Her lips didn't look so soft now.

'No. No! Anyhow, you wouldn't want to marry me.'

'Actually, I don't think I would,' she said. 'I've never had a guy talk tax with me on a first date before.'

He was really making a balls of this. 'Well, that's it! I mean, I'm lousy husband material. I don't talk enough, I've been told, or share emotionally, whatever the hell that means.' He gave a little laugh. 'And I'm rude, I don't do my half of the housework, I break wind . . . I steal. All the time.' Menus mostly, but he took stuff from hotels too.

Now she looked kind of disgusted. 'But I still might want to sleep with you? Despite all that?'

'What? No! That is not what I am suggesting.'

'It's exactly what you're suggesting. Because you don't want marriage, isn't that what you've said? Not that I would in a million years. So, really, you're looking for someone to shag.'

'Absolutely not!' He had totally misread her. He watched in dismay as she picked up her bag and grabbed her shawl from the back of the chair. She thought he was an idiot. Right now, he'd have to agree with her.

'Charlie, just because I don't believe in marriage any more doesn't mean I don't want a long-term relationship, I do.'

She snorted. 'How many times have I heard that before.'

'I can see I've gone about this all wrong. I was just trying to be honest with you. Charlie, please wait.'

The waitress approached, alert. 'Is everything OK here?'

Henry said, 'Fine, thanks.'

But Charlie rose and pointed a scarlet-tipped finger at him accusingly, and announced at the top of her voice so that the entire room could hear, 'This man is a restaurant critic!'

Then she turned on her heel and left.

In the end Jackie wrote him a letter.

Dear Henry,

You're probably surprised to hear from me after all this time.

I'm writing to tell you that, in view of our marital breakdown, I think it best if we finalise matters by divorcing. If you are in agreement, which I'm sure you are, then perhaps you could appoint a solicitor to act for you. I enclose my own solicitor's business card for your information.

I would greatly appreciate your speedy response to this letter.

Yours sincerely,

Jackie

Then, because everything from now on would go through their solicitors and it was unlikely they would be communicating again, she added:

PS: I read your reviews from time to time. I hope everything is going well for you.

She was pleased with the letter. It was polite and detached and to the point, and there were no ink blobs that would suggest that she had cried inconsolably all through the writing of it – which she hadn't. For once she had managed to resist irrelevant asides, although she had been very tempted to ask whether he would mind sending on her gold earrings that she'd left behind. She was almost positive they were in the little bowl of pot-pourri on the bedroom shelf. In which case he had probably thrown them out. He was the kind who detested pot-pourri, and scented candles, and anything that tinkled in the wind. The man didn't know how to live.

It was a shame about Velma's business card, though. She appeared to have only one, because she had handed it over to Jackie very reluctantly, and it was all smudged and dog-eared and had what seemed to be a cigarette burn on the back. It was unlikely to scare Henry, or his battery of London lawyers, one iota.

Still, the important thing was the letter set the whole thing in motion. She had made the first move, which everybody always said was the hardest. In fact, she didn't even *have* to write him a letter. It was a purely voluntary gesture of maturity on her part. She could just have let the divorce papers land on his mat unannounced. He need never know that she had already spent many pleasant, vengeful hours imagining just such a scene: his shock upon opening the envelope, his utter anguish. His screams of pain. Then, blinded by tears, his accidental fall down the stairs and the tragic diagnosis that he was paralysed from the waist down and would never be able to walk or have sex again. The whole thing ended up with her sparing a few minutes to go and visit him in a rehabilitation centre somewhere, where he had antagonised the staff so much that they wheeled him into a corner every morning and left him there for the day. In Jackie would sweep, looking stunning in a red dress and high heels, and carrying a bag of grapes, and she would smile victoriously and say, 'Well, Henry, you've only got yourself to blame!'

God, it was tempting. But no, the point was that she had gone beyond all that sort of petty thought this past eighteen months. Re-reading the letter now, she marvelled at how mature she sounded, how even-tempered. How she didn't bear grudges, despite everything, when he was probably a festering boil of recriminations himself. If he thought about her at all. He had never once made an effort to contact her after she had left, not even to send on a bill, or a phone message, or a lousy Christmas card.

She got some Tippex and blanked out the last line. She didn't wish him well. Not at all.

Chapter Four

'I don't know why you didn't tell him you were getting married again,' her sister Michelle said.

'Because it's none of his business,' Jackie said airily. 'Anyway, I don't want him thinking I'm looking for a divorce just because I'm getting married again. I want him to think I'm looking for a divorce because I can't bear to be married to *him* any longer.'

This was only partly true. She didn't want to confess that she was afraid that he would fall down laughing.

Michelle was impressed. 'You're so good, Jackie. I wouldn't have been able to help myself. I'd have said, look what I bagged after dumping you! A business banking . . . what was it again?'

'Manager.' Jackie was pleased by Michelle's approval, and wondered why. Probably because none of her family had liked Henry. He had never really recovered from that very first remark he'd made about hoping that Jackie's mother's lunch was up to scratch. In the dead silence that had followed, he had scrabbled about helplessly: 'It was a joke. More on me than anything . . . I mean, of course I'm not going to be critiquing the food . . . it smells lovely.' He'd told Jackie afterwards that he'd blown it. She had laughed her head off. But he'd been right. He'd always been viewed with a slight air of suspicion after that. Well, more outright dislike.

'I'd send him a photo too,' Michelle continued with relish. 'An eight-by-ten, in full colour. In it, I'd be draped all over Dan. Or maybe having sex with him or something. And I'd write on it in pink highlighter pen, Husband Number 2! And then I'd have sat on the couch for days just imagining his face.'

'I don't suppose he'd care much either way.'

'Men always care about their successor,' Michelle said knowledge-ably. 'Henry just wouldn't show it.'

Jackie said, 'Anyway, it doesn't matter. It's not like I'm going to invite him to the wedding.'

'Oh, do,' Michelle implored. 'The last wedding I was at, I thought I'd die of boredom. The speeches went on for two and a half hours, and then everybody got plastered, and I ended up shagging Gerry Butler just for something to do.'

'Mum's hairdresser?'

'Only don't tell her. You know the way she still thinks I'm a virgin.'

Mrs Ball came hurrying back in from the sitting room to refill the teapot. There were two high spots of colour on her cheeks and her Alice band had slipped with the stress of it all, giving her a slightly drunken appearance. She hissed, 'Would you two stop going on about Henry? We can hear you in there. It's making Dan very uncomfortable.'

They looked past her to where Dan was in the sitting room, perched stiffly on the sofa and talking drill parts with Jackie's father. So far it was the only thing they had found in common. But it was only their first meeting. Things were bound to improve.

Jackie said, 'He knows all about Henry, Mum. He's fine with it.'

'I don't know. Every time Henry's name comes up he kind of flinches,' Mrs Ball fretted. 'And it didn't help with your father getting the names all muddled up like that. I said to myself, please God let the floor open up and just swallow me. Oh, get out of the way, Michelle, you're sitting on the ginger snaps.'

She never gave out to Michelle. Michelle drew her mouth into a little O behind Mrs Ball's back.

Jackie pulled out a kitchen chair. 'Mum, would you sit down and relax for a bit? I'll take the tea in.'

'Relax. Relax, she says! After telling me yesterday that she's bringing her new fiancé for lunch! We didn't even know you were going out with anyone. We thought you were too busy setting up that flower shop, and "going off in a whole new direction" like you explained to us at Easter. When I spoke to you last week the big news was that you were going to try and get your hair straightened, and now *this*.' She abandoned the ginger snaps and flopped down onto the kitchen chair anyway. 'Honestly, Jackie, I haven't been able to keep up with you since you were about five.'

Michelle looked on with great interest, the cow. She could afford to, of course. She was the darling of the family, having managed to stay in further education whereas the rest of them had got distracted by fast cars and loose women, according to Mrs Ball. That was only because Jackie's brother Eamon had bought an old Mustang when he was in Boston fifteen years ago on a holiday visa, and then taken up with a woman from Arizona. They'd subsequently got married over there and had three children, and he drove a Mercedes now, but that didn't stop Mrs Ball worrying about him. Oh, she hadn't had a night's sleep since the lot of them were born. And it wasn't as though they hadn't been given the very best start in life! Breastfed, all of them; sent to the best schools; a proper dinner on the table every evening at the same time. They'd had every opportunity to turn into responsible adults with decent jobs who would cease to worry their mother upon turning twenty-one.

But Eamon had set the standard for them all, and Mrs Ball's heart had been broken as, one by one, the Ball children had failed spectacularly to go on to university and take up permanent, pensionable jobs. Instead they had driven her to the brink of despair by becoming yoga instructors and florists and 'performance artists' – that was Dylan out in South Africa. She was still sending out postal orders to supplement his rent. They had taken up with unsuitable men and divorced women – Dylan again – and two more of them were living openly in sin, not a sign of them wanting to get married. Not to mention Jackie, who was going the other way and becoming a serial wife.

It was all right for Mr Ball, retired at sixty and fiddling about with his DIY. But a mother never stopped worrying, especially when you looked at the bunch Mrs Ball had produced.

Except for Michelle, bless her, who had come along eight years after the rest. She was a mistake, of course (Mr Ball hadn't been forgiven yet) but pretty as a picture, and with a head stuffed full of brains. She was four years into a law degree, as Mrs Ball would tell anybody who listened. More importantly, such a *good* girl. Never bothering with men or alcopops or drugs or any of that. No, she only took an aspirin on a Saturday night before she went out, the better to bolster herself against the noise in some of those pubs, she said. Mostly, she didn't come home after these nights out, but usually that was because she stayed over with her friend Bernadette, she would explain, and they would drink cocoa and play Snap. Out of the lot of them, she was the only one that Mrs Ball truly felt she didn't have to worry about.

And worry she did. Her face was criss-crossed with hundreds of tiny lines, each one of them evidence of the many sleepless nights caused by her unruly children. Sometimes her worry was so great that she had to take to the couch, like Mrs Bennet in *Pride and Prejudice*. In fact, if she swapped her Alice band for a bonnet, she could actually *be* Mrs Bennet, Michelle maintained.

Mrs Ball looked at Jackie now – the one who had caused her more sleepless nights than the rest put together, except perhaps Dylan – and gave a little sigh. 'But I suppose we should be used to you by now. Your father always said there was never a dull moment with you in the house. And, to be perfectly honest, he didn't always say it in a good way.'

It must have been hard raising all those children. That was the excuse Jackie always made for her mother. 'Yes, but do you like him, Mum?'

'Dan?'

'Yes, Dan!'

Mrs Ball looked into the living room. Eventually, she said, surprisingly definite, 'He's very nice.'

Well, of course he was: he ticked every box in Mrs Ball's criteria of an Ideal Husband. Somehow it seemed very wrong to have chosen a man her mother approved of.

'I think he's gorgeous,' Michelle declared.

Jackie thought: if Michelle likes him, he must be OK. She had never needed to use anybody else as a barometer before. But after Henry, she found she didn't trust her own opinion any more. After all, she had thought he was the most perfect man in the world. Talk about getting it wrong.

'Does he have a brother?' Michelle enquired.

'He does, actually. Four or five of them, I lost count.' She had met them at a hastily convened family lunch to announce the engagement. They had all roared up in big corporate-looking cars, and had immediately launched into some kind of ritualistic behaviour that involved a lot of punching to the upper arms, and tackling each other violently on their way to the toilets. Their wives were all well-groomed blondes called Fiona who had kept rearing away like some kind of appalled Mexican wave every time Jackie crossed her red-booted legs.

Dan had laughed afterwards and said she'd started a new fashion craze and that next time they'd all be wearing the same. But she hadn't worn the boots since.

'Are any of them good-looking?' Michelle demanded.

Mrs Ball said to Jackie, 'For God's sake, don't be encouraging her, and her with only a year more to go. Her tutor said only this week that she had the makings of a barrister in her.'

'So if ever any of you are up for murder, give me a buzz,' Michelle said.

'Don't even say that!' Mrs Ball was appalled: something else to worry about. She said to Jackie, 'So don't go asking her to be bridesmaid again this time, Jackie. She honestly doesn't need the distraction. Anyway, you'll hardly go for the full thing again, will you?'

Jackie remained smiling through all this, to her credit. 'No, we thought we'd just do it in the garage if Dad could clear away a couple of boxes of rubbish.'

'You're joking, I suppose,' Mrs Ball said – she was never quite sure with Jackie. 'Take those ginger snaps in, will you, Michelle? And tell him there's more if he wants them.' More ginger snaps! Dan must have made quite an impression.

Michelle went off with the plate.

'You look tired, Mum,' Jackie said, conciliatory.

'Well, I suppose I am. What with the lunch and everything. And I'm not complaining or anything, but I had to send your father out to find a chicken at seven o'clock last night. A big one, I told him specifically, but you know what he's like without his glasses and that's how we ended up with roast turkey. In July! I don't know what Dan thinks of us at all.' Then she seemed to run out of steam, and she said to Jackie, 'Are you sure about this, love?'

'Yes.'

'Well, naturally, I'm worried.' It was possibly the most overused word in her dictionary.

'About what exactly, Mum?'

'Well, here you go again!'

'Just twice, Mum.'

'Don't get all prickly now. It's just, you know what you can be like. You go at things with such enthusiasm. Such energy! And I admire that. Remember that project you all had to do in school? Sewing that big quilt thing together? Although to be perfectly honest, I never quite saw the point of it; it's not as though it would fit any normal-sized bed, as your dad said. But do you remember you got the prize for sewing the most of those little squares? Your fingers all chapped and blistered from the needle! You won a Cabbage Patch doll. We were so proud of you.'

She often brought that up, usually at Christmas when she'd had a sherry or two. As though winning a Cabbage Patch doll had been the highlight of Jackie's life to date, her biggest achievement, and nothing else since had ever quite measured up. But Jackie didn't want to spoil the moment and so she just smiled and said, 'Zorabelle.'

'What?'

'That was what I called the doll.'

'Oh, yes. Zorabelle. If that wasn't just you, Jackie. The rest of us wanted to call her Jane.' And for some reason this seemed to tickle her, and she burst out laughing, and so did Jackie, and they egged each other on, until Mrs Ball ended up crouched over in the chair with tears coming from the corners of her eyes. 'Oh, stop!' she said, and she scrabbled for a tissue, and blotted her face dry.

Dan put his head in the door. He seemed pleased to find everybody in such good form.

'I was just wondering where you keep your axe,' he asked.

Mrs Ball sobered. She shot a cross look in at Mr Ball. 'I hope he hasn't been annoying you,' she said to Dan.

'No, no.'

'Because sometimes I could take an axe to him myself.'

'He was pointing out that dead tree in your garden,' Dan explained. 'I said I'd go and chop it down for him.'

'Well! That'd be great,' said Mrs Ball. 'Because I've been terrified that it's going to fall over and kill Michelle or something. She's only a year to go of her law degree, you know.'

'Yes, you told me,' he said. He winked at Jackie and went on out.

'He's a lovely fellow,' Mrs Ball declared. 'You couldn't find fault with him, no matter how hard you tried.'

'So I've got your approval then?'

'Since when has my approval ever mattered to you?' Mrs Ball said.

'I'd still like to have it, Mum.'

Mrs Ball adjusted her Alice band. 'I suppose I just don't want to see you getting hurt all over again.'

'I know, Mum.'

'The nights I listened to you cry in your old bedroom upstairs when you first came home from England. Broke my heart. I said to your father, if only she'd *think* a little more before she went and did things.'

'Think what, exactly?' Jackie enquired. 'Think that it might all end up a failure? None of us would ever do anything in that case. And I *do* think about things before I do them.'

'Yes, but you don't think the way the rest of us do.'

Which usually meant pensions and security and early saving for a retirement home. Jackie got a headache just thinking about it.

Mrs Ball mistook her silence for further annoyance, and she said hastily, 'Oh, I blame him too. Henry.'

'For my balls of a marriage?'

'I said to your father, that fellow turned her head – which wouldn't be hard, let's face it – with phone calls and letters and making all those dramatic trips across at the weekend. It was like the pair of you weren't in the real world at all, you were on some kind of . . . planet of love!' Jackie looked startled. So did Mrs Ball. She added stoutly, 'I like Dan. You can talk to him. He's someone you'd always know where you stood with.'

This was the ultimate seal of approval. And, actually, her mother's viewpoint sounded disconcertingly nice for a change – knowing where you stood with people, instead of always wondering, always hoping, and then being let down.

Mrs Ball added, with satisfaction, 'And, you know, I think you've settled down a bit even in the six months since you've met him.'

'You didn't even *know* about him until yesterday,' Jackie retorted.

Mrs Ball said, 'You're very hard to please, Jackie. If I'd said I didn't like him, you'd have been offended. I'm after telling you that I *do* like him, and that won't do either.'

'Your dad has a one hundred and thirty-seven piece drill set,' Dan marvelled on the way back across town in the car. 'That's what I want for Christmas.'

'Oh, shut up.'

Dan looked over at her, surprised. 'What?'

'You can stop pretending now.'

'I don't know what you're in such a bad mood about, Jackie. And I told him I'd get him a ticket for the Ireland–Argentina friendly next month if he'd like to come along.'

'Dad? Rugby?'

'He seemed very interested.'

'He just says these things. But he won't go. He never does.'

'We'll see. And your mother's turkey! Amazing. I won't need to eat for a week.'

She was very suspicious now. 'Dan, I know you're just trying to suck up to me through my parents. Pretending that you had a great time.'

Dan was magnanimous. 'They're going to be my in-laws for the next God knows how many years, Jackie. Might as well start off on the right foot.'

She was forced to crack a smile. 'You're devious.'

'I'm not! I mean, I thought they were OK.'

'They're very dull,' she said.

'Do you think?' said Dan, genuinely surprised.

He likes my parents, Jackie thought; her second little shock of the day, after finding out that her mother approved of him. Still, maybe it was just her. Maybe she *didn't* think the same way as everybody else. For all the good it had done her: one failed marriage under her belt already. Maybe originality wasn't all it was cracked up to be, maybe she should just knuckle down and get on with it like everybody else. It was still possible to have fun – look at Michelle, for goodness' sake. The shining hope of the family, while still managing to get completely off her head every weekend and shag unsuitable men. She just had the wit not to marry them and give up her entire life and move to London.

Dan said, 'Why didn't you tell me who Henry was?'

Henry's arrival into any conversation was always a rather rude shock. 'I did tell you,' she said.

'You didn't tell me he was a food critic. You didn't tell me he was semi-famous.'

'Come on, Dan.'

'Even *I've* heard of him, and I don't go in for all that food reviewing business. Food is food, as far as I'm concerned. None of that cordon bleu stuff that you have to hunt around on your plate for.' He looked at her. 'You just told me he was a writer, like he put together computer manuals, or the blurb on the back of cereal boxes.'

'I suppose I didn't think it mattered.'

'That your husband is a big-swing media type in London?'

'He is not a big-swing media type.'

'He has his picture in the paper every week! Not that I buy any of those tabloid-type papers.' He added quickly, 'And even if I did, it's only for the sports sections.'

'Henry's a food critic who got himself a reputation by being controversial, OK? He writes mean, nasty stuff and gets paid for it. Big deal.'

'I just think it's interesting, that's all. That you didn't mention it. Maybe you think I'm going to get all jealous or something.'

'I don't think that.'

'Because I've got a good job too, you know. I mightn't be *famous* but I do OK. I don't do badly.' If his chin jutted out any further he would need treatment. 'I mean, writing about food . . . what kind of a job is that, anyway?' Not much of a one, from his tone.

'He used to be a chef. I suppose it was a natural progression.' She wasn't defending him. She was just setting out the facts.

Dan's sneer deepened. 'So, what, he likes to go around the place with a little apron on, whipping up omelettes that melt in your mouth? I'll tell you, it wouldn't be a job for *me.*'

Not if his own cooking was anything to go by. Last night's curry was still hanging around unpleasantly in Jackie's stomach.

'Yes, well, each to their own,' she said, hoping he would drop the subject.

He didn't. 'I suppose you went to lots of parties. Openings and galas and the odd "glittering ball".'

Jackie kept her voice nice and even. 'I suppose we did in the beginning.'

They'd been out every night of the week. She had thought it was great at the start. Then she began to get tired of it. She began to suspect that they went out only because Henry didn't really want to spend the evening alone with her.

'What, meeting lots of celebrities and A-listers?' Dan said. He was almost green.

'Dan, could you please keep your eyes on the road?'

'And pop stars too, I suppose!'

'Dan! Mind that truck!' She was forced to grip the dashboard as they almost rear-ended it. She waved apologetically at the driver as they drove past.

When they were back on their side of the road again, Dan muttered, 'Sorry.'

They had both had a fright.

'Dan, you have to stop this, OK? It's not really making either of us feel better.'

'I know.'

'We have a wedding to look forward to. We're getting married! Who cares about Henry and what he does for a living?'

'You're right. I really am sorry, Jackie. Maybe it was just meeting your family today. I felt like I was an impostor or something. That Henry had got there before me.'

'Well, he did. But my family couldn't stand him, OK?'

'Really?' He immediately perked up.

'Really. So no more Henry, please?'

'No more Henry.'

Jaunty now, he reached over and laid his big hand on hers, and she had the fleeting sensation of being crushed.

Chapter Five

Lech said that in his country – he didn't specify which one – it was traditional to hold a big party whenever someone got 'the ring'. He described how a great crowd would gather, and enormous amounts of food and drink would be consumed, and people would drunkenly sing and wish the bride all the best for the future.

'It's called an engagement party,' Emma said coolly. 'It's hardly a unique Polish tradition. We have them here too, you know.'

'In that case, why have you not organised one for Jackie then?' he enquired as coolly.

For some reason that got Emma all fired up. She spent the whole week ringing around Jackie's friends, and hiring a room over a pub, and ordering rakes of sausage rolls and bits of cheese on sticks.

'But I don't want an engagement party,' Jackie protested. It sounded very permanent or something. 'And anyhow, I'm not even divorced yet.' Was it not a bit unseemly?

Dan's family and friends obviously thought so, because none of them was able to make that particular date, due to various other commitments such as chiropractor appointments that couldn't be rescheduled, and the unavailability of babysitters. That excuse was from Big Connell and Fiona.

'She hasn't even had her baby yet, has she?' Jackie said to Dan.

'Well, she's due soon. I suppose they were just making sure.' But he looked embarrassed and angry by the whole thing. There was nobody at all coming from his side except his younger brother Rory. And he always said he would come to things but never actually showed up. It was his trademark, apparently.

'I'll ring them up again,' he said. 'Tell them I'd like them to be there. That I *expect* them to be there.'

'Dan, listen.'

'No! We're getting married, and they can't be bothered to come to our engagement party? What kind of a message does that send?'

A fairly obvious one, Jackie would have thought. She had to salvage this.

'You know, I don't even *want* an engagement party,' she said loudly. 'It was all Lech's idea. I'd much prefer a . . . a bridal shower!'

'What's that?' Dan asked cautiously.

Jackie wasn't at all sure, but she said confidently, 'It's where the bride's friends gather and give her useful things for her marriage. Like toasters and diaphragms.'

'You'd like that?'

'I'd love that! But not if you desperately *want* an engagement party . . .'

'Me? No, no.'

'And you wouldn't mind if it was girls only?'

He was greatly relieved now. 'I could handle that. And we'll really pull out all the stops for the wedding, OK?'

'Great!'

She was pleased to see him happy again. She had been worried for a while there that he was developing some kind of an obsession about Henry. But their little blow-out in the car on the way home from her parents' house that day seemed to have cleared the air. Dan was his old self again, relaxed, and looking forward to the wedding. In fact, he was doing most of the planning. Jackie was relieved, but didn't show it, as somehow it didn't seem right for a bride-to-be to be uninterested in the arrangements. He showed her brochures and price lists, and she made enthusiastic noises, and otherwise hadn't a thing to do with it.

Emma was stoic when informed that the engagement party was now a girls-only bridal shower. 'I'll just cancel the cheese on sticks. And disinvite Lech.'

But, as bad luck would have it, the proposed date didn't suit most of Jackie's girlfriends either. At least they gave more plausible excuses.

But when even Michelle cried off, citing an important exam she had to cram for – although Jackie could swear she heard a man's voice in the background, or possibly two – the whole thing seemed a bad omen.

'Let's go to the pub anyway,' Emma said comfortingly. 'And get completely . . . scuttered!'

Jackie was touched. The most Emma ever drank was a half of lager.

'I love drinking,' Lech declared cheerfully. He was wearing a red vest today and his right arm was deeply tanned from where it rested on the car door all day long in the sun. 'Come on, girls!' he said. 'Get some powder on your noses and I will give you a lift down to the pub.'

They looked out the window at his car – a rusting green Ford, circa 1989, that habitually smelled of flowers and pizza. A pink rabbit hung from the rear-view mirror and there was a bawdy sticker on the bumper that wasn't quite legible at that distance except for the word *Girls*. It all added weight to Emma's argument that he was unsuitable as the public face of Flower Power, and that they should hire someone classier, and who wasn't likely to hit on clients on their own doorstep.

Jackie said that was very unfair and that Lech wasn't a bit like that; in fact, it was their female customers who got a bit fresh around him. As for Lech, he had shown no interest in any of them, even that woman who had tucked a red rose down his vest last week and told him to call her. He insisted that he was a romantic at heart, just looking for the right woman.

And if you believe *that*, Emma had said to Jackie.

She said to him now, coldly, 'Thanks anyway, but I think I'll walk to the pub.'

Lech looked at her for a long moment. 'Ever since I start work here, I try to be nice to you. I talk to you. I'm friendly. But you seem to have some kind of a problem with me.'

'I don't have a problem with you,' she said back steadily. 'It's just that it's a girls-only night.'

'Even if I *was* a girl, you still wouldn't want me there, would you!'

Jackie couldn't imagine Lech as a girl. Dan, maybe, as a sort of strapping, hockey-playing girl with an iron jaw. Henry would make a gorgeous girl, of course, all sultry and smouldering and with thighs that would never run to fat. He had it every which way!

She dragged her attention back to Lech, who was squaring up to Emma now. And look at Emma! Kind of red-cheeked and hot looking.

'Or maybe you don't like Polish people, is that it?' he said.

'What a load of rubbish!' Emma spluttered.

'Some very good people come from Poland. The last Pope was Polish. And everybody knows he was a top quality guy!'

'Now! The pub!' Jackie said gaily. She didn't want this to descend to blows.

But Lech just gave Emma a very dark look. 'Maybe we both have preconceptions. Because I come here thinking that Irish people are very friendly. I was wrong.'

Jackie said desperately, 'The first round is on me!'

'Maybe I'm not in the mood for drinks any more.' He picked up his car keys and left.

After that, Emma didn't look much in the mood either. Neither was Jackie, but the room over the pub had been hired, and there were all those sausage rolls to be eaten, so she dutifully went to the little bathroom at the back of the shop and put on a fresh layer of Wild Cherry lipstick and patted down her hair. It sprang up again immediately. Crossly, she dug out a canister of extra-hold gel from her bag and set to spraying vigorously.

Henry hadn't replied to her letter. Not that she had expected him to. Well, maybe she had. Just something! After all, it wasn't every day that a person received a letter informing them that they were going to be divorced. In terms of drama, it certainly beat electricity bills and incredible offers from DIY chains.

She had found herself checking the post every morning, not knowing quite what to expect. Obviously nothing too startling, such as a long, rushed, breathless reply begging her not to do it, that he was sorry about everything, and that he would love her until his dying breath. Henry had never been one to show his hand emotionally; Jackie was often left to decipher a cryptic crook of his eyebrow, or a little sigh that might have been one of ecstatic happiness or else grim despair. She had thought in the beginning that it was part of being a critic; that he had some kind of duty of care not to let anybody know what he was thinking until it was published in the newspaper, and that somehow it had bled over into his private life. And it was kind of sexy back then; all that inscrutability, and the many pleasant hours spent wondering what he was *really* thinking. She knew now, of course, that it was all a power trip on his part, and that mostly he would be contemplating nothing more than a mild case of indigestion.

Whereas she, on the other hand, had always been overemotional, according to Henry. Getting unnecessarily involved with stray animals and strangers in shops and generally making too much fuss about life in general. Sometimes she would catch him looking at her as if she had no decorum, or something. But imagine if the world was full of Henrys! People who went around looking all enigmatic and unreadable and totally in control. There would be no fun at all.

Really, his failure to reply to her letter was just another example of it: let her wonder whether he'd really received it at all, or if he'd moved, or the postman had accidentally dropped it down a drain somewhere. The best way to rattle her was not to acknowledge it at all. After all, that would mean recognising they'd had a life together. A shared past. He wasn't going to do that either.

The way he could cut her off so cleanly took her breath away. After everything he had done to her! Oh, he was a cynical, hard-boiled person and he always had been.

Velma said it didn't matter. She was just about ready to file divorce papers in England and then it would all move like clockwork. Set the wedding date, she had told Jackie. Jackie hadn't wanted to. Call it superstition. But Dan had seized upon it, and had gone on and on about it until eventually she had caved in, and they had decided on 14 October. It would be a white wedding, albeit a civil one, and they would take three weeks' honeymoon afterwards.

'Where are you going, anyway?' Emma enquired, when they were sitting, alone, in the vast empty room over the pub looking at four plates of sausage rolls and a plate of mini pizzas thrown in for good measure. Her voice echoed a bit. It all seemed a bit sad after all the great arrangements, but neither of them was going to admit it, of course. 'The Costa del Sol again?'

'Oh, no,' Jackie said. 'No, Montana, we think. Or maybe Nepal.'

There was a little silence.

'It depends on the temperatures, of course,' she amended airily. 'In the winter it can get pretty chilly, particularly in high altitude. But it has beautiful scenery! And, um, monks and things, not to mention Everest, which Dan thinks we might climb. Well, to base camp anyway.' She bit into a sausage roll nonchalantly, and added, 'Montana is absolutely spectacular. And there's Yellowstone Park, of course. For treks and things. Apparently you can spot bears if you stand still enough.'

'This is his idea, isn't it?' Emma said at once. You could never pull the wool over her eyes.

'It is not! We talked about it and decided that we wanted to do something a little different. Experience nature.'

'But Jackie,' Emma protested, 'remember we found a mouse in the storeroom once, and you fainted? How are you going to manage against a bear in Yellowstone Park? Or halfway up a mountain?'

'I don't know!' And she'd have to wear horrible big boots and everything, Dan had shown them to her in an outdoor magazine. She conceded, 'All right, so it *was* his idea.' Perhaps it was a mistake not to have been more involved in the wedding arrangements. Now she was stuck with an activity honeymoon.

'I hope you're not going to let him change you, Jackie,' Emma lectured.

'Of course I'm not!' She swiftly changed the subject. 'What about you?'

'What about me?'

'Emma, you've been in a terrible mood for a couple of weeks now. Is there something wrong?'

Emma looked like she was going to deny it, but she eventually admitted, 'Maybe it's all this wedding talk. I mean, I'm delighted for you and Dan. But it's hard on us singletons, that's all.'

Jackie was surprised. 'But I thought you didn't want anybody. You've never really seemed interested.'

'I suppose I haven't been,' Emma mused. 'But that doesn't mean I don't have . . . needs. Like everybody else.'

They'd never spoken about Emma's needs before. Jackie had always believed that all that Emma really needed was a trowel and a couple of bags of topsoil.

'I suppose you could . . . find someone to, um . . .'

'Ride?' Emma said.

'Yes.'

Emma crinkled her nose. 'But I don't know any men. Except for the guy living over me, and he's weird.'

'Think a bit harder.'

She did. She trained her gaze on the ceiling.

Jackie prompted, 'Surely there's someone else you've overlooked? Someone you see every day?'

'Oh, yes! The guy in the corner shop who sells me my lunch roll.'

'No! Lech.'

'Lech?'

'Yes.'

There was a little silence. Then, 'I can't believe you suggested him.'

'Why not? It's obvious you two fancy each other rotten.'

But Emma was looking at her in complete disbelief. 'I can't stand Lech. Everything about him makes me sick. In fact, if he were the last man on earth, I wouldn't give him a turn. How could you possibly think I fancy him?' Her bob was quivering about her chin indignantly.

'Sorry,' Jackie muttered. 'I obviously completely misread the signals.'

'I might be desperate, but I wouldn't sink that low!'

Jackie let it drop. It just showed you again how wrong she could be about people! It was very disconcerting, given that she had always believed that the older you got, the wiser you became. She'd kind of relied upon it, really; it saved her from having to think about pensions and retirement funds and all that. She had figured that she'd be so wise then that she could make a living from clever new inventions or something. She had never really considered the fact that she might get more stupid. And she was only thirty-four now. What would she be like at seventy? It didn't bear thinking about.

'I don't know how you would possibly think I would fancy Lech.'

'We've moved on from that, Emma.'

'Oh.'

'Unless you want to talk about him a bit more?'

'I do not!' But she went red, and blustered, 'Will we have another drink?'

'Is that wise? You've already had a half.'

'I can manage another half,' Emma said bravely.

Sitting there with her best friend, gossiping about men and whether to have another drink, Jackie suddenly felt very content. It only mattered

53

that Henry hadn't replied if she let it matter. She had a new place in the world now, a new relationship, and she would cut Henry out of her life as precisely as he had cut her from his.

She thought of Dan now, at home making dinner, one eye on the sports results on the TV, and wondering what time she would be home. Waiting for her.

She realised how selfish she had been. Completely absorbed in Henry and leaving Dan to organise the whole wedding! And he had been so patient already, whereas a lesser man might have decided she was just too much trouble. Even the embarrassment of presenting a married woman to his family hadn't deterred him. And look at the way he had put Henry so completely behind him, while she had so far spent her engagement party wondering why he hadn't replied to her letter!

They would go to Nepal. It would be enough just to be with Dan. And a dozen sherpas, halfway up to Everest base camp.

'What are you grinning about?' Emma asked suspiciously.

'I'm getting married,' Jackie said, smiling hugely. 'I'm happy.'

For the first time since Dan had proposed, she truly felt that things were finally working out.

Dan was at home alone in the dark, hunched over the video remote control, his breathing hard and fast. The pizza beside him grew cold as the telly flickered in the corner, throwing out jumpy images into the room. The noise level was uneven and the lighting poor, but that didn't matter – this movie would never be up for an Oscar. A boring bit now; Dan waited impatiently for the action to start again. The camera moved jerkily, then panned across before starting a slow zoom in. Dan licked his lips and leaned forward. *Oh, yes. There. Just there. Stop it there.* He aimed the remote control and the screen froze.

Henry Hart looked back steadily at Dan. He wore a grey morning suit and a formal white shirt and surely to God those teeth weren't his own. But after ten years of club rugby Dan recognised good orthodontics when he saw them and he glumly concluded that Henry's brilliant smile had not thus far been enhanced. And look at all that hair! Tons of the stuff, wavy and crisp, when already Dan was finding lumps of his own in his hairbrush every day. Henry's face wasn't all that perfect, though, he was glad to note; no Roman nose or cheekbones you could cut bread with or anything like that. In fact, it was his eyes you looked at most. They were very blue and sharp and charismatic, fuck him. You could see why a woman might be taken in by those eyes all right.

On the plus side, Dan was taller – much. In fact, if you compared him with the people standing around him, Henry was really very short. Remarkably short. A squirt! But, hang on, when Dan moved the frame forward a bit, he saw that Henry in fact was leaning casually, sexily, against a pew, and that when he languidly hauled himself upright, he topped six foot. The bastard. Dan wondered what he was like under that suit. Was he all lean and sinewy? Or maybe he was already beginning to run to fat. Oh, give him half an hour with Henry – on the pitch, obviously – and he would soon find out what kind of a soft, city boy he was!

With an unsteady breath, Dan bit into a slice of greasy, cold pizza and hit the play button again. He knew he shouldn't be watching this. Or he should have told Jackie that he'd inadvertently come across her wedding video while he was searching high and low for a blank tape to record *101 Greatest Rugby Moments Ever*. It wasn't as though she'd hidden it away. But it hadn't been left out casually either.

He just wanted to see what this Henry guy was like, that was all. It was natural curiosity. Just five minutes, then he would put it back. It might even be cathartic, he'd reasoned, like lancing one of those great big boils after a practice session.

The video moved on to typical wedding stuff now, as the camera followed Henry's progress up the church. Dan got to look at his big broad back, and all that hair again, as Henry was accosted on either side of the aisle by relatives and guests. There was the usual wedding blather: 'Good luck', and 'It's not too late to change your mind!' Henry smiled, pressed hands, delivered a line here and there that had them laughing. Come on, thought Dan, it wasn't that fucking funny. Eventually, finally, after making a total meal of the whole thing, he arrived at the front of the church and took up position beside a big, well-fed bloke in another morning suit. The best man. Dave, he'd heard someone calling him earlier. They had a bit of a hug, some back-slapping, then Henry said something that had them both smiling. A fucking comedian!

The camera, mercifully, left Henry there, and did a slow, pompous pan of the congregation, row after row, as if telling the viewer, look at how popular and important the groom is! Look at how many people turned up, made the journey over to Ireland, all brushed up for the occasion. Fleet Street types, Dan thought dismissively, even though he had never set foot in Fleet Street, and couldn't point it out on a map. But he recognised class, all right, and this lot didn't have much, for all their expensive clothes. Dan's own wedding guest list might be light on celebrities, although his second cousin was a popular local country & western singer, but, by God, none of them would turn up in a dress like *that*.

The camera found Jackie's mother now, sitting in the front row, huddled right into the corner of the seat as if afraid that someone would come and tell her she was in the wrong place. And she in her own church, at her daughter's wedding! Dan felt sorry for her. A variety of other relatives flanked her, stuffed into new suits and with red, shiny noses. Mrs Ball, aware of the sudden scrutiny, sat up straight and adjusted her dress, which was curiously similar to what Dorothy had worn in *The Wizard of Oz* – and managed a tight, false smile for the camera.

Only Michelle looked in any way confident at all. The camera cut to the back of the church and there she was, having snuck in in her frilly peach bridesmaid's outfit to pass on some message to the usher. She saw the camera, and smiled and trilled her fingers cheekily for the camera. Good girl, Dan thought fiercely. As far as he was concerned, she was sitting on his bench now. He made a mental note to fix her up with his younger brother Alan.

Where were Henry's parents? Dan fast-forwarded the tape a bit. Was that them, in the second row? They looked too friendly and modest to have produced someone like Henry. But the woman had those very blue eyes too, and they were about the right age. They were holding an animated conversation about a small gold plaque screwed to the pew in front of them, and the camera zoomed in to pick it up.

'"Pray for Patricia O'Leary",' she read out.

'Does that mean she's buried under here?' he wondered.

They both had a look under the pew, as if expecting a pair of feet to be poking up through the floor.

'I think it just means she donated the pew,' she said.

'Ah!' he said. 'Let's pray for her anyway.'

The camera moved on to Emma, whom Dan had met only days ago. Wearing brown, for God's sake. Still. In amongst the sea of violent pinks and reds and purples, she looked somewhat normal.

Then the camera stood to attention as the officiating priest arrived out on the altar in all his finery. He wasn't alone; two more swiftly followed. Three priests officiating! Even the priests themselves appeared to think this was excessive, because they kept looking at Henry as if desperately hoping to recognise him. Eventually they gave up and shuffled off to the podium, a task in itself given the number of altar boys and girls crowded around – ten, at Dan's count – and the dozens of flower arrangements dotted about, and the hundreds of candles, which at that moment were presenting a serious fire threat to the swinging robes of the priests. You could be forgiven for thinking some kind of a royal wedding was about to take place, Dan thought darkly.

Then the camera was on Henry again and, disconcertingly, Dan saw his own distaste reflected for a brief moment on his face. And then Dan realised: the whole thing had been organised by Jackie. Right down to the bosomy choral singer who was at that moment limbering up her vocal cords in anticipation of 'Here Comes The Bride'. And God only knows what the bride would be wearing when she finally *did* arrive. The full works, no doubt, and flanked by a couple of dozen bridesmaids. Dan could picture now how it had all come about; the rifling through the bridal magazines, the pillaging of wildly conflicting themes and ideas, and the whole lot put together at considerable expense and with great enthusiasm, but oh, what a mess. It had been nothing to do with Henry at all. He was, Dan saw now, almost immune to the entire thing, standing over to the left with his best man, and watching the whole circus out of those cool, blue eyes. Even more peculiarly, the guests, *his* guests, the newspaper crowd, seemed entirely separate from him, as though he had had no hand in their being there today. He didn't even seem to like them very much. Indeed, it was hard to know what he was doing there at all, in that overdressed church swamped by gaudy wedding trappings, and guests he did not appear to care about.

He was there for Jackie.

Before the choral singer had sounded the first note, before she had even drawn breath, Dan watched as Henry swung round to the entrance door on instinct. On his face was impatience, a need to see Jackie. He didn't look at the camera, or the priests, or anybody else. He didn't give a hoot, Dan knew. In fact, ideally he would have preferred it had the church been empty, and it had been just him there, waiting for Jackie, with none of this pomp and ceremony to steal even a moment of her attention away from him. The wedding was just something to get through, an obstacle, before he got his hands permanently on Jackie.

Dan was gnashing his teeth without even realising it. A piece of pizza seemed to be lodged somewhere in his windpipe but he couldn't swallow. He remained rooted to the sofa as the church door slowly opened, and there was just the briefest glimpse of a white dress. The camera was no longer on Henry, but Dan imagined he could hear his hateful breath, getting faster and more lusty as he waited for Jackie to come through that door—

'Dan? Where are you?' Jackie. She was home.

Dan scrabbled to turn off the video recorder. 'In here!'

Just in time. She peered round the living-room door. 'What are you doing sitting in the dark?'

'Oh, you know. One of my headaches.' It was difficult to look sick with a big slab of pizza in your hand, and he put it down. 'Come sit down and watch, uh . . .' He snuck a glance at the TV to see what the hell was on. 'An Irish language programme with me.'

She shook her head admiringly. 'You watch such good TV.'

'Yes, well,' he said modestly. 'Nice night?'

'Yes.' She snuggled in and he knew she was tipsy. 'I was thinking in the pub. About Henry.'

He gave a bit of a nervous little jump. The pizza in his windpipe began to work its way back up again.

She obviously misread his silence. 'I don't mean to bring him up again. I know you've been making a big effort to put him behind us. And you're absolutely right. I'm talking about *me*.'

Full of guilt, Dan just nodded.

'Maybe I haven't done as good a job as you. I've been giving him far too much head space and I've been ignoring arrangements and stuff, and I'm really sorry, Dan.'

'You haven't been.'

'No, no, I have! Dragging my heels, and leaving you to do all the work. I've been the most unenthusiastic bride ever. But all that's going to change, I promise. I'm going to follow your example. From this moment on, I'm going to leave things to Velma and just not think about him again! Ever, ever again!'

'Yes, well, there's no need to be too drastic.'

'As of now, Henry Hart is gone from my life!' She buried her head in his shoulder again, and did a little hiccup. 'We're going to be so happy together, Dan.'

'Me too. I mean, yes.' Over her shoulder, the red light on the video recorder blinked at him − winked at him! − and for a moment Dan fancied that Henry Hart was in the room.

Chapter Six

Henry was working from home that day, as it happened. Well, he almost always worked from home; he had found that it wasn't absolutely necessary to be at a desk in the hub of things when describing the taste of hollandaise sauce. Anyway, Friday was his day for letters. The office always posted them out in a big brown envelope, quite a good clatter this morning, and he was now working his way slowly through the opinions, meanderings, insults and righteous indignation of the British public. Or at least those who read his column. He would choose the best five of the lot. Not to *reply* to. He never replied to any of them, even though they all began expectantly with, 'Dear Mr Hart'. No, he handed them straight to Rhona on Mondays, who typed them up, and they would be published beside his column in the following Sunday's edition.

That morning Henry had already selected a couple of I–don't–know–who–you–think–you–are ones, one from a woman in Herefordshire whose local pub he had thrashed two weeks ago, quite rightly, and another from some old boy who seemed to think that Henry had no formal journalistic skills whatsoever. Well, of course he hadn't, but that was hardly the point. He was a guy who knew a bit about food and wasn't afraid to voice his opinion. Loudly. Insultingly, if at all possible. And with the odd bit of vitriolic wit thrown in for good measure, plus a smattering of bad language. That was pretty much Henry's job description, and damned cushy it was too. He'd got a hefty pay rise last year, a new two-year contract, a very flattering photo headlining his column, and expenses like you wouldn't believe. Not to mention the company car he'd talked them into. Try beating that lot writing worthy political pieces for the *Guardian* or *The Times*!

Sometimes Henry would put his head down on his desk in despair and wonder how on earth he had arrived at such a place. Worse still, was there any way out? And even if there was, would they let him?

On cue, the telephone rang. It was his agent.

'Henry! Adrienne here.'

'Oh. Hello, Adrienne.'

'You've been very, very naughty,' Adrienne scolded.

Henry always found Adrienne rather alarming but she never seemed to notice. 'Have I?' he said cautiously.

'Don't come the innocent with me. You know very well you were supposed to have those book proofs back in on Wednesday.'

'Oh. Was I?'

Adrienne was unimpressed by his memory loss, and reminded him, unnecessarily, 'They've paid a lot of money for this book, Henry.' Adrienne was particularly proud of the deal seeing as the concept had been her idea: *Henry Hart. The Guide.* His standing was such that there was no need to mention 'food' or 'restaurant' or 'reviewer' anywhere in the title. 'You're a brand name now, darling!' Adrienne had squealed. In it, he reviewed and passed judgement on one hundred of Britain's top restaurants. Adrienne was convinced that, overnight, it would take over from all of the other restaurant guides, maybe even – and she had lowered her voice reverentially – Egon Ronay and the Michelin Guide.

At that, he had told her to keep taking the pills. But she went and found a publisher who agreed with her, and she had signed him up for a two-book deal. He was unclear what the second book would be about. *Henry Hart: Yet Another Guide* or some bollocks like that.

'I'll ring them, apologise,' he said now.

'I've already done that. And I've told them you'll have it back to them Monday morning, first thing.' She burst out, 'They've had nine restaurants on the phone in the past week wondering if they made it in! Can you imagine? Shaking in their shoes, either from excitement or fear. Go and buy the book, they told them!' She laughed uproari-ously. Sometimes Henry thought she was unhinged. 'Oh, I can feel it in my waters, Henry. This book is going to be big!'

'Wonderful,' said Henry. 'Look, there's someone at the door.' It was his stock excuse.

'OK,' said Adrienne. 'And the people from *I'm A Celebrity, Get Me Out Of Here* were on again; are you absolutely sure—'

'I'm sure,' said Henry.

'OK,' Adrienne said, with a sigh that implied he was mad.

'One more thing,' Henry said. 'I was wondering. Do you do poetry at all?'

There was a brief, startled pause. 'Poetry?'

'Yes, Adrienne. Lines of text that sometimes, but not always, rhyme?'

'I know what it *is*. But we don't represent literature of any kind, darling, you know that. We just can't sell the stuff. As for *poetry* . . .' There was another brief, bemused pause. 'What kind of poetry are we talking about? Wandering lonely as a cloud and all that kind of thing?'

'No,' Henry said, as patiently as he could. 'Modern poetry. Love poetry, that sort of thing.' There was another long silence on the phone. 'Obviously it's not mine,' he told her. 'It's a friend's. I said I'd enquire for him.'

'Ah!' Adrienne sounded greatly relieved. 'Between you and me, darling, tell him to forget it. He's wasting his time. People don't want to read poetry any more. He wouldn't even get published in a magazine. Does he write thrillers at all?'

'No,' said Henry.

'Because I might be able to sell a good forensic novel.'

'He doesn't write novels. Just poetry.'

'You'll have those proofs for Monday?'

'Yes.' He hung up on her. Depression settled familiarly over him. Now he would be forced to spend the rest of the day, the rest of the weekend, doing the book proofs; reading his own reviews, only a longer version of them, and most of them starting with 'Well, I really *hated* this one . . .'

'Hey, girl,' he said to the dog, who wandered in. And actually, he wanted to check her for lice. She had been doing quite a lot of scratching yesterday and it was always best to catch these things early.

The dog, Shirley, gave him a kind of pitying look as he hunkered down and began to search through her stubbly, rough hair. He couldn't see anything, but he might check again later just in case they were camping out in the tail region.

'I think we should get that mole behind your ear checked out too,' he told her. 'We all know how these things can change shape and do nasty things to us, right?'

Shirley gave a little sigh.

'Well, OK,' Henry said to her. 'But you can't ignore these things for ever.'

He might as well make a coffee and get on with the proofs. Sometimes he wondered what his readers would think if they could see him now; the suave, arrogant, quick-tongued Henry Hart, the Butcher of Notting Hill, shuffling around his kitchen in his socks, pitied by his dog, and dithering between decaff or regular.

Some regular post had come with the readers' letters from the office, and as he cleared it all off the kitchen table so that he could spread out the proofs, his eye fell on a letter at the bottom of the pile.

Divorce papers. He knew immediately by the envelope, the weight of it in his hands.

He sat down heavily on a kitchen chair. Ridiculously, he found himself upset by the fact that they had sent it out second class. He paid his taxes, he had done a stint for Red Nose Day last year, and yet he wasn't considered worth the price of a first-class stamp.

Shirley must have sensed a further darkening of the general mood, because she looked over, alert. Maybe she somehow sensed the letter was to do with Jackie. Oh, those two, it had always been girly giggles and fun, and dressing Shirley up in hats. Hats! For a dog! And then taking her out in the freezing cold for a walk to the park. Henry never let her out of the house from November until at least March.

Divorce.

He had known it was coming, of course. There had been that odd little letter a few weeks ago warning that it was on the way. At least, the letter had been in Jackie's handwriting but maybe it had been dictated by her solicitor, that Velma Murphy person. It had been so odd and cold and not Jackie at all. Or maybe it was the result of her breakdown. Yes, very possibly.

This was a little fantasy that Henry often entertained; that Jackie had left because of some unexplained emotional crisis that had come upon her by surprise, kind of like a bout of coughing. Well, it wasn't all that unreasonable, when you looked at the kind of person she was! Always so skittery and unpredictable, rushing around the place, developing passions for this and that and going off them just as quickly; like the way she had gone off him, as though he were milk that had turned sour overnight. She was a person of excess, of extremes, of bad judgement and poor choices (apart from himself, of course) and really, it would be no wonder at all if her brain had one day screamed, Enough! and gone into meltdown. And she had packed one small bag, left a note on the table saying only 'Goodbye!' and gone back to Ireland to recuperate and drink Complan or something.

Sometimes, when he thought that way, he could almost understand her. He could almost forgive her for leaving him like that, in such an abrupt and shocking way. There was an explanation, a reason. You couldn't hold someone like that accountable for her own actions, could you?

But that was when Henry was feeling benign; when he passed a bunch of happy toddlers in the park, maybe, or saw a Coca-Cola advert, and the world seemed cuddly for a moment.

When he was feeling more robust, like today, he saw her flight exactly for what it was: a pretty brutal example of the woman's complete and utter lack of substance. Really, he should have seen it coming from the very start; if he hadn't been so head over heels in love, so flattered by her sheer admiration and attention. At his age, he should have known that that kind of intensity isn't real; that people who turn on so quickly turn off just as quickly, and once you scrape the surface, there's very little underneath. When she'd had enough, when he had failed to live up to her ridiculously grandiose notions of love and marriage, she'd simply hitched up her wagon and moved on. Just like that. Leaving him and Shirley behind, all used up.

'I still love you,' he told Shirley. 'Don't ever forget that.'

His solicitor had told him that because they'd been living apart for less than two years, she would have to cite 'unreasonable behaviour' on his part as grounds for divorce. Or at least some rookie solicitor called Tom had told him. He'd been filling in while Ian Knightly-Jones was in court fighting Microsoft, or someone like that. Tom had looked at his desk throughout and whispered to Henry that the courts were understanding, that their standards weren't too exacting, and that the unreasonable behaviour probably wouldn't be anything too personal.

'What, like my feet stink?' Henry said.

'Oh! Well, um . . .'

'I'm joking.'

'Ah! I see. Well, it'll probably be slightly more specific than that. Common reasons would be, oh, I don't know, you drank like a fish.' He was trying to be funny back, and Henry couldn't resist letting his face go leaden, and sending him into a spin. 'I didn't mean to—'

'It's OK. I don't drink like a fish. Only at weekends anyway.'

Tom had said hurriedly, 'Mr Knightly-Jones said to say he'll be back in the office next week, and that you don't have to open the divorce petition if you don't want to. Just send it in to him and he'll deal with it.'

Not open it? His own divorce petition? Pass up on all the juicy details, the instances of 'unreasonable behaviour'? He was looking forward to it! He might even break open a fresh box of Jaffa Cakes, take the telephone off the hook and have a good giggle.

He tore open the envelope carelessly, and said to Shirley, 'Bet you she mentions the way I drive. And that I didn't socialise as much as she wanted. Which would be impossible, let's face it. You couldn't keep up with her! As though I didn't listen to enough dimwits all day in the office without being forced out into their company at night. How many times did I try to explain to her – and you're my witness here – that I also had to do some work every now and again? That we couldn't both just shop all day?'

Shirley wasn't buying it. She gave a worried little whine.

'All right,' Henry said, shutting up. He took out the divorce petition and unfolded it. It was a bit of a shock to see her name typed on the front page. Jackie Ball. Petitioner. And then his own name underneath. It was doubly odd because he had never seen a divorce petition before. He couldn't quite get his head around it: *Jackie*, sending this stiff, typed-up court-printed document to him. Jackie, with her post-it notes, and scraps of coloured paper, and phone numbers scribbled down in lipstick. But *this*. He quickly flicked down through it, finding it easier if he pretended that it was his own work he was proofing. And he did OK on the first page, because it was all just legal guff, and then he came to the grounds for divorce.

Failure to participate fully in family life.

There was a short paragraph on that, nothing too dire, just some euphemistic guff that didn't really say much. Or at least nothing that made him want to howl with outrage before breaking up all the furniture.

Failure to emotionally commit to the marriage.

Another short paragraph on that. In it, she made him out to be more careless than outright negligent, as though it was something he'd forgotten to do, like mowing the lawn. Which, actually, he usually *did* forget to do. He found himself slowly releasing his breath.

He hurried to turn over the page to read the rest. But there wasn't any. Could that be it? Those two charges alone? Admittedly, they were serious, and could deal any marriage a mortal blow. But he had expected . . . well, more. All manner of character assassination and outright lies! She didn't even mention his moodiness, which towards the end had become intolerable even by his own standards. Had she just not noticed? Or maybe at that point she had ceased to care any more.

He found himself deflated. Disappointed even. Somehow it just wasn't like Jackie to be so restrained. And it seemed strange to end a relationship that had been so volatile with such a short, antiseptic little list as this. It seemed wrong.

Jackie was trying to choose between wedding dresses. Michelle had taken the day off college to help, which seemed to entail dragging out a great number of hangers and stuffing them back in again.

'Oh, my God,' she kept screaming. She hauled another one out. It took both hands just to hold it up. 'Here, this would save you the cost of a marquee. You could just hold the afters under your skirt.'

Emma had come along too, very reluctantly, and only because Jackie had said that she had to, because she was the chief bridesmaid since Mrs Ball had vetoed Michelle for the job.

'I won't be able to do it,' Emma had insisted. 'Not with all those people looking at me.'

'They won't be looking at you. They'll be looking at me.'

'So why do you need me at all then?'

'Because you're my friend, Emma. This is, like, an *honour!*'

But Emma had gone all white and watery looking, and so Jackie had been forced to ask her cousin, Chloe, to be bridesmaid number two. Then Michelle had pointed out, quite rightly, that Chloe was the best-looking girl in the whole family, probably in the whole country, actually, and that Jackie should have had the wit to ask their cousin Maureen, who was fourteen stone. But Chloe hadn't understood at all when Jackie had tried to shaft her, subtly, and now she was stuck with a bridesmaid who would undoubtedly upstage her. On top of it all, Chloe's mother had rung up Mrs Ball and said something to her – nobody ever found out what – that had Mrs Ball going around with her mouth all puckered up for a whole week.

If all that wasn't complicated enough, Dan was then left having to readjust the balance *his* end by getting his second eldest brother PJ to be groomsman, along with Big Connell. PJ's wife Fiona then got miffed that he had been asked as a kind of an afterthought, and said she felt slighted in front of the other Fiona, and could scarcely meet her eyes down at the club. Jackie had apologised profusely to Dan for causing family ructions, but he seemed oddly unmoved by Fiona's embarrassment and had tersely told Jackie that she could have as many bridesmaids as she wanted and he would match her, man for man, with a groomsman, and that he had a battery of first cousins lined up if he started to run out of brothers.

All this had Jackie wanting to run away to Tahiti and get married on a beach with just a pair of coconuts as witnesses. But she couldn't suggest scaling things down, not now that Dan had gone and added another hundred people to the invitation list, which had ballooned to four hundred.

'Do you *know* all these people?' She was beginning to wonder whether his organisational zest was running away with him.

'Of course,' he had replied. 'Bill and Cliff and Bugsy are from school.' She had later learned from his mother that they were from nursery school and that he hadn't seen any of them since he was five and that it had taken him weeks to track them down. His mother seemed to be rather surprised by the scale of things too, which was even odder given that she hadn't registered alarm in a number of years due to her pharmaceutical intake. During one of her more talkative visits, of which there weren't many, she revealed that he had badgered her for the addresses of third cousins in Australia whom he wanted to invite.

He certainly seemed determined to make a splash. For some reason Jackie had thought he would be very laid-back about things, but not a bit of it. There he'd been, on the telephone till midnight the night before, trying to talk some acquaintance into getting him the number of an eight-piece wedding band that played at all the snooty society weddings.

'It doesn't matter if we don't get them,' Jackie had soothed

'What, you want a DJ playing Madonna till four in the morning?' he had said, quite snappily.

Jackie liked Madonna. She liked DJs too and had rather hoped for one. She saw now that she wasn't going to get one.

'What about the cost of all this?' she ventured.

'Don't worry about the cost,' he said, picking up the phone again. 'By the way, we're arriving for the reception by helicopter.'

She made a mental note to keep her veil short, in case there was a sudden up-wind and she ended up decapitated.

Michelle was still rifling through the racks. 'Look at this one – a shepherd girl. Imagine if you could get your hands on a couple of sheep.'

'Are you just going to crack jokes or help me out here?' Jackie snapped.

Michelle was surprised. 'He's not worth losing your sense of humour over, Jackie.' It was the first bad thing she'd said about Dan. Jackie felt very defensive.

'It's not Dan, OK? It's just . . .' She managed a smile. 'It's just the sooner we're finished up here, we sooner we can go to the pub, that's all.'

'That's the spirit,' Michelle said approvingly. She had already tried to drag them into two on the way there.

Emma at least was taking things a little more seriously. She held a dress up for Jackie's inspection. 'I think it's kind of you.'

The dress was low-cut and floaty, with a chiffon effect that would make Jackie look all ethereal and dramatic, and the ivory would set off her skin just beautifully. But oh, it wouldn't do at all! Not for a wedding with four hundred guests and a seven-course dinner and third cousins and bitchy wives scrutinising every inch of her. The last thing she needed was a bloody helicopter whipping up her lovely, floaty, cheap dress to show them all her Marks & Spencer underwear. She felt damp under the arms just thinking about it.

'Why don't we have a look at the designer section?' she said instead.

Michelle and Emma exchanged looks. 'They'll cost ten times as much but won't have half as much material,' Emma advised.

'Let's have a look anyway,' Jackie said, leading the way. The shop assistant followed at a discreet distance. She obviously thought that Jackie was going to try to pilfer her best stock.

The designer section was low-lit and hushed and self-important. They found themselves keeping their voices down, and Michelle checked the bottom of her shoes for dog poo before stepping in. A nearby mannequin stood draped in a classic strapless creation that all the Fionas would utterly approve of, but it would have Jackie worrying for the whole day that it would slip down and launch her boobs into the middle of the speeches.

Michelle whispered, 'And look at the row of little hooks and eyes at the back. Can you imagine your wedding night, and having them opened one by one by Colin Firth?'

'Or by Dan, of course,' Emma chipped in diplomatically.

Dan would never get his huge fingers around those fiddly little things. He'd be going 'damn' and 'blast' and would have to put all the lights on.

She wondered how it all seemed to have got so complicated. Or maybe it hadn't. Maybe she just wasn't throwing herself into it enough – and after all her good intentions too. And it wasn't Dan's fault that he had such a big family, and so many business contacts, and so many people he seemed very anxious to impress. He couldn't be blamed for wanting a big day out. And here she was, dilly-dallying over a wedding dress which, when she thought about it, was the only thing she was actually required to do this for this entire wedding. Dan was doing everything else.

'I'll try it on,' she decided. She could always get some of that special boob tape, and just cross her fingers that it would withstand propeller pressure. Not that crossing her fingers would be any help if it didn't.

Emma saw her face. 'You don't have to do this today, Jackie.'

'But I do! I have to. Apparently I've left it far too late as it is to order a wedding dress! They need twelve weeks to make the thing, eight weeks for alterations, three weeks for me to lose weight, two weeks for them to make further alterations . . .' Then, it slipped out before she could stop herself, 'It was never this convoluted the first time around.'

Ooooh. There was a shocked little silence. Scandalised glances darted back and forth, with neither Michelle nor Emma daring to draw breath.

'I just meant the dress,' Jackie amended calmly. 'Mrs Brady made it, do you remember, Michelle? It seemed a lot easier than all this shopping.'

There was a little collective out-breath from everyone.

'I suppose,' Michelle said doubtfully. 'But it wasn't as classy as any of *these*, Jackie.'

She didn't remember caring. Her overriding memory was of excitement and sheer happiness. But it was ridiculous to draw comparisons. This was her second wedding, after all. Things were bound to have become a little, well, routine.

'Maybe it's just the whole white thing,' she said, for the benefit of the girls. 'Maybe it feels wrong, like I'm pretending to be a virgin.'

'Virgin!' said Michelle with a snort. 'I can guarantee you that you won't find a single virgin in this entire shop.'

Several brides-to-be looked over guiltily, and their shocked mothers. The shop assistant's hand hovered around the panic button.

'I don't know why you always have to be so cynical, Michelle,' Jackie hissed.

Michelle looked languidly around the shop. 'I just don't believe in all this happy-ever-after stuff.'

'And I suppose I'm a walking example,' Jackie said stiffly.

'No. In fact, you've done well. You've met not one but two men you'd consider spending your life with. I haven't met anyone I'd consider staying for breakfast with.'

'When you meet the right one, you'll know.' She felt kind of false, spouting platitudes.

'But how? How will I know?'

'Don't ask me,' Emma said.

Michelle persisted, 'I know you can't stand Henry now, but take Dan. How did you feel when you first met him? Was it, like, a thunderbolt?'

'Um, not exactly. It was more a . . .' She couldn't say it was a case of them both trying to convince each other that he wouldn't be too boring for her. And anyway, that was just the first day. After that it was, well, great. Fantastic! 'Oh, look, when it happens you'll know.' She decided she wasn't going to go there.

But Michelle looked very gloomy. 'I honestly don't think I'm ever going to feel that way about anybody.'

'Of course you will. Just keep looking.'

'I am, but at this stage it's hard to find men I haven't already slept with,' Michelle complained.

'Where did you find them?' Emma suddenly enquired. She tried to look casual. 'I mean, is there a place you would go? To find men to sleep with?'

At that point the shop assistant stepped up firmly. 'Can I help you there at all?'

'Yes,' Michelle said firmly. 'We're looking for something for a second wedding.'

'Ah,' the shop assistant said, understanding immediately. 'For yourself?'

'You must be joking,' Michelle said.

The shop assistant then alighted on Emma. 'You?'

'Certainly not,' Emma said, offended.

'Me,' Jackie confessed reluctantly. They all turned to look at her benignly. The shop assistant gave her a sweeping glance from head to toe, as if mentally measuring her.

'Have you considered tulle?' she said.

'No,' she said honestly.

'Just try to imagine it.'

Jackie did. She had a brief vision of herself, maybe with a modest veil, trotting up the aisle to meet Dan in his morning suit; and it all went perfectly well and the tulle was working out just fine – in fact some guests did a few oohs and aahs, and she was gratified, even if it was a little itchy – until she got about halfway up the church, and then she could see Dan at the top of the church, turning round to admire her . . .

It wasn't Dan at all. Somehow her brain had transplanted Henry into his place instead.

Appalled, she blurted, 'You know, I think I'm going to have to leave this till another time.'

'If you don't like tulle, we can always go for satin.'

'No. Thanks. Honestly.' And she ran out of the shop.

Chapter Seven

Jackie met Henry in a pub in London. It was one of those chance meetings that would never have happened had Emma not been mean with money and made them get the tube instead of a taxi from the Royal Horticulturist Society to their cheap guesthouse, and then dragged them both off at the wrong stop entirely. Which was why, after a day traipsing around the Chelsea Flower Show, they had ended up in some pub called the Crypt, completely lost and carrying two begonias, a tropical palm tree and a selection of ferns.

'Surely there'll be a King Edward further up the road? Or a Horse and Hound or something?' Emma asked, looking around nervously. The lighting in the pub was red and erotic, and the music throbbed. Occasionally, a strobe light flashed across her face, making her freckles look raised.

'We're staying,' said Jackie firmly. She liked the place; there was a slight air of danger about it, a feeling that anything might happen which, after a day diligently plodding around artificial gardens with Emma, was quite attractive. Anyway, she needed to take the weight off her feet, squashed and battered beyond all recognition in a gorgeous pair of silver pumps that hadn't been designed to cover great distances. Or any distance at all, really. When would she ever learn her lesson about wearing sensible shoes? And how was she going to get the palm tree past the air stewardess tomorrow?

'Cigarette smoke won't do these any good,' Emma fretted, laying down her precious plants on top of the bar, and firmly pushing away an ashtray. 'Still,' she said, 'the whole trip was really useful. In fact, I've jotted down all my ideas for when we open our own shop.' She busily took out a notebook. Jackie tried to look interested. You had to admire Emma: so earnest, so focused, while Jackie stood, with her tongue guiltily hanging out for a drink, and checked the place out.

The pub was packed. The other drinkers seemed to be very stream-lined, and they drank quickly. A lot of them seemed to know each other, and the women waved at each other in a kind of tinkly fashion. Jackie had never seen so much lipgloss in one room before. Her own make-up lay in crusty ruins around the region of her chin, and her raincoat, so bold and red this morning, was damp and dirty at the hem. Oh well. She looked away from the glossy women to a gang of men over in the corner drinking bottled beer and flexing their muscles under designer shirts. They'd obviously had a competition earlier to see who could get the most gel into their hair.

'Stop,' Emma hissed, following her gaze.

'What?'

'They might get the wrong idea.'

'I'm only looking.'

'You're not. You're sending out all these signals. You have no subtlety about you, Jackie.'

Honestly! Just because a person smiled, it was suddenly a crime? But Jackie had always been completely hopeless at any kind of coyness when it came to the opposite sex, or playing hard to get. It wasn't for the lack of trying; she had spent many hours in front of the mirror practising bored looks, and attempting to watch people in her periph-eral vision. But it gave her migraines, and made her feel all false and silly.

The men were looking back now and Jackie hastily turned away, for Emma's sake. Besides, on closer inspection they were a bit dodgy looking.

'There's no harm in it, Emma. Besides, it's ages since we had a man.' She was being diplomatic. Both of them knew it had been several years in Emma's case, and with no light on the horizon at all.

Emma's shoulders hunched over defensively under her brown coat. 'Look at *your* last one,' she said.

'Well, yes,' Jackie was forced to concede. In April she'd had a short, unsatisfactory fling with a lecturer who she had somehow imagined would be profound and deep and with whom she would end up discussing the meaning of life at four in the morning over a bottle of bourbon. But he had liked cheeseburgers and indecently early nights and had had an interest in *Buffy the Vampire Slayer* that had verged on the creepy.

'We just weren't suited,' she said.

'You might have more success if you chose a little more carefully,' Emma said.

'What?'

'Your problem is that you go for men with . . . I don't know, an "aura" about them.'

'An *aura*!' This was a new one to Jackie.

Emma didn't usually get drawn into conversations about men and romance and things. She'd much prefer to discuss geraniums. But tonight she was standing her ground.

'It's true. You never choose men on the basis of anything useful, like they're good-looking, or have a great job, or they're fantastic in bed. Instead, you fall for guys with sad eyes, or a wild streak, or because they're pseudo-philosophers, or because they look like James Dean.'

She had to bring that incident up, of course. 'He *did* look like James Dean,' Jackie said strongly. It was nobody's fault that the man in question hadn't been able to string two intelligent sentences together, and really only looked like James Dean when the lighting was dim. Very dim.

'You let yourself get all swept up in the moment,' Emma went on. 'You just don't stop to think.'

Why were people always saying that to her? 'Think' meant assess, of course. Weigh up, analyse, measure, gauge, calculate – all the things that Jackie was completely hopeless at – until the very last drop of spontaneity and passion was wrung from every wretched thing! Could Emma seriously be suggesting that potential mates be held up against some silly set of requirements? That love could somehow be ordered to plan?

'I'm not going to settle down with someone just because they have a job and a car and a face that doesn't make me scream,' she said loudly. 'Mr Reliable. Mr Steady.'

'Who, then? Some idiot with an aura?'

'I'll choose someone who makes my heart sing!' Jackie said grandly.

She knew true love was out there somewhere. Why else were so many songs written about it? So many films about boy-meets-girl? So much great literature and art and poetry dedicated to the bone-crushing, heart-twisting feeling that was love? She just had to hang around long enough for it to show up.

'Excuse me!' She waved for the barman.

He came over slowly, and with a slight attitude, Jackie thought. Still, he was young and slick and easy on the eye.

'Are you ladies with the private party?' he enquired, in a way that meant he knew full well they weren't.

'Sorry?'

He threw a look at the ferns. 'Or are you just here to do the flowers?'

'What?' Emma shot frostily. She could be very fierce when anybody put down her profession. She had said once that florists walked a lonely path, along with hairdressers, actresses and astrologists. And possibly wedding planners, who weren't taken seriously at all. When you looked at it like that, Jackie had said, the path wasn't that lonely; there were quite a lot of them when you added them all up.

'We didn't know it was a private party,' Jackie told him.

He arched an eyebrow disbelievingly. 'There's a red cord across the door.'

'Well, yes, but we just climbed over it.'

'I know. You were captured on CCTV.' He lifted his head, the better to look down his nose at them. 'I'll have to ask you to leave. It's *Globe* guests only. The deputy editor is leaving – Norma Jacobs.'

They should have said, 'Norma! Of course!' and acted all knowledge-able, but they weren't that desperate for a drink, and it had been a long day, and Jackie would have been quite happy to call it a night had a blast of icy wind not blown around her legs as the pub door opened sharply, and in marched a tall, slightly crumpled, grim-faced man who ignored greetings from left and right and made straight for the bar.

'For heaven's sake,' Emma muttered, shielding her precious plants from the breeze.

He wasn't alone. Another man followed, shorter, fatter and much less good-looking, and he seemed rather exasperated.

'There's no point blaming yourself, Henry,' he called.

Henry. Jackie turned the name over in her head as Henry swept past them without so much as a glance, leaving palm tree fronds fluttering in his wake. He flung himself onto a bar stool further up. The slick barman promptly abandoned Emma and Jackie and went scurrying over.

'Charming,' Emma complained.

The barman needn't have wasted his energy. Henry ignored him completely. His friend had to order the drinks while Henry looked into the middle distance and smouldered. Jackie had never actually met a man who smouldered, and didn't really believe they existed outside period TV adaptations, but Henry was doing a beautiful job of it.

Emma was looking too. Well, it was hard not to. 'I suppose he's quite dishy.' She still used words like that, along with 'disco' and 'bonk'.

'If you like that sort of thing,' Jackie said nonchalantly, who most certainly did.

As well as smouldering, he also roused himself occasionally to throw the odd tortured glance around the place. Every time the pub door opened his very blue eyes would dart over at it longingly as though he wanted to run away. And the place stuffed to the ceiling with blonde-haired women smoking long thin cigarettes and wearing next to nothing! Lord only knows what it would take to win the interest of a man like Henry. A man who, right now, was lighting a cigarette and dragging on it in quiet, charismatic anguish.

'Crikey,' Emma said. 'Maybe his dog has died.'

The minute the barman put Henry's drink down – whisky, natu-rally – he grabbed it up and swallowed it in one go before settling back to the business of brooding.

Jackie couldn't take her eyes off him. Like Emma said, she had no subtlety about her. But what tragedy! What depth. Already she was entertaining secret fantasies of rescuing him from whatever private hell consumed him, and consoling him between her 36C bosoms. He must have felt her lusty gaze because he suddenly looked over, his deep blue eyes holding hers for a moment, and she felt her entire world skid noisily to a halt. He might as well have tattooed his name on her heart.

Beside her, Emma was saying something like, 'Come on, will we go? We're not going to be served in here.'

Jackie didn't reply.

Then Emma, always alert to impending disaster, looked at her sharply and said, 'Sweet Lord. You're going to fall for him, aren't you?'

It was too late. She already had.

Further up the bar, Henry Hart utterly disliked himself for the first time in his life. He wasn't just being melodramatic; this wasn't some piddly little moment of self-hate, the kind of minor irritation with yourself that would pass over in thirty seconds. He was used to that: he already had a list of character faults as long as your arm. He was a grump in the mornings, for example, and his temper could only be classed as short. His friends told him that his jokes usually went too far, and he routinely forgot his mother's birthday. Plus, he had slept with a girl once in the dim past and never called her again, ever. No, all in all, he had no illusions about himself. But on the big things such as honesty and loyalty and fairness, he thought that he came out pretty OK. He could look himself in the mirror in the morning, put it that way, and nothing much kept him up at night except a tight deadline, or sometimes Mandy from advertising (whom he always called first thing the following morning, of course).

He could still see the letter in his mind, every word.

Dear Mr Hart,

Do you ever stop to think of the harm a bad review can do to a restaurant? Do you ever spare a thought for the people who have worked their entire lives to build up a business that you take apart in two throwaway lines? Do you realise that because of you, jobs are lost, reputations ruined, family businesses gone overnight? I hope you sleep well at night.

Well, he certainly wouldn't ever again. Not a chance of that! He'd be chewing his pillow in anguish and attempting to kill himself by overdosing on goose down. The honeymoon was over. Let's face it, he was a bum. A shit. An arrogant, malicious, stupid, selfish, irresponsible, idiotic, brainless prick.

'It's your job, Henry,' Dave said beside him, washing down a mouthful of peanuts with a swig of beer. 'You're a critic, it's what you do.'

'Oh, fuck off.'

78

'I can't,' Dave said gloomily. 'My mission is to bring you back in.'
'What?'
'Old fat-arse in HR said you handed in your notice.'
'So?'
'So I'm the only friend you have in the whole office and I was told to talk some sense into you.'
'Go away, Dave.'
'Come on, Henry. Let's get drunk, talk this thing through, cry a bit, sleep it off and go back to work in the morning, eh?'
Henry stared at him. Dave really thought he was over-reacting.
'I closed a restaurant, Dave.'
'Good thing too, judging by the crap you were served up. What did you say their toad-in-the-hole was like again? Oh yeah, I remember – turds set in cement.' He chuckled.
Henry was bug-eyed now. 'We're talking about jobs here, Dave. Chefs. Bar people. A waitress called Rose!' He had a sudden vision of her serving him that day, and he blanched. 'She was pregnant too.'
Dave sucked in his breath impatiently. 'It's their problem, Henry. If they want to serve food, they've got to be prepared for some fair criticism.'
But there was no 'fair criticism'. No 'level playing field'. How could anybody have believed – Henry included – that country restaurants and minor hotels were ready and waiting for hotshot London food critics to descend upon them and compare them to their city brothers? They weren't ready at all, no more than the poor sucker who'd written him that letter (there was no signature on it but Henry could see the man's face. He could smell his breath.) Henry had one of his urges to lay his head down, but his drink was in the way, and everybody would notice. They were all out tonight, of course, for Norma's leaving. Henry hadn't wanted to come. But Dave had insisted, said it was his duty. They'd all be out next week for Henry's leaving.
'Do you know what your problem is?' Dave said now.
'Please enlighten me.'
'You think too much.'
'I've often thought that myself.'
'Shut up. Always analysing stuff. You should be enjoying your job. If you can even call it a job. I mean, you get paid to describe what

you ate for *dinner* last night.' Dave always got in a crack like that after two drinks.

Wondering why he was even bothering, Henry said, 'It's a little bit more than that.'

'Yeah, yeah – you have to say whether the pasta was *al dente* and what colour the fucking soup was. Listen, I read your reviews, I know exactly what you have to write. I could do it myself! In fact, forget this entire conversation. Hand in your notice. Leave! I'll take over your job, and eat out in posh joints every night, and sit on my arse the next day getting over my hangover before writing a line or two about it.'

Henry said, 'And I'll apply for *your* job. Standing on touchlines in blizzard conditions, watching players from the third division murdering the beautiful game, trying to write down all those unpronounceable foreign names, blah, blah.'

'Don't laugh. That's hard work. That's real reporting,' Dave said. 'And I don't get paid half of what you get paid. A fucking *eighth* of what you get paid. I don't have a hotshot agent after me.'

'I don't either.' How had word of that got out? Honestly. There were no secrets in a newspaper office. Besides, Henry hadn't even spoken to her yet, didn't really see what he, a food critic, had to offer some posh agent called Adrienne.

Dave said, 'In fact, I wouldn't be a bit surprised if this whole thing worked in your favour.'

'What?' Henry was mystified.

'You closed a restaurant, Henry. Not many critics can do that. When word gets around, and it always does . . .'

Henry looked at him very coldly. 'You think I'd want to *benefit* from this?'

'Spare me,' Dave said. 'If you'd really wanted to leave over this, you'd have already left. Cleared your desk and gone. We wouldn't even be standing here discussing it.' He picked up his drink. 'So just chill out and enjoy the party, OK? By the way, I think Hannah's got her eye on you. Lucky you.'

He disappeared off into the crowd. Henry was left with a nasty little taste in his mouth. Dave had to do it, of course. Strip away his comfortable cloak of anguish. Now he was forced into a decision: either to follow through immediately on his resignation and be done with it, or stay at this wretched party and admit that his crisis of conscience was merely cosmetic.

He looked around, as if hoping that someone would make the decision for him. Look at Norma over there, drunk already, and crying and carrying on as if these people were her lifeblood and she couldn't survive a day without them; when in reality she was off to a new life in Spain with a thirty-year-old. The usual group of sycophants surrounded her – air-kissing each other now but, oh, wait till Monday morning when Norma's desk came up for grabs.

The bar was already running low on vodka and bottled beer, and Henry knew this shindig would go on all night. He couldn't bear it; not one more second of this excessive, superficial, cheap, depressing carry-on that he had somehow let himself become a part of. He was done with it! Enough was enough. He would stand up for what he believed in. And besides, he could always find a job cooking school dinners or something. Honest labour for an honest wage! It would be refreshing.

Full of tipsy self-righteousness, he drained his whisky, slammed the glass down on the bar, and squared his shoulders. It was time to leave the OK Corral once and for all.

There was someone peeking at him from between a couple of potted plants. Leaves framed her face and obscured her neck, so that for a moment it seemed to Henry that her head was actually growing, like some beautiful, exotic flower. He blinked – could it be the whisky? But no, there she was again, bobbing out of the leaves to peek quickly at him once more. She had frizzy hair of an indeterminate colour and a delicate, angular kind of face that had a directness, a boldness that would make you look at her. And listen to her laughing! At him? He straightened defensively. She was guffawing, actually, and hurling back that mass of frizzy hair.

He wondered whether she was connected with the newspaper. But he'd have remembered her if he'd seen her around. Besides, everything about her, from her out-of-control hair to her bright red coat to her questionable shoes, set her at odds with the glossy girls from the office. And anyhow, she was too animated, too unguarded to be one of them. Plus, her friend appeared to be wearing wellington boots; fairly conclusive evidence that neither of them was involved with any form of media, except maybe a farming programme.

He watched her out of the corner of his eye. She had talked the barman into supplying them with drinks and she sat up boldly on her seat with her legs crossed, one leg swinging energetically back and forth in those extraordinary shoes. She was delighted to be here, he could see. She actually found these people fascinating! Most of them turned Henry's stomach, including himself. Especially himself. But she liked them. And suddenly, the room seemed to grow brighter for Henry, everything more acceptable.

Then she shot him another of those wide-eyed, open looks and he knew that she liked him too. He found himself thinking *yippee*, a word he hadn't used since he'd been about nine.

But he had been about to leave. In fact, he still was. This was his moral fibre at stake, after all, a very serious matter. Plus, of course, other minor things like his job and his big house and his Coupe and his expense account and probably several casual girlfriends – they wouldn't want to go out with a school-dinner cook – and his growing reputation in the culinary world.

No matter! His mind was made up.

He threw back his shoulders, and marched across the pub. Just as he reached the door, some incredible, irresistible force, probably testosterone, made him swing sharply to his right and he skidded to a halt in front of the woman with the hair. He stared at her; she stared at him, and finally he managed, 'Can I buy you a drink?'

It was probably the sex, he told himself afterwards. Well, what else had him rushing up the aisle three months later? Chemistry wasn't in it. They were rampant, always jumping on each other every chance they got. Entire days went by with them holed up in the bedroom, the phone off the hook. He'd had to reinforce the base of the bed twice, and apologise to the neighbour next door who had complained about the noise. Weird thing was, if you were to press him on it now, he couldn't even say exactly why he'd fancied her so much. She was attractive, sure, in a kooky kind of way, but she wasn't stunning, not like Mandy, whom he hadn't seen since. And that damn hair of hers got everywhere; he was always picking strands of it out of his privates. She had a voice that drove him crazy, all scratchy and squeaky like some kind of demented mouse, and she was incapable of closing a door – a car door, a house door, the fridge door – after herself.

Or maybe all those things had just annoyed him afterwards: when things had started to go wrong. Maybe in the beginning everything had been perfect. Yes, he was sure it had been. Because surely he hadn't stayed in the pub that night, against all his better judgement, for someone who had merely irritated him? Hadn't they been in love?

'Not that she's admitting to it,' he spat out.

Tom, the rookie solicitor, looked up, startled. They were sitting in his little office waiting for the return of Mr Ian Knightly-Jones who was tied up in court doing battle with *Hello!* magazine, or *OK!* – one of those. Tom held a copy of Henry's divorce papers delicately by its very tips.

'I'm just thinking aloud,' Henry clarified. 'According to her, we never had a happy moment!'

'Um, yes. Unfortunately, divorce petitions tend to focus on the more negative aspects of marriage.'

'The way she's going on, it's like it was torture from start to finish. Now, I'd be the first to admit that it went bad – I want a divorce as much as she does, let's get that clear. I just didn't get around to asking for it first. But I'd like to think I'm big enough to admit that at one point I *loved* the woman. However misguided it might have been.'

Tom swallowed, looked at the door, and said, 'I'm sure Mr Knightly-Jones won't be much longer.'

'Let's just get on with it,' Henry said, gruff. He was embarrassing himself, and this man.

Tom hesitated. 'Don't you want to wait for Mr Knightly-Jones?'

'Why? I've agreed to buy her out of her share of the house. I can give you a cheque now if you want. So as far as I'm aware I've just got to acknowledge receipt of the papers and all that.'

'Yes, that's correct . . .'

'So? You can handle it, can't you?'

'Oh, well, certainly . . .' Puffing out his chest a bit, Tom fluttered about, gathering files and papers and pens, and even a paper cup of water, as if Henry might pass out shortly after signing. That'd be the day. As far as Henry was concerned, today was the first step to moving on. Not that he hadn't already, of course. Absolutely! He'd only thought about her twenty-seven times today, and it was practically lunchtime.

Tom eased a form across the desk, making no sudden movements. His voice dropped to a whisper. 'The D10. Acknowledgement of Service. If you could just sign where I've marked an "x". Then we'll return it to court and they'll let us know when the date is set for the hearing. You don't even have to show up for that. Most people don't. The decree nisi should be issued a couple of weeks later, and the decree absolute six weeks after that.' He paused. 'Have you any questions?'

'No.'

'No?'

'That seems perfectly clear.'

'Oh!' Tom seemed startled and rather pleased at Henry's confidence in his explanation, and he sat a little taller.

'Pen, please?' Henry eventually had to ask.

'Oh! Sorry.' Tom produced his own fountain pain and handed it over.

'Thank you.' Henry pulled his chair in closer and bent over the form.

Tom watched over him, prattling on, more confident now. 'You're my first divorce. Well, my first client ever, to be honest. Not that you're *my* client, of course . . . Anyhow, Mr Knightly-Jones will be very pleased that we've managed to tie this up between us this morning. And it's nice that it's all ended so well for you, isn't it?' He rushed on, 'Not that divorce is ever a *happy* occasion. I suppose for some people it can be very traumatic, very unpleasant. But I do think it's helpful that Miss, um, Ball has been pretty decent with the old unreasonable behaviour, don't you? Saves all sorts of unpleasantness.' He must have taken Henry's silence as some sort of encouragement, because he went on, in quite a jolly tone now, 'I mean, Failure to Participate Fully in Family Life. Can't get much nicer than that!' He sat down on the side of the desk now and swung a leg back and forth. Henry wanted to amputate it. 'It's always much easier when people don't go to town on things, don't you think? What's the point in getting all malicious and hurtful and scoring points off each other, especially when the whole thing is dead in the water anyway?'

That was exactly the thinking behind it, of course, Henry suddenly realised. Get it all over and done with as quickly as possible without getting anybody stirred up. Which meant not really telling the truth in those divorce papers. It meant soft-soaping Henry with her little list of non-offensive 'faults' on his part in the hopes that he would shut up and sign.

Well, he wouldn't. Not only had she denied that their marriage was ever happy, but she was now denying, blatantly, in court papers, the very things that had turned the marriage bad in the end! To look at that pathetic petition, you'd think the whole thing had crashed and burned on a few trivial offences that a good chat over a bottle of wine wouldn't have sorted out.

'I need another sheet of paper,' he told Tom.

Tom's foot stopped mid-swing. 'Sorry?'

'To write down all the things that *she* did wrong in the marriage.'

'I'm afraid I don't . . .'

'How come she gets a little box to write her list in?'

'Well, you see, she's the petitioner. She's the one divorcing you.'

'So she gets a box and I don't? Even if she contributed as much to the marriage breakdown as I did? More, in fact! Did you know that she walked out on me after making a dinner date?'

Tom threw a desperate look at the door. 'Well, I—'

'I am not agreeing to all these . . . these lies!' He rattled the divorce petition 'If she wants a divorce, she can take her share of responsibility too! She can face up to the facts of the marriage, not some silly crap her solicitor dreamed up.'

Tom had gone quite pale now. 'But . . . but there's nothing you can do. Either you agree to the divorce or you defend it. And you can't do that.'

'Why not?'

'Because . . . because nobody ever defends a divorce!'

Henry waited patiently.

'You have to have serious grounds! You can't stop someone divorcing you just because you didn't get your own box!'

Henry said loudly, 'Well, I want my own box! I want a fair and accurate portrayal of our marriage, and I'll defend this thing until I get it!' And in a rather nice dramatic touch, he aimed squarely and threw the petition in the bin.

Chapter Eight

Velma was livid. Her anger was so great that she seemed swollen by it, puffed up to twice her usual size, and she spilled out majestically over her swivel chair.

'This is most unusual,' she thundered. '*Most* unusual.'

Dan piped up, 'That's what I said. Didn't I, Jackie? I said people don't normally go around contesting divorces.'

'Defending,' Jackie said, again. 'You defend a divorce.' But Dan kept insisting on using the word 'contest', adding to the confrontation of the whole thing. In fact, ever since they'd got Velma's phone call that morning he had been going around hunched over in a semi-rugby tackle. Then insisted on coming into Velma's office to 'discuss tactics'. She had been so taken aback by everything that she had let him.

'I've never had this happen to me before,' Velma confirmed, looking again at the offending letter. 'Not once! And I've been in this business, oh, let me see, how many years now?' They waited expectantly as her brow puckered. 'Two, at least.'

'He can't stop her, can he?' Dan enquired hotly. 'I mean, this thing will go through, won't it? He can't insist they stay married?'

'Good God, no!' Velma shuddered as though the very notion were unspeakable. 'But it means he'll have to get his day in court, unfortunately. It will very likely hold everything up.'

'What?' Dan had that very week paid a hefty deposit to the Spring Courts Golf Hotel (non-refundable, non-transferable, and two more nons he couldn't remember at that moment, but they weren't nice).

'By a considerable amount of time,' Velma added.

'The bastard,' Dan ground out. 'Oh, sorry, Velma.'

'That's perfectly fine, go right ahead,' she said graciously. 'I encourage clients to let it all out. I had a woman sit there last week saying "scumbag" for half an hour. I can't tell you how much better she looked when she left.' She jerked a finger towards the ceiling. 'Just mind the volume. There's a prayer group upstairs.'

Jackie had said very little so far. She had not expected this. He hadn't even replied to her letter, yet he was now going to defend the divorce? Until now, the whole process, and Henry, had all seemed rather removed and distant, and somehow in the past. Something to be tied up. But with one short, rude letter, Henry had announced his arrival back in her life. Silly, but she could almost feel him in the room, skulking about and brooding, and out to make her life as difficult as possible. Well, he just . . . wouldn't!

She swung her steel-tipped shoe back and forth rather dangerously, and said to Velma, 'What exactly does he want?' Because it certainly wasn't her. He'd had ample opportunity in the past eighteen months to try and win her back. As if she would have gone back, anyway! If he had even dared, she'd have tossed him on the compost heap out the back of Flower Power. 'Is it the house? Well, he can have it. All of it! Write back and say I don't want my half.'

The minute the words were out of her mouth, she thought, oh feck. She'd raised half the loan on Flower Power on the basis of it.

Dan shifted in his chair. 'Let's not be too rash here, Jackie.'

Well, yes, but rash was her middle name, and she couldn't backtrack now, not without losing considerable face, and so she added, in a cavalier fashion, 'Tell him I don't want a penny from him!'

'He doesn't want the house, he doesn't mention it at all,' Velma said.

'Oh.' She felt weak with relief.

Velma added, 'That's what makes it all so baffling. You see, usually the only time people contest divorces is if there's some advantage to themselves. Financially maybe, or else access to any children.'

Dan shot Jackie a searching look. 'There isn't . . . ?'

She didn't dignify that with a response.

Velma went on, 'They can threaten to defend until those things are sorted out to their satisfaction. But in this case, he doesn't appear to have anything to gain at all. Except –' and she peered at the letter – 'accurate representation, as he puts it.'

'That is so unfair!' Jackie exploded. 'And I was so nice and everything!'

Velma tut-tutted. 'I know. You didn't put down half what you could have, in my opinion.'

Velma had wanted to 'beef things up'. She had strongly advised Jackie to throw plenty at him, in the hopes that some of it would stick. She had asked all sorts of leading questions about Henry's drinking habits, and whether he'd had any unhealthy fixations which mightn't look too good to a judge in a court of law. 'Everybody does it,' she'd assured Jackie.

But Jackie had resisted all attempts at exaggeration. In fact, in another show of remarkable maturity, she had watered down some of the complaints. When she thought of it now! At one count, there had been at least twenty-two serious examples of 'unreasonable behaviour' that would easily have sufficed, and that wasn't counting that week in Spain, in which he'd exhibited a special 'holiday' code of bad behaviour.

But she hadn't used any of them. Even the very big ones. The worst one of all. No, she had been mindful of further acrimony. She had thought that it would be better for everybody if she didn't hold up all of his bad bits to scrutiny. And after all her efforts, all her maturity, he wasn't going to let her divorce him? Well! She tried to stamp down on her anger, but couldn't. Her fists balled up, her face went hot, and in another moment her hair would spring loose from the gallon of hairspray she had applied that morning. Henry was the only man in the world who could bring about her entire disintegration in ten seconds flat.

To add insult to injury, Dan reached over and squeezed her hand. 'You did your best, honey.'

'What's that supposed to mean?'

'Just that this isn't your fault.'

'I know it's not my fault, Dan. It's Henry's choice to defend. I can't do anything about that!'

'Well, I suppose if you'd hit him a little harder in the first instance . . .'

'Sorry?'

'Sometimes it doesn't pay to be too soft on people, you know? They can come right back at you if they sense any weakness at all.'

'It wasn't being soft, Dan. I was trying to be humane.'

'I know that. Don't take it out on *me*, Jackie.'

Across the desk Velma cleared her throat, as if sensing she might be in for some repeat business even at this early stage. 'I think we need to register our absolute disbelief and disgust at this pathetic attempt to thwart the due process of law,' she thundered. 'I'll write to his solicitor immediately. I'll tell him that we are not prepared to wait around twenty-eight days at his client's command! I'll curl the hairs on his head!'

'Twenty-eight *days*?' Dan enquired.

'Well, yes. If Henry Hart wants to defend it, that's how long he's got to file what is called an Answer.'

Dan, who had only been waiting for an excuse to explode afresh, did so now, magnificently. 'This is ridiculous! We have a wedding to plan! A hotel booked! I have five hundred invitations at the printers right now! Oh, you'll come, won't you, Velma?'

'Me? Oh, no . . .'

'We absolutely insist, don't we, Jackie?'

'Dan, you said the hotel warned you they can't fit a single other person.'

'They can surely fit Velma!' Then, suddenly aware that he might have touched on some sensitivities, he blundered on, 'And a guest!'

'I don't want to impose . . .' Velma said.

'Nonsense! We have to have all our friends at our wedding!' Dan insisted, who hadn't met Velma until ten minutes ago.

'Well, in that case I'd be delighted.' She confided, 'I don't often get to see happy endings in my line of business. To be honest, you start to lose your faith after a while. I try to remain detached and all that, and not let it affect me, but when I walk down the street and see a couple holding hands and totally besotted with each other – kind of like you two folks, so obviously in love – well, I can't help thinking to myself, *that's* not going to last. It might be all fine and dandy now, but sooner or later, he's going to cheat on her, or she's going to hen-peck him to death, or they're just going to wake up one morning and find that the sight of the other person makes them want to throw up. They don't *think* it's going to happen. Nobody does when they walk up the aisle. But it's a fact of life. Especially now when fifty per cent of all marriages in the UK end in divorce. Course, it's not as bad here, but it's getting that way.' Her voice dropped to a new, gloomy low. 'Honestly, if I'd known it was going to affect me this badly, I would never have chosen to be a divorce lawyer. I'd have trained as a beautician, or a childcare worker maybe. Some happy job.' Then she gave herself a little shake and sat up. 'Anyhow, thanks for your invitation! But it'll just be me on my own. There's no way I'm going down *that* road, thank you very much.'

There was a depressing little silence. Dan looked as though he might be about to say something but couldn't muster the energy. Jackie was in no mood to cheer him up.

Velma stood chirpily and made for the door. 'If you'd like to wait just a second, I'll get my dictaphone and we'll get a letter off to Henry's solicitor today.'

Jackie and Dan were left alone. Jackie stared studiously at the peeling pink wallpaper behind Velma's desk.

'Sorry,' Dan said beside her.

'Sorry for what? For calling me too soft? Or for going on about wedding invitations in the middle of my divorce?'

'Jackie . . .'

'Or maybe for strutting around like you're in some testosterone contest? Treating me like my value has suddenly shot up because my ex-husband might not want to divorce me?'

Dan looked appalled. 'Jackie, I think you've totally misread my intentions.'

'Have I? How come I feel that I've got absolutely no support from you during all this?'

'I *am* supporting you! I'm just so angry about it all.'

'Because I'm upsetting all our plans.'

'No!'

'I was the one who wanted to wait, Dan. I said we shouldn't make plans until I was divorced.'

'I know! I'm sorry I didn't listen to you. Because you were absolutely right: it looks like we're probably going to have to delay things at this stage. And before you say anything, I'm not just thinking about practical matters, OK? I love you, Jackie. I want to marry you *now*, not when your ex-husband says I can.' He tried to touch her but she stood up and collected her bag.

'You know, maybe it's not such a bad thing that we'll have to post-pone the wedding. Because right now I think that we probably rushed into it in the first place.'

'Jackie!'

'Tell Velma I had to go.'

She went straight to the gym, even though she hadn't gone in four months and had forgotten how to use most of the machines. In fact, she really wasn't a gym person at all, but had been seduced by a neon billboard at the traffic lights near her apartment which had promised her a *New You!* for only seven euro a week. That was about the time Dan had arrived on the scene, with his passion for jogging and all things physical, and she had recklessly signed up for a whole year. After two near-fatal mishaps on the stairmaster, and no sign at all of a *New You*, she now confined herself to the pool, where she floated on her back, hardly sending a ripple out, as if to counteract the way she seemed to conduct the rest of her life.

Things had seemed simpler years ago, when you could get up to all sorts of things and there were very few consequences, or at least none very serious, unless you were particularly unfortunate. You could fall in love with idiots with impunity, or jack in your job, or do any number of foolish things without somebody sending you a solicitor's letter. Mind you, she had never gone so far as to *marry* any of her passions before.

She wondered again what he wanted. Not a swift and clean ending, that much was clear. Revenge? But why? She hadn't done anything wrong! She hadn't cheated on him, or treated him very badly, or boiled any household pets. *He* was the one who had let *her* down! Appallingly. Unforgivably. She had every reason to throw the book at him, while he was prepared to hold up her marriage to Dan over a bunch of words that nobody in the whole world would read except themselves. Arguing over syntax! Just for the hell of it because what she had done didn't please him! And so he would waste thousands of his own pounds, and thousands of hers, dragging this thing through the courts with absolutely no gain for either of them except to his own foolish pride.

When she thought about it like that, she wasn't even surprised. Obtuse, crooked, miserable soul that he was! She felt a bit superior now. You'd think after eighteen months he would have mellowed:

forgotten about her and moved on to his usual selection of Mandys and Ninas and Hannahs. He wasn't a man who could bear his own company for too long. He liked the distraction of women, as she very well knew; attractive, glossy women to take his mind off himself, to tell him he was great and witty and famous and a fantastic ride. Really, the man had never needed a wife. He'd just needed a prop, someone who would orbit around him adoringly while he was busy being Henry Hart. And the minute she had stopped doing that, the minute she'd had the tenacity to hold up her hand and say, 'What about me?' he had opted out of their marriage.

Or, rather, to other comforts, where everything was less demanding.

He had said to her on their honeymoon, 'You make me so happy.' But it wasn't a statement, one of those flowery, passionate things people say on those occasions. It had sounded more like an order at the time, and a rather tall one too. In retrospect, she supposed that he was used to women making him happy, without any effort or inconvenience to himself.

Maybe she had been reading too much into it. After all, there were so many other things he threw out without really meaning them. 'Anything for you' was another Henry favourite. Materially, yes. But she swiftly came to realise that with Henry, you only got as much as he was prepared to give. So it was just another line that he trotted out, to mask what he might really be feeling. For a man who made his living from words, he used them sparingly at home. Sometimes he would come home from work, black-faced, and you couldn't get a syllable out of him! Jackie, who had been at home all day by herself looking at the four walls, would press and press until eventually he would snap something cryptic, something cutting about her keen interest in his work – she was only making conversation! – before going upstairs in a huff. Into his study in the attic where the door would be soundly closed and he wouldn't emerge for hours, some-times dishevelled and in a sweat. At first, she had thought he was the kind of person who needed to unwind alone after coming home from work. She'd made every excuse in the book for him.

Lying in the pool, the water lapping at her, she felt very superior. Well, look at all the lessons she had learned from the whole miserable experience! She hadn't sat around for eighteen months brooding and plotting and planning; she had picked herself up, taken a long, hard look at herself, and set to weeding out all the things that had led to the disaster in the first place. And, a scant eighteen months later, she had turned herself into practical, sensible, non-excitable, straight-haired (almost) successful entrepreneur. Her fecklessness was a thing of the past. She would never again fall for a man on the basis of a pair of tortured eyes. She was *happy* now.

And it was all down to Henry, really. In fact, she ought to call him up and thank him for being instrumental in her transformation. Imagine, if she had never met Henry, she would never have met Dan, if you wanted to think about it like that. And she did. Badly.

Still, every now and then something would come along that would pierce her to the heart; 'their' song playing on the car radio, for example ('Karma Chameleon', you kind of had to be there) and she would sit, frozen at the traffic lights until someone hooted her from behind. Or the aroma from the open door of a restaurant as she passed by; after all, they had spent most of their brief marriage scoffing bakes and gratins and tagines. Which were not to be confused with tangerines, as Jackie had learned. But Henry hadn't made a show of her that time; he had spared her blushes by pressing her head tenderly into his shoulder, and she had scarcely felt his body shaking with suppressed laughter.

But they were only moments. And a few small moments didn't make up for the something that was rotten at the core.

When she got home, she slammed the door closed loudly behind her, and stomped across the hard tiled hall in her high heels, lest anyone be in any doubt that they were in the doghouse.

In the kitchen, she found Dan bent over the sink, applying two ice packs to his puffy face. His skin was blotchy and red, and his nose bulbously swollen. He straightened quickly when she came in.

'Dan! My God, what happened to you? Did you get in a fight?'

He waved her away. 'I'll be fine in a minute.'

'Should I call a doctor?'

'No.' Even his neck seemed twice its usual size.

'But . . . you're sick!'

In a voice that was all choked and hoarse, he admitted, 'I went to the shop this afternoon.'

'What? Flower Power?'

'Yes.'

'Oh, great!' She was cross. 'You know what they said in the hospital! That another brush with flowers could be lethal!'

'I am not going to get killed by a bunch of fucking flowers,' Dan snapped back. 'Don't make me out to be a complete idiot, Jackie.'

'Well, you obviously don't listen. They warned you that the allergy would get worse. And now look at you!' She dabbed at him with the ice pack.

He brushed her off and said, 'I wanted to talk to you, OK?'

'And you couldn't have phoned?'

'I figured you'd take that the wrong way too. You'd say, oh, he couldn't be bothered to apologise in person!'

'Oh,' she said grudgingly. 'Well, it could have waited till I got home.'

'But that wouldn't have done either!' he said. 'Then I'd have been accused of being lackadaisical! Complacent!'

'I would not have accused you of that!' Jackie said, even though she probably would have.

Dan went on loudly, 'So I put on my protective plastic jacket, bought a big box of chocolates, four tabs of Sinus Eze and I went around there in person, Jackie. To the shop. To apologise. To say sorry for behaving like a pig today. And throw myself at your feet and beg you not to call off our engagement.' He gave a torturously congested sniff. 'But those damned hanging baskets outside the door got me before I could even make it in.'

'Oh, Dan.'

'Turns out you were at the gym anyhow,' he added neutrally. 'I saw your car there on the way back.' He looked at her. 'So there you go. I'm sorry the apology has come a little late in the day, but I assure you I mean every word of it. Now, if you don't mind, I think I need to go to bed. But I'm pretty sure I'll make it through the night.' He hobbled towards the door.

'Dan. Wait.'

He turned and looked at her through alarmingly red, slitted eyes.

'Why would you think our engagement was off?' she said.

'Why? Maybe because you gave a whopping great hint that you regretted the whole thing!'

'I most certainly did not!'

'No? You said that it wasn't such a bad thing that we might have to postpone the wedding! That maybe we'd rushed into it!' Just when you might begin to underestimate Dan, he would display remarkable powers of clarity and memory, right down to the full stops. 'How was I was supposed to feel after that, Jackie?'

'I was hurt, Dan, OK? Sometimes I say things I don't mean.'

'Isn't that a fact.'

She was starting to feel less sorry for his painful-looking face now. 'If you weren't going at this wedding like some kind of steamroller . . . I'm in the middle of a divorce, Dan, in case you haven't noticed.'

'Oh, I've noticed. Your divorce has been the single biggest defining feature of our engagement yet, Jackie. Every last thing has been carefully planned and decided with reference to your divorce. I haven't made a single move without first thinking, how will it fit in with Jackie's divorce? And then today, after all our plans are in place, your ex-husband sticks his oar in and decides that, actually, he's going to drag the whole thing out for months longer, and we'll have to postpone our wedding!'

'I know.'

'And the remarkable thing is, you don't seem all that upset about it!'

She stared at him. 'How could you think that? Of course I'm upset!'

'So upset you go off to the gym? While I'm at home here on the phone all afternoon cancelling all our arrangements?'

She couldn't believe they were arguing like this, and with their whole wedding arrangements in tatters around them. And Dan glaring at her, his jaw jutting out aggressively although she knew by the glint in his eye that he was desperately upset. Well, so was she! She had a tight little pain in her stomach, and given much more provocation she would very likely burst into tears.

And all because of Henry. He rushed into her mind like a nasty, sly cat among the pigeons. Causing trouble and upsetting her life, and he wasn't even living in the same country.

'Let's not fight,' she said. 'Please.'

It was all either needed, really, and they rushed into each other's arms in an awkward tangle of limbs, words tumbling out over each other.

'I'm so sorry.'

'I'm the one who should be sorry.'

'But you're perfectly right, we can't let this stupid divorce take over our whole lives!'

'No, I'm getting too upright about it. I should probably just relax. I mean it's going to happen sooner or later.'

'Well, of course it is! We might still be able to get married in, say, six months.'

'If you still want to.'

'Of course I do! I want nothing more.'

'Me too.'

'Your poor face.'

'To be honest, I'm finding it hard to think straight.'

He wanted to order in a meal and open a bottle of wine and have a romantic night in, but was forced to go to bed instead with enough medication to stun a horse. Jackie tucked him in tenderly.

'We shouldn't let him get to us, Dan. Even though that might be hard.'

But Dan was in an upbeat mood. 'I don't care about him so long as you still want to marry me.'

'You know I do.'

'Well, then We'll just have to wait until he gets fed up and leaves us alone.'

'Yes,' Jackie agreed, and they said goodnight tenderly, each of them anxious to reassure the other that everything was OK.

She again waited until Dan was asleep before tiptoeing downstairs and shutting the living-room door soundly. This time she didn't dither or forget the number, and Henry answered crisply on the second ring.

'Hello?'

She took a swift breath and ignored the flapping in her chest. 'Henry, it's Jackie.'

There was the briefest of pauses and then he went on, in exactly the same tone of voice, without fluctuation or hesitation, 'Oh. I suppose you're ringing about the divorce.'

Obviously no time was going to be wasted on pleasantries or

enquiries about each other's health. Well, good. Because she wasn't in the mood for it.

'Of course,' she said coolly. 'What else?'

He said, 'Your solicitor has obviously received the papers so shouldn't you be talking to her?' How well she knew that lofty little upswing that he liked to use at the end of his sentences! To make herself feel better, she tried to imagine him in his ratty old dressing gown, with sleep stuck in the corner of his eyes, and his hair on end.

'I thought maybe we could iron out our differences on the phone,' she said.

'And you'd be confident doing that?' he said. 'Ironing?'

For a moment she thought she'd misheard him. Then she flushed a furious red. Imagine bringing up her domestic shortcomings! And the ironing had never been her responsibility anyway. What, did he think he'd married a maid?

'That was cheap,' she said.

'Yes,' he admitted. 'I guess old habits die hard.' It wasn't exactly an apology.

She took a breath. 'Henry, I appreciate that this might be difficult for both of us. But surely you agree that it's best if we try and bring things to a conclusion in the most civil way possible?' Surely he couldn't argue with that?

'Did you rehearse all that?' he said, eventually.

'I did not!' Of course she had.

'I'm not being sarcastic. It's just that you don't really sound like yourself. You haven't for a while, actually.'

'What's that supposed to mean?' she snapped coldly.

He didn't elaborate, just said, 'Look, I'm not going to change my mind, Jackie. I presume that's why you're ringing me up. To try and persuade me against my better judgement. You were always good at that.'

Another barbed dig that she chose to ignore. 'I have no intention of persuading you.'

'What, then? To suggest that we be "friends"?' He snorted.

'No.'

'Good. Because you . . .' He stopped, amended it to, 'Because I think things have gone too far for that.'

She couldn't agree with him more but refused to be drawn into it. 'I just want my divorce, Henry.'

'And you can have it. Be my guest! I'm as anxious as you are to resolve all this.'

'Oh? Strange that, seeing as you're going to defend it.'

'I'm not defending our *marriage*,' he said, dismissive. 'We both know what a shambles that turned out to be. But I object very strongly to being blamed for the demise of the whole thing.'

He was incredible! Unbelievable. If he wasn't to blame for her leaving, then who was? The guy was living in some kind of denial, or else he thought that what he had done was OK.

But she didn't say any of this. What was the point? She didn't care any more. She just wanted her divorce. And so she said, 'Tell you what. Why don't *you* divorce *me*?' She had already checked this out with Velma. 'It's exactly the same process. And you can write anything you like about me. All my so-called faults and failings, all the things I did that drove you completely mad. Blame the entire thing on me!' She added under her breath, 'Even though we'd both know what a whopper that would be.'

He laughed. 'I have to hand it to you, Jackie. You're innovative.'

'Well, why not?' she challenged. 'That way I'll get my divorce and you'll get to vent your misguided spleen, Henry.'

'And you wouldn't care?' he said back. 'Even if I said things that weren't true?'

'No,' she said, cavalier. 'Go ahead. You're a good liar, Henry.'

'And you're good at avoiding unpleasant realities, Jackie. Just like you're doing now.'

That was what did it. Before she knew it, she found herself saying sweetly, even though she had never meant to tell him, had sworn she *wouldn't* tell him, 'You see, Henry, I'm getting married again. Naturally, I'm very anxious to get this matter out of the way as soon as possible. And if it means that I have to put up with a few insults from you, well, I don't mind at all.'

There was a long silence, satisfyingly long, and then Henry said evenly, 'Congratulations. But I'm still not divorcing you, Jackie.'

She lost her cool. And she had been doing so well, too. 'Just tell me what you want! Because I know you, you must want something!'

'Like I said. The truth.'

'If you want the truth, why don't you look at yourself?' she fired back.

'Believe me, I am. I have no problem taking my share of responsibility for our marriage breakdown. What I want, Jackie, is for you to take your share.'

He was unbalanced, she decided. He thought her wrongs could possibly compare to his? They didn't come close!

'So you want some stupid list of things that went wrong?'

'You never know,' he said, 'you might find it useful. You mightn't make the same mistakes with hubby number two.' He sounded amused.

She said scornfully, 'I'm not making any mistakes with number two. Because my new fiancé, thankfully, is completely different to you. The very opposite, in fact! He's warm and decent and *fun* and . . . and we're going to be very happy.'

'Who are you trying to convince here, Jackie? Me, or yourself?'

She said, 'Oh, shut up, Henry!' and slammed the phone down.

Chapter Nine

Dear Ms Murphy,

We acknowledge receipt of your letter of the 20th.

Mr Ian Knightly-Jones is in court this week, but has asked me to inform you that he is quite unused to the tone used in your correspondence and, indeed, some of the language. He also strongly rejects any insinuation that we might have influenced our client in order to 'string things out and line our pockets'. He further feels that his client's position needs no further clarification: Mr Hart is legally entitled to defend Ms Ball's divorce petition and advises us that he will do so.

Finally, Mr Knightly-Jones is not in a position at this time to take you up on your generous offer of 'putting a bit of business our way' if he would return the favour, as suggested in your postscript.

Yours sincerely,

Tom Eagleton

On behalf of Mr Ian Knightly-Jones

'He is a pig,' Lech complained. 'Nothing from him for eighteen months and now this! He waits until somebody else wants you, then he starts kicking up a fuss.' He was taking the whole thing very personally, which was sweet of him. 'Why can he not let you marry the man you love?'

He had no problems at all talking about love. In fact, he was a great man for airing his feelings on matters of the heart, his own and other people's. Emma could only take so much of it before she went red in the face. Just like now.

'It's probably his solicitor,' she said curtly. 'You know what they can be like. Whipping everybody up into a frenzy just so they can clock up enough hours for a second home in France.'

But Lech shook his head. 'I don't think so.'

'You've never even met him,' Emma challenged.

'No, but I am a man.'

'So that somehow qualifies you to talk about Henry?'

'It qualifies me to talk about love. About what a man feels for a woman. About his needs, his wants, his desires.'

She was puce in the face now. 'If you don't mind, I haven't had my lunch yet.'

It had been like this all week: sniping back and forth at each other. Jackie finally felt compelled to intervene.

'Relax, everybody. So he's defending the divorce. I've come to terms with it, OK?'

She must have sounded convincing, because Emma said, 'And you're not in the least bit curious? About why he's doing this?'

Like she had thought of a single other thing the whole week!

'I just don't know, Emma.'

Emma said, 'You don't think it could be some kind of knee-jerk reaction?'

'He knew it was coming. I wrote to him.'

'Ah, yes, but knowing something is going to happen doesn't necessarily prepare you for when it *does* happen. People do very strange things in fright.'

'Does he frighten easily? Henry? Is he a nervous type?' Lech enquired. He was still there, even though a bouquet awaited delivery.

'No. The pressure cooker exploded in the kitchen one day and he never moved a muscle,' said Jackie gloomily. She had been cooking, naturally.

Emma mused, 'And to think that we believed they were such simple creatures; that they would be quite happy once you gave them food and sex.'

Lech exploded, 'That is the most sexist thing I have ever heard in my life!'

'Just kidding,' said Emma.

He glared at her. 'You think that women have some kind of prerogative when it comes to feelings? That we are only out for one thing?'

'You have a girl sticker on the back of your car,' Emma pointed out clearly. It had obviously been bugging her for weeks.

'What?' He looked very confused for a moment, and then his face cleared. 'Ah! That came on the car when I bought it. What, you thought I went out and got it and stuck it on the car?'

She looked a little embarrassed now, but retaliated with, 'I don't see you out there on your hands and knees scraping it off!'

'I will go and do it now! This minute! If it offends you so much.' And off he went.

'Two days to go,' Emma said through gritted teeth. 'Then his probation is up and he is *gone.*' Then she said, 'Are you OK?'

'I'm fine.'

'It must be a shock, though. I mean, what's his game then? Henry?'

Jackie didn't know, except that he would absolutely love this, the fact that they were all huddled around trying to figure him out. It was like a crime investigation. What could he be up to? What could he possibly want? And the canopy not even rolled down outside the shop yet for the day because they were all too busy trying to see inside Henry's head!

Still, it was disconcerting to have actually been married to someone, only to realise that you didn't know them at all. To have shared a house and a bed and body fluids with a person, and then not have a clue as to what really made them tick! And there was Lech and Emma, and Dan, and Mrs Ball, and five hundred wedding guests, all demanding explanations that she couldn't give. Henry had mortified her in front of the lot of them! He got to look all cryptic and elusive and dangerous, while she ended up the blithering idiot of the piece: a woman who, in the course of her entire marriage, hadn't managed to grasp much more than her husband's name.

Maybe she didn't know Henry. She had to face that possibility. Certainly on the phone the other night he had seemed like a complete and utter stranger. Even his reaction to the news of her engagement, her trump card, had been anticlimactic to say the least. Instead of falling to the ground, whimpering and traumatised, as she had so fondly imagined, he had come right back with that horrible insinuation that she was destined to make a balls of that too.

It was infuriating, and shocking, the way he could still pierce her like that. That she had let him! No, it was obvious that her solid, untouchable core had developed some serious patches of rust, and needed shoring up immediately. So, as kind of an interim measure, she had gone right out the following day and had a facial, a new sleek hairdo, and a manicure that left her nails pointy, hard weapons. Her hair had sprung back out within the hour, of course, but she'd felt better nonetheless, shinier and less vulnerable, and Dan had seemed pleasantly surprised. Or, at least, he had taken her down to the club that night, and all the Fionas had sat a bit closer than usual. She, for her part, had listened attentively to the story of how Fiona, Big Connell's wife, had had to grow a fringe very quickly after her last Botox job which had left her forehead with a distinct overhang. Jackie told herself defiantly that she belonged with these people now – although she would definitely use a different plastic surgeon. And not one of them had mentioned the wedding postponement, which was very decent of them, even though Taig and Fiona had put off their month in South Africa just so they could attend, and now all the best villas were gone. Nobody enquired as to when a new date might be set. All of them knew it was a waiting game, and that the ball was very firmly in a court in London (this was from Rory; it was impossible to get through a night at the club without balls being mentioned in some context).

'Twenty days to wait,' Emma said.

'I know.'

Then Henry would have to file his Answer in court. It was as if their entire lives were on hold. Even Dan had stopped talking about the wedding plans. He just went around with a kind of controlled stoicism and, apart from that brief night in the club, busied himself on his computer in the evenings, sometimes long after Jackie had gone to bed.

'It's obviously getting to him too,' Emma added.

'I know.' Jackie sighed deeply. 'But he's being good about it.'

'I meant Henry.'

'What?'

'Well, he took the whole of last week off work.'

'What are you talking about?'

'He didn't write his column in Sunday's newspaper.'

'How do you know that?'

'I read the paper. You left it on the counter.'

'I did not.'

'Well, somebody did.'

'I didn't even buy last Sunday's newspaper.' It would have made her gag.

'I figured you were going to throw darts at his picture or something. Where the hell has it gone?' She searched under the counter.

They eventually found it in the compost heap and spread it out, soggy and wet. She was right; Henry hadn't done his usual review. It was written by someone called Wendy Adams.

'She has a much nicer turn of phrase, in my opinion,' Emma said stoutly.

Jackie closed the newspaper and threw it in the bin. Some customer must have left it behind. 'He probably had a head cold,' she said dismissively.

'Or else he's in bed crying his eyes out.'

'Oh, Emma. You should know by now that Henry doesn't have any tears ducts. Only bile ducts.'

They laughed, and Jackie felt better.

'He'll probably be back next week,' she said. 'He couldn't stand the idea of someone else taking his throne.'

Still. It was slightly unsettling. It would be just the sort of thing he would do: launch his defence, then disappear from sight completely. She imagined him now, holed up in his house with a stack of paper making long, vitriolic lists of her marital misdemeanours.

Lech was back in. He looked triumphant. 'There is one other possibility,' he said.

'What?'

'About why he is defending this divorce.'

'Stun us,' said Emma.

'He could be doing all this because he's still in love with Jackie.'

There was a startled little silence. Then Jackie gave a loud snort of disbelief. 'I really don't think so.'

'Well, why not? Holding up the divorce . . . it's obvious!' Lech was giddy with the romance of it all. 'He's just buying some time so that he can win you back all over again!'

'And how exactly is he trying to win me back?' Jackie enquired. 'By insulting and offending me?'

Lech looked less certain now. 'Well . . .'

Emma had the final say. 'Don't be ridiculous, Lech. Didn't he have eighteen months to win her back if he wanted? No, that's all water under the bridge.'

'Absolutely,' Jackie said firmly, and went off into the storeroom, thinking uncharitably that Emma used far too many clichés and hoary old sayings and that really, sometimes, it was very hard to listen to her.

What sickened Dan altogether was that it always seemed to be Complete Shits who bagged the best women. Oh, he knew them well: those swaggerers, those strutters, the kind who led with their pelvis into a room and looked around as if the world owed them a favour. Alert, wolfish, predatory and opportunistic – he was only getting started here – these guys almost always had a full head of hair, the shits. But good looks weren't absolutely necessary. In fact, some of them were astonishingly ugly, with big knobs of noses, or hideous, fleshy lips, or no chin at all. But did that hold them back? Did it heck! They just pumped up whatever minor aspect of themselves passed muster, such as matching eyes or a full set of limbs, and relentlessly pushed it until it outshone all the bad bits, and women would say breathlessly, 'There's just something about him, isn't there!' Never mind that he was a dog-ugly, nasty, cheating, toerag of a man who would probably end up shagging their sister.

Complete Shits got away with infidelity too. And, in Dan's experience, rudeness, tardiness, hypocrisy and, sometimes, tax evasion. They would walk all over you, crush you, stamp you into the ground, leave a boot mark on your face – he was warming up now – and then say, in a cheery way, 'Oh, sorry, I didn't see you all the way down there!' Obscenely, the worse they behaved the more popular these guys were with the opposite sex. Unbelievable! Dan wondered what kind of a chemical mixture they had in their veins. Because they must give off a waft, like an air freshener, only poisonous, that had otherwise sensible women stampeding towards them in their hundreds. Perhaps it was something in their sweat, or their breath, that rendered women completely unable to make an informed choice, and would throw themselves at their feet instead. Naked.

Or maybe it was their rakish smiles, their arrogant strut, their self-sufficiency, their cruel lips, their sheer, utter certainty that the world revolved around them, and them alone! The shits. Dan almost felt faint at this point.

Where were the Nice Guys in all this? The guys who believed in loyalty and decency? The guys who worked hard at the nine-to-five jobs (let's face it, somebody had to) and provided for their families, and contributed to the community, or at least the sporting community? The kind of guys that Dan had grown up with, and gone to school with; the guys he threw a ball around with on a Saturday morning at the pitch, or had a pint with at the club. These lads didn't go around shouting, 'Look at me!' They didn't send glowering looks or reek of animal magnetism. They wouldn't know how. Instead they mowed their lawns on a Saturday morning, and washed their cars and drove their mother to the dentist to get her crowns replaced. They played fair and they expected you to do the same. Where were all these honourable, good men in the greater scheme of things? Standing at the back of the room, that's where, lost, neglected, forlorn, while the Complete Shit took centre stage. They were lesser men, somehow. Penalised just for being nice.

Dan clicked his computer mouse again. On the screen in front of him, Henry Hart was dancing with Jackie Ball, the pair of them pressed up tight to each other in passionate, silent embrace. Her wedding dress, some multi-layered net effect topped by a huge, dramatic veil, swirled around them romantically, almost obscuring his legs. Dan clicked the mouse again, and the image began to play at double speed, so that it looked as though Henry had nothing below the waist at all. But that was just silly. Still, it was amazing all the things you could do with a plain old wedding video once you got it professionally copied to a hard disk.

He brought up an image of Jackie now. It was later in the proceedings, judging by the state of her hair. The veil was nowhere to be seen. She was smiling hugely for the camera, her whole face gleefully puckered and creased. Dan wasn't sure if he'd ever seen her smile like that before. But then he wasn't sure of very much these days. Instead he felt a distance now, a gap, where Henry Hart had insinuated himself between them.

Still, one of the advantages of being a Nice Guy, Dan thought as he looked for his address book, was that you tended to maintain friendships over the years, do favours, extend loyalty, and then get it back in spades. And one of the advantages of being a Rugby Playing Nice Guy was that those friendships tended to be with very large, hairy, frightening-looking men who were good with their fists.

He had three or four good friends like that in London. They wouldn't mind at all if he gave them a ring; they were all very nice.

If food is the new religion, then restaurants are the temples where we gather to worship. Henry blinked. Could he possibly have written such horseshit? He scribbled it out, tried again. *A good restaurant should feed not only the body but also the soul.* But that just made him want to puke.

He tore the sheet out of his notebook, lifted the toilet lid under him, and tossed it down into the bowl. There were quite a few pages down there already, and he hoped the thing wouldn't flood when he flushed it. But at least it was quieter in here than at his desk.

Adrienne was parked outside the building in her car. She had said she wasn't leaving until he handed it over.

'It's a preface, Henry. Five hundred words. I could nearly write it myself.'

'Be my guest.'

There was a rather stiff silence her end. 'Henry, do you realise when your deadline for this book was? Three weeks and two days ago.'

'Relax, Adrienne. The world will survive a little longer without knowing my opinion on one hundred of Britain's restaurants.'

'Henry, I know that you're having a little . . . trouble at the moment.'

'Sorry?'

'Listen, I've been through three divorces myself, and I felt every single one, believe me.'

'My divorce has absolutely no relevance to this conversation.'

'I'm just saying—'

'How many words do they want again?'

'Five hundred. Oh, just give me four and we'll call it quits.'

He flipped to a fresh sheet and hunched over it, trying to ignore the noises from the next cubicle. He gritted his teeth as a zip was zipped, hands were washed and dried, and he was left in blessed peace again. Staring at his pristine white pad with not a word in his head. Him, who could cut you in half with a precisely aimed noun. It was maddening.

It was her, of course, back in his life again. Only this time she'd brought writer's block with her. Great! Why not take the one small thing that he had left?

You see, Henry, I'm getting married again.

Telling him like that, as though he'd still harboured hopes! That'd be the day. And of course she was getting married again: eighteen months was a very long time between husbands in the world of Jackie Ball.

He should have said that on the phone. Why hadn't he said that? Where had his brain been? Afterwards he'd gone over and over the conversation, berating himself for all the things he should have said but didn't. And for the things he *did* say but shouldn't have. Still, he supposed he was bound to have been a little off kilter: the last time he'd spoken to her, eighteen months ago, the night they were going out for dinner for their first wedding anniversary, it had been to say, 'You use the shower first.' Of course, when he'd come down from his attic office a little later, expecting a scene of cosy domesticity, she had scarpered. He hadn't believed it at first. Her stuff was all over the place, and the shower curtain was still wet.

Only when he found the note on the kitchen table did he realise that the idea of dinner with him was so repugnant to her that she'd had to skip the country. Naturally, a telephone call with such a person was bound to be a little tense.

And as for her, her voice was still like a cupboard door opening and closing, but apart from that, she had been pure ice. He'd poked and prodded a bit, sure it was all a sham, but she wasn't giving an inch. Until the end, when they'd got on to the subject of her new fiancé, and she'd started to unravel. But her anger wasn't for him, not for Henry.

It wasn't until that phone call that he knew that he had really, truly lost her. He wondered now whether he had ever actually tried *not* to lose her. He had always just assumed that she had wilfully left. Was it possible that she had, in fact, been mislaid?

His mobile rang. 'Henry? It's Adrienne. How much longer do you think—'

'Soon!'

The blasted woman just wasn't going to give up. He turned his mobile off, and bent over the pad again. Every word was excruciating. He sighed and groaned, and at one point banged his head on the cubicle wall. This stuff should roll off his tongue! And surely he should find it refreshing to be positive for a change, instead of ripping places apart? But Henry found himself untouched by happy pheromones today. He was about two shades more miserable than usual, which was saying something.

He hunched over the notebook. Toilets flushed here and there, and voices came and went, and someone at one stage pushed at his door. He ignored it all and went on writing until eventually his pen nib was bent and his shirt was sticking to his skin, and every hair was standing out from his head.

There was a sharp rap on the door.

'Henry?'

'Adrienne, go away.'

'It's Dave. Adrienne gave up and drove off half an hour ago.'

'Oh. Good.' He opened the cubicle door.

'She says she's going to wait for you outside your house instead,' Dave said.

'Can I stay with you tonight?' Henry begged.

'No.'

'I'll sleep on the couch.'

'No!'

'I haven't got this shagging thing done, you have to help me out here.'

'Look, it's my wedding anniversary, Henry. Me and the wife are having a meal in.'

'Oh, right. Sorry.'

Dave knew that wedding anniversaries were a sore point with Henry and he said, 'We'll have a pint tomorrow, eh?'

'Yeah.'

But he still hung around. 'Listen, I hear on the grapevine you've taken leave.'

'Yeah.'

'For how long?'

'I don't know yet.' Henry went over to the sink and splashed some water into it. He felt as if he hadn't washed in a week, although he was pretty sure he'd had a shower the day before yesterday.

'I suppose it's not a bad thing. Just until you're over this thing with, um . . .'

'Jackie is her name.'

'I know. I just didn't want to go upsetting you.'

'Do I look upset?' Henry scoffed, patting down wild, greasy hair, and blinking bloodshot eyes. Fuck it, who was he kidding? He smelled.

'You know, maybe you should shoot off somewhere,' Dave said. 'A week in Spain. Get a bit of sun.'

Henry stared at him. Did Dave really think he would fancy a pina colada on a sun lounger at a time like this? When his whole life seemed to be coming apart at the seams? Which was quite odd, really; up to a couple of months ago everything seemed fine. Well, all right. He had starting writing the restaurant book. He had started dating again, for goodness' sake. And now he couldn't even write his own name.

'No,' he said. 'I want to see this thing through.'

Dave said sagely, 'Yes, yes. Probably best. Then, you know, get back in the saddle and all that.'

'Maybe,' Henry said.

'It's just, you don't want to be gone from the column for too long. They've short memories out there.' He was warning him.

'Thanks, Dave.' And they both nodded manfully.

'Right, well, see you tomorrow, then?'

'Sure you can't make a beer?'

'No, I can't. Sorry, mate.'

He could hear them in the kitchen, trying to keep their voices down.

'I'm really sorry, honey.'

'It's our *wedding* anniversary.'

'He has nowhere else to go.'

'He has a big posh house with a flipping hot tub out the back.'

'It's the divorce. I think it's hitting him hard.' Dave was trying not to slur his words. 'Ten minutes and I'll ring a taxi, OK?'

Then the kitchen door swung open and out they came, all careful smiles. Dawn was bearing a raspberry cheesecake she'd made in the shape of a heart, and which she looked vaguely embarrassed about now. She'd already had to divide up the two sundried tomato tartlets and redistribute the asparagus spears.

'Now!' she said, with remarkable cheer. Dave subserviently held out her chair for her, swallowing a hiccup. She jerked the chair out of his hand and sat down under her own steam. He sighed and reached for his beer.

'You two are lovely,' Henry blurted. He knew he should go and leave them in peace but for some reason it seemed desperately important to be around people tonight. Friends, people who cared about him, even though they were obviously dying to get rid of him.

'Yes, well,' Dawn said. She was sober.

'I mean it,' Henry went on, emotionally. 'Just a lovely, regular, honest-to-God couple.'

'I don't suppose we're much different to anybody else,' Dave said, then cast a look at Dawn to be sure that he hadn't exasperated her further.

'Well, that's just it!' Henry said. 'You're *normal*. You have your little rows and arguments – Dave tells us all about them in work, Dawn – but they're just spats, really, aren't they? And then it all blows over and you kiss and make up. You'll probably end up making mad, passionate love tonight!'

'I don't know about that,' Dawn said tightly.

Henry said gloomily, 'Jackie and me, we weren't normal that way. I'd come home from work and she'd be waiting for me with this great air of, I don't know, expectation. Waiting for me to entertain her with stories about my brilliant, exciting day, my wonderful job, the glamorous people I met, all in witty one-liners. And I'd feel like such a fucking fake. Because that wasn't me, not really.'

'What?' Dave said, confused.

'I wasn't Don Corleone, or Robert de Niro or Richard Branson – actually, I'm glad I'm not him. I wasn't even Henry Hart!'

'Do you know what he's on about?' Dave asked Dawn.

'How could you tell someone like Jackie – a woman who doesn't deal in realities, might I remind you; a woman who once spent three hundred quid on a pair of shoes – how could you tell someone like her that you weren't what she thought you were? Burst her little bubble? Can you imagine *that* row? So I didn't tell her. And we never rowed. It wasn't very healthy, was it?'

'Well . . .' said Dawn, obviously struggling to find some kind of reply.

Henry leaned over the table and demanded, 'Do you think I'm fun?'

'Fun?' said Dave.

'You know, am I a bit of a laugh? A joker? When you're with me, do you have a giggle?'

'No,' Dave said.

'Oh. Jackie said that I wasn't any fun either,' he said stoically. It had been torturing him for two days now.

'She put that down on the divorce petition?' Dawn was appalled.

'No, no – you can't divorce someone just because they're not any fun.'

'Can't you?' muttered Dave.

'What's that supposed to mean?' Dawn snapped.

Henry ignored the infighting at the other side of the table; after all, he'd started the conversation and felt that it was about him. 'Her new fiancé is apparently great fun. Well, I don't care. I would never have described myself as a flippant man in any case. And that's nothing to be ashamed of.'

'You're a miserable git, Henry,' Dave said.

'Dave!' Dawn elbowed him.

'What? He asked for my opinion and I'm giving it.'

'She was probably just saying that,' Dawn said to Henry diplomatically. 'We can't all go around laughing and cracking jokes the whole day long.'

'Why do you always try to couch things nicely?' Dave said to her. 'It's not helping, you know.'

'Well!' she said.

Dave said to Henry, 'How many years have I known you now?'

'You always ask this question when we're drunk and neither of us has a clue.'

'All right, then. Loads of years. At least ten.' He paused. 'I've forgotten what I was going to say.'

Dawn butted in, 'Oh, Henry. You were so happy when you met Jackie. The happiest we saw you in years. We thought, great! It was just a question of you meeting the right woman. But then it turned out that it wasn't.'

'So I picked the wrong woman.' Henry was defensive.

'You're so miserable no woman would make you happy,' Dave declared. 'You can't blame it on poor Jackie.'

Now it was 'poor Jackie'! Henry wondered when the conversation had turned upon him.

'If it wasn't for her I wouldn't have stayed stuck in that job!' he retaliated.

'What, she *made* you?'

'No, but she expected it! If I hadn't got married I could have left! Done things. Other things.'

'Like what?' Dave challenged.

'Anything,' Henry said grandly.

'Name something then.'

'All right! I could have gone back to being a chef.'

'I've seen the inside of your fridge. You don't even boil an egg any more.'

'I could have changed career, then. I could have been, I don't know, a . . . sales rep!' It was the only thing he could think of.

Dave chortled. 'Selling what? Insurance? Lingerie? Trips to the moon?'

'Shut up. All right, forget that one. I could have . . . I could have written other things.' There, it was out.

'What, like a novel?' Dave was giggling now.

'No.' Just say it. *Say it*. But Dave was smirking so hard that he couldn't. 'You're right, it's a joke. Forget it. I'm stuck where I am.'

'You could still leave if you wanted,' Dawn said.

But Henry suspected that after a while you went so far down a particular road that there was no turning back. You kind of turned into your job, you fossilised, until you became what you had practised for so long: miserable, grumpy, unhappy and unwashed, in Henry's case. Which was strange, because deep down he knew he wasn't like that at all. The complete opposite, in fact.

Dave was contrite now. 'For God's sake, Henry, let it go. Jackie, the whole thing. Get yourself a haircut. Some decent clothes. Then get your ass back into work and put the whole thing behind you.'

'Leave him alone,' Dawn scolded. At least she seemed to understand that sometimes you had to go back before you could go forward.

Henry stood to go. He felt very tired, and distinctly unfunny. How it rankled: to be blamed at this sorry stage of the game for something that he had never been asked to provide in the first place! A house, a glittering career, famous friends and loads of hard cash – all these things he had supplied in abundance and on request. But fun? Maybe he should just ring her up and go, 'Ha ha ha!' down the line. Ridiculous.

But he thought about hearing her voice on the phone all the way home.

Chapter Ten

'I spoke to his mother,' Mrs Ball blurted out.

Jackie's heart missed at least two beats. 'Whose mother?'

'Henry's. I rang her up in Somerset. It seemed like a good idea at the time.' She was wearing a short frilly dress, and had had her hair curled, and she looked like an ancient Shirley Temple. At least now the redness of her cheeks was explained, and the way she had refused to meet Jackie's eyes all through lunch.

'Mum,' Jackie groaned.

'Well, I can't get a decent night's sleep until this thing is sorted!' Mrs Ball declared. 'So I rang her up. And I said to her, do you know what that scut is up to? He's only holding up my daughter's second wedding out of pure evilness and spite! Well, she was mortified. And rightly so. None of *my* children might have made anything of themselves, bar Michelle, but they would never dream of holding up a divorce, I said to her.'

Jackie felt weak with horror. 'You know what's going to happen now, don't you? She's going to tell Henry straightaway, and he's going to think I put you up to it! That I got my *mother* on the case!' She wanted to die. She wanted to curl up on her mother's lino floor and just pass on peacefully. Henry's anger she could live with. His hatred, even. But his pity? His peals of mirth?

Mrs Ball was addled now. 'All right, so I shouldn't have interfered, but I just don't trust that solicitor of yours! Not after what Michelle found out.'

'What exactly did Michelle find out?' said Jackie, dangerously.

Her mother looked nervously towards the kitchen to summon back-up. 'Michelle!' She said to Jackie, 'She went looking to see what other cases Velma has handled. But there wasn't a single mention of her name! She turned the whole Four Courts upside down – didn't you, love?'

Michelle stood in the doorway with a tea towel. She was drying a piece of the good china, which had been dusted off in honour of Dan. 'Don't bring me into this.'

'Looked in wastepaper baskets and everything,' Mrs Ball elaborated. 'That woman mightn't even be qualified. Although Michelle could look that up for us too. Couldn't you, love? In that Law Directory book of yours.'

'Give over, Mum.' Snappily, for Michelle.

Jackie glared at her mother. 'Velma was doing just fine until you went poking your nose in. Wait till she finds out that you went behind our backs to the opposition!'

'Oh, Jackie. Mrs Hart isn't the *opposition*. I sat beside her at your first wedding, remember?'

'I've only had one so far.'

'Lovely woman altogether, although she only talks about antiques. She sent me a Christmas card last year and everything, with robins on it.'

Her naivety further irritated Jackie. 'She's Henry's mother, Mum! Naturally she's on his side!' Then, just to frighten her, she said, 'Velma's going to hit the roof when she hears this. You've probably lost us the whole case!'

Mrs Ball didn't understand that you couldn't actually win a divorce, and duly looked terrified.

Jackie didn't care. 'In fact, you could be put in jail for interfering with witnesses!'

'I haven't interfered with anybody, have I, Michelle?'

Michelle didn't spring to her aid, for once. From the look of her, she had very probably been out scoring drugs and sleeping with men the night before and hadn't the energy.

'And anyway, Henry will never find out that I spoke to her,' Mrs Ball said. 'That lot, they don't talk at all. He didn't even tell Mrs Hart that you two were getting divorced. *I* had to tell her!' She saw Jackie's surprise, and was bolstered enough to add, 'They wouldn't be a close family at all, not like us.' She was obviously going to gloss over the fact that four of her offspring lived on different continents, and that her husband was in the garage at that moment caressing drill parts.

'So, basically, you've achieved nothing?' Jackie concluded sarcastically. 'Apart from making me look like an idiot and running up your phone bill?'

Mrs Ball's cheeks began to glow again. 'I thought that *someone* ought to act a little concerned at the hold-up. For Dan's sake, if nothing else.'

And they all looked out at Dan. He had been digging a trench in the front garden for Mrs Ball's rose bushes since after lunch. It was spilling rain and he was soaked to the skin. But he was already wet from fixing all that broken guttering that morning, he'd said, so he might as well just keep going. He was already being spoken of by Mrs Ball as the son-in-law-who-would-put-the-rest-to-shame. Not that she had any other sons-in-law. Ursula, her second youngest, refused point blank to marry that Australian ski instructor she'd been shacked up with for the past five years. That set-up worried Mrs Ball about once every couple of hours. Plus the fact that she wasn't at all sure there *was* any snow in Australia.

'I've already explained, Mum,' said Jackie. About ninety-two times now. 'We can't do anything until Henry files his Answer. We just have to wait.'

Mrs Ball pursed her lips. 'And tell me, when have you ever been able to wait for anything?'

'Yes, well, you know me. Miss Instant Gratification.'

'At least fire that Velma woman,' Mrs Ball begged. 'And hire Michelle here instead. In fact, I'm sure she'd do it for free, wouldn't you, love?'

'I can't,' said Michelle. She looked a bit bloated around the chin.

'Think of it as a wedding present. A divorce for your sister.'

'Mum, I can't. I'm not qualified yet.'

'Neither is Velma, for all we know.'

'If I *could* have acted for Jackie, don't you think I'd have offered to do it already?'

Mrs Ball's eyes misted up. 'Of course you would. You're a good, good girl, Michelle. The best.' She turned to Jackie fretfully. 'Poor Dan is not himself. Did you see the way he hardly touched his meat loaf

119

at lunch? What worries me is that all this will put him off so much that he might change his mind and marry someone else.' She patted Jackie's hand. 'Don't worry. I'll take him out a cup of tea and talk you up.'

When she was gone, Michelle said, 'Don't mind her. Dad says she hasn't slept since last Tuesday.'

'Anyone would think I was enjoying all this,' Jackie said loudly. 'That I was delighted the whole thing was being dragged out by Henry! I've written to him, I've phoned him – I've done as much as I can do!'

'I know,' said Michelle. Doubtfully.

'What?'

'You're right. You have.'

'No, go on. If you've something to say, then say it! Everybody else bloody has.'

'Well, you could always just give him what he wants, Jackie.'

This was so simple, so obvious, that Jackie felt obliged to retreat behind a series of disbelieving splutters and puffs. 'Well, pardon me for dragging my heels! For not wanting to enter into a dissection of my marriage, long dead, might I add, with a man that I can't stand to be in the same room with.'

'Nobody's asking you to dissect your marriage.' Michelle waved a hand.

'*He* is!'

'He probably wouldn't like what might crawl out of the woodwork any more than you. Look, the guy is bitter and twisted. Or else he's got masochistic tendencies, who cares? Just give in, Jackie. Capitulate. Redraft the divorce petition whatever way he wants, and I can guarantee you he'll drop the whole thing in a matter of days.'

'Do you think?'

'That way you'll get your divorce and Mum will get her wedding.'

'So will I,' Jackie felt obliged to point out.

'Yes, but Mum really wants it. And Dan, of course.'

Outside, Mrs Ball had Dan pinned up against the garage with a cup of tea and a plate of fig rolls. She had been right, Jackie thought, he did look a bit off. The pet! Plus, he had started to grind his teeth at night. And then there was that incident two nights ago when he'd jack-knifed up in the bed and swung a punch at the air. He'd said afterwards that it was just a mosquito, even though the nearest swamp was in Dun Laoghaire.

Michelle flopped down on the couch. She really didn't look at all well.

'I hope you're not taking too many drugs again, Michelle,' Jackie scolded.

'Jackie, I'm pregnant.'

On reflex, Jackie looked out at their mother. 'Oh my God,' she said.

'It's twins.'

'Oh my *God*.'

'Wait till you hear who the father is.'

Jackie clamped her hands over her ears. 'Don't tell me, don't tell me, I don't want to know!'

'Justice Gerard Fortune. We had a one-night stand at the Legal Eagles Ball.'

His name was horribly familiar. Probably from the newspapers and television. 'Is he the one with the black hair and the thick glasses?'

'You're right about the glasses. But he doesn't have any hair. Well, not on his head.'

'Michelle, he's ancient!' That was the kindest thing she could say about him.

'He didn't look too bad in the dark,' Michelle said with a sigh. 'I don't know what his wife is going to say.'

'Does this get any worse?' Jackie enquired. 'Just so I'm prepared.'

'No, I think that's pretty much it. Except that so far he's been reluctant to sign up for ante-natal classes with me.'

'Michelle, this isn't funny.'

'Who are you telling?' complained Michelle. 'I haven't a pair of jeans left that I can fit into and I'm only just gone sixteen weeks.'

'Sixteen weeks? You're nearly four months pregnant!'

'Oh, stop!'

'You've obviously decided you're going to keep it.'

'Them. Yes, I suppose so. Although Justice Fortune has offered to do the dishonourable thing in terms of coughing up to go to England.'

'Do you call him that?' Jackie asked. 'Justice Fortune? Even though he's the father of your twins?'

'I suppose it's a bit odd all right,' Michelle mused. 'Especially as on the night in question I called him Spanky.'

Jackie looked at her. 'I just can't understand why you're being so calm about this. I mean, this is the sort of thing that would happen to me.'

'I know,' agreed Michelle.

'But you always played things so cleverly, or something. You toed the line but you still managed to do exactly what you wanted. Whereas I just rush in without thinking and make a total mess of things.'

'You had fun, though,' Michelle challenged.

'So did you. Too much by the looks of it.'

'I mean you had a life of your own once Mum knew you were a hopeless case. She left you alone. Then the rest of them skipped the country, and it was up to me to make her happy. Do you know what it's like, being the apple of Mum's eye?'

'Having the blood sucked from you drop by drop?'

'Worse,' Michelle said gloomily. 'Having to sneak around all the time, and hide my drugs in the sugar bowl, and invent a friend called Bernadette just so I can have a shag in peace. Well, I'm sick of it.' She stuck her chin in the air. 'I'm delighted I'm pregnant! I couldn't be happier!'

'You don't really mean that, Michelle.'

'I do! Well, maybe not twins. One would have done.'

'When are you going to tell her?'

'I don't know. But I'm hoping the judge thing might impress her.'

'I wouldn't count on it.'

'Either way, I'm finished in her eyes. So it's up to the rest of you to carry the can now.'

'What?'

'And unless Eamon or Dylan or Ursula or one of them in Europe decides to come home, which is pretty unlikely, it's down to you, Jackie.' She begged, 'Go on — give her a big flashy wedding and she'll have something else to focus on. And I can quietly grow bigger in the back-ground.'

'I'm not getting married just because you're pregnant by Justice Fortune.'

'I hope that's not another excuse.'

'Sorry?'

'Anybody would think you didn't want to divorce Henry.'

That very week Jackie purchased a new A4 pad and a clatter of pens. If Henry wanted the truth, then he would get the truth. She would do exactly what she should have done in the first instance: hit him hard and fast! Leave no stone unturned when it came to exposing his numerous character flaws and hideous personal habits. She would redraft the blessed divorce petition if it killed her, and then she would stick it in the post and be done with him. While she was at it, she'd send a copy to his solicitor, all his ex-girlfriends, his workplace and his agent.

'You can't do that,' Velma said on the phone. 'It's illegal.'

'Then I'll post it up on a website for the whole world to see!'

'That's illegal too.'

'Oh. Can I send it to his mother?'

'Nope. The contents of a divorce are completely private to the parties involved.'

'So he gets it every way!'

'Jackie, you're very angry today.'

'Yes, I am, Velma.'

'He hasn't got in touch with you or anything, has he?' Velma demanded.

'No.' Jackie found it difficult to explain even to herself. 'I suppose divorce tends to make people angry. You know, in general.'

'Oh, yes, it does. And bitter too,' Velma said, warming up.

Jackie hastily made her excuses and rang off: Velma could work herself into a right old state if you let her. Sometimes Jackie wondered whether she'd been divorced herself. But Velma seemed to hate men so much that it was unlikely she had lowered herself to marry one.

'How are you getting on?' Emma enquired now.

When Velma had said 'private to the parties involved' and nobody else was to see it, Jackie was sure she didn't mean Emma too. She was her friend, for heaven's sake. Plus, it was kind of hard to keep it from her, seeing as it wasn't something Jackie wanted to do at home, under Dan's nose, and so she'd taken her pad and cleared a corner of the counter in Flower Power. And, actually, it would have been quite pleasant sitting there amongst the flowers, with all their smells and colours, were it not for Henry.

'I'm just trying to decide where to start,' Jackie told her nonchalantly. 'Maybe I should do it alphabetically. A for Arrogant and so on. And wait until I get on to the Bs! I'll be spoiled for choice.'

But Emma just said, 'I suppose maybe it's not a bad thing. You know, to write things down.'

'I'm doing this so that I can get a divorce, Emma. That's the only reason.'

'I'm just saying that you and Henry, you never really resolved things between you, did you?'

'There isn't anything to resolve.'

'Are you sure?' She was giving Jackie one of her canny looks.

'Emma, I appreciate your concern. But whatever happened between Henry and me, it's in the past. I've dealt with it, OK? I'm completely fine. This petition thing, as far as I'm concerned it's a clean-up operation. That's all.'

Emma shrugged. 'OK.'

Jackie put her head down and set to it. But she found the alphabetical thing didn't really work. Then she tried to group his faults under a series of headings, such as Biological Defects, which, in fairness, he couldn't do much about, and Fundamental Character Flaws. She spent another hour listing those particular traits that had driven her crazy: his cynicism, his sharp tongue, the way he would hide behind his image. For example, name one instance when he had lost the run of himself and done something mad! Spontaneous. Such as go along with her suggestion to paint the entire house in a shade of lilac which apparently did wonders for the nerves. Or tell her passionately how much he loved her, and that he would die if she ever left him. Instead of the few meagre, thought-out crumbs of affection he flung in her direction. Even when they had first met, he had been cool and reserved like that, as though he'd had to make sure he didn't give too much away. While she, of course, had blabbed her heart out!

But how could she write that down? For him to read? She would die.

She must have moaned or something, because the next thing she knew Lech was standing over her, bouncing nervously on his white runners, his hands dug into his very tight, faded jeans.

'Are you OK?' he asked, concerned.

'Yes! Sorry.' She put her notepad away.

'I just want to say I finished those deliveries. Is it all right if I go now?'

It was five to five.

'Sure. But actually, Lech, I think Emma wanted a word.'

As if sensing him – those two always seemed to know when the other was in the building, they were like a pair of dogs – Emma came in from the storeroom. Her bob looked more severe than usual and she was dressed in her most sober brown trousers and top. She held an envelope that Jackie knew contained Lech's P45.

She cleared her throat, very much the bearer of bad news, and said, 'Sit down, Lech.'

'Where?' He looked around. There wasn't actually anywhere *to* sit down.

'Oh, it doesn't matter,' she said, caught out.

'I can get a couple of buckets and turn them upside down . . .'

'Leave it! It's fine. We'll, um, stand and talk instead.'

'OK.' He shrugged, and looked at Jackie. But she wasn't getting involved. She liked Lech. If Emma wanted to fire him, she could do her own dirty work.

Emma began, 'As you know, your probationary period is up today. And Jackie and I, we've reviewed your position here, Lech.'

His eyes darted from Jackie to Emma. 'Yes? I hope everything is OK?'

'Well,' Emma said grimly.

But Lech went on, 'I turn up on time, I do my deliveries, I make no more mistakes with addresses, right? And your handwriting – it's getting much better, Emma.' He cracked a big, white grin at her. Jackie marvelled as Emma managed to withstand his toothy charms. 'And my car – all the stickers are gone, see?'

'Yes, very good—'

'In fact, if you look more closely, you will see that I have stencilled on the driver's door FLOWER POWER.'

They looked. He had. In red, with the phone number underneath.

'Wow! That looks great,' Jackie said.

'It cost me fifty euro,' he said. He waited expectantly.

Jackie looked at Emma. 'Well, naturally, we'll reimburse you . . .'

But Emma glared back. 'Lech, you weren't asked to do that.'

But he waved a hand graciously. 'It's no problem. On the other side, I advertise the pizza company people.' He added, 'They pay me for that. It's advertising, after all. On a private vehicle.' Again he looked directly at them.

Jackie said, 'He has a point, Emma.'

'I'm not paying for advertising on a 1989 Ford! Fine, if it's a *company* car.'

Lech's face lit up. 'You'll provide me with a company car?'

'No! Look, this is not what I wanted to talk to you about.'

'But I am allowed bring up things too,' he challenged. 'As an employee.'

'He has a point, Emma,' Jackie said again.

'I think you should look into a company car,' he said. 'Something sporty, maybe. Something I can take girls out in.' He clicked his tongue. 'Joking!' He slung his denim jacket on over his tight, white vest, which rode up obligingly.

Emma, who had been about to thrust the envelope at him, looked away.

'It's good we have this talk!' he said cheerfully. 'I like talking. And one more thing. I want a proper contract of employment.'

'What?' Emma said.

'I'm over my probationary period.' He added nicely, but firmly, 'I know my rights.' Before anybody could say anything else, he looked at his watch and exclaimed, 'Ah! I've got to scoot. I'll be late for my date.'

Jackie said, 'You have a date?'

'Yes. With Aisling. She's beautiful.' He rolled his eyes passionately, and made for the door with his springy, energetic, confident walk. 'See you Monday!'

When he was gone, Jackie gave Emma a meaningful look.

She bristled. 'All right, so I didn't fire him!'

'Not only did you not fire him, but we're stuck with a pay rise and a company car too.'

'He will not get a company car.' She got very busy then, tidying up the counter jerkily.

'Imagine. He had a date,' Jackie said.

'So.'

'With *Aisling*.'

Emma snorted. 'God help her.' Then she reached under the counter and brought out a rolled-up newspaper in plastic. 'It came in the post for you Wednesday. I forgot about it until now.'

It was perfect diversionary material: a copy of the previous Sunday's *Globe*. It was mystifying. Her name was on the label all right, above Flower Power's address. It would explain last week's newspaper too. Jackie looked at Emma.

'Don't ask me,' Emma said. 'Unless, of course, you don't want Dan to know that you're buying it. It's understandable.'

'Emma, I did not order this newspaper to be sent here.'

'Well, somebody did.'

Henry hadn't written his review this week either. That Wendy woman had filled in again. There was no explanation as to his absence, no little by-line saying *Henry Hart is away*.

It was very unsettling. Who on earth would be sending her a copy of Henry's newspaper?

Only Henry, of course. And yet he hadn't written a review.

'He must still be crying in his bed,' Emma offered, trying to lift the mood.

Jackie didn't believe it for a moment. No, most likely he was hatching up some nasty legal assault behind the scenes, and sending her copies of his newspaper just to let her know that he hadn't gone away.

'Just ignore it,' Emma advised.

'I intend to,' Jackie said, and threw it in the bin.

'You've very quiet,' Dan said. He had picked her up from work and they were in Le Bistro at their usual table by the window.

'Am I?'

'You didn't even exchange the usual pleasantries with Fabien. He's quite offended.'

Jackie managed a little smile. At least Dan seemed to have cheered up somewhat since lunch at her mother's house. In fact, he was positively sunny, and seemed to have developed an air of expectation, as though he were waiting for something. At any rate, she didn't want to spoil his mood and so she said, 'I suppose I'm worried about the Michelle situation.'

'Yes,' said Dan. 'I was thinking. Maybe we should be there when your mother is told. Stand behind her and help catch her.'

'It's Michelle I'm thinking of. One year to go of her law degree, Dan. I know we're all sick to the back teeth hearing that, but it's true. And now she's going to be saddled with two babies. And no father. What kind of a life is that going to be for someone who loves drugs and going out?'

'Maybe you're underestimating her. She seems very calm about it.'

Far too calm. Jackie suspected that it was the shock of it. Once that wore off and Michelle realised the enormity of the situation, she'd probably be scrabbling about for the number of the nearest private clinic and her supply of ecstasy.

Dan said, 'Maybe your mother will soften. Help out.'

'Not if they look like mini bald versions of Justice Fortune,' Jackie said grimly. She looked at him. 'I'm sure you're wondering what kind of a family you're marrying into.'

'No, no,' he said, very convincingly. But Jackie guessed he would wait until his mother was high as a kite on samples before breaking this latest scandal to the family. (Actually, she and Michelle had a lot in common.) And as for the Fionas! None of them would sit near her in the club again, no matter how respectable her shoes were. And Dan would gamely laugh and pretend that it didn't matter.

'Sorry,' she said to Dan.

'For what?'

For everything, really. Perhaps she would suggest that they go away for the weekend, just the two of them. To a country retreat maybe, or a hunting lodge, where he could shoot at things, and go for long wet jogs through impenetrable forests, and eat eighteen-ounce sirloin steaks. She didn't know what she would do: sit at the bar and drink gin and tonics, she supposed.

'I've been thinking,' said Dan. 'Maybe we should go away for the weekend. Shopping, or something. Maybe New York, where you could do Bloomingdales and all that. I could, I don't know, sit in a bar or something.'

'Oh, Dan.'

Wasn't he the sweetest! The important thing was that they were prepared to put themselves out for the other. To compromise; to share. Surely those were vital ingredients of a good marriage. More important than, say, passion, or lust or obsession. Which often passed in the blink of an eye.

Then, as if a bad smell had crept over the table – bloody Henry again – Dan asked, 'How are you getting on with that thing for Velma?' They never called it the divorce petition. It was the you-know-what, the yoke, thingamajig.

'All right. Taking longer than I thought.'

Dan squeezed her hand. 'Jackie, you don't have to pretend. I know it's all very upsetting. It's unbelievable, really, that you should be put through this. If I could get my hands on that, that . . .' Then he seemed to snatch himself back. He took a breath, and gave her a cheery smile. 'Still! What goes around comes around, I always say. It's the circle of life, isn't it? Do unto others, and they'll do it back unto you. In spades.' He ground that last out.

'I'm not sure that's the actual saying, Dan.'

But his jaw was jutting out so far that it practically cast a shadow over the table.

'People *should* get their just deserts, Jackie. Do you not agree? And I'm not talking sherry trifle here. Mind you, sherry trifle is nice and soft, isn't it? If you didn't have any teeth, for example.'

'I have no idea what you're talking about, Dan.'

But he didn't elaborate. He just said, 'I wouldn't worry too much about that whatsit petition thingy. You never know what might happen in the meantime.'

It was all right for him to be cavalier. He didn't have to write the damn thing. A whole document dedicated to a man she detested! And to herself. It was her own role in the marriage that had caused her to lie awake in the middle of the night last night. She had fought it: clamped her eyes shut and told herself she absolutely would not engage in this kind of . . . enforced self-analysis! But Henry had kept drifting in and out of her dreams, waving the divorce petition at her gleefully (for some reason they were both on a double-decker bus), and she had tossed and turned, and eventually had blurted crossly at him, 'Oh, fuck off.'

'Sorry,' Dan had mumbled, and shifted over a foot or two in the bed.

Then, about five o'clock, just when the birds were starting up outside the window, she saw it all with queasy clarity: her arrival home to Dublin eighteen months ago off Flight FR 219, in high heels and full make-up, magnificently tragic in her hurt, her betrayal, her innocence of any wrongdoing whatsoever! She was the wounded party and let nobody forget it. He was the bum, the wrecker of a perfectly good marriage that she had poured her heart and soul into! And let nobody forget that either.

And how everyone had scurried around to commiserate with her over her bad luck in devoting herself so completely to a man whose first love was, and always had been, himself! Nobody pointed out – except Emma, of course, you couldn't stop her – that maybe if she hadn't devoted herself so entirely, then she mightn't have ended up so hurt. Even her mother had refrained from pointing out that Jackie should have taken heed of one of Mrs Ball's favourite sayings: always have something to fall back on. Apart from her backside, that was, which had grown two sizes through lack of motivation and too many mid-morning digestives in the house in London.

It was difficult to see, now, what she had done with all those empty hours. She, who was always buzzing from one thing to the next, who had taken her first job stacking shelves in the local supermarket at fourteen. But London was new, different. She didn't know anybody. Still, she'd been gung-ho, sure that she would make a go of things. Had even tried to transplant her business idea of opening her own florist shop. But who needed another florist in an area that had twenty-six listed in the local directory already? Then she'd looked for a job in one of them, as an employee. No luck there either. Packing shelves became an attractive option again only it didn't seem fitting, given Henry's position. She became aware of her lack of a university degree for the first time in her life. She had no contacts, no circle of acquaintances to help her out, or even just to listen. Some days it was easier to stay home and watch the TV.

Meanwhile, Henry's star was growing brighter and brighter. You'd nearly need a pair of sunglasses whenever he would walk into the room. What was someone with no job, no friends to tell her to get a grip, and two stone heavier than usual, to do? Fawn, that's what. Kind of scuttle around him in little circles, hoping that some of it would rub off on her. That he would make her feel better; fulfilled, and happy, and successful, all those things she had thought you were automatically entitled to once you got married.

Last night it all came back to her in horrible detail: the key turning in the lock, her leaping up off the sofa with her wobbly bottom, running to the door as though her whole day had revolved around that moment. Around Henry. It made her blush to think of it.

In fairness, he could have encouraged her a bit more. He could have said (jokingly), 'Get off your arse and find a job.' It wouldn't have hurt him to look up the employment pages for her every now and again. He could even have found her something in that newspaper office of his but when she'd mentioned it, his face had gone kind of grey and mottled, and he had said that he didn't think it was a good idea that they worked together.

Looking back now, he just didn't want her hampering his style.

'Is your dessert OK?' Dan asked, concerned by the look on her face.

'Fine. Lovely!'

She wouldn't write all of that down on her list of 'faults', naturally. She wouldn't give him the satisfaction! Absolve him of the responsibility of supporting her, like any normal husband? No. But she might write down that she had failed to make an effort to integrate more with her new surroundings. Just as he had failed to make provision for the fact that his wife actually *was* in new surroundings.

She felt better now. Maybe it was because it was a small nugget of truth between them. She wondered would he see it too.

Once again she waited until Dan was in bed before sneaking downstairs. At least he seemed to be in the middle of some happy dreams for a change; he was grinning away and drooling into his pillow.

Downstairs, she opened her handbag and took out the copy of the newspaper she had rescued from the bin. Emma had dumped wet flower cuttings on top of it, and Jackie plucked a few bits off as she unfolded the damp pages gingerly. It had been bugging her all day. Why would he send her a copy of his newspaper? If it were him at all. But who else could it be?

By the light of the lamp, she started on the front page and began to work her way carefully to the back. There wasn't a mention of him anywhere. She even trawled through the Horoscopes and Female Health in case he might be lurking in there somewhere, ready to jump out and go, 'Boo!' But, nothing.

Then something *did* jump out at her: a bright red box in the Personal Ads on the second to last page of the newspaper. It was just above an ad for a Midlands gent seeking a lady for 'discreet afternoons'. Inside the red box was a five-line poem. A jaunty limerick.

> *So you think that I'm no fun?*
> *That I'm gloomy and moody and glum?*
> *Well, my fun anecdotes*
> *Witty stories and jokes*
> *Will light up your face like the sun!*

Then, at the end: *For Jackie.*

Chapter Eleven

'I want to speak to Ian Knightly-Jones,' Velma demanded.

'I'm afraid Mr Knightly-Jones is in court this morning,' said the hushed, male voice at the other end of the phone.

'What about this afternoon?'

'I don't believe he's going to be back at all today.'

Velma gave a mirthless little laugh. 'Scared stiff, is he? Terrified to come to the phone?'

There was a nonplussed silence now. Good. Let them know that they weren't dealing with some country hick.

Eventually, he said, 'I can assure you that isn't the case. Mr Knightly-Jones is fighting an action against a multinational food corporation this morning.'

Velma threw her eyes to the cracked ceiling. Honestly, she'd heard it all now.

'Right,' she said with heavy sarcasm. 'Well, when he's free fighting this "multinational", then maybe you'd get him to give me a buzz.'

'Perhaps I can help you instead?'

'Who are you?' Velma demanded.

'Tom Eagleton.'

Oh, yes, the guy who'd written those rude letters. He certainly didn't sound like a solicitor. The guy in the corner shop who sold Velma her three doughnuts every morning had more authority.

'Are you qualified?' she demanded suspiciously. 'Because I'm not going to be palmed off with a law clerk here.'

'I most certainly am.' He sounded affronted. Well, let him. How was she to know what kind of an outfit she was dealing with over in London, unless she checked? They might use heavy cream embossed paper, but that was no indication of anything. She could do that too, if she could afford it. But she didn't have airs and graces, not like this shower, with their double-barrelled names and the way they'd kept her on hold for over two minutes, just to give the impression they were mad busy. Velma knew every trick in the book.

'I rang you up because I thought that we could talk this thing over. Solicitor to solicitor.'

There was another long pause. 'I beg your pardon?'

She injected a chummy note into the conversation. 'You know, see if we can settle our differences without all this nastiness.'

'Ms Murphy, I really can't share confidences with you without consulting my client.'

'Tosh,' Velma scolded. This guy would be putty in her hands. 'Let's face it, clients are more trouble than they're worth sometimes, aren't they? And as for *our* two clients, well, I've seen headless chickens with more direction!' She chuckled down the line.

'I simply cannot agree with the description of my client as a headless chicken.'

God, he was a tight-arse.

'The point is they need good advice, Mr Eglinton.'

'Eagleton.'

'Whatever. And advice is what we're here to provide, right? So, let's say you were to advise your client as to the futility of defending this divorce. And in return I would then advise *my* client to, say, give up all rights to the dog. How's that for a deal?'

'Your client hasn't claimed any rights over the dog.'

'Not yet,' Velma said sweetly. 'So, what do you say?'

'Ms Murphy, we are a reputable law firm. We don't engage in these kinds of deals on the phone. But if you'd like to put something down on paper for our consideration . . .'

Well, she had tried to be nice. He had had his chance! She puffed herself up in her chair, which creaked alarmingly. She had gained another half stone since Easter, and who could blame her? All that damn summer stock in the shops already; itsy bitsy floaty things taunting her from every window as she went past. And look at what was in fashion. Tiny sixties-style minis, halter-neck tops, skinny jeans and voluminous, hippy skirts, all the very worst things for a woman who had been medically classed as obese since her sixteenth birthday. Every year since, she'd added another stone to her frame, and lost another chunk of confidence. She hadn't had a date since that outing with Trevor, a guy she'd met through one of those awful support groups for fat people, and who was twice as large as her. He had taken her to a funfair, of all things. It had ended miserably with the pair of them being denied seats on the Ghost Train due to safety concerns. Trevor had half-heartedly suggested another date. But for Velma, the bitterness had set in.

Her only pleasure in life now – apart from food, of course, but that was a complicated relationship – was her career. After a number of years selling insurance over the phone where client contact was nil, she had stumbled across an American distance learning law course on the internet. And there Velma found her true calling: fighting the corner of other people who had been done out of love. Those poor souls who had been betrayed, disillusioned, rejected, scorned, cast upon the scrap heap of life – she wanted to clasp them to her chest and say, 'I know exactly how you feel!' But that tended to alarm people, and so she confined herself to doing the very best job she could in dispatching their other halves as swiftly and brutally as possible. And to watch her go! Fuelled by zeal, and packing twenty-four stone of pure rage, Velma was not a woman to be trifled with.

'Now listen here, buddy,' she said. The American law course had taught her many useful techniques, including Positive Confrontation, and Stealth Tactics. Her personal favourite was, Don't Make Me Angry. Which she was just about to kick into action, actually. 'I'm going to give you a chance to think my offer over, OK?'

After a timid pause, he said, 'But you haven't actually made an offer.'

Velma ignored that and continued, 'Have a little chat with your boss, once he's back from buying his sandwich or wherever he really is. I think you'll see that, on reflection, it's best if we settle this thing now.' She added heavily, 'While we still can.'

'Pardon?'

Velma flung her eyes heavenwards again. He didn't even understand a veiled threat! She felt rather sorry for Henry Hart, even though he was a total scumbag. But everybody deserved decent legal representation. She would have thought he'd have been able to afford a big law firm, not this two-bit outfit fronted by a man so meek she could feel him quivering down the phone.

She would have to spell it out for him. 'Before things get Very Nasty for your client.'

She had his full attention now. Good. Because Jackie Ball had called by that morning to tell Velma that she still hadn't redrafted the petition, and she'd had bags under her eyes that Velma could have popped her entire week's grocery shopping in. The woman looked like she hadn't slept in days. And to think that it was all Henry Hart's doing. It was enough to make Velma cry. But, as the American course said: Don't get mad. Get hopping mad.

Jackie Ball's divorce would be Velma's personal mission from now on.

'Was that a threat?' Tom said. At last! Bright spark.

Velma took a lungful of air, and thundered down the line, 'Do you want to find out?'

'Hold still, pet. That's lovely, pet.'

Henry tried not to sneeze as thick orange foundation was pressed into the lines around his nose. There was so much hairspray in his hair that he was afraid to light a cigarette in case he burst into flames. But then he remembered that he didn't smoke any more. He'd given up overnight after Jackie left. Strange, that: most people reached for forty Rothmans after a traumatic event. But maybe it had been tied in with his relief that she had gone. Yes, relief, underneath all the shock and horror and hurt. A little voice had whispered, hurrah! It had said, you can stop punishing yourself now, Henry; stop putting on a show. She's gone, taking all her expectations with her. He could be, well, himself!

It didn't quite work out that way. For starters, he wasn't all that sure who he was any more. Hadn't the guts to risk doing anything drastic to find out. So all his great notions of jacking it all in, and turning to yoga or taking up creative writing classes or something came to nothing. He just went on being Henry Hart: writing vicious reviews, nurturing his reputation, going to crap social gatherings with people he didn't like, and occasionally sleeping with Hannah (all right, once). Only now he had to do it all without Jackie.

Talk about shooting yourself in the foot.

Sometimes he suspected he had wilfully driven her away by his bad behaviour in order to free himself to undertake this dramatic transformation in his life. You stupid bollocks, he told himself now.

'Don't do that with your eyes, pet. I'm trying to put on mascara,' the make-up girl told him.

'I don't want mascara.'

'Don't worry, you won't see it on camera.'

'I don't care. I'm already wearing foundation, lipgloss, spot concealer and blusher. I'm not having mascara too.'

'It'll bring out your eyes,' she said stubbornly.

'Get away from me.'

Adrienne arrived at that point and moved quickly to smooth things over. 'Why don't you take a coffee break?' she said to the make-up girl. Then, in a soothing aside, she added, 'He can be very difficult.'

Henry heard and didn't care. He was trying to break up his hair, which looked like you could lift it off, like a lid.

'They're just tweaking the lights now,' Adrienne told him chirpily. 'It's going to look absolutely fabulous. Henry Hart at his own kitchen table!'

'I don't know why they couldn't just have used my column photo,' said Henry grudgingly.

'Darling! This is for your book! They can't use an *old* photo.' She kind of looked away and added in a rush, 'Look, they want you to be plucking a chicken.'

'What?' It had already been agreed that he would be sitting at the table, drinking a glass of wine. Simple and non-pretentious.

'I know, I know. I mean, fowl, I wouldn't go near it myself. But they're adamant. They want blood and feathers and fluff.'

Henry immediately understood. 'So it will look like I've just killed the fucking thing with my bare hands?'

'Well, someone has to.'

'What? You mean it's still *alive*?'

'It's pecking away in your pantry. The photographer guys are vegetarian and say they won't do it.'

'So it's up to me? Maybe they'd like me to drip saliva while I'm at it, for the photo? And wave around an axe?'

'Well, you do have that kind of a reputation,' Adrienne said. 'If you didn't, there wouldn't *be* any photo today, would there? Or a book. Or me!' She laughed, but Henry got her meaning all right. She'd got progressively more edgy as his absence from his newspaper column grew longer. She had repeated several times that it was their 'building block' and that 'everything grew from that'. He knew she thought that he was a self-absorbed minor star with a gigantic ego who needed to be reminded of reality every now and again. Worse, she was ninety-nine per cent right.

She was ready with another reality check now. 'Henry, they're not happy with the preface you wrote for them.'

'What's wrong with it? I managed six hundred words in the end.'

'I know. But, Henry . . . how can I put this? It's not exactly what they expected.'

'If they wanted something specific, they should have told me.'

'I suppose they assumed, logically, that you would know what kind of thing to write, Henry.'

'I really don't understand, Adrienne.'

She looked a bit tight-faced, as though she suspected he was having her on. 'Why don't I give you an example then?'

Henry was a little worried himself. 'I'd be obliged if you would.'

She took some folded pages from her briefcase and opened them up. With pursed lips, she read, 'Good food begins in the home. The simple ingredients of your fridge and store cupboard, put together with care and enthusiasm, and served with a dollop of decent conversation and laughter, is the best night in you'll have all year.' She lowered the page and crooked an eyebrow at Henry dangerously.

'What?' he said.

'This is a book about restaurants, Henry. Restaurants. Not cooking at home, or people's store cupboards, or having cosy nights in with friends around the bloody kitchen table! Otherwise, it would be a cookbook!'

'Now, there's an idea,' Henry mused.

Adrienne stared at him. 'And what's all this "decent conversation and laughter"? You're the Butcher of Notting Hill! You don't laugh!'

'I certainly do,' Henry said, offended. 'You've just never caught me, I have my fun side too, you know.' Or at least he was trying to develop it.

Adrienne was cold-eyed now. 'In fact, the publishers have indicated that there's a problem with the entire tone of the book. They feel there is a light-heartedness running through it, a warmth, and what can only be described as a –' she could scarcely bring herself to say it – 'a *benevolence* which is entirely inappropriate to your stature as the top restaurant critic in this city! And, I have to say, I totally agree with them!'

There was a little silence.

'Well,' said Henry. 'Sorry.'

'Sorry?'

'Yes. Sorry. I didn't mean it.'

'You didn't mean to be so nice?'

'No. It was completely subconscious. Maybe the sun was shining when I was writing it or something, and I didn't notice.'

Adrienne slowly pulled out a chair and sat down so close to Henry that he could see the crease marks in her make-up. And, actually, he was wearing more than she was.

She flexed her scarlet-painted fingernails and said softly, 'Henry, this is a tough game. It takes a lot of hard work and talent to get to the top, doesn't it? Hm? And sometimes when people *do* get to the top, they can become a little arrogant. A little cocky. They think, oh, I'm so big I can do anything I want! They believe they can change, Henry. Leaving behind the stuff that made them successful in the first place.'

'Is this a scary story?' Henry whispered, eyes wide.

'You bet it is,' she snapped, dropping her auntie bit. 'Because it's a big mistake to change, Henry. People don't like it. They want to know what they're getting, just like they know it's fish and chips on a Friday night.'

'I really think you're underestimating the public, Adrienne.'

'Don't talk to me about the public. Big, thick ignoramuses who can barely read, half of them, never mind get their heads around a new concept. People who get in a tizzy if their favourite cereal is repackaged and moved up two places on the shelf! Do you know how many new and innovative projects I've tried to launch over the years, Henry? How many times I've tried to "stretch" the public? When, frankly, there's not a lot there to stretch in the first place. So don't think they're going to hang around while you experiment with "tone" and explore your nice side. Because they won't. They'll get nervous and confused and dump you like a hot brick. And in a year's time you'll find it hard to get a place on a charity quiz show on the telly.'

'I hope you don't talk to all your clients like this,' Henry told her.

She gave him a scarily sweet smile. 'Only the ones I care about. But I know that you're too sensible to stray off the path, Henry. For all your tough talk and I-hate-my-job vibes, you know perfectly well what the alternative is – obscurity. You wouldn't last six months.' She stood perkily. 'Now! Why don't I go see if they're ready for you?'

She glided to the door, and paused briefly before going out. 'By the way, that friend of yours who writes the poetry. I've been rethinking. I'm sure I could find a little publisher for him somewhere. You never know, it might shift a couple of copies at Christmas. He wouldn't buy a pint of milk with the profits, but that wouldn't matter. Not if it was a vanity project; while he got on with his proper job, of course.' She gave him a knowing smile. 'See? Everybody can win, Henry.'

She exited, leaving a waft of cloying perfume behind. And, after eighteen months, Henry had a sudden and deep urge for a cigarette. It was so overpowering that he went to the dresser drawer and rooted around in the hopes of finding a forgotten, half-smoked pack. Not a chance. Instead, in amongst the screwed-up plastic bags and Indian delivery leaflets, he found a pair of dark sunglasses – the big, round, Hollywood kind, which would have been OK were the frames not bright pink. Tastelessly pink. And what do you know, a strand of long, frizzy hair was snagged on them.

He should be used to it by now, of course. For weeks after she'd gone, he had gathered her up: make-up, clothes, missed pieces of jewellery, the book she'd been reading and left on top of the locker (*The Complete Guide To Self-Hypnosis*). Not to mention shoes – he had a whole bag of those in the garage, most of them not matching. And her hair, of course, which she had wilfully left scattered over every square foot of the place. At one point the hoover had packed up under the strain.

He had thought he would feel better when he had finished. But instead the place took on the kind of soulless feel of a hotel lobby, and sometimes he was afraid to speak too loudly in case he might hear an echo. But he had refused to admit he missed her. Desperately. Even her voice. Even her hair.

Adrienne smoked. Unfortunately her habit hadn't killed her yet. On the bright side, she had left her handbag on the back of a chair. He knew it was scurrilous to go through a woman's handbag, but he was more worried that she would walk back in before he found her cigarettes.

They were Light cigarettes, long girly white ones packed with cancerous chemicals but scarcely any nicotine at all. He'd just have to make do, and hope that nobody saw him. He nipped out the front door just as he heard her making her way back from the kitchen.

'Henry? They've caught the chicken for you.'

'Back in a minute,' he called. Just as soon as he got his head together. Just as soon as things made sense again.

For some reason Dan hung around the house all morning Saturday, not even going out for a paper, and then invited two friends over for an impromptu lunch.

'For God's sake, Dan. There's nothing in the fridge. You'll have to go to the shops.'

But he was most reluctant to set foot outside the house. 'There're eggs,' he said. 'We'll fry them up and do them a couple of slices of toast.'

Then, just after they'd got rid of their rather dissatisfied and bemused guests, Mrs Ball got on the phone for an hour and a half to worry about Michelle.

'There's something up with Michelle. Your father heard her being sick this morning in the bathroom. And have you seen how much weight she's put on? I wish you'd have a word with her, Jackie. Maybe it's the stress of the exams coming up or something, but it's all going to her stomach. I saw her yesterday in tracksuit bottoms, it's all she wears these days, and these big, smock-like things, and she's like a beach ball. And it's no wonder, I said to your father, when she eats half a roast chicken and eight potatoes at lunchtime. You couldn't keep food in the house. And all these doctor's appointments all of a sudden. She went off into the hospital yesterday for some kind of scan thing, she said.' She paused for breath. 'I wonder what could be up with her at all?'

On Saturday evening Dan mentioned a traditional music session in the local pub that he expressed a sudden and rather inexplicable desire to see, and they spent three hours standing in a packed pub. Even when two seats became free over at the bar, Dan hadn't wanted to leave their position in the open doorway under a CCTV camera.

'Why do you keep looking up at it?' Jackie had enquired.

'I'm not. I've just got a crick in my neck.'

'Well, let's go home then.' She was freezing. And her drink kept spilling as people pushed in and out by her.

'In a minute,' said Dan, looking up at the CCTV camera again.

He relaxed a bit on Sunday, but still stuck to her like a leech.

'Do you not want to go to that match with your brothers?' Jackie said.

'No, no. I'd rather be here with you.'

'Oh.'

'Trying to get rid of me?'

'Hardly!' The poem was burning a hole in her bag. But short of locking herself in the bathroom, there was no chance to examine it that weekend.

Monday in work wasn't much better; four funerals and a wedding, and the first time she got a minute to herself in three days was when they closed up the shop at six o'clock.

'I could drink ten vodkas,' Lech declared. He had worked as hard as any of them. And with new vigour, now that he had been supplied with a proper contract of employment and a pay rise. Emma had given in, except on the company car. Even she didn't have a company car, she declared, and she co-owned the place.

'Who's coming to the pub?' Lech asked.

'Not for me,' Jackie said firmly. She was dying to get rid of them. 'But why don't you and Emma go for a drink?'

Emma and Lech looked at each other.

'I don't—'

'I'm not—'

They stopped.

'Try out that new bar they're talking about,' Jackie suggested, ushering them out the door.

'Let me stay and clean,' Emma begged under her breath.

'Go, Emma.'

At last she was on her own. She did a very cursory tidy-up and pulled down the shutters. Then she snatched up her handbag, her heart beating a little fast. She unzipped the small inside pocket where she kept very important things, like her driver's licence and spare sachets of Canderel. She found the poem, which she had carefully clipped out of the newspaper and which she had been turning over and over in her head since. It rested in the palm of her hand, flimsy and enigmatic. She hadn't shown it to anyone. Well, everybody would have gone jumping to conclusions, wouldn't they? All kinds of theories and motivations would have been put forward and discussed, not one of which would turn out to be true, don't you know.

Besides, there was something very private about this, even though it had been in the ads page of a national newspaper, and highlighted in red type. Somebody had wanted it to be noticed, all right, but only by the intended person.

For Jackie.

She was probably being silly. There must be hundreds of women named Jackie who read that particular newspaper. Thousands, maybe. The poem could have been intended for any one of those. Yes, when you thought about it logically, most likely it was nothing to do with her at all.

The hot leather of Lech's cheap car seat beat into Emma's back. She held her knees rigidly together in case they might brush against his fist, which was working the gear stick like he was a Formula One driver. The smell of pepperoni pizza and fresh flowers threatened to suffocate her.

And the smell of Lech. She got sweat and deodorant and minty breath. He must have popped a Tic-Tac before he got in the car with her. He was so . . . obvious.

At that thought, she felt better. Back in control. It was just Lech, after all.

'So!' he said. He sounded nervous.

'So what?' she said coolly.

'So, poor Jackie. That divorce petition.' He tutted and shook his head.

Anyone would think he cared.

'I suppose these things are never easy.' She looked out the window, hoping to God that nobody would see her riding along in this appalling car with a twelve-inch pizza on one side and a bunch of flowers on the other. And Polish music blasting out the window.

'Things went very wrong between them, yes?' he enquired.

'She's divorcing him, so I would have thought that was obvious.'

She felt him looking at her again. She refused to meet his eyes. They would get to the pub and she would make her excuses and cross over to the bus stop on the other side.

'I don't get that feeling, though. That she really hates him.'

There he went again! Spouting his opinions on love and feelings, like anyone had even asked him. You would think he was a diehard romantic himself, instead of a guy on the make who picked up women called Aisling.

'She has plenty of reason to,' she said shortly.

He shrugged. 'She doesn't seem to be writing many of them down. These reasons.'

'Maybe some things she doesn't want to write down. They might be too painful.'

'If she did, they might work things out,' Lech offered.

'You were saying only last week that he was a pig.'

He shrugged. 'Forget it. What do I know?'

They rode on in silence for ages. Then he said, 'Still, relationships are funny things, yes?'

'What?'

'I often wonder, what draws people together? What is the thing that makes them click? That makes them fall in love?'

'I have no idea.' She could not believe she was sitting there discussing relationships with Lech.

'Sometimes it is people who are the very opposite who attract each other the most.'

'Did you read this in a magazine somewhere, or did you make it up all by yourself?'

'I go by my own feelings. What do you think?'

'What do I think about what?' she snapped.

'Love.'

'I can take it or leave it,' she said shortly.

'Me, I think it is the best feeling in the world. Falling in love.'

'Good for you,' she said. Where was the blasted pub? 'I hope Aisling appreciates that.'

'You remembered her name.'

'I have a very good memory, actually, yes. I can remember all sorts of things, not just the names of your girlfriends.'

'Just one,' he corrected. 'And anyway, it didn't work out. She was not the one for me.'

Why did he keep watching her like that?

'Well, keep looking,' Emma advised cheerily. 'You can drop me here.'

'We're not at the pub yet.'

'I know, but it's my bus stop. I've just remembered something I have to do. At home. Now, this second.'

'I see.'

He stopped the car. Her hand flew to the door handle.

'Goodbye, Lech. Thanks for the, um, lift.' She tugged at the handle.

'It's broken,' Lech said apologetically. 'Here, let me.'

And he leaned in across her, pressing his sweaty, muscular, white-vested body against her prim, brown, pressed blouse. And something very strange happened to her then, something dark and primeval, and definitely to do with the loin region. And in front of the crowd at the bus stop, and the drivers of the cars all around them, and the gang of smirking teenagers walking by, she completely lost the run of herself and she grabbed him hard and kissed him.

Chapter Twelve

Jackie dreamed about Henry again that night. This time they weren't on a double-decker bus. They were in a huge, white four-poster bed, naked, and bonking to beat the band. *I don't even like this man,* Jackie was thinking in the dream, as she encouraged him to do something very rude. For his part, he just kept saying her name over and over again; at least he was focused. Then at the end of it all, he produced two ice creams. 'How did you know that was exactly what I wanted?' Jackie marvelled. 'Because, even though you hate my guts, I'm your soul mate,' he said, very throaty and deep. And Jackie had such a funny feeling in her tummy that she thought she would cry. 'Why did you hurt me so much then?' she asked. For once he looked vulnerable. He said, 'You hurt me too.'

She awoke with a start, feeling guilty and too warm, and somehow disappointed that the dream hadn't reached its conclusion. It would be interesting to find out, for example, how exactly she had hurt him, apart from blowing a gigantic hole in his pride, of course. He wouldn't be the type who would relish having to explain his wife's abrupt departure to his co-workers in the coffee room over bourbon creams. But why should she have left explanations and excuses and drawn the whole thing out longer than necessary? The very fact that he hadn't contacted her afterwards was proof enough that he knew he'd been caught red-handed, so to speak.

No, he wasn't the one who had been betrayed and humiliated and left feeling like a fool.

There was a knocking on the front door below. That was what had woken her. The clock said it was ten past seven. Who could be calling this early in the morning?

'Dan.'

'Hmmm?' He didn't even lift his head, although they had been in bed at a very reasonable hour the previous night. It was left to Jackie to go down and answer the door in her Winnie-the-Pooh pyjamas.

Two policemen stood there. Or rather a policeman and a police-woman.

'Jacqueline Ball?'

She knew immediately what it was about. She turned to the stairs and shouted, 'Dan! Come quickly! It's Mum.'

Michelle must have told her about the twins and Justice Gerard Fortune, and she had collapsed with the shock. But surely the hospital would have phoned in that case. Unless, of course, she had been driving at the time, and the news had sent her into a tailspin, which had propelled her into the path of an articulated lorry. The incongruous image of an Alice band twirling merrily in the middle of a tarmac road popped into Jackie's head.

'We'd just like to ask you a few questions,' the policewoman said. She looked very stern, as though she had been warned during training never to smile.

'Come in,' said Jackie. This obviously wasn't about Mum at all. Could it be some traffic offence?

Dan arrived down the stairs, belting Jackie's white towelling bathrobe round him. It scarcely met across his massive chest, and big tufts of hair popped out. Further down, it was only a matter of time before something else popped out; it barely came to the top of his huge thighs. The policewoman swiftly averted her eyes.

'What's going on here?' he asked crisply. In fact, he was very sprightly altogether for someone who had been comatose sixty seconds ago.

The policewoman said to Jackie, 'Is Henry Hart your husband?'

'No. I mean, yes.'

'Yes or no?'

'Well, I suppose technically he *is*.'

Dan stepped forward protectively. 'She's in the middle of a divorce,

OK? Naturally, it's an upsetting time for her. Can I ask what this is all about?'

'He was assaulted on Saturday afternoon outside his house when he stepped out for a cigarette.'

The word 'assault' was slightly shocking. Jackie wasn't really sure how to respond.

'Henry?'

'Yes.' They were obviously waiting for more of a reaction.

'That's . . . well, that's terrible!' she said. It was best not to confess that she had entertained far more violent fantasies about him in the not too distant past. But now that it had actually happened to him, she wasn't half as delighted as she had thought she would be.

'Terrible,' Dan echoed. 'How badly assaulted?'

'Pretty badly,' the policeman said.

'Anything broken? Any disfigurement? Permanent disabilities?' They turned to look at Dan oddly. He said, 'He *is* still Jackie's husband. Naturally, we're concerned.' It was the first Jackie had heard of any such concern, and she gave Dan a look. But he just gazed steadily at the police.

The policewoman said, 'He should be discharged from hospital today.'

'Oh,' Dan said, rather unenthusiastic for one who had been so concerned. Then, 'See? He's going to be all right, honey.' And he put an arm round Jackie's shoulders and gave her a bit of a squeeze. The bathrobe rode up a couple of inches, and the policewoman switched her gaze to the ceiling.

'We were hoping you might be able to help us with our enquiries,' she told the light bulb.

Jackie said, 'Well, of course. Although I can't imagine we'd be any help. I haven't really had anything to do with him since we broke up.'

'Where were you on Saturday afternoon and evening?' the policeman asked. He had big bushy eyebrows that reminded Jackie of a couple of suspicious caterpillars. And that suspicion, she was only just realising, was aimed at them.

Beside her, Dan puffed up belligerently. 'I hope you're not accusing us of anything.'

'We're just trying to eliminate you from our enquiries.'

'Eliminate! You think we skipped over to London Saturday morning, biffed him around a bit, then popped back in time for bed?'

'It's possible,' the policewoman said.

Dan huffed a bit more, looked at Jackie dramatically as though the entire thing was preposterous and said, rather slowly and patronisingly, 'Jackie and I were both here all day Saturday. We entertained two people for lunch, and then went to the local pub in the evening, where we were in the company of about two hundred people. O'Reilly's pub, I'm sure they can verify it. I can also supply you with the names and addresses of our lunch guests if you'd like.'

'Maybe you'd drop them down to the station at some point.' They closed up their notebooks and prepared to leave.

But Dan couldn't let it be. 'You know, I've a good mind to ring up my solicitors!'

The policewoman looked him straight in the eye this time, refusing to be intimidated by vast tracts of nakedness and copious body hair. 'Ring them up away. They might be able to explain why one of the assailants said to the victim, "This one is from Dan."'

'Jackie, you're being silly.'

'Don't you dare tell me I'm being silly.'

'I didn't mean . . . please, Jackie. Sit down. Let's talk about this.'

'About how you arranged for a gang to beat up my ex-husband?'

'It wasn't like that!'

'What *was* it like then?'

'They were supposed to just frighten him off.'

She didn't believe him. She looked at him, boggle-eyed. 'My God, Dan, he could have been killed!'

'Don't be ridiculous.' At least he had taken off the teensy robe and put on a pair of tracksuit bottoms and a sweatshirt. Unfortunately they were both black, making him look large and thuggish. 'The lads know their stuff. It was all superficial. Jerry said they roughed him up a bit. Gave him a bloody nose, that sort of thing.'

'You checked in with him, then? Jerry? To see how the "job" went?'

He looked exasperated. 'Stop it, Jackie. It's not like we're a bunch of gangsters.'

'But that's exactly what you're like! You didn't get what you wanted through the proper channels, and so you decide to take the law into your own hands!' She stormed past him and grabbed another armload of clothes from the wardrobe. She hurled them into an open suitcase, hangers and all.

'I can't believe you're reacting like this!' Dan exploded. 'For God's sake, Jackie. Where are you even going to go?'

'I don't know. But right now I don't want to be anywhere around you, Dan.'

He sank down onto the bed. Oh, he was scared now: now that she was leaving. 'I'm sorry, OK? So it was a stupid thing to have done! But I couldn't let him keep on doing what he was doing.'

'What?'

'Ruining us, Jackie. Coming between us all the time. For God's sake, look what he's doing to us! We're facing a massive legal bill for starters. We've postponed our wedding because of him. Our friends and family think we're a fucking laughing stock!'

'I don't care what they think.'

'And what about what he's doing to you, Jackie? Humiliating you with that stupid divorce petition he's making you rewrite? He's making you crawl!'

'I can handle it, Dan.'

'Well, I can't! Do you know how hard it is for me to watch? And not be able to do anything about it? Not be able to help you, protect you?' He sat up straight now. 'So, yeah, I arranged for the lads to pay him a visit. I told them to give him a kick in the nuts for me. It was the only thing I could do in the circumstances, and I'm not a bit sorry.'

She looked at him. 'And what if the police get enough to press charges?'

He flicked a hand. 'They won't. The lads left nothing behind.'

'But what about me, Dan? What if I decide to go down to the station and tell them exactly what you've told me?'

He looked humbly at the floor. 'And are you going to?'

She slammed the suitcase shut. 'Oh, you're such a big thick fool, Dan!'

'I know. I can't stand myself right now. I'm morally reprehensible, and mindlessly violent, and—'

'Shut up. You know what this means, don't you?'

'What?'

'He's really going to have it in for me now. He's going to string this thing out for as long as he can just to get back at us!' She picked up her suitcase and glared at him ominously. 'So you can forget about getting married any time soon. For a number of reasons.'

'Why didn't you kick him out? Why were *you* the one who left?' Emma enquired.

Good question. In fact, Jackie felt rather foolish and deflated now, standing in Emma's tidy little living room at dawn, in her pyjamas with her red coat on over them, and carrying a suitcase that was packed only with high-heeled shoes and occasional wear. She hadn't even brought any knickers. Still, Emma would lend her some: good, sensible ones that would keep out the chill.

Defensive, she said, 'Well, he didn't offer!' Anyhow, at the time it had seemed so much more dramatic and satisfying to be the one to leave. The downside was that she now had nowhere to actually live, which was problematic to say the least. She was also starting to remember numerous other vital things she had left behind, such as her mobile phone and the keys to the shop. She'd have to call back and get them. In about an hour, actually. Fantastic.

'And is this arrangement permanent, do you think?' Emma asked cautiously.

'Stop asking me all these difficult questions!'

'I'm only asking so I can clear out the spare room, Jackie.' She hugged her bathrobe tightly around her. Jackie realised she had got Emma out of bed. But it was nearly a quarter to eight. Emma should have been up and dressed for work at this time anyway.

'Sorry, Emma. I didn't mean to crash in on you like this.'

But Emma waved a hand. 'Don't be ridiculous. Coffee?'

She set off fast for the kitchen. Jackie followed. She had forgotten how Emma liked to line up jars in order of descending size. And you could eat your dinner off that kitchen floor.

There was an empty wine bottle on the draining board. That was unlike Emma. Unless she had started to tipple at home by herself. Jackie made a mental note to get some more leaflets for night classes again. Emma seemed to enjoy the one on Cake Baking For Beginners last year, even though not one of her sponges had risen. Jackie thought she might be joining her this time, depending on how things went with Dan. How To Avoid Relationship Disasters, maybe.

Emma looked at her kindly. 'Are you worried about him?'

'No! Let him stew at home.'

'I mean Henry.'

Jackie gave a bit of a splutter. 'God, no! I mean, Dan said he was OK. And the police said he'd be out of hospital today.' She added carelessly, 'I just hope his jaw is not broken, that's all.'

'So? They'll be able to wire it back together,' Emma said.

'Yes, but he's a food critic, Emma. He'll lose his job if he can't chew.'

'They might puree it for him and give it to him through a straw,' Emma suggested.

Jackie burst into tears. It took her completely by surprise. But Emma, bless her, just found a wad of kitchen roll and pressed it into her hand.

'It's just the shock of it,' she said. 'He's still your husband.'

Jackie was glad she had said that. Because he *was*. And no matter how much she hated him, or how much everybody else expected her to hate him, they were still tied to each other.

'You know, in a way I wish I'd never met him,' she declared tearfully to Emma. Her nose was all bunged up and her voice sounded even more squeaky than usual.

'You're just saying that.'

'I'm not! I mean, when you think about it, we were only married for a year. One year out of my entire life! That's all it was from start to finish!' She sniffed loudly. 'And just look at the mess that's left behind.'

'Well, you know what they say,' Emma said stoically. 'It's better to have loved and lost and all that.'

'Why? Why do they say that?'

'Well, I don't know, do I? It's a saying. Maybe it makes you a better person.'

'It certainly hasn't made *me* a better person. In fact, I was much nicer before I met Henry.'

'True.'

'Maybe it means you get sex or something. As opposed to not getting sex.'

'It's a possibility.'

'Well, it wasn't worth it,' Jackie declared. 'I'd rather not have met Henry and had something with batteries from Ann Summers instead.'

'But you always said that side of things was great.'

'Well, I suppose it was,' Jackie said grudgingly. 'Comparatively speaking.'

'You said you were at it like rabbits!'

'All right, so we were! In the beginning. Before everything went pear-shaped.'

Emma tutted, before popping an extra spoonful of sugar into Jackie's coffee as some kind of consolation prize. 'Isn't it funny the way it worked out? I mean, when you two met, it was stars exploding in the sky and that kind of thing. I never thought it would go wrong.'

'I didn't either, Emma. Otherwise I wouldn't have married him.'

'I suppose. You know, it's a shame in a way you never confronted him.'

'Why?'

'Well, about all his shortcomings.'

'Aren't I doing just that in the divorce petition? I've written down reams of stuff! I might have to go on to a third page soon.' She crossed her fingers under the table. She had scarcely managed a paragraph so far.

'I know, but it might have been more satisfying to say it to his face,' Emma insisted.

'Well, I just didn't.' What was she getting at?

'You packed up and left?'

'Yes.'

'Without solving any of the problems?'

As though Jackie routinely ran out when the going got tough! The cheek of Emma!

Out of the corner of her eye, Jackie saw her suitcase by the door. Emma did too. The damn thing was red as well, and it seemed to throb accusingly, until Jackie was eventually forced to retort, 'This is not the same thing at all!'

'Of course not,' Emma said.

'You know, you don't know the first thing about why I left, Emma.'

'So tell me.'

And she was going to, she opened her mouth to pour out the final hurt and outrage, when Emma's bedroom door opened and Lech walked out, completely naked except for a pair of deep purple Y fronts.

'Do I smell coffee?' he said cheerfully. Then he saw Jackie sitting there in her pyjamas. 'Hey, Jackie! Did you stay over too?'

Jackie swung to look at Emma. Emma turned a variety of interesting shades before eventually going a violent pink all over. She said, 'I'm going to get dressed for work.' And she ran for the bedroom.

'Oh, Henry! Your poor face! Your chin, your lip . . . My God, your *nose.*'

'It's not broken. Just slightly bulbous. Ouch! Don't do that.'

'Sorry.' Dawn was dabbing at him here and there with antiseptic on a piece of cotton wool. Henry had a woozy sense of déjà vu; it seemed only a minute ago that the make-up girl was dabbing at him. Then something horrible happened: three brutes appeared, like out of a grim fairytale, and here he was, back in the same chair, only with a couple of bruised ribs, a loose tooth, a variety of cuts and bruises and a nose the size of a turnip. And he hadn't even had his cigarette.

'Will I make you a cup of cocoa?' Dawn murmured.

'Yes. That would be lovely.' He had already refused her chicken soup and Marmite jelly and he didn't want to hurt her feelings. She and Dave had picked him up from the hospital and insisted on staying, even though Henry was dying for a moment's peace. He had never been on a trolley in an A & E before, and it hadn't been very pleasant. Apart altogether from the fact that every bone in his body ached, people had kept looking at him as though he were some kind of yahoo who had got caught up in a drunken row. People had avoided him, and drawn any small children away.

It could have been a lot worse, they kept telling him in the hospital. He could have ended up like that bloke who came in earlier and practically had to be stitched back together. Or that guy who went straight up to surgery to have a six-inch kitchen knife removed from between his ribs. Oh, just get on with it, Henry had eventually said. They hadn't liked that, and he had been left on his own with a thermometer under his armpit for nearly an hour. Then one of the nurses recognised him from his picture in the paper and there was a flurry of whispering and pointing, and eventually she came over and produced a book for him to sign. It wasn't even a book he himself had written; it was bloody Jamie Oliver. But he had signed anyway, and she had brought him a cup of tea and told him that, in most cases, hair grew back. What are you talking about? Henry had said, before reaching up and realising that a lump of his own was missing.

The phone rang again out in the hall.

'Do you want me to get that?' Dawn murmured. She kept speaking in a very soft voice, as if Henry was a sick child, and he kind of liked it.

So he stuck out his lower lip, playing up a bit, and said, 'Tell whoever it is that I'm not here.' Honestly! What was it about injuries and tragedies in general that prompted people you hadn't heard from in six months to suddenly clog up your phone line with their sympathy and concern? Half the newspaper office had already been on. 'Get better soon, Henry! We miss you!' Even though he had already been gone three weeks. Hadn't they even noticed? Then his editor had phoned up, and his publisher, and his mother, although that was only to ask if he minded if she converted his bedroom. She didn't say what she was converting it into and he didn't enquire. Probably something to do with antique china dolls or her vast period rug collection. He didn't tend to visit her planet very often. The last time they had spoken she told him that Mrs Ball had phoned her up to tell her that she was getting divorced.

'Jackie's parents are getting divorced?'

'I think so, yes.' She always managed to sound very far away. Which usually she was, in her head.

'I'm getting divorced too, Mum.' Might as well break the news to her.

'Are you? Oh, dear.' And then they'd moved on to talk about the *Antiques Roadshow*.

Adrienne had been on the phone today too. Oh, that woman! But she was the one who had discovered him, as she breathlessly told anybody who would listen. In a pool of blood in the middle of the road! Well, more of a puddle, really, and he had actually been sitting up on the pavement when she found him. And the cigarette wasn't even broken, which was a mercy, because Lord knows she needed it while they waited for the police to arrive. She hadn't seen the assailants, of course, and she wasn't ashamed to say that she was glad. Police lineups weren't her thing. But what really got to her was that if she had walked out a minute earlier, she could easily have been caught up in the fracas. She could have been *injured*.

But the real problem now, she told Henry, was the photo. She had managed to reschedule. They had said they could airbrush out the black eye, but if he lost that tooth they were in trouble. On the plus side, she told him, she would rework the offending preface. She'd already been through the entire manuscript on her computer and deleted all the words 'nice', and 'impressed'. Already it had much more punch. Oops – sorry, darling, she had said.

Dave appeared from the kitchen, wearing an apron and an old pair of Jackie's pink rubber gloves. Henry had to blink a couple of times, wondering was he hallucinating. But no. He found he was disappointed.

'Where do you keep your bleach?' Dave enquired.

'Under the sink. How's it looking?'

'Don't talk to me.' He shook his head from side to side in disgust. 'You know, I've a good mind to report that photographer lot to the RSPCA. Imagine walking out of here leaving a live chicken locked in the kitchen with a fucking dog!'

Shirley slunk by, her belly dragging on the floor with shame. At least Dawn had managed to get most of the feathers off her. And the kitchen wouldn't have been so bad either, Dave insisted, if those photographer jokers hadn't left the bloody heating on full blast. The chicken was so decomposed that you'd nearly need dental records to identify it.

'It wasn't your fault,' Henry told Shirley. But either her chicken guilt was too much or else she hadn't missed Henry at all, because she trailed out into the hall after Dawn. 'We'll catch up later,' Henry called after her, aware that he sounded desperate.

'So, have the police been by again?' Dave demanded. He was very worked up about the whole thing. Dawn said he'd been acting all primitive and testosteroney the whole weekend and it was driving her bonkers.

'No, but my guess is they're too busy catching murderers and violent criminals.'

'So what are those guys who beat you up? Litter louts? You even know who they are!'

'I don't. I never saw any of them in my life before and would probably never recognise them again. Well, maybe their knuckles, if I saw them at close range.'

'Henry, this isn't fucking funny!'

'Language,' Dawn called from the hall.

'Sorry! But seriously, Henry, they have motivation on this Dan guy and everything. Why aren't they on a plane over there to arrest him?'

'He's already been questioned. Denied the whole thing, of course. Alibi and the whole lot. They don't have any hard evidence, apparently.' He thought he might need a couple of paracetamol. Things were starting to throb again.

'Well, I think it's fuck— bloody disgraceful. And if the police can't catch them, I say we should go over there ourselves and sort him out!'

'You mean start some kind of a turf war?'

'Well . . .'

'Over a woman that I don't want anyway?'

Dave looked at him. 'That's a horrible thing to say.'

'What?'

'All right, so you're injured and we should make allowances, blah, blah. But Jackie's a decent woman. The best thing that ever happened to you, mate. Don't talk about her like that.'

Henry was incredulous. He'd been hospitalised and she was getting all the sympathy! 'For all we know, she might have set her boyfriend on me! She could have been behind the whole thing!'

'That woman wouldn't hurt a fly and you know it,' Dave said. 'And if you don't mind me saying so, if you'd given her her divorce when she'd asked for it, none of this would have happened.'

'So I brought it all on myself?' His nose began to drip now, as well as throb, and he felt stung at the injustice of it all.

'Yeah,' Dave said, planting his hands on his hips combatively, undeterred by the rubber gloves. 'Like you bring most things on yourself. You treat people like shit, Henry, and then you wonder why it backfires on you.'

'Fuck off home with yourself if that's how you feel.'

'You know something? I think I will.' And he ripped the pink rubber gloves off majestically and threw them on the floor. 'You can clean up your own fucking chicken!'

This time Dawn didn't shout in to correct the stream of bad language, even though he sensed she was listening. Dave turned and left. A moment later, Henry heard the front door open and close.

He sat there for a moment. All right, so Dave had to let off a head of steam. Fine. He'd ring him later, agree that he was being a prick, and everything would be fine. At least Dawn was still here. He wondered had she forgotten about his cocoa. She was taking a long time out in the hall.

'Dawn?'

There was no reply. Had she gone too? But he didn't want to call out again. For some reason he was more afraid of Dawn than Dave. If *Dawn* had left . . .

After a moment, he called, 'Shirley? Shirley!'

But she didn't appear either. She detested him too. She probably thought, along with everybody else, that he had brought the whole thing on himself – the divorce, the bashing, the swollen nose.

He sat there in his chair, in his empty house, having driven away every single person in his life. Having driven away his dog. And with his nose throbbing like a big red cauliflower in the middle of his face.

The phone started to ring again. And no Dawn to answer it. He could let it ring out, of course. Or let the machine pick it up, like he usually did. Keep them all away. He hated everybody!

But he got up and hobbled out to the hall and picked it up.

'Hello?'

'Henry?' It was Jackie. With her squeaky voice, as if she had breathed in an entire helium balloon before coming on the line.

'Oh. Hello,' he said. He hoped he hadn't sounded too enthusiastic.

There was a big long silence.

'Look, I'm ringing to see if you're all right.' Her concern came bubbling out of the receiver, warming him up, making him feel he wasn't such a piece of crap after all.

'How did you know there was anything wrong with me?' He shouldn't have said anything, but bloody hell! Her boyfriend had beaten him up.

She was game about it, to her credit. 'I heard. From some friends of friends.' There was a little pause. 'I was shocked to hear it.'

It was her way of saying that she'd had nothing to do with it. He supposed it was never really a possibility; the same woman used to trap mosquitoes in a glass and let the buggers gently out the window. But at the same time she was associated with the culprit, and he knew it, and she knew he knew it.

'Let's just hope they find whoever was responsible,' he said meaningfully. 'And bring the full weight of the law to bear on them. Over here, I think it's about six years for this kind of assault.' He had no idea, but it had the desired effect at the other end, because she gave a kind of an 'Oh!' and he could just see her in his mind, winding the telephone cord into nervous knots. He hoped she would pass his words on to that thug of a boyfriend of hers. Fiancé, he corrected himself.

She said, 'Are you OK? Have you . . . someone to look after you?' She really had perfected the whole efficient, bland thing. He wondered was she really as indifferent as she sounded, or was she fishing to know whether he had a woman in the house – her replacement. Why not? Lord knows she'd replaced *him* quick enough. He wondered suddenly whether she thought he was very sad that he seemingly hadn't got a new girlfriend. Did she think that he was hanging around for her to come back?

'Oh, yes,' he said smoothly. She might read something into that. 'And my mother is coming up too.' Well, she would surely come up the year after next for his fortieth. At this point it looked as though he'd be pulling in all the favours he could get.

'Good, good.'

There was another long silence. He was sure that she was about to hang up, so he said, prevaricating, 'I haven't heard from your solicitor yet.'

'Well, no.'

'It's only about ten days until I file my Answer.' She needn't know that the Answer, as such, didn't actually exist yet. There was a big meeting scheduled with Ian Knightly-Jones on Tuesday.

'I know. I just need a little more time.' There was a rapid tat-tat-tat noise in the background.

'Jackie, what's that?'

'What?'

'That noise.' It sounded like rapid machine-gun fire.

'Nothing! Just some . . . gangs outside having a bit of an argument.'

'You live in a neighbourhood with gun-toting gangs?'

'All right! If you must know, I'm at the movies.'

There was another sound that resembled a grenade going off in an ammunitions arsenal. 'What's the movie?' he asked.

'*Supreme Justice 3*.' She sounded a bit embarrassed.

He laughed aloud; he couldn't help himself.

'I happen to like the occasional mindless Hollywood action movie, actually.'

'Jackie, you've watched *Casablanca* twenty-seven times.'

'I've moved on from all that, Henry.'

He felt he had stepped over some kind of mark, and she was gone all frosty again, and he was sorry, and before he could help himself, he said, 'Jackie, I didn't really mean to do all this.'

'Then why are you?' She sounded tired and hurt.

'Because you left me and I don't know why. Or maybe I do, but I need it pointed out to me.'

But she didn't come back all vulnerable like him. She was white-hot angry and loud.

'Oh, grow up, Henry. This isn't join-the-dots here. Do you think I'm a fool? That I wouldn't find out? Or, if I did, that I wouldn't *mind*?' She hung up.

Two things struck Henry: firstly, he hadn't a clue what she was talking about. Then, if she was at the movies at six o'clock in the evening on her own, there was something wrong with her and Dan.

Chapter Thirteen

Dear Ms Murphy,

Mr Knightly-Jones feels he has no apology whatsoever to make, given the tenor of your last telephone call, which, we repeat, was routinely recorded for training purposes, and not in any attempt to 'entrap' you. He felt he had no option in the circumstances of our client's assault but to pass on your verbal threat to the police. Rest assured we had nothing whatsoever to do with them calling to your office and publicly embarrassing you in front of your neighbours Rent-A-Vehicle and Philomena's Hair Creations. We are sure business will pick up again for you soon.

We are, of course, relieved to learn that you, and your client, had nothing to do with the matter.

Yours sincerely,
Tom Eagleton
On behalf of Mr Ian Knightly-Jones

'She's not here,' Emma kept insisting. At least this time it was the truth; Jackie wasn't cowering behind a door or in the storeroom, but on her way across town to the Ball family home in a taxi.

Dan said, 'Well, did she say when she'd be back?' His voice was all muffled and funny underneath the biker's helmet he wore. The visor was down to protect him from any stray pollen and he had a scarf wrapped tightly round his neck and tucked up into the helmet as a precautionary measure. He had warned Emma upon entering

163

that he would only have about two minutes before he ran out of air.

'No. Her mother isn't well,' Emma said neutrally. In fact, Jackie had assured her that she would be away until tomorrow at least. She had repeated that a couple of times meaningfully as though clearing the way for her or something! Emma had told her crisply that she had nothing planned for that night except some midweek telly, and there was no need at all for Jackie to vacate the apartment on her account. But apparently Mrs Ball had taken an accidental overdose of a herbal medicine called Sleep Tight and had been dead to the world for thirty-six hours. Jackie's presence was required.

'Oh, come on, Emma!' Dan implored. 'She's my fiancée. She walked out on me over a week ago! She won't answer my calls, or my texts. She even sends back my emails. Please, I need to know what's going on.'

'I wish I could tell you, Dan.'

'You're lying.'

'Well, yes, I am. But I'm certainly not going to repeat to you any private conversations that I might have had with Jackie.' Especially as Jackie had left strict instructions not to weaken should he show up in her absence.

'Give me an indication,' he begged.

'No.'

'A hint then.'

'No!'

'Has she said, I never want to see that fat-head again, or, I'll send him to hell and back and then I might see? A or B?'

'Stop it! Look, you two are going to have to work this out between you.'

'I would if she'd talk to me! I can't eat, I can't sleep, I can't concentrate on any mergers in work!' He abruptly flipped up the helmet visor and thrust his face into hers. 'Look at these eyes! I'm a broken man!'

Then he flipped the visor back down again.

'Dan, I don't know what to say.'

'I'm not asking you to break any confidences, Emma. But just tell her, that's all. Tell her how you saw me and I was only a shadow of my former self. That I'm riddled with guilt. That I've just got two grey hairs over the whole thing – look! Well, you can't really see them under the helmet but they're there.' He made an odd, swallowing sound. 'OK, I'm starting to run out of air here. Please, Emma. I love her. I need her back.'

'OK, Dan.'

'Tell her we don't even have to get married. That I'm perfectly prepared to live in sin.'

'Fine—'

'And that I'll attend an anger management course.'

'Yes, Dan.' He had gone slightly blue.

'Promise me.'

'I promise. Now go!'

He staggered out, ripping off the helmet as he went. Emma debated ringing Jackie and filling her in. Then she decided she wouldn't. Whatever way she described it, it would look like she was taking sides.

Two hard, tanned arms grabbed her round the waist. A warm mouth nuzzled at her neck. She was so shocked she just gripped the counter hard.

'At last we are alone,' Lech murmured.

'Lech! What . . . ?'

'It's OK, I know you feel the same. All week I've been watching you, remembering what you are like under your brown skirts and blouses. Hot and passionate and wild. But you want to play it cool in the shop, and that's OK. And Jackie moving into your house . . . that woman has terrible timing! But now she is gone and there's no stopping us!'

Emma slapped his arms away and spun round to confront him, furious. 'For God's sake!'

He was taken aback. 'What's wrong? Are you worried about a customer walking in?'

'Sod the customers!' she spluttered. She couldn't ever remember using the word before. But it wouldn't be the first time recently that she had acted completely out of character. 'How dare you grab me like that! You're behaving like a loutish, brutish, rude, ignorant, sexist Neanderthal!'

'I will have to look up some of those words in my English dictionary but I have a feeling they're not very nice,' Lech said, his ardour diminished somewhat. 'What's the problem, Emma?'

'What's the *problem*?' Had he not read any of her signals during the week? Her refusal to look at him, speak to him or otherwise acknowledge in any shape or form that he was actually alive? Had he not noticed that there was something seriously amiss when she had slammed the shop door in his face yesterday? Or did he think, unbelievably, that she was being coy?

But obviously some major wires were crossed here, because he said, very wounded, 'I thought you enjoyed our night together as much as I did.'

The very words 'night' in conjunction with 'together' made her want to throw up. She couldn't believe she had done it. Slept with Lech. Kissed him. Torn his clothes off. Let him put his . . . oh, she couldn't go on or she would have to sign up for one of those dodgy experimental studies where they erased your entire memory like it was a floppy disk.

She might have had some excuse if she'd been off her trolley. But all she'd had was two glasses of wine and a cheese and ham pizza (he'd got one of the lads from the pizza company to deliver it for free), which they had eaten naked on her bed, licking tomato sauce off each other – another terrible, burning image that wouldn't go away. In fact, the entire night would haunt her until she died, alone and neglected, in some old folks home somewhere, having first made her own wreaths.

He said, almost indulgently, the fool, 'I think maybe you are a little embarrassed about that night, yes? That's OK. I am too.'

'You are?' This one she had to hear. He certainly hadn't seemed embarrassed, as he'd roamed around her apartment buck naked, before rooting in her fridge for dessert after the pizza. Sex, he had declared proudly, always made him ravenous.

'Well, yes.' He looked at her in that very direct way of his. 'Look, I will be straight with you. I have made love with a lot of women. Maybe twenty, which is not bad for a guy my age. I think I am experienced, yes? I think I am a macho guy, that I know it all.'

Emma could not quite believe she was standing there listening to this, but some kind of morbid fascination made her say sarcastically, 'Really?'

'But then I meet you. And hey! You blow my mind! We end up making love the whole night long until five a.m.!'

Emma wanted to gag again.

'It was like some kind of weird connection for me. Like it was something very special, not just sex. And I am embarrassed by my feelings.' He shrugged. 'But there you go. I had to tell you.'

Emma smiled pleasantly, then cleared her throat and said, 'I have to tell you a few things too. I'm . . . pleased that you had such a good experience. As for me, I bitterly regret it. I can assure you now that it will never be repeated. And I'd be very grateful if you wouldn't mention it again, ever, and that we all just get on with work, OK?'

She turned back to the counter and the bouquet she was arranging. She knew Lech was still there. She couldn't not know. The guy gave off some kind of radar when he was in the vicinity of women. And he stank of aftershave too. He had all week. For her, she knew. Oh, he had no class at all.

Eventually he said, 'I get it now. You are the boss and I am the employee, is that it?'

'No. I am the boss, and you are . . . *you*!'

He was really hurt now. 'What is wrong with me?'

She looked at him in his vest, with his cropped haircut and tattoo and white sneakers, and it was as if an electrical charge ran through her body, and she grabbed him hard, and snogged him.

'Twins,' Mrs Ball kept moaning. 'Twins!' Then, in an accusatory aside, 'There's no history of twins in either side of the family going back three hundred years! You'd have to be smart, wouldn't you!'

Michelle just looked stoically at the ceiling. To add insult to injury, she had ballooned in the past week, and her belly practically blocked out most of the light from the windows. Mrs Ball closed her eyes briefly, the better to shut the sight out. She added, 'Maybe *his* side is teeming with multiple births. Not that we're likely to find out, are we?'

Mrs Ball was dressed most incongruously in dungarees, and had her hair in pigtails. The older she got, the more childlike her clothing became. She would eventually end up in romper suits, Michelle often maintained. It was obviously a subconscious regression on her part to the worry-free days of her childhood.

But she looked very tired today, and shrunken under her dungarees,

167

and Jackie felt sorry for her. 'Mum, why don't you go and have a lie down.'

'I told you, I can't sleep! Not without my pills.'

'You're not having any more of those.' Jackie was firm.

'Anyway, I've flushed them all down the toilet,' Michelle said. She told Jackie, 'It said take one at bedtime. She was washing down handfuls of them with mugs of tea. Dad found her flat out on the ironing board.'

'That's right, make a skit of me,' Mrs Ball said. 'But whose fault is it that I can't sleep?' She glared at Michelle, as if there were any doubt about the matter. 'After this latest, I'll never get eight hours again.' She hadn't had eight hours since Eamon was born forty-two years ago, but nobody pointed that out. 'What I want to know is, what are you going to put on the birth certificate?'

Michelle informed Jackie matter-of-factly, 'He's disputing paternity.'

'What?'

'He says it could be any number of men, including other judges.' Her forehead crinkled. 'And, you know, he's probably right. Plus, I was pretty off my head that night. But no, on the whole, I'm fairly sure it was him.'

Mrs Ball stared at her as though she were some alien thing with horns that had crawled out of a swamp somewhere: not her lovely, clever, *good* girl. It was worse than when Mrs Mooney up the road discovered her fireman son dressed in a French maid's outfit and licking whipped cream from one of those canisters.

'What are you going to do?' Jackie asked.

'I don't know. He says that he has a very important public job to do putting criminals and amoral people in jail, and that he can't have his reputation sullied like this. Oh, and that he'll sue if I ever repeat my allegations to anybody.'

Jackie was appalled. 'What, does he think he's living back in the time of the Vikings?'

'The Vikings!' Mrs Ball said. 'Don't get her started, because she's probably slept with half of them too.'

Michelle laughed. 'Good one, Mum.'

Mrs Ball's lips quivered. 'Stop it!' But then she was laughing too, bent over, and going, 'Oh – oh – oh!' slightly hysterical, and saying, between bouts of laughter, 'It's not funny, it's not funny,' which of course made Michelle laugh more, until they were all cackling so loudly that Mr Ball down in the shed lifted his head from his drill parts and looked briefly out the window, wondering whether the neighbourhood cats were at each other again.

'Give me a tissue, someone,' Mrs Ball eventually said weakly. The box was passed around and they mopped themselves up. She added piously, 'This doesn't mean everything's all right, you know. Just because I manage to keep my sense of humour in a situation like this doesn't mean I think any better of you.'

'Well, you couldn't think any worse of me,' Michelle said.

'Taking money like that! Off that fellow!'

'What's this?' Jackie enquired.

'Justice Fortune gave me five thousand euro in a brown envelope to be getting on with.'

Mrs Ball said to Jackie, 'And she took it. She's already spent some of it.'

'I had to buy some maternity clothes, Mum. And some little outfits for the babies.' She looked a bit soft, or shy, or something: nothing that Jackie had ever seen before, anyway.

Mrs Ball begged Jackie, 'You talk to her, Jackie. Tell her to make him take a paternity test, or whatever it is. Otherwise those two children are going to grow up with no father.'

'They're going to grow up with no father anyway,' Michelle pointed out reasonably.

'You see?' Mrs Ball said to Jackie despairingly. 'I've a good mind to go round there myself and tell him exactly what I think of him.'

'Forget it, I've already tried,' Michelle told her. 'He lives in a mansion with electronic security gates and two Rottweilers.'

'I'm not afraid of Rottweilers,' Mrs Ball said loudly, but she didn't voice any more plans to confront him. A huge yawn overtook her. She'd had so little sleep in the last few days that she had yawned eighty-two times yesterday. But do you think she could get a wink? Not a bit of it! She was inclined to think at this stage of her life that she wouldn't get any rest until she had passed away. Knowing her luck, she would wake up six feet under, in a coffin, and start worrying. And, at that stage, there certainly would be something to worry about.

And there was Mr Ball tinkering out in the garage as if none of it had a thing to do with him! That Michelle was somebody else's daughter entirely. But he'd always been that way, Mrs Ball thought darkly. Even when they were little she'd catch him looking at the lot of them as though he scarcely recognised them.

Jackie said diplomatically, 'I suppose all this, it's a bit of shock to you, Mum. Wait till you get used to the idea.'

It was a very bad idea to have drawn attention to herself, because Mrs Ball was overcome with a fresh burst of worry. 'Just like I've had to get used to the fact that you've broken up with Dan? I had a turkey defrosted for him and everything.'

There was a whole clatter of rakes and shovels lined up against the garage wall, and the lawnmower was out, so it was a fair guess that she'd had some gardening lined up for him too. And was that a bag of cement?

'I haven't broken up with Dan. We're just having some time out, that's all.'

'Time out! Don't be using your euphemisms around me,' said Mrs Ball, who watched *Neighbours* and was well up on these things. 'I know exactly what it means – the whole thing has gone to the wall but you're letting everybody down gently, including yourselves.'

'That's not true, Mum.'

'Why aren't you wearing your engagement ring then?' She looked like she was going to burst into tears.

'Because I didn't feel like it,' Jackie said. 'Oh, look, I had to take a stand! Otherwise he would have thought that what he did was OK.'

'Well, I think he's a saint,' Mrs Ball declared. 'For putting up with as much as he has. You couldn't really blame him.'

'For organising a vicious assault?'

'Don't tell me you wouldn't have liked to give Henry a good thump yourself.'

'Well, yes but—'

'When you arrived back here from London first, we all prayed to Saint Francis that he would trip into the path of an articulated lorry, do you remember?'

'That was then, Mum. I was upset. I didn't really mean it.'

'You sounded like you did. You were hopping off the ceiling with rage. That's when you weren't lying on your bed up there drenching the pillow. I said to your father, you'd wonder what in the name of God he did for her to be in *that* state. Not that he replied or anything. Of course, we all knew things weren't going that well over there – you weren't working, and he was working too much. Always a recipe for disaster. Any time I'd ring you'd take the head off me. There's something up with that pair, I said to your father, they're not happy at all. Not that he gave any indication that he heard me. But then for it all to end in such disaster! He did something big to her this time, I said to Michelle.'

Michelle jerked at the mention of her name; she had drifted off somewhere, now that the heat was off her. 'Yes,' she agreed. 'Something very big.'

And they looked at Jackie expectantly.

She said neutrally, 'I suppose it was just . . . the final straw.'

Mrs Ball persisted, 'What straw, though? You never actually told us.'

'For God's sake, Mum, it was nearly two years ago. I can hardly remember the ins and outs of it, and to be honest, I'd rather not try!'

Mrs Ball's mouth puckered up like a cat's bottom. 'Just trying to show a bit of motherly support, Jackie.'

'I wish you'd show some to me,' Michelle complained. 'I'm about to become a single mother.'

'You should have thought of that before you lay down under Justice Fortune.'

'Well, actually,' Michelle began, but thought better of it, and stopped.

Mrs Ball hadn't finished with Jackie. She asked, 'So how long is this "time out" going to last between you and Dan?'

'She has her wedding outfit bought,' Michelle informed Jackie. 'But unless you get a move on, it'll be all the wrong season and she'll have to get another.'

Mrs Ball's worry was sent scurrying in another direction. 'Oh, stop. And there's me size ten on top but size twelve on bottom . . . you might as well be at nothing. And some of those sales girls can be very sniffy about separating up outfits.'

Jackie was fed up with the conversation now, and so she announced, 'Right now, I don't know if there *is* going to be a wedding.'

Mrs Ball's hand flew to her throat. Her eyes, already burning from lack of sleep and worry, took on an other-worldly glow. She implored, 'For goodness' sake, Jackie, we all have our little failings! If I were to list everything that I've put up with from your father over the past . . . oh, I don't know how many years, and to be honest, it'd sicken me to count.' She looked at Jackie as if she couldn't understand her at all. 'And to think that you got a second chance. The whole thing, handed to you on a plate!' She added, bewildered, 'But only you, Jackie, could make such hard work of it!' She flopped back in her chair, red-cheeked, confused, worried and spent. She closed her eyes and a moment later an odd, whistling noise came from her.

'Is she . . . asleep?' Jackie enquired.

'I don't know. Give her a poke.'

'I will not. Be grateful for the peace.'

Michelle said, 'So *are* you going to go back to Dan? Or were you just saying that to rile her up?'

'I suppose I will, eventually.'

'Don't sound so enthusiastic.'

'Maybe Mum is right. Maybe I do make hard work of things. I get engaged before I'm divorced, I goad Henry into defending the thing, and now I've gone and left Dan. The whole thing is a mess.'

'At least you know you're alive,' Michelle said.

Jackie looked at her suspiciously. 'What's got you so philosophical?'

'I don't know. Maybe it's all the hormones. But I feel happy or something.'

'Happy?'

'I know. Isn't it strange? Without having to take an E or anything.'

'And you're not worried about Spanky?'

'There's isn't much I can do until the babies are born. Anyway, Mum is worrying enough for both of us.' She patted her belly contentedly, and Jackie felt envious of her unexpected bliss. Why couldn't she get it right? Why did she always make a total mess of things?

'Do you think I run out on things?' she asked. 'You know, in life generally?' Beside her, Mrs Ball's mouth had fallen open, and she was giving big, lusty snores. In the dungarees, she looked like a toddler having a mid-morning nap.

Jackie went on, 'Maybe I have some kind of, I don't know, commitment phobia.' She tried to sound flippant. But Emma's comment had been festering since last week. Was it possible that every serious relationship ended abruptly with her walking out with a suitcase?

Michelle snorted. 'Listen, I've been with enough men to recognise a commitment phobe when I sleep with one. And you're not, Jackie. For goodness' sake, you upped sticks and went to London for Henry!'

'Thank you!' Jackie cried, feeling much better. Emma had been talking a load of old cobblers. Hadn't she herself come to the conclusion that she had invested far too much in Henry? Certainly not the actions of someone shy of pitching in! It wasn't her fault that the men she wholeheartedly fell in love with let her down so badly, and with such depressing regularity. Anybody would pack a suitcase and leave.

'No, I've always thought your main problem was setting your sights too high,' Michelle went on.

'Sorry?' She had thought they were talking about her virtues here.

'Well, you know what you're like. All caught up in the romance of the moment.'

'That's not a fault, Michelle. It's what people do; they fall in love. Just because it's never happened to you.'

'That's because I'm a realist. I don't want to end up constantly disappointed like you.'

Jackie gave a bit of a laugh. 'I am not constantly disappointed!'

'Let's face it, you do expect a lot from men.'

'You're saying I should lower my standards?'

'If you did, you mightn't end up walking out the door with a suitcase so often.'

Jackie was astonished. And very defensive. 'You've never even been in love, Michelle. So you don't really know what you're talking about. And anyway, if I had wanted to pick someone who was going to shatter all my so-called romantic illusions, then Henry was the man.' She sounded very bitter.

Michelle said, 'Did you give the guy a chance?'

'Of course I did. Several! Hundreds! It wasn't my fault that he turned out to be a bum!'

She badly wanted to believe that. Otherwise he began to look a little bit better in all this. Less black, anyhow. And she began to look a little less white.

'He came in again yesterday. That's three visits in two days,' Emma said when Jackie arrived back at work on Thursday. 'Maybe you should take pity on him and, I don't know, talk.'

'Dying to get rid of me?' Jackie enquired.

'Hardly,' Emma said gruffly. 'No, I'm delighted to have you back.'

She was wearing a polo-neck sweater, brought right up to her chin. It was rather odd, in this weather. But she explained she'd been doing a bit of gardening in the evenings while Jackie was at her mother's, and had caught a chill.

'Why has Lech got a polo neck on too, then?' Jackie enquired. 'Was he helping you?'

Emma did the varying shades of pink thing again, and wrung her hands a bit.

'It's nothing to be ashamed of,' Jackie said.

'It is!' Emma hissed. 'It's deeply shameful! Promise me that you won't tell anybody we know. Please, Jackie. I'd have to leave town.'

'Oh, Emma.'

'I don't know how it happened again. I mean, once was bad enough. Maybe I need to go and see somebody. Or maybe I've neglected my . . . needs so long that they're out of control, and I'll have to get neutered or something.' She was in a right old state.

'So you've met a great guy. Why can't you just enjoy it?'

Her eyes popped. 'Enjoy it? It's Lech.'

'Yes?'

'I'll say it again. *Lech.*'

As though he'd been summoned, in he walked from a delivery.

'Hey! It's a beautiful day out there!'

'St James's Hospital,' Emma said, thrusting a bouquet at him for delivery. She looked fixedly at a point three feet to his left.

'I'm due for my coffee break,' he said. He was hurt and watchful and Jackie felt sorry for him.

'Get a takeout. Now go, please.'

But he lingered. He flicked a look at Jackie and said to Emma, low, 'Will I see you later?'

'No. No, no, no!'

When he took the bouquet from her she snatched her hand away fast. He gave her a stiff look before he walked out, without his customary bounce.

'Poor guy,' Jackie said.

'I'd like to change my shifts,' Emma said. 'If that's OK with you. I thought maybe I could do more mornings.'

Lech didn't work in the mornings.

'That's fine by me,' Jackie said. 'But I really think you should give him a chance, Emma.'

But for Emma the conversation was over. 'Now, two things while you were away. We're behind with the accounts, again, and another one of these arrived for you.' She took out a plastic-covered copy of the previous Sunday's *Globe*. 'Looks like somebody's got you a yearly subscription.'

'Yes, well, they needn't have bothered, because this is exactly where it goes!' And she launched it scornfully at the bin. She missed, of course, and had to retrieve it from a bunch of roses before dispatching it.

'Do you want to go on a coffee break?' she asked Emma.

'OK, thanks.'

It was only an excuse, of course, to get her out of the way. The minute she was gone, Jackie scrabbled in the bin and got the newspaper out. She tore the plastic off. First she checked the food review section. He hadn't written it again, but that wasn't surprising, given that he'd mostly been eating hospital food. Then she turned to the back of the newspaper to the Personal Ads, her heart doing a little skip in her chest. She told herself there probably wouldn't even *be* anything. And even if there were, it wouldn't be intended for her. In fact, the first poem could have been some marketing gimmick, dreamed up by some little whippet in a suit to test public awareness of God knew what –

There was a new one.

> *You're on my mind constantly*
> *In everything I do*
> *Days and nights and thoughts and dreams are*
> *Sweetly full of you.*

Then, like the first one: *For Jackie.*

Chapter Fourteen

'The only *good* grounds for a defence are that allegations of unreasonable behaviour are untrue,' Mr Ian Knightly-Jones intoned importantly. He fixed Henry with his watery grey eyes set in a deathly pale face. 'And are they, Mr Hart?'

Henry would have loved to fix him back with a look of his own, but that would be a tad difficult given that his right eye was black and blue, and bloodshot in the middle. It was all he could do to squint.

'Yes,' he said arrogantly. The main thing was to look confident when dealing with legal matters, even if he hadn't a clue what he was talking about.

'You can prove in a court of law that what your wife has accused you of in the petition is a pack of lies?' He had the knack of making Henry feel like a naughty schoolboy who had been caught cheating at maths. And as for rookie solicitor Tom, he was in contortions on the edge of his seat, every muscle straining obediently in the direction of the great man.

'Yes,' Henry repeated loudly.

Knightly-Jones gave a little sigh, and shot a malevolent look over at Tom as if to admonish him for foisting this particular domestic matter upon him, when he should really be in a courtroom defending somebody truly important. Tom withered a little.

'The petition,' he commanded.

Tom darted forward, bird-like, and placed the petition on the desk, just so. In another lightning move, he edged Knightly-Jones's bifocals

177

an inch nearer. The whole building seemed to breathe in expectantly as Knightly-Jones lifted the petition, put on his glasses, and read.

Henry rudely interrupted the awed silence with, 'You see, that's only rubbish, what's she's written down there. It's not what *really* went wrong.'

'We can only defend what is in the petition, Mr Hart.'

Henry said meekly, 'OK.'

'Let's start with the first instance of unreasonable behaviour.' He read, portentously, '"Failure to participate fully in family life."'

'She never complained about that at the time,' Henry interjected quickly. 'Just so you know.'

That earned him an admonishing look from both Tom and Knightly-Jones.

'Can you defend it, Mr Hart? More importantly, will *I* be able to defend it? Because I'll tell you this, I do not like to be caught in open court with my pants down.'

Henry had a brief vision of such a spectacle, before confidently saying, 'Yes.'

'How?'

'What?'

'How do you suggest that we defend it?'

'I thought you guys came up with all that?' He was paying them a fucking fortune.

Mr Knightly-Jones lowered the petition. 'I can't just stand up and say that it's a load of nonsense. We need arguments, evidence. We have to disprove her witnesses – she's got a short statement here from someone called Emma Byrne. Tom?'

Tom dived into the file. 'I have it here.'

'Don't mind Emma,' Henry said. 'She's her best friend, she'll say anything for Jackie.'

'I can't put that in our answer, Mr Hart. "Don't mind the best friend."' Knightly-Jones gave another little sigh. He reached for his glass of water, but stopped just short, and it was up to Tom to jump forward and edge it closer.

'You have to leave for court in ten minutes,' he whispered.

'Yes, yes.' Knightly-Jones flapped him away as if he were an irritating fly. 'If you insist on defending this divorce, Mr Hart, then these allegations will come under a great deal of scrutiny in court. From her side *and* yours. And so we need to back up our defence with a certain degree of proof, do you understand?'

Henry began to feel under pressure. It was never like this in John Grisham books. Then he hit on it. 'I can say it was the nature of my job! As a food critic. That I couldn't always be there when she clicked her fingers.'

'And did she? Click her fingers?'

Henry felt on much safer ground now. 'God, yes. Needy was her middle name. She was never like that in the beginning.'

'Why do you think that was?'

'Well, I don't know. I mean, she was living in London, she loved London, all those shops, and things to do and see, the buzz. She had a lovely house and all the money she could spend.'

'So as far as you were concerned, she had no reason at all to be "needy"?'

Henry looked at him. 'I don't think I like your tone of voice.'

'I'm simply wondering if you ever asked her why she wasn't the way you wanted her to be.' His grey eyes seemed to bore into Henry. His face had grown even whiter. He reminded Henry of an angel of death.

'I didn't want her to be anything! Just . . . happy.'

'And were you upset when she refused to be happy? After every thing you had done for her?'

'What is this, fucking therapy?'

Knightly-Jones winced. 'I'm simply asking some of the questions a judge might, Mr Hart. Failure to participate fully in family life covers rather more territory than simply you counting up numbers of hours.'

Then Henry caught Tom giving him a look. Of pity? But then Tom swiftly averted his eyes and whispered to Knightly-Jones, 'Five minutes.'

Henry said, face burning, 'I don't want to hold you up with my petty little problems. Go if you have to go.'

'No, no.' Knightly-Jones looked a little less stern. Sympathetic almost, which was even more sickening. 'Would you like to go on to the second allegation? Let me see, "Failure to emotionally commit to the marriage".'

Henry began to hate him.

Knightly-Jones said, 'At the end of the day, Mr Hart, this one will come down to her perception of whether you committed to her emotionally or not. And it's very difficult to argue with that. Do you see?'

'No, I don't!' He knew he sounded querulous and loud, like someone refused entry to a late-night bar. 'I'll give you an argument! That it's impossible to emotionally commit to someone who thinks that she's married Don fucking Corleone!'

Both Knightly-Jones and Tom looked mildly startled at this.

'I wasn't what she wanted, OK?' he muttered.

Knightly-Jones said, 'Then I would advise you to think very carefully again about this course of action, Mr Hart.'

'So, what, you're saying it's all over? We're licked?' Henry doggedly said. Well, fuck him. Giving in just like that. This was supposed to be a firm of lawyers who won more cases than they lost. And now they were saying that there was nothing he could do? That he just had to stand by and swallow all this . . . stuff? Without even putting up a fight?

Ian Knightly-Jones folded his white, soft hands together and said, not unkindly, 'Mr Hart, it's quite clear that Miss Ball wants to be divorced from you. And no matter how brilliant our defence, how convincing our evidence, it's not going to change the fact that Miss Ball wants to be divorced from you.'

Hearing it put like that, so detached and objective, gave Henry quite a shock. They were looking at him, waiting. He managed, 'Yes. You're making yourself perfectly clear.'

'Of course we will act on your instructions, but I should warn you that no judge is going to insist that she remain married to you.'

'I get it. Thank you.'

They were all saved from further mortification by the door opening and a secretary appeared. 'Your car is here, Mr Knightly-Jones.'

There was a great flurry of activity. Tom hummed and buzzed around the place like a graceful little bird, getting files, pens, diaries and umbrellas. Other assistants appeared to speed the exodus. Finally, one of them reached up, took off Knightly-Jones's bifocals, popped them in a leather case, which was then slipped reverently into Mr Knightly-Jones's breast pocket. Henry sourly wondered if one of them was employed to wipe his backside.

'Do let me know what you decide, Mr Hart,' he said. 'And there's always the option to take a civil action for assault. I wouldn't mind getting a crack in at that odious solicitor of hers – what's her name again? Vera? Verucca?'

'Velma,' Tom supplied eagerly. 'Or I can do it. I don't like her a bit either.'

Knightly-Jones waved a thin, white hand. The guy didn't look well, Henry decided.

'Fine, whatever Mr Hart decides. Good day, Mr Hart, Tom here will finish up.' And then he was borne out by the clatter of secretaries and assistants.

Henry was left looking at Tom.

'If you *did* want to start a civil suit—' Tom began.

'No.'

'Oh. OK.'

There didn't seem to be anything left to say. Tom fiddled nervously with a pen. Henry knew he was waiting for him to make his excuses and leave.

'You think I was a fool too, don't you?' he said to Tom. 'Along with Mr Knightly-Bigshot-Jones.'

Tom looked terrified. 'Me?'

'Yes. You.'

Tom dithered and squirmed and wavered. Then he said, 'Actually, no. I think if I were getting divorced from someone, I'd like it if they tried to stop me. If they put up a bit of a fight.'

'I wasn't fighting for her,' Henry said gruffly.

'No, of course not,' Tom agreed readily. 'Will I . . . tell them?'

'No,' said Henry. He felt like a child about to take some nasty medicine. 'I will.'

'It's over,' he declared to Dave. 'But you know something? I really loved that woman. And I'm not embarrassed to say it. Not now that it's over. I mean, really over.'

He was delighted with himself. Perhaps he was already 'healing', although usually he had no time for all that crap. He went on emotionally, 'You know the way you *think* you love someone? Or even several women? But then you meet the One –' he held up one finger to drive the point home – 'and you realise that you didn't love any of the other ones. You only lusted after them. With Jackie it was lust *and* love. Quite a good combination, I have to say. I'd recommend it.'

'I'll take that on board,' Dave said. 'If ever I'm in a position to remarry. Which, actually, I might be. I was supposed to be home four hours ago to fix the washing machine for Dawn, and look at me. Pissed out of my head again.'

'She'll forgive you.'

'Easy for you to say that. You don't have to go home to her.'

'Sorry for being a prick the other day,' Henry said, cracking open two more beers. He'd have to go down the off-licence in a minute. Although he might have a bottle of Scotch or something somewhere. After the day he'd had, his defence gone up in flames, he needed it.

Dave was magnanimous. 'That's OK. Most of my friends are pricks, Dawn says. Mind you, she's very fond of you. I don't know why.'

'I'm very fond of her too,' Henry said. Actually, he was a bit afraid of her.

Dave suddenly squinted at him. 'I hope this doesn't mean you're going to go chasing after her. Now that you'll be divorced. Do you remember Andy Carroll? He made a play for everybody's wife as soon as he got dumped. Except for Dawn. She was very offended over that, you know.'

The word 'dumped' rankled with Henry. 'I haven't decided whether I'm going to drop my defence yet or not,' he said.

'Bollocks,' Dave said. 'Jackie has you whipped and you know it.'

'But I put up a fight,' Henry said.

'You did, mate. You did her proud. It's just that she can't see it at the moment because she's so angry. But she will in time.'

'I'm going to tell her,' Henry said. 'Personally. That she can have her divorce. And marry that jug-head if she wants.'

Which she probably would. It was only wishful thinking on Henry's part that she went to afternoon movie showings in order to escape him. They were probably bonking morning, noon and night.

Dave was admiring. 'You know, I'm really proud of you, Henry. I said to Dawn, knowing Henry, he'll take this thing to the bitter end. I didn't think you'd actually come around like this.'

Henry didn't feel the need to go too deeply into his bruising at the hands of Ian Knightly-Jones earlier. 'Yes, well, I suppose I see that maybe she was right. About some things. I *did* let her down emotionally, and with the family stuff.'

'Listen, we're all guilty of that, apparently,' Dave said. 'It's a wonder there aren't more divorces.'

'I kind of wish I could say sorry,' Henry said impulsively. He knew it was the drink talking, but he was kind of enjoying all this self-flagellation.

'Why don't you?' Dave encouraged. Dave was obviously enjoying it too. 'Ring her up! Apologise.'

'Naw,' Henry said.

'Do. You have to tell her that you're dropping the whole thing anyway. You'll feel a whole lot better. Cleansed.'

'Cleansed?'

'Yeah. Dawn is reading this book at the moment – you know the way she's into all that spiritual stuff – and I was reading a chapter of it, just while I was on the bog, and it said that in order to properly let go, you have to apologise to everybody you've wronged.'

'What, in your whole life?'

'I think so, yeah. Although, hang on, I wouldn't even have the phone numbers of half of them.'

'Maybe it just meant women.'

'Like I said. I wouldn't even have the phone numbers of half of them.' He cackled, before adding hurriedly, 'I was only joking. For Christ's sake, don't tell Dawn I said that.'

'Anyway,' Henry said, 'like Jackie's going to be impressed if I ring her up now and cry down the line that I'm sorry.'

'Wait until the morning then.'

Then Henry hit on it. 'I know. I'll write her a letter!'

'You just can't forget for a fucking minute, can you? That you're a writer?'

'It's not that! It's just, I think better when I write. I can really say how I feel, you know? It's always been that way with Jackie. Whatever I couldn't say to her I wrote down. So I'll write it down. Everything! And in a way it'll be ironic, you know? Seeing as my writing was part of what drove us apart.'

Dave yawned hugely. He was obviously riveted. 'Can I ring a taxi?'

'I'm in the middle of a fucking epiphany here and you're going to walk out on me?'

'What epiphany?'

'I'm going to reveal myself to her, Dave!'

Dave looked mildly alarmed. 'This book, it didn't say anything about revealing yourself. Just saying a simple sorry, Henry, can you not do that? Do you always have to go making things out to be more complicated than they actually are?'

'I don't make things complicated.' He was already hunting about for a piece of paper.

'You do! You're always moaning about your job but you don't do the obvious, simple thing, which is to leave. You don't get divorced through the post like everybody else, you have to go making a song and dance about it. I'm starting to think you're a fucking drama queen.'

'I am not.'

'Go on, you love it. All the theatrics, and wandering around the house like a lost soul, and having a hissy fit any time your week looks like it might be getting a little too dull. I'm starting to think you don't want to be happy!'

'I want to be happy as much as the next person!'

'Do something about it then. Because you're driving me crazy.'

'I have plenty of changes up my sleeve,' Henry announced grandly. 'I just haven't put them in motion yet.'

'Do it soon. Because my liver can't stand any more of these drinking sessions.'

Henry was barely listening to him. 'Jesus Christ! I can't find a sheet of paper in my own house! Get up off your arse, Dave, you might be sitting on a notebook or something.'

'I'm not,' Dave grumbled.

Eventually Dave produced a telephone bill from his pocket and Henry spread it out, blank side up, and found a pen.

'You're my witness,' he told Dave fervently. 'I'm going to cleanse myself. And then I'm going to reveal myself.'

'Forget it, I'm not hanging around for this,' Dave said, hitching up his trousers and making unsteadily for the door. 'By the way, HR is muttering that if you're not back at your desk next week, they're going to fire you for non-fulfilment of contract. They'll properly write to you, but I'm just giving you a jump on it.'

'All that will be taken care of,' Henry informed him.

184

Oh, yes, he was going to ring in the changes in his life. And to think that Jackie had brought it all about, by trying to divorce him. She was a fine, fine woman, he thought almost tearfully, and he had never deserved her. And now it was time to grow up and let her go. To that gangster of a Dan, unfortunately, but there was nothing he could do about that. As for himself, well, he would be a better person after it all. Still alone, but better.

With a religious-like fervour, and a bottle of beer at his elbow, he lifted his pen and began to write

Jackie and Henry went on honeymoon to Tenerife. Henry thought it was tacky, overpriced and the food was terrible. Jackie loved it, and came home with a tan and ten assorted pairs of flip-flops.

'And what the hell is that?' he asked in the car on the way back from the airport, pointing to something round her wrist that looked like a piece of rotten seaweed.

'A good luck charm,' she said. 'It brings the wearer good health and happiness, the woman at the stall said.'

'But only if you pay ten quid first.'

'Fifteen,' Jackie admitted. 'But she looked like she needed the money.'

He looked at her angular face, smattered with hundreds of tiny freckles, and framed by frizzy hair that the sun had turned a lighter shade of . . . whatever her hair colour actually was.

'I know what you're thinking,' she said, defensive.

He was actually thinking that she was good and pure and high-minded, and he was grubby and nasty and cynical in comparison. And smelly. That was another thing about Jackie; not only did she worry about old ladies who successfully conned her, but she never smelled either, any part of her, no matter how long she went between showers. Or at least she never smelled appalling, not like him. In the heat of Tenerife he had gone around stinking of old cheese the whole time, and he'd had to keep taking furtive showers, because somehow he just knew that a whiffy bridegroom wasn't part of her honeymoon agenda. Other elements of that agenda had involved walking barefoot in the moonlight across a beach that turned out to have fucking razor shells all over it. A whole night of sex wasted poking at the undersides of his feet with a pair of tweezers! She hadn't stepped on a single one, of course. But then again, he was learning fast with Jackie that her feet never really touched the ground. He had mentioned this once, delicately.

'I'm a Pisces,' she said. As though that explained everything! 'What are you?'

'Gemini,' he said back, scarcely able to credit that he had allowed himself to get drawn into a discussion about star signs.

'Ah,' she said, nodding sagely. 'That explains everything.'

It was all very baffling and confusing except for one thing: Jackie Ball seemed to have very high expectations about things, including marriage, and romance, and him. In his case, she seemed to think that he was some kind of cross between Heathcliff and Mr Darcy, and while it was flattering, it was bloody hard work. All those rakish smiles and inscrutable looks . . . He was worn out.

Still, the important thing was that she seemed to really love him, which was amazing. A woman like Jackie! So different to the cold fish he met in his working life, women more obsessed with their waistlines than their own happiness. Jackie had no pretensions, or airs or graces. She was just . . . unbridled, was the word. Sometimes, when she gave him a big, wide, toothy smile, she took his breath away.

He must be careful not to do anything that might diminish that, at least until they knew each other a little better. Then, surely, they'd be able to relax a bit. After only three months he was already finding it a bit of a strain, the constant pressure to be suave and arrogant and cool the whole time. Luckily, he was naturally a moody so-and-so, and rude with it, so no problems *there*. But in time – well, any day now – he hoped to be able to reveal that, in private, when he wasn't trying desperately to impress her, he liked to stick his stockinged feet up on the coffee table, and watch trash TV, and occasionally belch. And that coarse black hairs grew abundantly from his nostrils and ears except that he beat them back. That he didn't brood twenty-four hours a day; indeed, if you tickled his tummy, he would collapse into uncontrollable titters. That most of his friends, who so impressed her, were no more than acquaintances, and bloody irritating ones at that, and that he had no intention whatsoever of inviting any of them round to the dinner parties that she was already enthusiastically planning. And that he smelled like a hog if left to his own devices.

The bigger issues, like hating his job, and the utter lack of meaning he felt in his life, he might save until further down the line. At least until she'd unpacked her suitcases and settled in.

When he laid it out like that, he got a bit of a shock: she'll think she's married a total stranger.

In the passenger seat, Jackie was thinking, there he is, brooding again, probably about Third World poverty and thinking that I'm such a ninny for spending fifteen quid on a piece of dried seaweed.

Sometimes she would catch him looking at her as though she were an amusing oddity; the kind of person that he didn't often come across in his line of work or social circle but who intrigued him all the same. She wondered if the day would come when the intrigue wore off. Already she'd caught him wincing once or twice on honeymoon, usually when she would sing along loudly with the hire car radio that only seemed to play eighties holiday hits.

But, apart from that, what an absolutely perfect time it had been! Just them, no deadlines, or phone calls, or that new agent of his with the peroxide hair who gave Jackie the willies. It had been a little cocoon of happiness where she'd shamefully indulged her romantic side and made him do the same. And he always thought he had to be so macho and moody all the time! No man could look too tortured in the Kiss Me Quick hat that she'd bought him at the market stall. By day three, he'd stopped frowning, and by the end of the first week she'd started to think that they were really opening up to each other. But no matter how many glasses of cheap red wine Henry had, he never went all the way, in her opinion; even after she told him some of her most private childhood experiences, including the one about the moving statue of Our Lady at the local grotto. This was at the time when statues were moving all over Ireland, and Jackie had wanted it to happen to her so badly that she told the whole school that she had seen Our Lady's right hand slowly rise in the international V sign for peace.

But Henry wouldn't go that far. He held things back. He was secretive and reserved and careful, as if he was terrified of what might happen if he let himself go.

She had never had that problem, of course. She was always letting herself go, to the point of gaining about eight pounds on honeymoon.

And now here they were, back in London. It was a grey, cold day and she shivered in her light sundress and three-inch wedges. She should have put on more clothes at the other end. But she'd wanted to hold on to the honeymoon as long as she could. It would be different here. She already knew that. She was used to being elbowed aside at parties as people descended upon Henry. 'Tell us, Henry, where's your absolutely *favourite* place to eat?' A gaggle of women would surround him at any gathering in five seconds flat, holding on to his every word, begging for a tip on the latest hot restaurant. Which he nearly always gave them, along with a charming smile. Sometimes Jackie felt like asking these people what did it really matter, it was just food, but then they would all know how unsophisticated Henry's new wife really was, how uncultured, uncouth. Henry himself would doubtless be appalled at her lack of regard for his career. And so she kept up her side of things by smiling brilliantly and nodding at all the tedious functions, and trying to invite his plethora of superficial friends round. She didn't really like any of them, but they all talked the way Henry did, in short, witty sentences, and they were part of her new life now and so she would just have to learn to like them. Or pretend to.

And she didn't care anyway, so long as she was with Henry. She still couldn't believe that he had picked her above all the Hannahs and Mirandas and Tanyas, with their lipgloss and cosmetically whitened teeth. And so what if he held a little back? She would give enough for both of them. When she put her mind to it, she could melt a stone. She reached over and squeezed Henry's hand. 'Oh, look, there's Big Ben!'

'I see Big Ben every day,' Henry said.

She felt as though she had let herself down. The country hick. 'Well, I don't.'

'Sorry, honey.' He was raging with himself. He had hurt her. But the further they got from the airport, and the honeymoon and the sun, the more his claustrophobia grew. His mind clicked into the familiar, depressing triangle of work, sleep and − what was the third? Oh, yes; bloody work. He'd almost left it behind for a fortnight to frolic on beaches with Jackie, and ogle her in that bright, tight yellow bikini she'd worn, and splash cold water at her until she got into a huff and went off shopping instead.

'Jackie,' he said suddenly.

'Yes?' She turned to him.

He didn't know what he was going to suggest: that they turn the car round and go back to the airport, maybe. And jump on a flight to somewhere. Anywhere. Back to tacky Tenerife, he wouldn't care.

But she was waiting, the keys to the house in her hand, and her face so full of expectation and optimism and the absolute sense that everything was as it should be, that he just couldn't do it. She had left everything behind in Dublin for him. And he was going to tell her that, really, he'd rather be a beach bum?

She'd run home screaming that she had been misled.

'What is it, Henry?'

He gave her another one of his lopsided smiles. 'Just, I love you.'

'I love you too,' she said, with such passion and such feeling that he thought, this is OK. If I have this, then the other stuff won't matter so much.

In the passenger seat, Jackie was thinking, everything's going to be just fine. She was in a new country, with no job, no friends, no family, although that was a blessing, and with her new husband already behaving a little peculiarly, but she had love, and with her usual breathtaking optimism she just knew that love would always save the day.

In one of the honeymoon photos Henry was standing on a pier, and at the moment the shutter had clicked he had pretended to lose his balance and fall off. The person taking the photo, Jackie, had obviously screamed in fright and begun to run towards him because the photo was all lopsided and fuzzy. And if that wasn't just typical of him! She had set up a lovely romantic shot, and at the last moment he had confounded her expectations.

And look at him in the next one, ducking below the waves just as she had taken the shot. Further photos showed him wearing his sunglasses backwards, or dipping his tongue into a big pint of beer, or modelling her bikini top. She rifled through the whole pack, but there wasn't a single photo in which he was truly himself. He seemed determined not to play along with the whole honeymoon thing. As though he was above it or something.

Not her, of course. No, in every single photo she'd embarrassed herself by practically swooning for the camera, her eyes only half-focused and her lips permanently moist. She was like an advertisement for some cheap holiday destination, except for her thighs. They would never find their way into a holiday brochure.

And these were the rejects too. There were three big photo albums in the house in London with more of the same, her misty-eyed in every single one. She would be too mortified to look back on them now. She didn't even know why she had brought this discarded pack with her when she had left that night. Or, indeed, why it was one of the few things that had made it into her pink suitcase when she'd walked out on Dan, along with her shoes and ball gowns.

Looking back on the rejects now, she saw how doomed the marriage had been from the start. Henry couldn't even take the honeymoon seriously, or was intentionally *not* taking it seriously, while she looked like she was living out some lurid happy-ever-after fantasy she'd had since she was seven.

But then, at the bottom of the pack, she came across a photo of them together. It had been taken on the beach by a passer-by who wasn't all that gifted with photography, because both Jackie and Henry's legs were cut off at the knees. And two teenagers appeared to be mooning in the background, which further went to explain its exclusion from the official album. The whole thing was the very opposite of Jackie's idea of romantic.

But look at their faces. They had eyes only for each other, oblivious to the photographer and the teenage mooners. And Henry looked so . . . besotted by her that you would almost think that his heart had been in it as much as hers. You would believe that they had, indeed, been made for each other.

Oh, bugger it! Her eyes were suddenly full of tears and she lurched sideways in Emma's narrow single bed for a box of tissues. She sobbed lustily into a handful, and decided that she would burn the photos tomorrow in a big barrel with a can of petrol. Well, that was probably overkill, but it would be symbolic, she told herself. She'd even burn the one where he was looking at her like that because, knowing him, that was only pretend too.

To add insult to injury, Emma and Lech began to bonk in the room next door. She had heard Emma sneaking him in just after she had gone to bed – as though she wouldn't hear the pair of them at it three feet away through a wall that seemed to be made of cornflakes boxes.

There was a curious twanging sound through the wall. What were they up to now?

'Oh, baby,' Lech murmured through the wall in delight.

Oh, God. Jackie stuffed her fingers into her ears and burrowed under the pillow. She struck herself as faintly ridiculous. Not, not faintly: completely ridiculous. There she was, into her fourth decade, sleeping in her mate's spare bed while she and her boyfriend got it on next door. Was this really where her life had arrived at? After all her great hopes and dreams? And, to cap it all, there was a big, hard spring sticking up into her bum.

She bet Henry was having no such difficulties sleeping. They'd installed a six-foot bed shortly after she'd moved in, and stocked up on linen and a lovely, big, fluffy duvet. He was no doubt benefiting, too, from her brief flirtation with feng shui, and would rise in the morning well rested after his feet had pointed in a soothing northerly direction all night. Jackie had no idea what direction her own feet were pointing in. Probably towards the local festering dump, or a home for sad losers or something.

And there was Dan across town, alone and hurt in another double bed (why did the guys get the double beds and she was stuck in this lumpy thing? Another important question.) He was probably cursing her, and making a small doll with frizzy woolly hair to stick needles into.

'When are you coming back?' he'd asked tersely on the phone earlier.

'I don't know.' Oh, he wasn't forgiven yet.

She waited for him to prostrate himself at her feet again. To beg or plead or something.

But he said, a little snappily, 'And I'm supposed to be happy with that?'

That deserved a response, she felt. 'I left because of what you did, Dan!'

'Are you going to hold it against me for ever?'

'I just need to sort out some things, OK?'

'What things?'

She dodged again. 'Well, my divorce for one.'

'So you've rewritten the petition then? Finally?' There was a note of incredulity in his voice. Was he, too, going to suggest that she was somehow dragging her heels?

'I'm working on it,' she said coldly.

'When is he filing his Answer? Three days' time?'

'Four,' Jackie said.

'You'd want to get a move on then, wouldn't you?' he'd said sarcastically. 'Unless you've got something to hide.'

'Me? Most certainly not!'

'Well, then. I don't know what you're afraid of.'

Grief, that's what she was afraid of. And confrontation, and pain, and failure. Such things had no place in the world of an idealist. Hadn't she a perfect track record of extricating herself as dramatically as possible from undesirable situations, and partners, and moving swiftly on to the next, red suitcase in hand? It seemed such a shame to sully that record now. And she could easily just beef up that divorce petition, stick it in the post and be done with Henry. And nobody would blame her! He was a pig and beast and everybody would say how much better off she was without him. No, nobody at all would point the finger at her and call her a coward. Especially if they knew the whole truth.

Lech, damn him, was picking up pace next door and the whole apartment block began to shake. She peered at the clock. Ten past three! Had she dozed off, or had they been at it nearly three hours now? It was the last straw for a soon-to-be-divorcée! She flung back the duvet and went into the kitchen to make some tea.

While she waited for the kettle to boil, she took out the cutting from the Personal Ads section of the previous Sunday's newspaper. It was baffling. *'Days and nights and thoughts and dreams are / Sweetly full of you.'*

She might have believed that Henry wrote the limerick. He could be clever and funny like that, and he might have found it amusing to put it in the paper just to stir her up. But this? Love poetry? He'd sooner write a piece for *Motorbikes Today* complete with expletives and vitriolic put-downs. Nothing ever came from his pen except bile. Anyway, to write poetry you had to feel things, you had to be capable of empathising, sharing, appreciating. You had to be romantic. And how often had he laughed at her for being too starry-eyed and altogether too soft! But, of course, he had banked on that, with the divorce. Her softness. Her aversion to confrontation. He had thought, well, she'll never have the bottle to bring up the *really* nasty stuff. And so he got to look lily white in the whole thing, bar a few minor offences, and she ended up the feckless villain of the piece who had run out on a perfectly good man!

And she had played along so far. Or tried to. No wonder she couldn't rewrite the blasted divorce petition; she wasn't writing down what she was really divorcing him for. Not the Class A, uncondensed, unabridged version of their marriage that, so far, he had not admitted to.

Well, for nearly two years now she'd been working on a new, harder, more worldly-wise version of Jackie Ball. A woman with dangerously high heels and a look in her eye that said, 'Just try it, buster!' Never again would she be taken in by moody, artistic eyes, or any resemblance to James Dean. She couldn't do much about the fuzzy hair or the squeaky voice, but by God they wouldn't hold her back! She had, she thought, finally grown up.

Which was all a load of old rubbish, she saw now. Her entire trans-formation had been merely cosmetic. Why on earth was she still carrying around a batch of honeymoon photos so? Why had she rushed into another marriage without even finishing off the first? More to the point, why was she still letting Henry Hart dodge the truth and run the show?

Lech was going at top speed in the bedroom now, and the ensuing vibration set off a burglar alarm in the apartment below. But Jackie scarcely noticed. She scrunched up the love poem, and pushed it down Emma's waste disposal unit.

It was time to divorce Henry Hart once and for all.

Chapter Fifteen

Velma had a ferocious itch all over her body. She'd had it for the past couple of weeks now. Perhaps it was that new duvet she'd purchased for the upcoming winter months. Contrary to popular belief, layers of fat did not act like some kind of lagging jacket, and Velma was getting to an age where she felt the chill around her ankles in the evening time. And her bed, while cosy, did not have the same warmth were there another person in it besides just her.

Oh well. Mr Bear would have to do for now, although he was beginning to look as tired and lonely as Velma these days.

These thoughts would have begun to worry her – they smacked of dotage, and going soft – were it not for this constant itch that Velma felt. She went back to her old duvet, and changed her brand of bubble bath. She wore only cotton against her skin. And still it was there. Irritating her, all the time. Causing her to wriggle in her seat, and rub and scratch and swipe angrily at herself, and yet it would not go away. Could it possibly be something that she ate?

She was gloomily reconciling herself to a process of elimination, which could take some considerable time, years perhaps given the range and volume of her food consumption, when her eye fell on a file one day and she knew in an instant what the cause of her annoyance was: Henry Hart.

What a merry dance he had led them! Rarely had Velma come across a wicked Other Half with quite the cunning and cruelty of this particular one. And so nice to look at! (Jackie had shown her a photograph.

195

Velma liked to put a face on her adversaries. He had a dimple in his left cheek.) He had called their bluff beautifully for the past three and a half weeks now, with no sign of letting up. Could he seriously be going to take it to court?

But it wasn't his legal trickery that got Velma's goat. It was the fact that she simply could not understand why he had thrown away such a fine woman as Jackie. Velma could never admit it, of course, but most of her clients were, well, flawed. To be perfectly frank, practically everybody who walked into her office looking for a divorce jolly well deserved one. She would have divorced them herself if she had ended up married to most of them. There they sat, frumpy and self-absorbed and fractious, and complained bitterly about their husband or husbands having strayed. Would you blame them? Velma sometimes wanted to say. Nobody wanted to come home to a spouse with a poker face, and where the only joy was to be had in the television, or a bottle of wine. Or at the bottom of a biscuit tin.

But of course she would never voice these opinions, and in fact she didn't often even think them, because the fact that her clients were by and large a pretty unlovable bunch made her understand them more, and draw them closer to her big, empathetic heart.

Jackie Ball wasn't selfish or moaning or controlling or self-pitying. In fact, Velma couldn't really find anything wrong with the woman, apart from her dubious fashion sense, but that wasn't a crime yet. The woman was just plain nice. Unless she had some fundamental character flaw that Velma had thus far failed to spot, she surely did not deserve to be used and abused in such a fashion, and Velma found that she took personal issue with it. Grave personal issue.

And, deep down, there was the thought that, if Jackie Ball wasn't appreciated, with all that hair and a waspish waist, then what hope was there for the likes of Velma?

She wanted to crush Henry Hart like a bug.

And as for Mr Ian Knightly-Jones . . . She wondered whether he had changed his name by deed poll, and whether he was really called Arthur Dash. He was quite possibly the most arrogant, rude, dismissive person Velma had ever come across. But was she cowed? By God, no! She welcomed it. She thrived on it. Let those two wiseguys bring this thing to court! Then they would get their day of reckoning.

If she were honest, she might be just the teensiest bit nervous if it *did* go to court. It was just that the American law course didn't really go into the specifics of courtroom practice. In fact, Velma had never actually been in a courtroom, except for that speeding thing ten years ago. She wasn't too up on English divorce law either. Thank God for all those divorce solicitors' websites, otherwise she'd have been in a right pickle. Still, she'd rather not go head to head with Ian Knightly-Jones over some finer point of law.

And there was Jackie depending on her. Lovely, decent, good Jackie, who was desperate to offload her toerag, scumbag husband so that she could be with . . . whatever his name was. Velma never concerned herself with incoming partners, just outgoing ones. If only she hadn't made Jackie so many inflated, rash promises in the beginning. And only three days to go before Henry Hart filed his Answer, which Velma would be expected to . . . well, she wasn't sure. Did she answer his Answer? Or did someone else answer it?

The itch had turned into a cold clammy sweat now. She desperately wanted some biscuits, or a triple-decker toasted sandwich with fries on the side. And Jackie was due in the office any minute. It was urgent, she said, That rugged boyfriend of hers had probably gone and booked another hotel for next month or something, and the heat would really be on.

In a panic Velma began to rummage through the file. She needed some leverage, something to come back at Henry Hart and his solici-tors with. Was there anything at all she could threaten them with? One of the tabloids, maybe, or a trashy magazine? He was a minor celebrity after all. Oh, what would they care whether he was getting divorced or not? Who wasn't, these days.

Through her grimy window she could see Jackie Ball coming down the street. You'd never think she had a divorce weighing on her mind, to look at her: hips swinging and hair flying, and high heels plonking confidently in the puddles. In fact, there was altogether an air of purpose about her, of resolve, that Velma hadn't really seen in her before.

Better buck up, thought Velma. She looked like she meant business.

By the time Jackie was sitting at the other side of the desk, Velma was in the groove. She bluffed smoothly, 'Naturally, we'll be sent a copy of his Answer by the court. That should be a laugh, I'm quite looking forward to it. And then I should imagine the court will fix a date for the, um, hearing.'

Luckily, at that point, Jackie intervened. 'Velma, you've done so much work on all this, and I don't want it to go to *waste* or anything.'

'No, no,' Velma said graciously.

'It's just, I haven't been entirely straight with you.'

'Have you not?' Maybe the woman wasn't so lily white after all. Velma's mind immediately raced down all kinds of murky avenues.

'It's about Henry,' she added.

Ah. And then Velma knew that the case was about to turn around. Henry Hart was about to be squashed like a bug.

'What is it about Henry?' she asked, holding on to the underside of the table with her fingers.

Jackie hesitated only a second, before saying clearly, 'I think he was seeing somebody else.'

Henry tried to lift his head off the pillow. But he couldn't. Some jackass seemed to have left a couple of hundred pound weights on top of it. Possibly the same person had also poisoned his food because he desperately wanted to throw up. But that would mean lifting his head off the pillow, which of course he couldn't.

Also, he wasn't able to see. Now that was scary. Then he managed to unstick one gluey eyelid and peered out, but everything swam alarmingly, and so he clamped it shut again. At least now he knew he was in his own bedroom and not under a truck or in a decompression tank or something.

Things weren't much better on the mouth front. His lips were stuck to the pillow, and his tongue was so dry and swollen that it had given up the ghost and just lolled there in his cheek like something dead for a week.

He didn't even want to go into the whole area of his brain. It was enough to say that it felt battered and deep fried, and gave off little screams of pain every couple of seconds. But mostly it hadn't the energy to do anything, like the rest of Henry.

At least his sense of touch still functioned. He could distinctly feel something nestling between his arms. He wondered briefly, wildly, whether it might be a woman. Had he gone out on the town and picked up a stranger? But no, unless she was an extremely skinny, short woman with a neck, but no head. Still, at this stage he could hardly afford to be choosy. He felt around a bit more. Hang on, and with a label around her middle?

It was an empty bottle of Scotch. The contents were in Henry's stomach, he now recalled. In fact, they were making their way back up now. Right this minute. He wrenched his head from the pillow and ran for the bathroom with a yell.

Later, much later, he became aware of the telephone ringing. He lifted his head from the toilet bowl, where he had fallen asleep again.

'Go away,' he moaned.

After a while they did, and Henry tried to go back to sleep, but the toilet bowl was cold and unfriendly and not all that clean. He hadn't felt this bad since, oh, he couldn't remember; that part of his brain seemed to have been permanently erased. But there was some reason why he had got himself into this state.

Jackie. And the divorce. And what was it that shite Dave had been on about last night? Cleansing himself. It would be enough to make him titter if he didn't feel so close to death. Still, maybe he'd needed to do it. Go on the batter, that was. Get ratted. Get her out of his head, his system, his life. Spend the day in bed getting over it and wake up tomorrow and get on with his life. Hurrah!

It sounded so easy put like that. But surely he was supposed to feel all light and free in that case. And not think about her any more.

Hang on, here came another puke.

When he extracted his head from the toilet for a second time, the telephone was ringing again. He knew who it was. Adrienne. She was completely undeterred by the fact that he never answered her phone calls. She would just keep ringing at five-minute intervals until eventually he lost all patience and would pick up. 'You're there after all!' she would say cheerfully. Not that she was cheerful these days. At least not when it came to Henry. He had cancelled two follow-up photo sessions for the book. 'I can't work with people who care so little about chickens, Adrienne.' But now the book publishers were clean out of patience, apparently, and Adrienne was threatening to supply them with an old photo of Henry back when he had a mullet. He had no idea where she'd got her hands on it.

She said to him that he was making her look very bad. Unprofessional. And that she was reconsidering whether she cared to represent him any longer except that she was in important talks with a television company about a possible project for him and would see how that panned out first.

And another thing: when was he going to get himself back to work? She had managed to buy him an extra week on the grounds of 'mental stress' but they knew damned well he was neither mental nor stressed, and if he lost his job, then he needn't blame her. They wanted a meeting with him at nine o'clock next Monday morning to discuss his future with the newspaper, and she would personally pick him up and drive them there. And could he please have a wash and comb his hair and wear matching socks?

The phone stopped but started up again three seconds later. He decided he would fire her. There and then. She couldn't go ringing him up any more if she no longer represented him.

He crawled to his penis-shaped phone and picked it up.

'Henry?' It was Tom. His voice erupted down the line in a babbled rush. 'There's been a bit of development I don't really know how to tell you this but the thing is I got a phone call this morning and I thought I'd better let you know as soon as possible—'

'Tom. Stop. Please.' He crawled back to the toilet just to be on the safe side. 'Who was the phone call from?'

He could hear Tom take a few shaky little breaths on the other end of the phone.

'Velma Murphy. They're divorcing you on the grounds of adultery.'

There was a little moment in which nothing at all happened. Then Henry laughed. He laughed and laughed. But it hurt too much and he stopped abruptly.

He said, 'Adultery?'

'Yes.'

'Me?'

'Yes.'

'Why?'

'*Why?*'

'Why are they divorcing me on the grounds of adultery?'

Tom whispered, 'Velma Murphy said that you'd left them with no choice. By refusing to accept the grounds of unreasonable behaviour, which she said were very reasonable. And so apparently they are withdrawing their original divorce petition and will be filing for a new divorce on the grounds of, um, adultery.'

'But I haven't committed adultery.'

'They say you have.'

'But I haven't.' His voice was loud now, and querulous.

'The thing is, we have to decide what to do,' Tom said.

'Are you saying you don't believe me?'

'I'm saying we have to respond!' He really was on the edge today.

'Well, what does Knightly-Jones say?' Knightly-Jones would mash the pair of them, and their false allegations, into the ground. In fact, Henry would *instruct* him to do just that. Because this was . . . preposterous! What kind of sick fantasy world was the woman living in at all? That she thought he had actually had an affair? With whom, for God's sake? When? *Where*, even?

His head was spinning with it all, and it was an effort to focus on what Tom was saying. Which seemed to be, 'Intensive care.'

'What?' Henry said sharply.

'He collapsed during rigorous cross-examination in court yesterday, just after he left us. The stenographer managed to catch him before he hit the ground. He's having a triple bypass first thing this morning.' Tom tried to sound practical, but the hysteria was just barely below the surface. 'I have to look after your case, apparently. But don't worry! You're in safe hands!' Then there was a loud crash and a mumbled expletive, and then Tom said, 'Sorry. I dropped the phone.'

Henry put his head back into the toilet bowl. He couldn't deal with any more of it. Not today.

'Henry? Mr Hart? Are you still there?'

'Look, Tom. I don't know what this is all about.' The toilet bowl made his voice echo eerily. 'But it's guff, OK? It's not true. I don't know why they're even doing it, seeing as we're not defending the divorce any more.'

'But they don't know that yet.'

'What? You mean you haven't told them?'

'You said you were going to,' Tom said timidly.

Henry's heart stopped altogether. The letter. The fucking letter. He dropped the phone into the toilet and ran.

'I can't do that, mate,' the postman insisted again.

'Please,' Henry begged. He was in his pyjamas with a denim jacket hastily pulled on over them, and a pair of dirty old runners he'd found by the door. He'd already endured many curious looks as he'd waited by the postbox for thirty-five minutes for the delivery van to arrive. 'It was all a mistake.'

But the postman was firm. 'Once a letter goes into the postbox it's our property, so to speak. I can't give it back to you. It goes on from here to the addressee.'

Jackie. Henry wanted to vomit again as he imagined her receiving it the day after tomorrow, with all its drunken ramblings of apology and regret and what-might-have-been. Embarrassing, dreadful, revealing things. And he could distinctly remember elaborating on the love/lust theory he'd put forward to Dave. Jesus. At one point he had run out of room on the electricity bill, and had continued on the back of a shopping list. So she would read that too, and know that he bought spaghetti hoops, and too much wine, and shampoo for men that promised to fight off grey for as long as possible. Now he *did* do a slight retch. The postman looked wary.

'Sorry,' Henry said. He had an idea. 'I'm sick, you see. Very sick. In fact, the doctors say I may not have all that long. But I managed to find the strength to get out of my bed this morning in my pyjamas to come down here to try and retrieve the letter. It's a very personal letter about my illness. To my sister.'

The postman was scooping letters out of the postbox and into a big brown sack.

Henry added pitifully, 'She doesn't know about my illness, you see. The letter was to tell her. But then I got word this morning that she's been made redundant.'

'From where, Santa's toy factory?' said the postman.

OK. It was time to tell the truth. 'Look, it's a drunken letter to my ex, OK?'

At that the postman brightened. 'Never post a letter when you're drunk. Or make a phone call. You'll always regret it.'

'Yes, well, I *do* regret it,' Henry said. 'Which is why I need it back.'

'Can't do it. I could lose my job.'

'She's divorcing me for adultery,' Henry said. How could he worry about his job at a time like this?

The postman's brief good cheer died abruptly. 'I divorced my wife for adultery. She broke my heart.' And he looked at Henry as though he were something he'd discovered on the bottom of his shoe.

'But I didn't do it,' Henry said desperately. 'It's lies. All lies!'

'That's what my wife said too. And all the time she was boffing my best pal. You should be ashamed of yourself.' He gave Henry another disgusted look and continued to pile letters into his bag.

Henry watched helplessly. The injustice of it all now was beginning to bite. He couldn't believe it. And he had to have that letter back. Telling a woman like that – a woman capable of manufacturing blatant lies, porkers, scandalous untruths! – about his innermost feelings? Thinking she might understand? She'd probably show it to that Velma one and they'd have a right giggle over it.

He couldn't bear it.

'There it is!' he yelped. 'There. In the white envelope with the little robin on the front.' He couldn't find an envelope either last night and had resorted to pillaging one from his leftover Christmas card selection, and had dithered for some considerable time between the robin and one with a bunch of holly with berries on it. He had been very drunk at that point.

The postman extracted the letter. He turned it over slowly and held it up, the better to see the address. 'Ms Jackie Bell.'

'Ball.'

'Poor woman.'

'I told you. I didn't do it.'

The postman gave him another withering look. 'And your handwriting is a disgrace. I mean, what's that supposed to be, Ireland or Iceland? We get this kind of thing all the time, people just not taking the trouble to write clearly and legibly. And then we get our ears chewed off about late delivery.'

'Sorry . . . look, can I just have it back, please?'

'No. It's against rules.'

'But nobody would know, would they? I mean, come on, it's just you and me here. Nobody is actually going to see you handing that letter back to me. Which is mine in the first place.'

But he knew that words were wasted on the postman, who opened his big bag to chuck Henry's letter in.

'Fifty quid,' Henry said.

'Are you trying to bribe me?'

'A hundred then. But you'll have to come back to the house. I've no cash on me except . . .' He felt around in his denim jacket. 'Fifty pence.'

This was the last straw for the postman, apparently. 'You screw around on your wife, and you expect sympathy? And now you're trying to bribe an employee of the state? There's a word for you, do you know that?'

'Scumbag?' Henry supplied.

'Bugger off home with yourself. You're not getting your letter back and that's that, OK?'

'Oh, look!' Henry exclaimed suddenly, pointing into the sky.

'What?' said the postman, swinging round to squint up at the sun.

Henry snatched the letter from his hand, and ran.

Chapter Sixteen

Maybe Jackie had been waiting for something to push her over the edge. Some excuse to leave Henry, and her marriage, behind. Because Lord knows at that stage she was close enough, what with the atmosphere in the house, and his unhappiness, and her unhappiness, and everything going so flat and wrong. But, despite all that, she had still felt that it was just some kind of maladjustment, like a zip done up wrong. Any number of things could be blamed for that. The sudden domesticity. The politics of married life. The pressure of his job. The lack of *her* job. A new city, a new relationship, a new life together, all of these things could have momentarily skewed them off course. But she had never thought for a second that they wouldn't get back on track. Because surely something so perfect and right in the beginning couldn't all go so horribly wrong?

She had believed that he felt it too. Their first anniversary was approaching fast and both of them knew things had not quite gone according to plan. Then he had invited her out for dinner. Not one of those working dinners where he would scribble things in his little notebooks and she would gaze off into the middle distance. This would be a proper dinner date. A first anniversary dinner, he had told her, rather meaningfully, where they would talk. Properly. Like they hadn't in a while.

It had the air of anticipation and excitement and romance. All week long he had given her a series of meaningful looks and the odd intense, warm glance. He got his hair cut in anticipation, something he never usually did. Then he went and got a silk shirt dry-cleaned especially for the occasion, which was totally out of character. She had thought, this is it. They would go out and talk, air their grievances, be honest with each other. Then he would declare, 'I can't believe I've been so stupid!' and hurl the table aside and snog her wildly. Well, perhaps that was jumping the gun slightly, but she could hope, couldn't she?

She bought a new outfit in anticipation. And shoes, which hardly needs mentioning. She got her hair professionally straightened, even though it took nearly two hours, and the girl doing it was red-facing and puffing at the end.

Then she saw that the shirt that had come back from the dry-cleaners was purple, the very same colour as her new outfit, and the pair of them would look like matching aubergines. And she so wanted everything to be perfect for that night – she now called it the Second Chance – that she decided to venture upstairs to the attic study where Henry had said he wanted to finish something off. Perhaps he could be persuaded into the burnt orange shirt, or the pale blue, even though he maintained it made him look ill. But he had worn blue that night in the Crypt, the night Jackie had fallen in love with him. Surely he'd do that for her? Tonight of all nights?

So out she got from the shower, wrapped a towel around herself, and set off in her bare feet. The study door would be closed as usual. And that was another thing; she would tell him tonight that there would be no more closed doors in their house. Plus he could stuff those vibes that seemed to tell her that the attic was out of bounds to her. You'd think he was at brain surgery up there or something, and dare not be interrupted.

Oh, she had her list of hurts all made out. Twelve months' worth in fact, and she was determined to get them off her chest. She decided that the best course of action was to start with the minor items such as his refusal to be a passenger seat in any car that she drove and his slovenly bathroom habits. That ought to get them through to the main course, when things might get a little more intense. By dessert she hoped to be firing on all cylinders and would bring up the serious stuff, which was why in the name of blazes had he married her at all? Because sometimes he gave the impression that he wasn't all that sure himself. The way he would look at her sometimes! You'd think she had done something to him, something terrible, that she had ruined his whole life, when in reality she had bent over backwards to accommodate him. It just goes to show you, she would tell him over coffee, that the more you put into something, the more you got taken for granted!

Well, actually, being taken for granted wasn't on her list of faults. But she would bring it up anyway, just in case.

He would probably have his list too. She knew he was kind of geared up tonight. He'd been fussing, ringing up the restaurant for a quiet table and organising a taxi to pick them up. Then he'd checked his watch periodically over the day. He was going to say his piece too, she knew. He was welcome to! The only way this thing would work was if they both had their say. Absolutely.

Still, she wondered what would be on his list. Her kitchen habits, probably, and the way she could never remember to put things back in their proper places afterwards. Spices, usually, which tended to drive him mad. And the piles of clothes she left around on the bedroom floor, meaning to put on hangers at some point but never getting around to it; he would definitely mention those, which he maintained had become a health and safety issue. Plus her sense of décor; but wasn't it time to face it once and for all? She and Henry would never see eye to eye on colour schemes. Or curtains. She liked frills and he did not, and that was really all that needed to be said.

But surely that would be about it. He couldn't go giving out about her thighs or anything like that, could he? Anyway, he'd known what they were like when he'd married her. It would be very low to bring them up now.

Deep down, despite all the complaints, she knew that the night would end up well; as in they would retire to bed for the whole weekend, just like they had in those early days. In anticipation, she had cancelled all her other plans for the weekend, such as they were, and stocked up on delicacies in the fridge. She was glad, too, that she had taken the trouble to shave her legs properly, all the way round. If she had time she would give them a spray with Easy-Bronze, too, to shake off their deathly pallor. After all, there was a chance that she would be spending the entire weekend naked and her legs would come under a great deal of scrutiny.

It was on this optimistic note that she skipped happily up the last couple of narrow attic steps and stopped outside the study door. She quickly adjusted the towel to best advantage (it was a shame she hadn't already easy-bronzed, but thankfully the lighting up here was dim) and she put her hand on the door handle, about to go in, when she heard him talking.

There was something so intense and fervent about his tone that she waited. He stopped speaking, as though listening. He was, she guessed, on the phone. She pressed her ear closer to the door, feeling guilty and shameful, but who was he talking to in that low, furtive tone?

Then she heard him say something like, 'You are beautiful, beautiful.' Or maybe he said it just once but she got such a shock that the word reverberated around her brain like a horrible echo.

Without making a sound she turned and went down the stairs again.

Mrs Ball said that if the ceiling fell down on top of her at that moment, she wouldn't be a bit surprised.

'I don't know what's going to happen next,' she fretted. 'Maybe Eamon's going to phone to say he's been deported for un-American activities and is moving back home. Or Dylan, from South Africa, wanting to know if he can have his old bedroom back. Maybe the whole shooting lot of you are going to move back in.'

At that moment, the phone in the hall began to ring, and Mrs Ball let out a little worried yelp and bolted out, tripping over Jackie's suitcase on the way. But it was only the telephone people asking if she wanted broadband so that she could surf the internet twenty-four hours a day.

'Don't be annoying me,' she told them, and hung up. Although, on reflection, she told Jackie and Michelle, all-night internet access might be handy given that she hadn't slept since Tuesday week, thanks to her offspring. And as for all the notice she'd been given! Well, as she'd told Jackie when she'd picked her up at the bus stop, she needn't expect the bed to be aired.

She said now, 'I don't know where I've gone wrong at all. I send you all out into the world to make your own way, and you all blessed well keep coming back.' She shot a look at Michelle. 'As for you, you never left.'

Michelle replied, unbowed, 'I'm pregnant. I need my mother at a time like this.'

'What about all the money the judge gave you?'

'It wasn't to buy an apartment. Anyway. I've already spent it.'

'Five thousand euro?' Mrs Ball was shocked.

'Do you have any idea how much a double buggy costs?' Michelle complained. 'Plus, I need two of everything. It's not cheap, you know, having a couple of babies.'

'I don't know what you're telling me for. Try telling the judge.'

'I have tried. I've left seven messages and he hasn't phoned back.' She seemed unperturbed. In fact, not much at all perturbed Michelle these days, Mrs Ball had told Jackie in the kitchen. Even when Mr Ball had short-circuited the entire house yesterday with one of his drills, she had scarcely budged. She just sat on that couch all day, reading baby books and magazines, and eating pickled gherkins out of a jar. The whole house stank of vinegar, Mrs Ball said, and you could be forgiven for thinking you were living in a chippers.

Michelle added, 'Anyway, the hospital told me that I should stick close to home. To be in close proximity to my birthing partner.'

Mrs Ball stiffened. 'What?'

'Mum, we talked about this last night.'

'We did not.'

Michelle said to Jackie, 'She kept turning the volume on the television up louder and louder, but I know she heard me.'

'I heard nothing!' Mrs Ball objected. 'And anyway, I don't want to be your birthing partner. I wouldn't know what to do or anything.'

'Didn't you have a whole clatter of your own?'

'Yes, but in those days you were just left to get on with it. Nobody expected you to write out birth plans and provide your own music.' She was practically wringing her hands now.

'Come on, Mum. I don't have anybody else I can trust.' She thought about that, and amended it to, 'Anybody else I can be sure will show up.'

'I don't know why you don't ask Jackie. Now that she's moved back in.'

Jackie was quick to point out, 'I haven't moved back in. I just need a temporary base for a couple of weeks, that's all. And I didn't want Emma to get caught up in the crossfire.' More importantly, the single bed with the dodgy springs was driving her mad. Not to mention Emma's nightly sex sessions with Lech.

Mrs Ball said, 'What are you talking about? Bases and crossfire? You'd think you were going to war.'

'Well, I am in a way, Mum.'

'I hope there's not going to be any more unpleasantness, Jackie.'

'Of course there is,' Jackie assured her cheerfully. 'Plenty of it, I would say.'

Mrs Ball's hand flew to her throat. 'And you think this is wise, do you? This whole adultery thing?'

'It's not a question of being wise, Mum. It's what happened.'

'I can't believe it,' she said. 'Henry! With another woman.'

'Or man,' Michelle interjected. 'Let's be fair here. He could have been talking dirty to either.'

'I'm pretty sure it was a woman,' Jackie said. He'd never have called another man 'beautiful'.

'And, like, he *admitted* it?'

'Not yet. But he'll have to now that he's being divorced for it,' Jackie said.

Mrs Ball let out a little moan. 'And supposing he defends it again? You're happy for all this . . . stuff to come out in open court?'

'All what?'

'Stop it now, you know exactly what I mean! Sex. Adultery. Willies and bonking and all that.'

'There was a time when I'd be quite excited at a conversation like this,' Michelle remarked, flipping a page in her baby magazine.

'I'm perfectly happy,' Jackie declared. 'I'm not the one in the wrong.'

'Yes, but your sex life will come into it,' Michelle said. 'Regularity, any problems, preferences, fetishes.'

'Stop, I feel sick,' Mrs Ball said.

'I feel perfectly comfortable with that,' said Jackie, who wasn't at all. Especially if the judge was old and crusty. But, on the other hand, Justice Gerard Fortune was old and crusty, and just look what he had got up to.

'I don't know what the neighbours are going to think,' Mrs Ball fretted.

'The neighbours won't know. It's not like it's going to be on the front of the *Sun*, Mum, with pictures.'

'He took *pictures*? He's even worse than I thought! But I said that to your father, when you announced that you were marrying him, I said I hope he doesn't run rings around our Jackie, what with him being medium-famous and media savvy and sharp, and generally too clever for his own good. And there's our Jackie, a poor girl from the sticks of North Dublin, I said – a wonderful girl, don't think for a minute we weren't proud of you – but not on the same level as that lot over there in London.'

'Thanks, Mum.'

'There's no need to get offended, Jackie. We brought the whole lot of you up to be decent and truthful and not to sleep with loads of people, although I know now we failed miserably with Michelle, and I'd have thought much less of you if it was you being divorced for adultery.'

Michelle commented, 'There's a compliment buried in there some-where if you can be bothered to dig it out.'

'You know, Mum, you're wrong,' Jackie said. 'Just because I was a big, thick, naive hick going over there doesn't mean it was my own fault that I was cheated on.'

'Hear, hear,' Michelle said.

'I never said that! Did I?' Mrs Ball was in fresh pet now. 'No, this is entirely his fault.'

'Glad to hear it.'

Mr Ball arrived in then and, as usual, when he saw everyone gathered in serious discussion, he tried to back out again quickly.

'Larry!' Mrs Ball was too fast for him. 'Jackie has just told us that she thinks Henry was cheating on her. And that's why she left in the end.'

Mr Ball said, 'That's terrible, Jackie.'

Everybody waited, but that appeared to be the extent of his input.

'Thanks, Dad,' Jackie said.

He went off out again.

'I still can't believe it,' Mrs Ball said. 'Henry never struck me as the type.'

'They don't go around with a sticker, Mum.' He hadn't struck Jackie as the type either.

'I know, but I like to think I have some experience of men.'

Michelle challenged, 'What men have you experience of? You only know three.'

'I wouldn't have your vast knowledge, that's true,' Mrs Ball shot back. 'What I'm saying is, we always knew that Henry was a very unpleasant person, not the sort you'd want to be around for any length of time, but he never gave me the impression he would cheat.'

Jackie felt very defensive. 'Great! My own mother doesn't believe me!'

'I didn't say that.'

'What do you want me to do, produce phone records?'

'You'll have to, for the court,' Michelle interjected.

'What?'

'You can't just point at him, and say, "That's the creep, milord!"'

Mrs Ball tittered, despite herself.

'Velma and I will work on all that,' Jackie said confidently, even though Velma was turning out to be scarily light on hard information of any kind. 'The main thing is that I'm not running away this time. I'm going to see this thing through to the bitter end for once in my life.'

'You sound very hard, Jackie,' Mrs Ball said.

'I'm just facing up to realities. It's a good thing, Mum.'

Mrs Ball obviously couldn't see the liberating side of all this. 'You don't want to turn into one those women you see on afternoon TV, cursing and giving out about men all the time, and fighting among themselves.'

'I'll try my best,' Jackie assured her.

'And I suppose if it brings you and Dan back together . . .' Definitely, the whole point of the thing was lost on her. 'I mean, does he even know about this latest development?'

'Not yet,' Jackie conceded. She had been putting it off. But she'd have to face up to the reality of that whole relationship, too. And soon. It wasn't fair on Dan otherwise.

'Where exactly do the two of you stand now?' Mrs Ball enquired.

'I'm not quite sure,' Jackie hedged.

'I mean, are you still engaged to each other? Or is that too much to hope?'

'On reflection, I think we're probably not engaged.' Best to break her in gently.

'But you're still an item, obviously?'

'Mum, I don't want to talk about this right now, OK? I'm trying to get rid of one husband, so just leave me alone.'

Michelle looked up from her baby magazine and asked Mrs Ball, 'If the babies are boys, what do you think of Ernie and Bert? As names?'

Mrs Ball pursed up her lips, considering. 'Do you know, I quite like them. Although they remind me of someone, I can't quite think who . . .' She added, 'They're better than those girls' names you came up with yesterday – what were they again?'

'Cagney and Lacey.'

'Oh, no. I never heard of any girl called Cagney, did you, Jackie? Except that one from the TV, she was a detective, what was the programme called again? Oh, it'll come to me.' And off she went to the kitchen to make a cup of tea.

Michelle told Jackie, 'I've just given you an opportunity to laugh at her. You might as well take it.'

'Maybe I don't have much to laugh about right now.'

'Neither do I. According to the hospital, I won't be able to move after thirty weeks and labour's going to be hell. That's if they don't have to slice me open before then.' She said all this with relish, and patted her tummy contentedly. Then she checked that Mrs Ball was out of earshot, and she looked at Jackie very seriously. 'I never slept with Henry. Just so you know that.'

'What?'

'Well, you'd have been perfectly entitled to wonder. *I'd* have wondered. Because obviously he liked to put it about as much as I did. Not that I knew that at the time.' She added hurriedly, 'Even if I *had* known, I wouldn't have touched him with a barge pole. I have a very strict rule: I don't do men that belong to other people.'

'What about the judge?'

'I meant men that belong to relations and friends. Anyway, I just wanted you to know that.'

'Right. Well, thank you, Michelle.'

'Phew!' With that off her chest, Michelle settled back on the couch and popped another gherkin into her mouth. 'So,' she said. 'He was playing away?'

'Looks like it, yes.'

'Why didn't you say anything before now? Why have you kept us all in suspense for eighteen months?'

'I suppose I just didn't feel like talking about it.'

'Talking about it? Jackie, you never even mentioned it. It is true? Velma didn't put you up to it or anything?'

'I can't believe you just said that.'

'Don't get into a huff. I'm just saying that as a solicitor I'd have advised you to throw anything you could at him.'

'I would not accuse him unless I thought he did it,' Jackie said fiercely.

Michelle looked at her. 'You're really on a mission, aren't you?'

'I wouldn't put it like that.'

'No? Looks to me like you're going after him with all guns blazing.'

'Look, I don't care about Henry. Well, I *do* care about Henry, but not in a nice way. But I'm not going to get over this thing until every rock is turned, not just the ones he wants. Then maybe I can see where I go wrong with men, and not make the same mistakes.'

'Why didn't you tell me? Why did you keep it to yourself?'

'I got such a shock,' Jackie said truthfully. 'It was our wedding anniversary. I didn't know what to do. I just threw a few things into a bag and left.' Not even anything useful, like Henry's bank cards, or a few pairs of clean socks. She might as well face it: she would never be a good packer in a crisis. 'And then when I got back here, I just needed some time to make sense of everything. Not have everybody clamouring around for the gory details and whispering behind their hands, "Oh poor Jackie, did you know that she was cheated on?"'

'People wouldn't have said that.'

'They would,' Jackie argued. 'I felt enough of a failure as it was. My whole marriage down the Swanee! After a bare year!'

'Oh, Jackie.' Michelle was all sympathy. Then she ventured, 'Who was she?' She added out of obligation, 'If it's not too painful, of course.'

'I never found out,' Jackie confided. 'Somebody from the office, probably.'

'And obviously very good-looking, if he said beautiful twice,' Michelle said. 'Not that I want to rub salt into any wounds . . .'

'No, no. You're right. She was probably gorgeous and skinny and with flat hair. In fact, I don't even know why I'm surprised! He should have married someone like that in the first place!'

'Now, now,' Michelle scolded.

'Well, let's face it. He obviously regretted marrying *me*. Otherwise I wouldn't have caught him red-handed whispering to another woman on the phone!'

'That's men for you,' Michelle said, and she should know.

Actually, Jackie was glad to be finally talking about it. She should have done it ages ago. What was the sense in bottling the whole thing up when she could have had an almighty bitching session and got the whole thing off her chest?

'Thinking about it afterwards, he must have been talking to her three or four times a week. I used to hear his voice sometimes when *Coronation Street* would have the occasional silent scene. Murmuring through the ceiling, all tortured and low. I thought he was reading his reviews back to himself. And all the time he must have been talking to her!'

'The dirty louse!' Michelle said, gratifyingly.

Jackie felt better now, lighter. She said, 'I could have forgiven almost anything else, you know. But not that.'

Michelle nodded sagely. 'How has he taken it? The adultery thing?'

'I don't know. There's been nothing yet.'

'You could use it as leverage, you know. Or did Velma explain that to you? You could tell him, settle the original petition, or else.'

'I don't want to "settle". I really want to fight this time. For me.'

'You know, a nasty divorce really isn't the best way to promote inner growth, Jackie,' Michelle advised. 'It'd be much easier to try therapy, or yoga or something. And cheaper.' Then a funny look came over her face and she kind of sat up straight. Her hand went to her stomach.

Jackie said, 'Michelle? Michelle, what's wrong? Will I call an ambulance? Mum!'

'Shut up,' said Michelle. She pressed her tummy again, a most wondrous look on her face. 'I think I just felt the babies move.'

Chapter Seventeen

Dan knew that Jackie was going to break up with him. Well, it didn't take a genius. Dan wasn't a genius but he did have an IQ of 139, which not many people knew. It was enough to get him into Mensa if he chose to apply. Not that membership of Mensa would change Jackie's mind. No. She had already decided.

The dual carriageway was coming to an end at the roundabout ahead. His runners hit the tarmac with a hypnotic thud thud thud. In his head, it sounded like *it's over it's over it's over.*

She had rung at lunchtime. Said she was moving back into her mother's house for a while. That she needed some time to think, and that she hoped he'd understand. She might as well have lifted a megaphone to her end of the phone and bellowed at him, get lost, sucker!

But of course Jackie wouldn't do that. She was too kind. No doubt she was in a right lather about the whole thing. She had probably tossed and turned for nights, wrestling with her conscience and her decision. Soon, the only question clouding her big grey eyes would be, how to break it gently to poor old Dan.

Well, there was no gentle way. No nice words or platitudes or explanations that would make him feel better. She might as well bring a hedge trimmer over with her when she eventually came to break up with him, and fire it up in his direction. Because that's what she would be doing to his heart!

Briefly he wondered at this gory and violent image. It was a bit unsettling. He used to be such a steady, peaceful guy, who collected for Daffodil Day and recycled. Since he'd met Jackie, his world had become darker and, well, bloodier. Even his brothers had all been very taken aback after the Henry assault (you could keep nothing secret in rugby circles). Them, veterans of hundreds of brutal attacks and broken bones! But they hadn't seen it like that at all. 'Let's keep it on the pitch, Dan,' Big Connell had murmured to him at the club.

A car slowed down. Someone rolled down the window and called, 'Excuse me, could you tell me the way to—'

'No,' Dan snarled, and thundered on. He had been running for over an hour now and was drenched in sweat. Steam came in little puffs from the sides of his runners each time they hit the ground. He should turn back soon. But at the roundabout he took the slip road to the left and ran on.

He tried to figure out what he had done wrong. Apart from having Henry beaten up, of course. She just couldn't let that go, no matter how many times he said he was sorry. In fact, he was beginning to suspect that she was using it as an excuse to buy herself some time away from him, while she sorted out her feelings.

Maybe he had tried too hard. Frightened her off by being too pushy, wanting too much. But how was a guy to get a date unless he asked? Repeatedly, in his case, in those first weeks, until she eventually caved in. There was no question of her suggesting a date. You could almost have called her reluctant. Which of course whet his appetite more – she was unavailable! A challenge! Kind of like those businesses he went after in work who stubbornly refused to lodge their money with him, until after an intense courtship he eventually wore them down with promises of ridiculous growth projections and future security.

Hmm. He was feeling a little uncomfortable with this line of thought. Most likely his upset was skewing his memory, because surely she must have been a little more proactive in their relationship than that.

He wondered what she would say when they met. Oh, fuck it, he already knew. She would say that, temperamentally, they were too different. They didn't click. They weren't suited. And she would list things off on her fingers: that she was a dreamer and he was a realist. That she was an idealist and he was pragmatic. That she was a dessert person while he was firmly main course.

Well, so what? He had never misled her about any of that. She had known exactly what he was like before she'd put that ring on her finger, albeit reluctantly. And now she was going to turn around and complain that he wasn't exciting and volatile and dangerous enough for her? Didn't he have her ex beaten up for her, for fuck's sake? You'd think that would have impressed her, but no! He was still Mr Plod as far as she was concerned.

It made his blood boil. She would probably go on to complain that he liked *Sunday Sport* and she liked art (for that, read 'shoes'. He had never known her to darken the doorway of a gallery or anything like that.) She would say that they didn't share the same 'world views' – just because of that silly argument once about capital punishment. As if you could let mass murderers wander around the place freely! She would say she didn't like the club or the Fionas, although, in fairness, they tended to wince when they saw her coming too, in her pedal pushers and high heels. Well, that was only the once, but it was the instance that tended to be brought up at dinner parties after a couple of bottles of wine. Not when Dan or Jackie were present, obviously. But Dan just knew.

He slowed. Actually, when he listed everything out in his head like that, they *weren't* really all that suited.

She would probably wrap the whole thing up by apologising profusely and saying that she was very fond of him. Such a pathetic word, 'fond'. Almost as bad as 'nice'. Which Dan was.

And then the truth of the whole thing hit him hard. He was a nice guy that she was fond of. A steady, decent guy she had thought she really wanted. Indeed, had tried very hard to love.

But she'd never get there, Dan knew. She could try until the cows came home, but she'd never rustle up an ounce of genuine passion for him. She'd never love him wholeheartedly, truly, desperately. She would never look at him the way she had looked at Henry Hart on that wedding video.

A truck blasted past Dan, throwing up fumes and dirt into his face, but he didn't really notice. He was wondering what that felt like. To have a woman look at you like that. To really love you. Not just throw you what little scraps of affection she could manage.

Just imagine, thought Dan. Imagine what it must feel like to walk into a room and have a woman turn around just upon sensing you, and without having to repeat her name. Sometimes three or four times. Imagine if she rang you up looking for a date! And turned up in that little something you'd bought her on that business trip to Berlin, without complaining that it was a bit itchy around the boobs. What if her face lit up just upon hearing your voice; if she didn't complain endlessly about your passion for rugby; if she slept the whole night long snuggled right up against you, without at some point extricating herself from under you and going over to her own side of the bed, with a little sigh of relief.

Could someone like that be out there? For him? He felt giddy: lightheaded at the very thought. He skipped joyously along the hard margin, the backside of his shiny shorts reflecting the early morning headlights of passing cars, until it seemed as though he almost twinkled.

One of the cars cut in sharply in front of him. More directions, no doubt.

But no; it was a squad car, and the person getting out of the passenger window was the female policewoman who had called by the house a couple of weeks back. She was as neat as a new pin in her uniform, and she raked him from head to toe with her eyes, him bursting out of his vest and shiny shorts, and her tongue darted out to flick across her lips.

'Mr Lewis,' she said. 'Do you realise that, contrary to the Road Traffic Act, you are jogging on the motorway?'

'Cry any time you want,' Emma said generously, reaching for the box of tissues and putting in on the counter within handy reach. 'Let it all out.'

'I let it all out ages ago,' Jackie insisted. 'I cried bucketfuls. I couldn't manage another tear if I tried. Even if I peeled an onion.'

'Still, you never know when a fresh flood might overtake you.'

'Emma, I know you mean well, but I'm fine. Honestly. It all happened eighteen months ago.'

'At least take a few days off,' Emma encouraged. 'You need to build up your strength if you have a vicious divorce ahead. Put your feet up and drink Bovril or something.'

'No,' said Jackie firmly. Mrs Ball's house was not the best place in the world to build up one's strength. Endurance, perhaps – Mrs Ball had kept everybody awake the previous night by walking up and down the creaky floorboards on the landing at 2 a.m., like some kind of insomniac ghost. Then she had snoozed away the entire afternoon on the sofa in the living room. When Michelle had suggested she might get a better night's sleep if she stayed awake more during the day, she had gone off the deep end altogether.

'Anyway,' Jackie said, 'I want to be here. This is my job. My business. He's not going to take that from me.'

'Is he trying to?' Emma asked cautiously.

'You know what I mean. I gave up a lot for that man. Never again!' When she said things like that, profound things, she half expected a fanfare to start up from somewhere. But it never did, disappointingly. Even if Emma punched the air and let out a 'Yahoo' it would be something.

Still, Emma was probably too tired. She and Lech had had a heavy-duty week, judging by the rings under her eyes. And Lech looked like he'd been dragged through a hedge backwards. They were obviously making the most of her absence. Jackie wondered when Emma was going to go public. Surely she couldn't keep him under wraps for ever. Especially as things seemed to be going so well between them.

'How are you and Lech—'

'I don't want to talk about it.'

Obviously she wasn't ready yet.

'I've told you all about Henry.'

'There wasn't all that much to tell, was there?' Emma said, with her customary bluntness. 'Just one suspect phone call.'

'Sorry I don't have any more gory details,' Jackie said, stung. 'No detective's report with lurid telephoto shots of his naked bum bouncing up and down.'

'I'm just saying. Maybe it wasn't another woman on the phone. Maybe it was his mother.'

'He wouldn't tell his mother that she was beautiful down the phone. And anyway, I'd heard him through the ceiling loads of times before,' Jackie insisted. 'He would be all sort of passionate and anguished, and full of longing.'

'Jeepers,' Emma breathed.

He had never talked to her with any degree of anguish. Or longing for that matter. He might manage the odd bit of passion occasionally, but not so that he would lose the run of himself. Not in a really satisfactory way, in any case: not in the way she had been led to believe. All that brooding in the beginning! And him flashing his dark soul at her enticingly! Naturally, she had expected that life with him would be a roller coaster of emotion, full of passion and intensity and each of them baring their souls at every opportunity.

But did she get any of that? Did she heck. No sooner had they settled down to married life in London than the roller coaster slowed, got rusty, and then toppled over on its side. Pretty soon the only thing he was baring at her was his increasingly sour moods. It seemed that he saved all the good stuff for the woman on the end of the phone.

She was jealous, she found.

'I suppose you'll find out who she was,' Emma mused. 'If it goes to court.'

'Maybe. Maybe not,' Jackie said with admirable indifference.

'Oh, come on,' Emma said, not fooled. 'I bet you're dying to find out.'

'Cheating is cheating, no matter who you do it with.'

'Lots of women would have tracked her down and gone round there with a saucepan.'

'Yes, well, I felt that would be beneath me.' It wasn't often that Jackie was in a position to take the moral high ground, and it felt rather nice. Of course, there was the contributory fact that she had leaped on a Ryanair flight so fast that she had left skid marks behind.

'I wonder if it was someone you knew,' Emma said. 'Most people cheat with people they know.'

'As opposed to a complete stranger they pass on the road and give a quick jump to against the nearest tree?'

'I mean a family friend. Or a colleague, maybe. If you really thought about it, I bet you'd probably have it figured out pretty quickly.'

'I have better things to do with my time,' said Jackie loftily.

And anyway, she had already done that. She had gone through every last one of them in her head on the flight back from London, in between bawling into a tissue and requesting a third vodka and tonic. After a year in London, she had a pretty good idea of all Henry's female acquaintances and she'd held each up against a little list of incriminating questions. Was Henry spending lots of time with her?

Did she act strangely around her, Jackie? Did she ring up on flimsy pretexts, and corner Henry at parties? Did she have straight hair?

Only one woman fitted the bill: Adrienne. And Henry despised her, so there was no joy there. Unless, of course, that was all an act, and he was only *pretending* to dislike her to throw Jackie off the scent, and that really the pair of them were at it like rabbits. But no. Henry cursed Adrienne even when he didn't know Jackie was listening, so it was definitely not her.

It would have to be one of the women from the office. Someone Jackie didn't know. Or maybe one of his many exes. She had met at least twenty of them at various parties. They all looked remarkably similar, and after a while it was difficult to tell whether she was meeting new ones or just the same ones over and over again. 'Oh Jackie!' they all said. 'I've heard so much about you!' Probably about her flabby white thighs and her lack of knowledge about food and her strange passion for flowers and her extraordinary hair that looked like the Burning Bush.

'All right!' she burst out viciously to Emma. To hell with the moral high ground. 'I'm dying to know! I'd pay money to know! I'd love to crack the bitch over the head and throw her under a bus!'

Emma clapped. 'Good girl.'

She knew immediately that she had let herself down. 'No, I shouldn't have said that! This isn't about revenge!'

'Pull the other one,' Emma said.

'I mean it!'

'Don't forget to crack him over the head too. Harder.'

'Stop! Stop.' Jackie took a few quick, calming breaths. 'This is serious, legal, grown-up stuff, Emma. It's about taking responsibility for your actions, not going after people with saucepans.'

'I guess,' Emma said, a little disappointed. She was definitely more alive these days since Lech had taken her in hand. She was even wearing a white blouse today, which, for her, was a radical departure from the usual brown. 'I suppose it's the kind of thing that's best done at the time.'

And how many times had she regretted that too! Her dramatic and undignified flight down the attic steps, eyes full and towel flailing. The haphazard packing of her suitcase, the rummaging for money and passport. The discovery that nobody had done the ironing and so she was forced to dress in her new purple strapless evening dress, her legs poking out pitifully white underneath – no time for fake tan, dammit. The scrawling of the note, her head was so full of recriminations and accusations and hurt that in the end all she put was, 'Goodbye.' Then she'd walked out the door, and found that she had to wait twenty minutes in the drizzle for a taxi to take her to the airport. It was inglorious to say the least.

When what she should have done was marched right up those attic steps, hurled open the study door, and bellowed, 'Just what the hell do you think you're doing, buster.' It would have given her some satisfaction to see his shock and guilt. Caught red-handed! Then she would have demanded to know who the other woman was, and how long it had been going on. He would have cowered and squirmed under her inquisition, and then, on his knees, he would have begged her forgiveness (hopefully). But she would have brushed him off like a fly, magnificent in her rage and righteousness, and she would have told him to his face that it was over. O-V-E-R. No piddly notes for her. Then, leaving him crying on the floor, she would have marched back downstairs, where she would have had plenty of time to do a proper pack, taking all the best DVDs for instance, before ordering a limousine to take her to the airport and charging it to his credit card.

There would have been some closure that way, she'd thought. And it would have been a hell of a lot more glamorous.

But of course she had done things in her usual haphazard, scatty way, and had crawled home to Ireland like some kind of victim, and waited for him to ring. Because surely he would. Surely he would wonder why one minute she was in the house and the next she was gone with all her belongings? Or some of them anyway. At the very least he would be worried for her safety.

When he didn't ring that first day she had thought that he was so embarrassed and guilty that he couldn't bring himself to.

After a week, she realised that he was not going to phone at all. As if she was in the wrong. As if she had run out on him.

'Have a tissue,' Emma said, seeing that Jackie was blinking hard.

'I'm fine. Honestly.' But she took one anyway. 'I just want to get this thing over with, you know, Emma?'

'When will you hear?'

'What?'

'Well, from his solicitor. I suppose he'll defend it.'

Jackie lifted her chin. 'Oh, yes. Well, this time I'm ready for him.'

'You're fired,' Dave told him.

'You can't fire me,' Henry shot back.

'I don't mean *I'm* firing you, I mean the board is. You dug your own grave when you didn't show up for that emergency meeting last Monday.'

'I know. What do you think I'm doing here putting all my things into a cardboard box?'

'Oh,' said Dave. Then he said, 'Hey, that's my good pen. I've been missing it for months. You fucking thief!'

'Take it. And there's your stapler back too, and your secret stash of Jaffa Cakes.' Henry handed them over. 'In fact, here, take the whole lot, everything.' He lifted the cardboard box and plonked it into Dave's arms. 'I'm not going to need it again.'

'Don't be so dramatic, Henry.'

'I'm not being dramatic. I'm fired. I'm leaving.'

'Yeah, but they're just trying to frighten you,' Dave advised. 'Look, the word is that readership's down for your column big time. Wendy isn't cutting it with the punters. For starters, she *likes* everything, giving every greasy caff from here to Manchester four stars. The readers, they're missing you, Henry. They wouldn't tell you in editorial, of course, but the letters are pouring in – well, four anyway – saying that people's Sunday mornings just aren't the same without you giving some poor restaurant a pasting.'

'I'm touched,' Henry said.

'All right, listen. I was told to let you know on the nod and the wink that if you go crawling back to the MD then you'll get your job back. I can't be any blunter than that.'

'You mean lick his backside a bit?'

'Naturally.'

'Tempting and all as that sounds, the answer is no. I'm leaving.'

'Now when have I heard that before? Oh, yeah, about forty fucking times. And every time you change your mind and stay.'

'This time I mean it.'

He must have had a determined set to his jaw or something, because Dave stopped making fun of him and asked, 'And what are you going to live on? What are you going to do for money? Have you thought of that?'

'I have loads of savings,' Henry boasted.

'You had to borrow a hundred quid off me at Christmas to buy your mother a present,' Dave pointed out. 'Which, by the way, you never gave back.'

Henry whipped out his wallet and said, 'Fine! Here you go!'

'Stop it.'

'No, no, obviously it's been festering away with you!' Then he discovered he only had a tenner. 'I'll give it to you next week, all right?'

Dave said, 'If you give up here, what's going to get you out of bed in the morning? I mean, you have to have a job.'

'Why?'

'Why? Everybody has a job!'

'Doesn't mean I have to have one.'

'So, what, you're going to be a bum?'

'I haven't decided yet. What I do know is that I'm finished with here. And why are you looking at me like I've got two heads?'

'Because nobody in their right mind walks away from a gig like this! You work less than three hours a week and in return you get respect, success, and I don't know how many thousands of readers.'

'I can live without fame,' Henry said grandly. Actually, he wasn't sure he could at all. Maybe Adrienne had been right. Maybe he was all guff, and that after two weeks of anonymity he'd resort to living in a glass box over the Thames just to get some attention.

Dave said, 'Who said anything about fame? I'm talking about being able to ring up any restaurant in this city at ten to eight on a Saturday night and get a table. And the freebies! Remember that big hamper you got two Christmases ago with all that pâté and wine?'

'God, yeah.' A 1996 Margaux. Bliss.

'And the free concert tickets, and the theatre shows, and the comedy gigs.'

'Stop,' Henry begged.

'The point is, you're giving up a lot here, Henry. And I wouldn't be your best friend if I didn't try and talk you out of it.'

'Consider your duty discharged,' said Henry, resolve strengthened again. 'Because I'm absolutely sure of what I'm doing.' He wasn't really at all. But if he had learned anything recently, and sometimes he wondered whether he had, then it was that he couldn't expect anybody else to change his life for him. Even though Adrienne had tried, bless her. Still, he might never have had the courage to take this step had she not goaded him with veiled accusations of superficiality and being a junkie for minor fame.

He would show her. No, he would be very happy as an unemployed nobody, living alone with only his dog for company. Who wasn't that keen on him, if he would just face it.

Fuck it, he'd go and lick the MD's arse. He'd scrabble and say he was sorry, and he'd get his job back. He was too afraid to face the alternative.

Steady, man! he told himself. Look what cowardice had already cost him: his wife. Who was falsely accusing him of adultery, but there you go. Nothing was perfect.

And so he stood now and pushed his chair in for the last time. He closed all the drawers, and he put the telephone to voicemail.

'I'm finished!' he announced magnificently.

'Sssh,' somebody at a nearby desk said, and he deflated somewhat.

But Dave seemed to realise that this was the end because he said in a very hushed, sombre voice, 'I'll walk you to your car.'

'Thanks.' Then Henry remembered. 'Actually, I don't have a car any more. It belonged to the newspaper. I've had to give it back.'

'I'll walk you to the bus stop then. What number bus do you get home?'

'What? I don't fucking know what bus.' It was all beginning to go flatter and flatter.

Then he was forced to give in his security card and ID badge at reception and when he walked out the enormous automatic doors, he knew he wouldn't be able to walk back in again like any other staff member.

'Let's go to the pub,' he said to Dave, who still had his security card and ID, the lucky bastard.

'No. Absolutely not. Anyway, Dawn's having some people round for dinner tonight and I have to be home early to peel artichokes or something. Come round if you're doing nothing else.'

'I have plenty to do!' Henry said defensively. 'I'm very busy, actually.' He had a hot date with Shirley to take her for a walk, and someone might phone later on. Usually nobody did, but wait till word got around that he would be at home all day from now on. The phone would ring off the hook with all his friends wanting to chat and laugh and exchange views.

Actually, he would hate that. He made a mental note not to tell any of them that he had given up work.

They reached the bus stop. Henry had no idea what bus stopped here but he would get on it anyway. He waited for Dave to say goodbye but he just lingered.

'Henry,' he said, 'how many years have we known each other now?'

'Jesus, don't start that.'

'A good few years then. And, you know, I hate to see you like this.'

'What?'

'Defeated.'

Henry laughed.

'It's not funny, Henry. Dawn's worried that you've gone off the rails with this divorce business.'

'Tell her I haven't. I'm just giving my life a bit of a spring clean, that's all.'

Dave stared at him. 'You *have* lost it, haven't you? You're using words like spring clean.'

'You're always saying to me that I sit around moaning and don't do anything about it.'

'I meant change newspapers, Henry. Or take up extreme sports. Whatever revs your engine. I didn't mean for you to jack everything in!'

'There wasn't that much to jack in.' In fact, it had all been surprisingly simple. A trip to the office to collect his things, and a quick phone call to Adrienne telling her that he wouldn't be requiring her services any more. Easier still, he had got her answering machine and hadn't even had to speak to her. He didn't know why he had thought it was all so complicated. In the end it had just been a question of making the decision.

'Nobody believes it, you know,' Dave blurted. 'Not for a minute!'

Henry tried to catch up with the conversation. 'Believes what?'

'The adultery thing.'

'Good. Because I didn't do it.'

'I know you didn't,' Dave said, obviously trying to be supportive. 'And I've defended you in the strongest possible terms to everyone who thinks that you *did*.'

'I thought you said nobody believed it.'

Dave shifted guiltily. 'You know what people are like. They love a bit of gossip. The hot money is on Mandy, by the way. As the other woman.'

'Mandy? From advertising?' They'd only had a few casual dates before he'd met Jackie. 'For God's sake.'

'At least she's gorgeous,' Dave commiserated. 'It could have been Joanne from accounts.'

Henry didn't even know Joanne from accounts, never mind entertain the possibility that he might at some point have had sex with her.

'Still,' said Dave. 'You'd wonder, wouldn't you?'

Henry began to wish the bus would come along. Any bus.

'How did Jackie get it so wrong? I mean, obviously she thought you were having an affair.'

'Or maybe she's just lying. Have you thought of that?'

Dave looked troubled. 'Jackie never struck me as a liar.'

'What are you saying? I strike you as an adulterer?'

'Hardly. But I'm just saying. I wonder how she could have got the wrong end of the stick.'

As though Henry himself hadn't wondered. Furious, he'd gone over his daily schedule with a fine-tooth comb, taking out his personal organiser and work diaries and looking back over that entire year. And every second of his life was accounted for, in black and white! When he wasn't working, he was at home with Jackie. Or at home anyway, working away in the attic on his secret collection. So unless she thought he was boffing the girl down at the local shop when he nipped in for his morning paper, he was at a total loss to explain her allegations. Then his fury had turned to bafflement as he wondered whether he had ever said anything, however innocently, that had made her think he was playing away? Was it possible that a word or a glance had been misconstrued? But he couldn't think of a single thing. Finally, he wondered whether he had shouted out something in his sleep, like someone's name, or 'Shag me now!' which had inadvertently put him in the category of adulterer. Either way, he was now the baddie of the piece. Him, who had never even glanced at another woman! While Jackie, the blatant liar, had emerged smelling of roses! Imagine being so desperate to marry that yob Dan that she would sling anything at him to get her divorce!

There was one other possibility: that he had been so surly and remote and unhappy that she had hit upon the most obvious reason for it, which was that he was involved with someone else.

He didn't like this one much. But he kept coming back to it. Thinking about it, turning it over. Adding it to the first two charges of not committing emotionally and failing to share in family life. For all intents and purposes he *had* been involved elsewhere; with his own angst, to be precise.

He had bolted upright in the bed two nights ago and thought, right, that's it. It was time to get off his arse and sort his life out once and for all. Hence the dramatic life changes. At this point, he felt that the only way was up.

'Here's my bus!' he said. Imagine getting excited over a bus. Still, it would be the small things in life from now on for him.

He enthusiastically waved it down. He hadn't been on one in about seventeen years, and he presumed that things would have modernised to such an extent that they now accepted credit cards, because he didn't have any change on him.

'When are you seeing your solicitor?'

'Tomorrow.'

'Do you want me to go with you?' Dave offered.

'Why?'

'I want to offer myself as a witness. You know, for the defence. I'll stand up in any court in the land and say that as far as I knew you weren't having it off with Hannah.'

'I'll let you know,' Henry said, stepping up into the bus, Visa card in hand.

'Or Joanne,' Dave called.

'Goodbye, Dave.'

Chapter Eighteen

'I want to hand in my notice,' Lech said to Jackie the following morning. The weather had got cooler in the last week or so, and he wore a leather jacket over his collection of vests. He liked to roll the jacket up at the sleeves, so that he resembled an extra from *Miami Vice*. The look was completed this morning by a scowl.

'What?'

'I will work till Friday if that is OK and then I will leave.'

Jackie was very surprised. 'Are you going back to Poland?'

'No. I'm going to work in the pizza place full time. They have offered me a job.'

'Well, yes, of course . . . it's just, I thought you liked it here, Lech.'

Lech shrugged. 'I do. But it is better that I go.'

He was proud and resolved, she saw. And also deeply hurt. What could be the matter with him?

'Is it your working conditions?' she pressed. 'Because if you're not happy about something . . .'

'My working conditions are fine. But I find I have a clash of personalities. With one of my bosses.'

That hardly needed further clarification. But Jackie was even more mystified.

'I thought you and Emma were getting on really well. She tells me you've been seeing quite a bit of each other since I moved out.'

Emma had said nothing of the sort, but Lech agreed. 'Oh, yes. I am living round there now.'

CLARE DOWLING

'What?' This was a very juicy bit of news. 'That's great, Lech.'

'It is not great!' he exploded. 'She makes me go in and out by the fire entrance!'

'Oh.'

'I can't stand for her treatment any more. No man could!'

He really was very upset. But Jackie felt she had to stick up for Emma.

'She's just the kind of person who likes to keep her working life separate from her private life, that's all.'

'Is that why she does not speak to me during business hours?'

'Well, I wouldn't take that personally . . .'

'Why she can hardly bear to look at me?'

'Sometimes she doesn't look at *me*.'

'Let us be frank here,' Lech said. 'She is only after one thing. After that she does not want to know!'

It seemed to be a fair and candid assessment of the situation, on the face of it.

'Maybe she's just afraid to show how she feels, Lech.'

'Or maybe she just does not feel it. Is that not also a possibility?'

It was difficult to know exactly what Emma *did* feel. But Jackie would have to agree with Lech: all was not well.

'How about you, Lech?' she asked.

'That is easy. I am completely in love with her.'

She hadn't expected such a forthright statement. But Lech was a forthright kind of guy.

He went all kind of dreamy. 'I knew from almost the first moments. I have never met anyone like her. It's the combination of all that brown on the surface and all that passion underneath. It's irresistible.'

'Um,' said Jackie. It was disconcerting to have her friend described in such a fashion. 'And have you tried to tell her? How you feel?'

'I am always trying to tell her how I feel! But she won't listen. She just rips off my clothes and makes me have sex again.'

'I can see your problem,' Jackie sympathised. 'But maybe you should try discussing the situation outside the bedroom. In a restaurant perhaps.'

'Don't be ridiculous,' Lech scoffed. 'You know she refuses to be seen in public with me.'

'Now I think *that* is definitely an issue you have to tackle.'

But Lech was very downhearted. 'I don't want to love a woman who is embarrassed about me. I think I am better than that.'

'And you are!' Jackie said. Then she remembered where her loyalties were supposed to lie. 'But you can't just leave, Lech. That's called giving up.'

'Then I've given up,' said Lech, his chin at a proud angle. 'I am an attractive man. I will find somebody else eventually.'

'At least let me talk to Emma.'

'No. I do not want anybody to try and persuade her that she wants me. She should come to that conclusion herself.' And he loaded up a couple of wreaths for delivery. He looked at Jackie sorrowfully over them. 'I know exactly how you feel now, Jackie. To have loved someone, and then lost them. It is tragic, yes?'

He went out, leaving Jackie feeling rather depressed. And to think that she had been so full of resolve these past few days. On a high, really, fuelled by her new determination to get rid of her love rat husband (she liked 'love rat'; it seemed an appropriate term for someone who worked in the tabloid press). For once, she had the better of Henry, and by God, it felt good! She had worn her highest heels, her brightest skirts, and what with Velma ringing up every half hour and shouting, 'We have them on the run, we have them on the run,' it had all been one big adrenaline rush that had borne her along for three days now.

And now look what Lech had done, the fecker. Taken the lovely gloss off it all and made it seem a bit sad and loser-ish. Even though technically she had never actually 'lost' Henry in the first place. She was the one who had left.

Somehow, it didn't seem much of a consolation.

'Is he gone?' Emma hissed, peering out from the storeroom.

'I thought you were on your lunch break,' Jackie said crossly.

Emma ignored this and said, 'Did he really hand in his notice?'

'Yes. Apparently it's a case of unrequited love.'

Emma looked a bit stricken. Then she said, a touch defiantly, 'I didn't mean for him to go falling in love. I never let him think that it was anything more than just sex.' As the matted lump in the back of her sleek pageboy would testify. 'I thought he understood.'

'How do you know what he understands if you won't listen, apparently?'

'You know Lech. So flamboyant with his feelings. It'll be me this month and someone else next month.'

'I don't think so, Emma.'

Emma looked more troubled. 'We were never going to end up happy-ever-after. He's nice and he's sexy, I suppose.' It looked like it nearly killed her to admit it. 'But can you imagine me actually settling down with him?'

'I think you'd be kind of cute. Your brown granny shoes lined up beside his shiny white sneakers.'

'Stop.' Emma looked appalled. 'Oh, why couldn't he just be normal!'

'What does normal mean?'

'Don't get all high and mighty on me,' Emma complained. 'You know that none of our friends would ever dream of going out with a man like him.'

At that moment, Lech's car backfired loudly outside the shop. Then Brian Adams blared out the open car window as the radio was turned on full blast. Lech set off in a cloud of smoke and burning rubber, waving enthusiastically at Jackie and Emma as he drove past the window. In case they missed that, he hit the horn loudly a couple of times for good measure, and gave them the thumbs-up.

Emma just looked at Jackie.

Jackie said, 'All right, so he might lack a certain . . . finesse, but he's a good man, Emma.'

Emma shook her head rapidly from side to side. 'It's not going to happen, Jackie, OK? It never *was* going to happen. The whole thing was like a dodgy holiday romance, OK? And now it's over.' Her chin was firmly set. 'Him leaving is for the best. End things cleanly. It's not fair to give him false hopes.'

'Which nobody could accuse you of doing.'

'I think not.'

'And have you thought what you're going to do for sex now?'

'I don't know what you're in such a bitchy mood for. You were in great form earlier at the thought of getting rid of the love rat.'

'I can't be expected to keep up that level of excitement the whole time,' Jackie said defensively.

'You're probably a bit nervous about tonight,' Emma consoled.

'That's because I don't have a tough hide like you.'

'Don't be mean,' said Emma. 'Anyway, me and Lech are different. We aren't engaged, not like you and Dan.'

Jackie felt sick even thinking about it. Dear, sweet Dan, who had rescued her on the motorway and tried to persuade her that he was her knight in shining shorts. And she had let herself be persuaded, had wanted to be persuaded, and would probably have walked into that register office had Henry granted a divorce without a murmur. She supposed she should thank him for that, albeit grudgingly. Otherwise she might not have realised until it was too late, and she would have watched her life play out on a bar stool in the club with all the Fionas.

'I'm going to break his heart,' she said.

'On a practical note, at least it'll stop him calling round here all the time in his helmet and frightening the other customers,' Emma observed, always one to nip any dramatics in the bud. 'Although he hasn't been by in nearly a week.' She added, 'Maybe he knows it's coming. If you hang on another week or two, he'll probably give up altogether.'

'Emma! Just because you treat men like dirt doesn't mean the rest of us do. No, I'm going to do this thing properly. We'll meet up, have a heart-to-heart, and I'll let him down gently. It's the very least he deserves.'

'At least do it in a restaurant. That way he can't throw a fit.'

'Honestly, Emma. You really are the lowest of the low.'

'Now, monsieur. And mademoiselle.' Fabien poured their wine. He added to Jackie, coquettishly, 'Although I suppose it will be madame before too much longer!'

'Um, yes. Thank you, Fabien.'

'We have not seen you in a while. But you are very busy with the wedding preparations no doubt, yes?' This was directed at Dan.

'Mmm,' Dan said.

Jackie wished that Fabien hadn't discovered his romantic side and would leave them in peace. But he continued to fuss over them, opening their napkins, presenting menus, all the time making little clucking noises under his breath.

'Thank you, Fabien. That's fine,' she eventually said, firmly.

'Ah!' he said. 'I understand. You want to be alone.' And he backed away with a sickly smile.

Dan and Jackie looked at each other over the tops of their menus.

He seemed very unfriendly tonight, Jackie observed. Downright grim. Still, they had been living apart for weeks now. She hadn't returned any of his phone calls. Had refused to see him when he came to the shop. Anybody would look annoyed.

He said, very neutrally, to his credit, 'I heard from Emma when I called into the shop that you're divorcing Henry for adultery now.'

'Yes. I was going to tell you myself but I didn't think . . .' Well, she hadn't thought it was relevant, given that she had finally decided to give him the boot. But she said, 'It was too painful.'

Dan arched an eyebrow. 'Really.'

'He *did* cheat on me, Dan.' In all probability. But it would be handy if she had absolute proof. She hoped Dan wouldn't ask what happened because somehow the 'beautiful, beautiful' thing over the phone was beginning to sound less substantial with each retelling.

The very mention of Henry's name had always managed to light Dan's fire, and tonight was no exception. 'What a scumbag!' he said. 'A shit! A cheating, lying, two-timing . . . well, there's a word I'd like to use but I won't in front of a lady.'

'Thanks anyway, but I've already called him everything under the sun.'

'He doesn't deserve to be divorced. That's too good for him. He should be strung up by his testicles for a week! Or castrated, or something. Mind you, stringing him up by his testicles would probably do the job.'

But he calmed down rapidly. Too rapidly. And she saw that his anger was manufactured. Obligatory.

'If you want, I'll send the lads round again,' he offered. 'I'll tell them to concentrate on below the waist.'

'That's very sweet of you, Dan, but I don't want you to get into any more trouble because of me.'

'OK,' he said. Just like that! Like she wasn't worth the effort. A month ago you could hardly stop him getting on a plane and going over to mash Henry's head in. Just because she was going to finish with him didn't mean they weren't still engaged, for goodness' sake.

'So, anyhow, the divorce might come through a bit quicker,' she said, just as a little test.

'Good,' he said. Good? That was it? There was a time when he'd have whooped with joy and swept her off to bed. What the hell was going on here?

'Of course, knowing Henry, he'll probably defend it,' she said. It was a deliberate goad, like giving a bee a good poke with a stick.

'Probably,' said Dan. Unruffled.

She was getting annoyed now, even though she knew she must stop this right now.

'Which could drag the whole thing out for months. Years maybe.'

'I thought you just said it might come through quicker?'

Oh, Mr Mathematical! Mr Rational. How right she was to end things with him.

'So you *were* actually listening,' she said sarcastically. 'You hadn't nodded off, or fossilised with boredom.'

Dan said, lips pursed, 'What's up with you, Jackie?'

'There's nothing up with *me*. I just expected to come here tonight and have a meal with my fiancé and . . . and discuss our wedding plans!'

Sweet Lord. She hadn't expected anything of the sort. Discussing their wedding plans was the very last thing she had wanted to do tonight. All going well, she had hoped to have dumped him by the arrival of the starter and be out of there before the main course even arrived. And now look! How was she going to backtrack from this one?

'But I can see now that you don't want to discuss them,' she said loudly. Maybe she could say that she couldn't live with his apathy any more, and turn it around that way. Or that he was too big or something. Which was low and cheap, but she was scarcely in any position to be choosy.

Across the table, Dan's head collapsed into his hands and he gave a kind of low, animal groan that had nearby diners looking at their meals suspiciously as though the food might be off.

'Jackie, I don't know how to say this,' he said.

And then Jackie knew in a flash. And before her brain even processed her shock and surprise, she had one burning thought: she must get in there before him.

'Dan, I . . .'

But, blast him, he had already drawn breath and his voice rolled out over hers. 'I think we should break up!'

Unfortunately, just as he spoke, one of those eerie silences fell, and the entire restaurant transferred their gazes from their plates to Jackie. You could have heard a fork drop.

She opened her mouth to retort, 'I was just about to say that!' but thankfully she realised in time how ridiculous it would make her look, how pitiful. And so she closed her mouth, and just sat there, purple-faced, humiliated, and dumped.

Finally, she said cheerily, 'OK! I can live with that!' And she smiled and nodded at all the other diners, just to show them that she was perfectly fine with it. Not a bother! She even pulled a mock sad face at the couple at the next table, as a little joke. Inside, she said 'Stupid cow' to herself at least fifty times and wondered were there places you could go to get your mouth sewn up. Then, after all the nosy parkers had gone back to their meals, she lifted her menu and said, 'The pasta looks good.'

'Jackie,' said Dan solemnly. 'I'm really sorry.'

'Dan, it's fine. Really.'

'I didn't want to do it like this. Not in a public place. But when you were so insistent on meeting in a restaurant . . .'

'Don't beat yourself up about it.' She wondered whether she could plead a headache and go home. But then it would look like she was all upset and she wouldn't give him the satisfaction. The alternative – enduring an entire meal as the Just Dumped Fiancée – was scarcely better. Stupid cow, she told herself again.

And now Dan, revoltingly, went into caring mode. Relieved, no doubt, that he had got the dirty deed over with.

'Are you all right?'

'Me? Fine. Oh, look. They have salmon on, your favourite.'

'You don't have to be brave, Jackie. You can go into the loo if you want, nobody will notice.' Like heck they wouldn't. They were all watching the drama unfold in their peripheral vision.

'I don't find it necessary right now to cry, Dan.' She gave him a warning smile. 'If you must know, I'm more surprised than hurt.'

It was obvious he didn't believe her. He said, 'Well, to be honest, I was going to break it more gently. Suggest that we postpone the wedding till after your divorce came through. But let's face it, how likely is that to happen any time soon?' And he gave a little laugh. Like everything was OK! Like they were old friends now.

'What do you mean by that?' she asked coldly.

'What?'

'You think I want to stay married to Henry?'

'I'm just saying that you two seem to find it hard to let each other go.'

'That's what happens when you're married to someone, Dan. It's much deeper and stronger and more enduring. It's not the same as just being engaged.'

His smile dimmed. 'I suppose you should have ended it properly with him eighteen months ago. It would have saved a lot of pain all round.'

'You're absolutely right,' she agreed coldly. 'I should have.'

There was a long silence, and then she decided that she really couldn't bear a whole meal under these circumstances, and she was just about to think up some plausible excuse when Dan said, 'You know, I think I'm going to go. Under the circumstances.'

He had done it again!

'If that's all right,' he said, seeing her face.

'It's fine. Go.'

'I can stay if you want.'

'Go!'

He stood. Thankfully he refrained from asking whether they could remain friends. He said goodbye, and added, 'Good luck with Henry.'

'Thank you. But I'm sure everything will go smoothly from now on.'

'Well, whatever way it works out.'

As though there was some alternative.

When he was gone, Jackie sat alone at the table, stiff-backed and proud, in the full knowledge that this would be her lot from now on: dining alone, enduring pitying looks from people at other tables. Never being able to order the platter-to-share.

'Fabien! More wine please.'

She might as well enjoy it.

At five to six, Henry was sitting opposite Tom in Mr Knightly-Jones's plush office. Tom was trying to keep his nerves under control. And mostly he was doing a good job, Henry thought, except for when he lifted a sheet of paper and you could see it shaking like a leaf. Also, he kept swallowing compulsively, like there was something jammed in his throat. Which actually there was, and it seemed to be the word 'adultery'.

'Now, obviously you're maintaining that you didn't commit . . . what she's saying you did. Often in cases such as these, when the grounds for divorce are . . . what is written down here, there would be a co-respondent, but I see in this case nobody else is named. And it appears also the accusations have been made within the correct time limit; as in you and Ms Ball did not live together for longer than six months after the alleged incidence of . . .'

Henry watched him squirm around for a suitable euphemism until he could bear it no longer, and he said, 'Adultery. Say it. Please. Otherwise we'll be here all day.'

'Right! Um. Sorry.'

Mind you, Henry wasn't all that keen on the word himself. He was fast finding that adultery had a very bad image. People didn't think of glamour, and passion, and beautiful women; they pictured cheap hotel rooms and grubby little men. Bank robbers got better press, for goodness' sake, or football hooligans, or even the odd arsonist who had acted in a fit of rage.

No, adulterers were the lowest of the low. They shouldn't even be given the vote. How it rankled with Henry. Still, he'd better get used to it.

'Can we get on with this?' he told Tom gruffly. He would probably regret what he was going to say next. Undoubtedly. But he had come this far. It would be such a shame to turn back now.

'Of course,' Tom stammered, reaching into his desk and producing some kind of dossier. Face bright red, he whispered apologetically, 'Look, you may feel that this is not the right time for this. But it's just a little something that I've written myself. I was wondering if you wouldn't mind reading it, just whenever you have a minute, and giving me your opinion?' Humbly he handed it over. It was at least a hundred pages thick, and professionally bound.

Henry took it with a sinking heart. 'Tom, no offence, but I don't read other people's books. Or scripts. Or business plans for a new restaurant. But if you're looking for an agent, I'd be happy to introduce you to my own. Well, ex-agent. Adrienne Jacobs. Who might be in the market for a good forensic thriller, I hear.' He couldn't do fairer than that.

But Tom looked very offended. 'It's not a book. It's a strategy. For your divorce.'

'What?' The thing was so big you could use it as a doorstop. 'What the hell is in here?'

Tom said, rather excitedly, 'Plans. Legal arguments. Research.'

'Research?'

'You can't hope to defend a divorce successfully without doing your research. Because hardly any divorces *are* defended successfully. Which is why we need research!'

Henry turned over a page, more out of morbid curiosity than anything. 'Tammy Winthrop versus Bernard Pike,' he read aloud. They sounded like characters from a soap. 'I think you've given me the wrong file here.'

'No, no,' said Tom. 'That section there is a selection of our past case histories.' He confided, 'The Pike divorce was one of our most bitter. What that woman didn't want! The house, the car, the boat, the Swiss bank account and her own pension. But Mr Knightly-Jones played a blinder in court and we eventually won, even if legal costs swallowed up everything but the boat in the end. And that turned out to have a leak.' He peeped over Henry's shoulder. 'If you want to turn the page there – that's it – you'll see a whole section on court precedents involving cases similar to yours.'

Henry just looked at him in silence.

'Fascinating reading,' Tom went on. 'So much of it depends on the judge you get in the end. And whether he's having a bad day or not. Let's hope yours isn't!'

When Henry failed to smile, Tom did a little nervous flutter and said hastily, 'And I've finished up with an overview of the entire case, right from that first letter Ms Ball sent you months ago. Best to have everything together before we start to construct our defence.'

Henry slowly put the dossier back on the desk. 'You've certainly done a lot of work on this.'

'It wasn't just me,' Tom said bashfully. 'I roped in three legal assistants, and a senior partner. And then Yvonne out front typed it up.' After a little pause, he added, 'I didn't want you to think you were getting second best. Because Mr Knightly-Jones wouldn't be here.'

Henry managed a smile and said, 'Thanks, uh, Tom. So far you're doing a fine job.'

And Tom glowed. Which made Henry feel worse. But he couldn't change his mind for the sake of a rookie solicitor who had finally got out from under the boss.

'But I'm not going to defend the divorce.'

It took a moment for it to sink in. Then Tom's whole face fell. His eyes flicked mournfully towards his dossier, and for a moment he looked as though he might cry.

'I just don't feel it's in my interests to defend the allegations,' Henry said.

'Even if they're not true?'

'They're not true.' Henry was emphatic.

'But I don't get it!' Tom said, disappointment making him brave. 'You argue everything! We were only saying in the coffee room yesterday that you're the most contrary client we have!'

True. But back then he'd had something to gain, he had thought. Some notion of finding the truth and apportioning blame, both of which had backfired on him in recent days. If he were to defend this petition, wouldn't it only be a desperate attempt to hold on to a woman who didn't want him any more? A woman he'd let down in ways he was embarrassed and ashamed about now.

He would just have to live with the adulterer tag. Let's face it, most people believed it anyway.

'Sorry,' he told Tom. 'But I'm finished with this. Now. Today. Let me sign the thing and go.'

Tom had disintegrated into a kind of puddle on his desk. He managed to slide over the petition. Henry did his duty. He slid it back.

Tom said, face on his blotter, 'You can have a different solicitor. One of the partners will take on the case if you want.'

'Hey, come on, Tom, it's not *you*.' He was going to give him a little friendly punch on the shoulder, but that might knock him out altogether, and so he ended up giving him a sort of yucky pat instead.

'Contact them. Tell them we don't want to hear from them again,' he finished up.

Then he stood and walked out the door, with no wife, no agent, no career and no responsibilities whatsoever. Free as a bird!

And no car, fuck it. He'd have to get the damn bus home again.

Chapter Nineteen

The new girl in the shop where Velma got her doughnuts every morning had been giving her distasteful looks this past week, as though Velma really should do something about the state of herself, and not be taking up so much room in the shop. And Velma found that she was intimidated by her – a girl of eighteen! – and now she had to walk three blocks to a different shop where nobody knew her, and where the doughnuts weren't as nice. She had broken the heel of her shoe that very morning, too, and was trying to glue it back on when Tom Eagleton rang with the news that Henry Hart would not be defending the divorce.

'What?' she snapped, sure that there must be some interference in the line. She was convinced that the phone people deliberately did that sometimes when she hadn't paid her bill.

'He will grant your client a divorce.'

Velma covered her surprise and delight. Only that very morning she had decided that she would, in the end, have to hire a solicitor herself in order to make head or tail of the legal quagmire that Jackie Ball found herself in. One petition was tricky enough, but *two*. They had been very snooty about it over in the UK, telling her that their service was not designed so that petitioners could launch multiple divorce petitions willy-nilly, and that they were currently processing the *first* divorce petition, which Velma had thus far failed to withdraw. Formally. In writing.

At that point Velma had launched her Positive Confrontation, as learned in the American law course, but they were obviously used to confrontation of all sorts and indeed gave her quite a bit back. Hence the need for doughnuts this morning, and a six-pack of crisps which she had hidden under her desk and which she had told herself she would strictly ration out, one an hour. That hadn't worked either.

It was a morning when Velma was angrier at the world than ever. She couldn't even get much pleasure out of Henry Hart's capitulation. Why couldn't Ian Knightly-Jones have come on the phone himself? Was she that insignificant that he couldn't tear himself away from opening up his petty post, or defending somebody on a TV licence charge? Instead she had been palmed off with the lowest of the low, this Tom jerk.

'Well, that's big of him!' she bawled down the phone at him. 'After making such a song and dance about it these past weeks.'

There was a frightened little silence at the other end. Then Velma realised that there might be some advantage to be had from dealing with this excuse of a man. Seizing the moment, she said, 'Naturally, we'll be seeking costs.'

Another terrified silence. Then he bleated, 'Just a minute please.'

She could hear pages turning frantically at the other end. He was going through the file. Then there was a crash – there went the file to the floor, probably. Realising that this could take quite some time, Velma put her two fat stockinged feet up onto the desk and opened another bag of crisps.

Naturally, she'd hike up her fee to a hundred an hour. Normally she didn't charge her clients anything of the sort; she looked upon this as a vocation, and she felt it was morally wrong to profiteer out of other people's misery. But Henry wasn't her client and he must have pots of money. She'd throw in expenses too. Food. Petrol. The doughnuts.

She wondered if she might even be able to stretch to a little holiday after this case was over. She had been very down recently. Scotland for a week, maybe, or one of the Scandinavian countries. Somewhere cold where people covered up and she wouldn't have to go around in foolish tourist pants. She'd be alone, of course, but what else was new.

After a couple of minutes he was back on the line. 'Your client agreed to split the costs evenly right back at the start of all this. I have a letter here.'

Velma was ready for that. 'She didn't realise she'd have to bear the cost of a second petition.'

There was no need to tell him about the court mess. She'd get all that straightened out.

After a bit, he said tentatively, 'Nobody asked her to launch that.'

Velma took another lungful of air. 'She felt she had no choice because your client wouldn't play ball with the first one!'

'She didn't allow us our full twenty-eight days to file our Answer.'

'As if that was going to make a difference.'

'And—'

'Doesn't matter!'

'But—'

'I don't care!'

It took a moment before she realised that there was a *beep beep* noise on the line. Those damn telephone people. She gave the phone a shake, but he had been cut off. But when she lifted the phone again, the dial tone functioned normally. He had hung up on her. That weed of a man had actually hung up on her.

She sat there for a moment. Then she took her hand out of her crisp packet and dialled his number.

They put her on hold for nearly two minutes as usual – no wonder she couldn't pay her bill, this was an international call – before she was finally put through to him.

'Hi,' she said.

'Miss Murphy,' he said.

'We, uh, appear to have been cut off there.'

He said nothing to that.

'So, anyhow, about these costs.'

'Forget it. We're not paying your costs.' He sounded surprisingly robust.

'Even some of them?' Velma cajoled. 'You know your client is filthy rich.'

'My client's finances are absolutely no concern of yours.'

'Blah, blah,' Velma said. She was quite enjoying this. 'I bet you're stiffing him for a small fortune.'

'Miss Murphy . . .'

'What do you lot charge an hour anyway? A hundred?'

'I'm not discussing that with you.'

'Come on, we're both professionals. Pool our knowledge and all that. Just give me an indication.'

Tom said primly, 'I'm not telling you what we charge. But it's a lot more than a hundred an hour.'

Velma laughed in disbelief. They really put on airs and graces, that lot. They probably made do on closing the odd house sale, like most solicitors she knew.

'And you have a most irritating habit of not allowing people to finish their sentences,' he told her.

'Have I?' She was astonished. The American course had said nothing about allowing people to finish sentences. Imagine taking offence over a little thing like that! 'Anyhow, back to my expenses,' she said.

'I thought it was your client's expenses. Not yours.'

He wasn't playing ball here. She might have to go higher up.

'I want to speak to Mr Ian Knightly-Jones,' she demanded, her voice rising again. He wouldn't mind being shouted at.

'Mr Knightly-Jones has retired.'

'What?'

'During the course of open heart-surgery he, uh, apparently had a vision of a tunnel. And a white light at the end of it. He has since reassessed his life.'

'So I have to put up with you?' It hit an odd, flirtatious note, and she blushed wildly. To claw back some ground, she barked, 'I'm not happy about costs.'

'Neither am I.'

'How are we going to resolve it?'

'I'm in Dublin the day after tomorrow on business. We could . . . meet. Just if you wanted to. But maybe you're too busy.' That nervousness was back again.

According to her diary, she had nothing on until the second Tuesday in November. Of next year.

'I could squeeze you in,' she said. It was just a business meeting, for goodness' sake. People did it all the time. Then why did she feel so excited?

He suggested a coffee bar and a time, and they were just about to hang up when he said, 'Hold on. What do you look like?'

'What?'

'So I can recognise you when we meet.'

She thought quickly. 'I'll be carrying a copy of a newspaper.'

He laughed. 'So will everybody else.'

'I'll be wearing pink.' Damn. The pink was in the wash. 'Black.' That was always slimming. But in a size 24?

'I'm kind of tall,' he admitted sheepishly.

Fantastic, Velma thought. Another freak. 'How tall?'

'Six three.'

'That's nothing! I'm five ten myself.' She might as well come clean. She couldn't bear that look on people's faces when they saw her for the first time and hadn't been forewarned. 'Look,' she said. 'I'm big.'

'OK,' he said.

'Really big.'

'Right, well, I'll see you the day after tomorrow.' He sounded unperturbed.

'OK,' Velma said cautiously. 'The day after tomorrow.'

'Anyway, isn't it great news,' Jackie said The best! In fact, she might even go out tonight to celebrate.

'I suppose,' Mrs Ball said gloomily. She was still in mourning about the whole thing, Another son in law slipped through her fingers! And all the flower beds just begging to be weeded out there, and the wall only half built. She'd have to get Mr Ball to finish it off, but he couldn't draw a straight line, so how was the wall going to end up? Oh, it was endlessly worrying.

'Well, I'm shocked,' Michelle declared from her position on the sofa, which was rapidly taking on the imprint of her bottom, as well as listing dangerously to one side. 'Who would have thought it? Henry Hart giving in just like that!'

It was true. He had capitulated. Crumbled like one of those oatmeal cookies that Michelle was stuffing into her face at that moment. And Jackie *should* be delighted. There would be no court case, no painful airing of personal matters. No more delay either, and very little expense. She would be rid of him once and for all in about four months' time without ever having to set eyes on him again.

The flipside of course was that he was more or less admitting to having an affair. And she herself just starting to doubt whether he'd had at all!

There was no doubt now. He was holding his hand up, wasn't he?

'Anyhow,' she said bravely. 'I can get on with things now.'

'What things?' Mrs Ball said.

'Well . . .'

'You've no wedding to prepare for now.'

'I know that.'

'Unless you want to put your mind to finding yourself somewhere to live. The immersion is going to pack up with the strain of providing hot water morning, noon and night. And the pair of you wandering out of the house with wet hair every morning! You'll catch your deaths.'

'Getting somewhere to live is a top priority,' Jackie said sweetly. 'And I want to concentrate on work.'

Even though she hadn't actually gone in today. But it was Friday, and she hadn't expected Velma to phone with such startling news and she needed a little while to assimilate it. Unfortunately Lech was leaving and she'd wanted to have drinks for him after work or something, but Emma probably wouldn't have shown up anyway, and it would just have been embarrassing.

She told Mrs Ball and Michelle now, recklessly, 'I'm thinking of opening another branch of Flower Power.'

'What?' Mrs Ball looked even more worried.

'Obviously I'll have to do my figures and all that, but Emma is up for it.' Well, with Lech gone she'd need something to do. Jackie too: hard work and long hours, and the occasional Friday night in the pub with Emma, girls only. In fact, she felt quite excited at the thought of a challenge. And, in time, maybe when she was about forty-five, she would look back upon this time in her life and laugh. Hopefully not hysterically; not from the inside of a loony bin or anything. No, she'd be sitting at a hearth where a fire would be burning merrily, and she would have a flock of well-behaved children around her knees – her own, hopefully; surely she'd have met someone halfway decent by then? – and she would be looking over the accounts for her twelve branches of Flower Power and wondering whether they should go international. And just as she was idly wondering what nutritious dish to prepare for a cosy family dinner, Henry would pop into her head. And she would let out a little tinkly laugh, and the children would all turn to look at her, wide eyed and wondering, and she would say, very jolly, 'Don't mind me! Just thinking of somebody I used to know.' Some shit. But of course she wouldn't say that. Because she would be so *over* him.

Yes, that day would come. But right now, she just wanted to crawl upstairs to her pink single bed and bawl.

Unfortunately she had to look delighted, and so she said, 'So isn't it great news anyway!'

She needn't have bothered, because Mrs Ball wasn't listening. She was peering out the window, fingering her Alice band nervously. 'Who's that driving in? I hope it's not those Jehovah's Witnesses again.'

It was unlikely to be, given that the car approaching was a big swish Mercedes, an important dark blue, with tinted windows to keep the gawking plebs out. Mr Ball arrived in. He hadn't appeared for any of the Henry dramatics, or Michelle's little crisis about one ankle being markedly thicker than the other, but he looked out the window with great interest now and said, 'That's about a hundred and twenty grand's worth there.'

'What?' Mrs Ball jumped up, stiff with anxiety 'What do they want with us?' To her mind, it would have to be trouble; she couldn't entertain the possibility that it might be anything nice. Usually she was right.

They were all on their feet now, vying with each other to look out the net curtains as the car crunched up the gravel and came to a stop outside the front door.

For a wild moment, Jackie thought, Henry. Which was so ridiculous she blushed wildly every time she thought of it afterwards. As if Henry would come here, to her mother's house, in a Mercedes! He didn't even know she was living here now. He didn't know a thing about her any more. And why, anyway? To beg her forgiveness? She was furious with herself for even having the thought.

Only Michelle stayed on the couch, because it was too much of an effort to get up. She went on blithely eating her cookies as Mrs Ball clutched Jackie's arm and gave a running commentary.

'The door is opening! Someone's getting out. It's a man. Oldish. Nice shoes though. He's wearing a suit. Oh, it's very nicely cut, isn't it, Jackie? He doesn't have much hair, though, does he? And the face on him! You'd think he was after swallowing a lemon.' A fresh thought struck her. 'I wonder is he someone from the Revenue? We never declared that five hundred euro we have in the Isle of Man account.' She hissed, 'Here he comes. Don't answer the door, Larry! We'll pretend there's nobody here.'

Michelle finally stirred herself to have a look. She craned her neck as the man approached the house. 'My God. It's Spanky.'

It was five to five. Emma smoothed down her sombre brown blouse – no cheery white today – and wished she'd gone a little heavier on the deodorant. It wasn't that she was nervous as such; but it was a little awkward, Lech's leaving. Still, she would keep everything as professional as possible. She already had his final pay packet, including a generous bonus, in an envelope ready to hand over. A second envelope held a glowing reference. The third envelope contained a cross and chain which he had left in her shower tray this morning, and which was slightly embarrassing. But she didn't want him contacting her at some point down the line looking for it. No, this had to be as clean as possible for everybody's sake.

She tried to concentrate on a wreath, but her fingers seemed very clumsy that afternoon, and it was turning out suspiciously like a half-moon. She would have to start all over again.

The little bell over the shop door tinkled, but she didn't look up. She knew it was him because, as usual, every fibre of her being screamed, 'Hey, Lech's here!' But she was an expert at playing it cool, and she waited until he had come all the way up to the counter before she raised her neat, brown head and said pleasantly, 'Lech.'

'Emma.' He was wearing sunglasses, the kind they used to wear in *Chips*, and so she couldn't see his eyes, but his body language told her clearly enough how he was feeling.

She sympathised, she truly did. She just couldn't do anything about it.

'I've got your paperwork here,' she said, efficiently handing it over. 'And if you could just hand me back keys and stuff . . .'

She waited calmly as he rooted in his skin-tight jeans and produced a set of the shop keys.

'Thank you,' she said.

'I don't have keys to your apartment,' he said.

'I know.'

'There was no need, seeing as I never used the doors. The fire escape, yes. The windows, occasionally.'

'Um, yes.' There was no sense going down that road. Not at this stage. 'Now! Jackie sends her regrets that she's not here to see you off. There was a development on the divorce front this morning, apparently. But she wishes you all the very best for the future.'

Lech just looked at her from behind his black sunglasses. It was getting very awkward. Still, another minute and he'd be gone.

'So!' she said. 'I guess all that's left is for me to thank you very much.'

'For my services.'

'Let's not get cheap here.'

'Maybe I say cheap things because you make me feel cheap.'

She gave a little sigh. 'I had hoped we could part friends.'

'That is a lie. You hope I will go and you will never set eyes on me again. And you will find another toy boy to keep your bed warm and not give me another thought.'

'That is not true!' He wasn't her toy boy anyway; he was older than her. And she *would* think of him occasionally; and cringe, and wonder what in the name of God she had been thinking of.

He ripped off his sunglasses and presented her with a pair of black-rimmed tortured eyes. 'You lay beside me in your bed last night, and I was watching you sleeping, and I was asking myself, does she feel anything for me? A single thing? Could I be any guy – José or Andreas or Vladimir –' he was giving it an international flavour, true to his heritage – 'instead of me? Lech?'

There was a little pause, and then Emma said, 'I don't know what to say, Lech.'

'Something to make me stay,' he said.

Emma hesitated. And hesitated. And finally he put the three envelopes into his pocket and turned for the door.

'Goodbye,' he said.

She picked up the wreath again and listened as his footsteps retreated across the floor and then she heard the door opening and the little bell tinkling, and it was as though the noise woke up some part of her brain, and she hurled the wreath aside and shouted, 'Lech!'

He turned, 'Emma?'

And she took a running jump at him, and pinned him against the door, and they were kissing and pawing at each other like wild things, the bell ringing merrily over their heads.

'Let's go in the back room,' she panted. He smelled amazing, sweat mingled with cheap aftershave.

'What?'

'We can lie down on that tray of dahlias that came in earlier.'

He grew still. 'The back room where nobody will see us?'

'Well, we can hardly do it on the counter. We have to think of our customers, Lech, most of whom are elderly.'

He pushed her away. 'I cannot believe you! Nothing has changed!'

'Lech, please . . .'

But he left. Just like that! She watched through the window as he got into his ancient car. Eventually, he got it started. He drove slowly past the window, and looked pointedly the other way as he went by. The car backfired loudly for good measure. Then he was gone.

Emma went back to her wreath, on automatic pilot, neither realising nor caring that her brown blouse was open to the waist.

Justice Gerard Fortune said that he had never tasted apple crumble as good as his mother's until Mrs Ball came along.

'I don't want any of that kind of talk,' she told him sternly, even though her cheeks were rosy and her Alice band at a rakish angle. 'You're here to discuss my daughter's future, not my apple crumble.'

'You're absolutely right,' he said meekly, stealing a glance across the table at Michelle.

'Why do you keep looking at me like that?' she demanded. 'Do you not recognise me with my clothes on?'

'Michelle!' said Mrs Ball. He might be a spreading, middle-aged old codger but he was still a judge.

'It's true. He's been giving me these creepy looks ever since he walked through the door. Well, you're out of luck because I'm not jumping you again, OK? Once was bad enough.'

Mrs Ball looked as if she would faint. Jackie watched with interest. At least it was taking her mind off the fact that Henry had tacitly admitted sleeping with another woman. Or several. Who knew? He and the judge should get together. They had a lot in common.

Mr Ball said to the judge, 'What kind of mileage do you get to the gallon with that car?'

'I don't even know what you're doing here,' Michelle said. 'Unless it's to throw more money at me to buy me off.' She added, 'Which is all right by me.'

The judge looked convincingly offended, his drinker's nose quivering in indignation. 'I most certainly have not!'

'What, then? Are you going to threaten me again? Have you got a writ in your pocket there that you're going to whip out?'

'What's that?' Mrs Ball whispered nervously to Jackie. 'I hope it's not rude.'

The judge said, 'Michelle, you've a very bad opinion of me.'

'Well, would you blame her?' Mrs Ball rallied. 'You haven't answered a single one of her phone calls! I even sent you that scan picture of the babies in the hopes that it might jog your conscience!'

'Mum!' Michelle said, appalled.

'Somebody had to do something to break the deadlock,' said Mrs Ball, looking to Mr Ball for back up. But he remained staring out the window at the car. Mrs Ball would have to go it alone once again, and, after a shaky breath, she did. 'I think you owe our Michelle some answers. You're not the first man she's slept with, and you won't be the last by a long shot, but I believe her when she says those babies are yours and I think you're a cowardly, weak excuse of a man if you don't put your hand up and take responsibility!' Her Alice band slipped off altogether and tumbled into the apple crumble, detracting somewhat from her speech, but she remained defiant, even whilst swallowing a yawn. Stressful situations always made her extra tired.

The judge looked stricken, if you could believe it. 'I wanted to! Heaven help me I did! But I'm a married man, and an upholder of the law. Surely you understand my situation?'

'Balls,' Michelle said, reaching for another biscuit. 'Anyway, you've said your bit, such as it is. You've relieved your conscience. So go on off in your big car and I'll let you know when they're born. And don't forget to send a cheque every month.'

'It's sagging down a bit towards the back, that car,' Mr Ball observed, looking out the window. 'Have you checked your rear tyres recently?'

'I wonder if Michelle and I could have a word alone?' the judge asked, his frustration with the Ball family clear.

But Mrs Ball crossed her arms over her chest. 'I'm not leaving you alone with my daughter. Look what happened the last time.'

'We need some privacy,' he implored Michelle. 'To discuss the future of our children!'

Michelle eventually said, 'Oh, all right. But Jackie stays, OK? She's in the middle of a divorce and as angry as an Alsatian, aren't you, Jackie?'

Jackie didn't really know how she felt at that point, but gave a kind of snarl in the judge's direction so as not to let the side down.

He shrank back, moistening mottled red lips nervously. Honestly, how could Michelle have slept with him? Her drugs must have been twice as strong as usual.

Mr Ball vacated the room with indecent haste. It was left to Mrs Ball to whisper loudly to Jackie as she went, 'Keep an eye on his hands. If they go out of sight, let a shout.'

It was all very awkward then, with Jackie sitting between Michelle and the judge like some kind of umpire. Which was a bit of a laugh when you looked at how she had managed her own life in the last couple of months. But she put on her most mature expression and didn't react when Michelle kicked her under the table.

The judge began, very sombrely, and sounding suspiciously rehearsed, 'Michelle, contrary to what you think, I came to tell you that I've been feeling just terrible about everything. That I know I've shirked my responsibilities. In fact, I've behaved abominably!' He felt Jackie looking at him. 'I'm a judge. I can use those kinds of words.' He looked past her at Michelle pleadingly. 'And today I came to make it up to you.'

Michelle considered. 'How much are we talking about here?'

'I don't mean money, Michelle. I mean I want to be a proper father to this child.'

'Children,' she corrected him.

'Yes, sorry. Financially, emotionally, practically, you name it! I'm prepared to do a complete U-turn for the sake of the little, eh, chis-ellers.'

It all rang even more false. But Jackie didn't say anything. He deserved the benefit of the doubt. Obviously he'd had plenty to come to terms with too.

But Michelle evidently shared her scepticism, because she said, 'What's the catch?'

'There isn't one,' the judge insisted. 'Why do you think it's so strange that I might want to be a father to my own children?'

'Probably because you have four already,' Michelle said.

'They're all grown up,' he said dismissively. 'And, anyway, I don't like any of them. But with you, I feel like I'm getting a second chance, Michelle. To do it properly this time.'

'Whoa,' said Michelle. 'There's no "with me". There's no us.'

'Of course,' the judge retracted quickly. 'A slip of the tongue. But obviously you're the mother of my child. Children. And as such you deserve the kind of respect you haven't been afforded so far.' He gave a little laugh. 'I mean, look at you! Blooming! Those beautiful babies nestling in there!'

'No touching,' Michelle snapped. 'And what about your reputation? As an upholder of the law? You won't mind that they'll all be laughing their heads off at you in the Four Courts?'

The judge looked stoic. 'I understand there will be a certain dent to my reputation. Which to date has been sterling, I might add.'

'That's because you never got caught before. And what about your wife? How's she taking all this?'

'Naturally, it was a . . . surprise to her. But we've talked it over and she's been very forgiving. She feels very strongly that she, too, wants me to become involved.'

'She must be a saint then,' Michelle said baldly.

'I'm trying to take responsibility, Michelle. I'm not a complete cad. I thought you'd jump at the chance. And in a year's time, we could talk about childcare and maybe you could go back to college.'

In Mrs Ball's absence, Jackie felt compelled to inform him, 'She only has a year to go of her law degree, you know.'

'Exactly!' the judge said. 'You know it makes sense, Michelle. Let me be involved and I'll pay for everything! An au pair. A private nanny, whatever you want.'

'And what do I have to do in return?' Michelle said suspiciously.

'Because there's no sex or anything. Just so we're absolutely clear on that.'

The judge gave an impatient sigh. 'I'm doing this for the babies, Michelle. That's all. I want to be a part of their lives.'

Michelle looked at Jackie. Jackie shrugged. You couldn't fault the man for wanting to do the right thing by his children. And it would look selfish and unreasonable of Michelle if she were to deny him his rights.

'All right,' she said.

'Oh, thank you! Thank you. This means so much to me.'

'Hold your horses. We'll draw up an agreement. About access and things. Visitation rights. Financial details. All that kind of stuff.'

The judge deflated. 'Does it have to be all stiff and formal?' He added, over-familiarly, 'After all, we're going to be a mummy and daddy now!'

'What exactly do you have in mind?' Michelle enquired.

'I thought I could start spending some more time with you during the pregnancy. Support you. And get to know the babies a bit better. I could even stay tonight.'

'Here?' Michelle was bug-eyed.

'Just on the couch. If that's OK. I really feel I've already missed out on so much of this pregnancy.'

Michelle flashed Jackie a look that wondered whether he was losing it. Or else there was something else going on. But what?

It was Mr Ball who eventually shed light on the situation by knocking politely at the window, and calling in cheerfully, 'Good news. Your tyres are fine. It's just all those suitcases in the back seat weighing it down.'

Michelle whirled round to the judge, who had blanched. 'She's thrown you out, hasn't she? Your wife.'

'It's not—'

'She's packed your bags and kicked you out.'

'I wouldn't put it like—'

'And you thought you'd come crawling here to see if you'd have any luck with me. It wasn't about the babies at all!'

'It is! Partly. I want to be involved in their lives!'

But Michelle just waved a hand. 'I'll give you access when they're born. Now go on. Sling your hook.'

'But I've nowhere to go! Like it or not, you're in this mess with me.'

'I most certainly am not. I'm doing just fine on my own.'

He dropped his nice-guy act completely. 'It's all your fault! If it wasn't for you ringing me up all the time, and your meddling mother posting me that scan, which my wife opened, by the way. Why couldn't you just have left me alone?'

Jackie and Michelle looked on in a kind of horrified fascination. The man was clearly on the edge. Or just a creep, which was more likely.

'I should have sued you in the first instance! Those babies probably aren't even mine! Oh, your reputation is well known around the Four Courts. Do you know what they call you?'

'Not in front of the children,' Michelle warned, her hand going to her stomach.

'Sorry,' he said. 'But anyway. You think you're going to walk away from this scot-free?' It was a wonder how he had worked that one out. 'While my reputation is in tatters? I have to stand up there on Monday morning and pass judgement on all kinds of criminals and lowlifes! How do you expect me to do that effectively with this tawdry affair hanging over me?'

A voice spoke from the door. 'I'd like you to leave now.'

They all turned round. Mr Ball stood there, an electric drill in his hand. He must have heard everything through the window, and had, for once, been stirred. He cocked the drill dangerously towards the judge, and coolly pressed the trigger. There was a menacing whirr as its tip sliced the air.

The judge gave a little laugh. 'For God's sake—'

'Don't make me use this,' Mr Ball cut in softly.

It had the desired effect. The judge turned to Michelle, but he had well and truly burned his boats there. He grabbed his coat and car keys and, with a last angry look around, went to the door. He eased past Mr Ball. Moments later they heard the Mercedes start up and, with a clashing of gears, go off down the drive. Mr Ball didn't lower the drill until they heard it speeding off down the road.

Mrs Ball bustled in from the kitchen. 'What are you doing with that thing?' she said to Mr Ball. 'And where's the judge?'

Mr Ball didn't enlighten her. He merely put the safety catch on his drill, gave Michelle an embarrassed little salute, and left.

Jackie had had enough drama by ten o'clock and retired to bed, where she lay looking up at the ceiling. After the judge and Henry, she felt entitled to indulge in some very bad thoughts about men in general. But the judge didn't bear thinking about for too long and so she ended up thinking about Henry. Again.

She might as well admit it: he'd got the better of her again. Pulled the rug from right under her, and was probably laughing at the good of it at that very moment. He was giving her a divorce, all right, but in such a way that she had no proper closure at all! (He would laugh more at the word 'closure'. He was always accusing her of being influenced by too much daytime TV.) She wondered whether he had actually planned it that way. It seemed almost too crooked, but she wouldn't put anything past him. Not a thing!

And now here she was tonight: deflated, defeated and, yes, cheated once again. Denied her day in court where she had expected finally to confront him, question him, call him names and spit at him, even though Velma had assured her she wouldn't be allowed to do any of these things. But at the very least she would have been able to look him in the eye and let him see what she thought of him.

He was, she decided, a coward. He had challenged the divorce when it suited him, but he lacked the courage when the spotlight was pointed at *his* failings. Talk about crawling for the nearest stone!

Well, she wasn't going to let him. Not after all this. She'd get her divorce, but she'd get the boot in too.

She flung back the duvet. Everybody had gone to bed, except for Mrs Ball who was wandering around out in the garden in her nightie. Her latest thing was to listen for an owl whose tooting might make her sleepy.

Jackie put on her dressing gown and went downstairs. Some rational part of her brain urged her not to do this, to sleep on it, but she ignored it. After all, rationale had also told her to forget wild passion and gut instinct and marry Dan, and look how that had turned out. From now on she might as well let her life be guided by the horoscopes in the TV guide. Or the weather forecast, or something.

Downstairs, she quietly locked the back door on Mrs Ball, who was liable to wander in at the most inopportune moments. Then she hunted around for some hard liquor to fortify herself with, but there was nothing, only Cup-A-Soups, and so she settled down by the phone with a steaming mug of Farmhouse Vegetable. If she got his answering machine she would hang up, she decided. Leaving a stream of vitriol on someone's voicemail wasn't half as satisfactory as saying it to their faces.

She dialled his number. She found that she wasn't nervous at all. She was cool and angry and she wanted some answers.

It kept ringing and ringing at the other end. Typical. She was going to get neither him nor his answering machine. Her anger began to lose its edge. In another second her nerve would leave her altogether.

Then, finally, 'Hello?' he panted.

'Henry? It's Jackie.'

'Oh.'

'Not calling at a bad time, I hope?' She had probably interrupted him mid-shag.

'No, no. I just had to come down from upstairs. I was in the office.'

In the office! She couldn't believe he had said it. The scene of his crimes. Was it a deliberate attempt to goad her?

She said icily, 'My solicitor tells me you're not defending the divorce.'

'That's right,' he said. 'I hope you're happy now.'

Happy? Did the man have any feelings at all? Did any regular human emotions run through that bloodstream of his, or did he think every-body operated on his own twisted level?

'Actually no,' she announced. 'I'm not.'

He sounded angry too. 'You know something, Jackie? I'm not all that interested in your unhappiness. You're getting your divorce, however you insist on getting it, and now you're free to marry your loutish boyfriend. So what's the problem?'

'What do you mean, however I insist on getting it? I'm just going on the facts here!'

'What facts?' he scoffed. 'Because there isn't a single one as far as I can tell!'

'The usual facts where adultery is concerned! The fact that you . . . deposited your willy where you shouldn't have!'

259

He sounded a bit taken aback. Then he said, 'I'm not sure how to respond to that. Except to say that, for the duration that I considered myself to be married to you – until the night you waltzed out, on our wedding anniversary – I did not sleep with anybody else.'

It was a bit of a surprise to hear him deny it openly. She was less certain when she said, 'Henry, do you think I'm a total fool?'

'No,' he said. 'But I'm a little confused, Jackie. I don't know why you're ringing me up seeing as you're obviously so sure that I did it.'

'You've admitted it on the divorce papers!'

'I'm letting you have your divorce. I'm admitting nothing.'

So he wasn't really denying it. He was just digging in his heels, as always.

She said, 'You know, I rang you up in the hopes that, for once in your life, you might be straight with me. But I can see I'm at nothing.'

'So you're looking for the *truth*?' he scoffed. 'A month ago you didn't want to know about the truth, remember? You just wanted to get shot of me as quickly as possible so that you could get hitched again!'

She wouldn't tell him that everything had changed on the Dan front; it was far too embarrassing. And she didn't want to go into her personal reasons for the phone call, because she would be sure to mention the word 'closure' at some point and he would burst out laughing. 'Well, I'm after the truth now,' she said. 'And I don't know why you can't just let me have it. It's not some competition, Henry. We both know it's over. So can we not just be grown up about it?'

'I'm perfectly prepared to be grown up,' he said. 'But I'm not going to admit to something I didn't do. You must be joking.'

She was very angry again. Even now, he wouldn't stop game-playing; even when she had absolute proof. 'I heard you that night, Henry. I heard you on the phone to her.'

There was a very long pause. He knew the game was up.

But he said, 'To who?'

'You know bloody well who!' Even if she didn't. 'I heard you in the office upstairs on the phone. You were muttering away and then you said to her, you're beautiful. Beautiful. Twice, I mean. I heard it with my own ears, Henry!'

There was another silence now. It was him putting things together in his head. And they fitted. She knew him too well.

'I see,' he said, eventually. Just that. No further denials, or pretend bafflement. He might as well have waved a white flag.

She was astonished at the sharp pain she felt inside. 'Is that all you have to say?' No apology, no regrets? He didn't even make an excuse to get off the phone quickly and show her how embarrassed he was by all this.

He said, 'Well, it's just the phone in the office hasn't worked since the time I threw it against the wall, remember?'

'What?'

'Why do you think I'm down here in the hall freezing my ass off talking to you right now?'

She faltered. The ground was going from under her. 'Your mobile then!'

'What exactly was I supposed to have said again?' Listen to him! More interested in the gory details than how she might have felt.

'It doesn't matter,' she said.

'It bloody does matter. This is my reputation here. And it wasn't beautiful, beautiful; it was *beautifully* beautiful. At least quote me right.'

And she saw it all clearly now: the real things that had been wrong in their marriage. His reputation, which had its own place at the dinner table, was only one of them.

'You didn't come after me when I left,' she told him. 'You didn't even ring up to see was I still alive!'

There was a silence at the other end of the phone. 'I know. I'm sorry, Jackie.'

'So am I. Goodbye, Henry.'

'Jackie, wait. We need to clear this up. I can explain it all.'

'Why? It's not like it's going to make any difference, is it?' She hung up.

After a while there was a rapping on the kitchen window. She got up and opened the back door. Mrs Ball came in, blue with the cold.

'Don't mind me, I only came in for my cardigan.'

She must have known that something had happened, because she lingered a minute at the door.

'Come on out with me for a few turns around the garden, and if we're quiet enough we might get lucky with an owl. A good night's sleep will do you the world of good.'

Jackie looked at her. She managed a smile. 'You know something? You're probably right.'

She tucked her arm into Mrs Ball's and they went out.

A week later in work a copy of the *Globe* arrived in the post addressed to Jackie. Heart hurting, she went straight to the personal ads section.

> *You are perfectly perfect*
> *I admit I lag behind*
> *You are wonderfully wonderful*
> *Something I've yet to find*
> *You are beautifully beautiful*
> *So far ahead of me*
> *You are gloriously glorious*
> *. . . And mine, incredibly.*

And, at the end: *For Jackie, on our first wedding anniversary.*

Chapter Twenty

'I'd like to order a wreath,' the woman caller on the phone said.

'Certainly,' Jackie replied, her voice full of sympathy. 'That's our speciality.' But she couldn't resist giving Emma a jubilant little thumbs-up. Their very first customer! She said to the woman, 'And seeing as we've opened for business just this morning, there won't be any charge.'

On second thoughts perhaps she should have saved the freebie thing till the next customer; it was probably a bit tasteless when it involved bereavements.

But the woman was delighted. 'Thank you! I'll recommend you to all my friends.'

'If you could,' Jackie said modestly. She reached for her pad and pen, and asked, suitably sombre, 'What kind of arrangement were you thinking of? We do a lovely mid-priced one with carnations and white roses, or our own special bouquet which is slightly more expensive but is a beautiful mix of lilies, chrysanthemums, and snapdragons.'

It was one of her line of 'occasional' flowers, which she privately called *So You've Passed Away*, but of course Emma had no sense of humour at all and she insisted they call it their memorial wreath, which was unoriginal to say the least.

'I'll have the special,' the woman decided. 'No expense spared.'

The deceased must have been a very close relative, so Jackie upped her sympathy.

'Certainly.' To Emma she whispered, 'The special.'

Emma immediately set to work, bustling about the place in a blur of brown. Everything she wore these days was unrelentingly brown. You could be forgiven for thinking she was in mourning herself.

Jackie reached for her pad and pen and asked the woman, 'Would you like to send a message with that?'

'Yes, please. Could you put, "Wish you were dead."'

Jackie's pen stilled. Great – a weirdo. This wasn't good karma, not on their first day.

'He'll know who it's from,' the woman added briskly.

It was very tempting; they were desperate for business, and one good wreath could get a whole word-of-mouth thing going on.

But, blast it, she couldn't. Not in all conscience. And so she told the woman regretfully, 'We don't actually deliver wreaths to people who aren't clinically dead.'

Emma immediately abandoned the wreath, and slumped at the counter.

'Really?' The woman sounded astonished.

'Really.'

'Just make it up for collection then, and I'll deliver it to him myself.'

Jackie clamped her hand over the phone, and hissed to Emma, 'She'll deliver it herself.'

'Absolutely not.'

'Oh, come on, Emma.'

'No! It's unethical and you know it!'

'I also know that we're up to our goolies in a bank loan.' But she told the woman, 'We can't do it. I'm really sorry. But if ever you need a wreath for legitimate purposes, we'd be delighted if you'd consider us.'

The woman hung up.

Jackie said to Emma, 'I hope you're happy, now that you've driven away our very first customer.'

'There'll be another one,' Emma replied. *She* could afford to be laid-back. She'd had hardly a thing to do with this second branch, except stump up some capital. It was Jackie who had slaved over the business plan, got the bank loan, found the premises, which was an ex-Miss Leather outlet, and then discovered it had a leaky roof, which was why Miss Leather had moved, after losing half its stock to water damage. She had spent a whole month persuading builders into renovating the place, and had put the finishing touches to it only ten minutes before they threw open the doors at nine that morning to the general public.

So far the only person to come in was a middle-aged man asking where Miss Leather had moved to.

All in all, Jackie felt entitled to break into a cold sweat, and blurt, 'I hope we haven't made a terrible mistake!'

'I did try and warn you,' Emma said, annoyingly. 'I said, there are lots of easier ways of getting over men. You could have drunk yourself silly every night for starters. Or done the whole one-night stand thing. Or got a tattoo or something. But what do you do? You decide to go and open another branch of Flower Power instead!'

'Sorry for being so constructive,' Jackie said, feeling very superior. 'And anyway, I didn't do this to get over Henry. I'm over Henry. This is for me. It's about self-fulfilment, and proving to myself that I can be successful on my own terms.'

'I hate the way you keep doing that,' Emma complained. 'Speaking like you're on a recovery programme or something. It's sickening to listen to.'

Talk about begrudgery! People just hated it when you came out the other end of a relationship intact. Well, Jackie had.

And to think that it had all been a misunderstanding in the end. She had very nearly weakened. But had those words of love, in black and white in the newspaper, really been for her? She could hardly believe it, after everything. For a week afterwards she had half expected to hear from Henry. A follow-up phone call or something. But when there was no further contact from him, the whole thing had the feel of being too late. She had, she decided, no real reason to turn back.

After that, it hadn't been all that hard in the end. Once no defence had been entered, the whole thing had proceeded efficiently. And very impersonally too, helped in large part by the fact that Velma seemed to have established a surprisingly good working relationship with Tom, Henry's solicitor. Between them, they had ironed out any minor issues without bothering Jackie. All in all, it had gone like clockwork with no more blunders or angst at all.

And now there was only one legal hurdle left to be jumped over: some final application to the court had to be made, and then the whole thing would be over and done with. Velma had been pressurising Jackie to come in. Well, she didn't have time that week to waste on Henry! He could wait until she could squeeze it in.

'You know,' she observed now, giddy with her own coping skills and general all-round brilliance, 'if I gave up men entirely, there would be no stopping me. I could open new branches of Flower Power all over the city!'

'You'd never last without a man,' Emma said sourly. Honestly, just looking at her these days would bring you down.

'Excuse me,' Jackie pointed out, 'but I haven't been on a date since Dan and I broke up four months ago.'

'That's because you haven't been under any serious pressure,' Emma argued. 'You've only been associating with bank managers and land-lords and great big sweaty builders. You just wait till some guy comes along with big wet dreamy eyes, or some bleeding heart story, and you'll fall for him like a ton of bricks.'

'I will not.' She felt very cross that her entire transformation wasn't being taken seriously. 'Do you think I've learned nothing this past two years? You really think I'm going to fall into bed with the first pair of moody eyes I see? Well, I've got news for you: the most important person in my life from now on is me!'

Emma sighed and enquired, 'When are you actually going to be totally recovered? And start speaking normally again?'

But Jackie just looked at her very kindly. 'Do you not think it's time you looked after your needs again, Emma?'

'What?' Emma snapped.

'Let's face it. Lech has been gone a long time.'

'So?'

'So you've been miserable ever since.'

'I am not miserable!' Emma lashed out. 'I'm happier than ever. Ask anybody. I sang a song only the other day – one of the neighbours heard me, so there.'

'OK—'

'Just because I don't go around opening new branches doesn't mean I'm not recovered too, you know.' She sniffed disdainfully. 'And don't think I didn't realise you tried to hire that Phil guy for me.'

'I did not.'

Phil had interviewed yesterday for the vacancy of delivery guy, which had lain open since Lech had quit. He had been nice enough, and easy on the eye (all right, so she *had* been thinking of Emma) except for the fact that he had an opinion on everything and didn't hesitate to give it. It was because he spent so much time in his car, Emma reckoned, and had confused himself with a taxi driver. On and on he had droned until, at the end of the interview, Jackie and Emma had been rendered comatose by his pronouncements on politics and why cannabis should be made legal.

'I am perfectly reconciled to being alone again,' Emma declared. 'And I'd thank you to stop meddling in my love life.'

She looked pretty fierce. Jackie let it drop. She was coming round to the view that some relationships were fated, and nothing anybody could do would save them. And she should know. Some people started off their lives together on the wrong foot entirely, and their whole relationship seemed to be nothing more than a series of misunderstandings and botch-ups, and the kindest thing to do at the end of the day was put it out of its misery.

'Anyhow!' she said. She had also become practised at recognising the onset of black moods, and heading them off at the pass. 'Let's put some balloons up outside to let the whole world know we're open.'

'For a minute there you looked normal,' Emma commented. 'Instead of going around the whole time like you're on amphetamines.'

'I refuse to be brought down to your level,' Jackie said, and bustled off to fill some balloons with hot air.

'Velma phoned again,' Emma called after her.

'OK, OK.'

'Are you nervous?' Michelle asked a week later.

'No.'

'You're allowed to be, you know.'

'I know. But I'm perfectly fine with it.'

'It's just a matter of signing the thing, that's all,' Michelle told her kindly.

Velma had finally nailed Jackie down to an appointment to apply for the final legal document, which went by the rather grand title of decree absolute. For some reason Velma was unable to apply for it herself. Her repeated abusive phone calls to the courts office had led to an investigation of some register, which apparently she wasn't on. As if she had time to be registering right, left and centre! Very niggly altogether, she had huffed to Jackie, but that was the English courts system for you.

'You really didn't have to come along, you know,' Jackie told Michelle lightly. 'I'm pretty sure I'm not going to burst into tears.'

They were having lunch in a rather posh restaurant down the road from Velma's. The last supper, Michelle had joked, before she officially became a divorcée.

'I know, but I couldn't bear another afternoon on the couch watching Oprah interview poor, pregnant white trash. It reminds me too much of myself.' She snapped up the last hunk of bread, having polished off her own lunch and half of Jackie's. When the restaurant manager had seen them coming, he had seated them at a booth for six, right away from everybody else. 'Anyway,' she said, 'I wanted to make sure you weren't going to back out at the last minute.'

'Hardly.'

'It's been known to happen.'

'Michelle, I've just spent the last six months trying to divorce the guy. Today is the final step, that's all. If you want to know the truth, I'm relieved.'

'I suppose,' Michelle said in commiseration. 'And at least you found out that he wasn't throwing his leg over anybody else.'

'Sorry, am I supposed to be grateful for that or something?' The number of people who had said that to her! As though she should be delighted that he had not been panting down the phone to some mysterious paramour at all, but apparently only writing some bit of a poem to her, quite a flattering one at that, and now let's everybody give him a big round of applause.

'Don't get in a huff,' Michelle complained.

'I'm not. I've just come round to the view that whether he had an affair or not is a mere technicality.'

'What?'

'Because what kind of marriage was it, where he was behaving as though he *were* having an affair, and I was behaving as though I expected him to have one?'

Michelle thought hard for a minute, before hazarding, 'One without

268

trust?' Trust was an alien concept to her given that she had slept with half the country.

'Exactly!' Jackie threw back her head. It wasn't half as satisfying now that she had had her hair radically restyled last week – very 'programme', Emma had said, but so what? Her mane of fuzz was now gone, replaced by what the hairdresser had assured her was a sophisticated layered effect, but what Jackie suspected was really just shorter fuzz.

Still, it was a change. It was different. It was leaving scatty old Jackie behind. And after today, she would be completely free!

But Michelle had to go spoiling the moment by saying, 'Could you not build all that up again? The trust thing? Now that you know for a fact he wasn't shagging anybody else?'

'It's not as simple as that.'

'Why not?'

Everything was just so black and white with Michelle! She wasn't the one who had languished on the sofa night after night in her just-married negligée, with her new husband upstairs muttering to himself in the attic room. Apparently writing torrid poems about feelings that he had never had the bottle to confess to her face. And her only dying for a bit of romance. Forced to live vicariously through the passionate entanglements of emergency room doctors on the TV.

But that was her and Henry all over: never quite connecting. One of them always out of sync with the other. There was no reason to expect that things would ever change.

She complained to Michelle, 'Are you trying to talk me into *not* divorcing him?'

'Hardly. You know I can't stand the guy. Besides, you'll definitely have more fun single.' She looked at Jackie. 'You seem so cool about it, that's all.'

'What, I should be rolling around on the ground in anguish? Look, I'm ready for this, OK?'

'OK.' And she threw down her napkin energetically, and said, 'Let's go divorce Henry Hart!' Then she looked down, and said, 'Oops.'

Jackie looked too. There seemed to be some kind of liquid slowly dripping down Michelle's bare legs.

'Did you just spill a glass of water or anything?' she enquired.

'No,' Michelle confirmed. 'Did you?'

'No.' They pondered it for a moment longer. Jackie asked, 'And it's not some kind of . . . bathroom thing?' It was a delicate subject, due to the number of mysterious wet patches that had been discovered around the house in recent weeks. But with two babies sitting on top of her bladder, was it any wonder it was weak? Michelle had argued.

'I don't think so.' She looked very apologetic. 'I'm really sorry, Jackie. You probably think I did this on purpose. But maybe if I crossed my legs, I could hang on until you get your appointment with Velma over and done with.'

'Don't be ridiculous,' said Jackie, her heart beating fast. She wondered should she ring Michelle's birthing partner: Mrs Ball. But then she remembered she was on the golf course today. She had taken it up after somebody told her that it was marvellous for emptying the mind and that she'd sleep like a baby after a round. But instead of it having a calming effect on her, she now had a whole new set of worries, to do with handicaps and quality tartan trousers. Mr Ball, on the other hand, had taken to it beyond anybody's expectations and had grown even more detached and serene.

Jackie took a deep breath, and said, 'I suppose we should get you to the hospital.'

Michelle waved a hand. 'It could be hours before I go into labour yet. We'll easily have time for dessert.'

'No. I think we should go now.' Jackie waved authoritatively for the manager. 'I'll get them to ring for an ambulance.'

But the restaurant manager was most reluctant to have an ambulance pull up outside his establishment. He pretended he didn't know the number, even though Jackie told him twice that it was 999. He suggested a taxi or, better still, a hackney, which would be unmarked and which he could arrange to have arrive at the back entrance. He would ring one now.

'And could I get some kind of a container for the fluid?' Michelle called after him. 'They tell you to try and catch some and bring it in with you to the hospital. An espresso cup or something would do.'

He quickened his step towards reception.

'Disgraceful,' Jackie said. 'I won't recommend this place to any of my friends!'

'You're very cheerful all of a sudden,' Michelle said suspiciously.

'It's a momentous occasion, Michelle. You're about to give birth.'

'And you get out of going to see Velma.'

'The thought never crossed my mind.'

'Actually, I do feel a bit strange,' Michelle admitted, hand on her stomach. 'I think this might be it. Imagine! I'm going to be a mum.' And she looked all soft and excited.

The restaurant manager soon wiped that off her face with the news that the hackney office had told him that no car was available for at least half an hour. When they heard that it was for a pregnant woman who looked like she might be going into labour, they changed their story and said it could be up to two hours. But in the meantime, the restaurant manager told them they were perfectly welcome to wait inside.

Then Michelle announced suddenly, clutching her stomach hard, 'I think I might need to get there faster than anticipated.'

'I'll call an ambulance,' the restaurant manager reluctantly conceded.

'Wait,' said Jackie. When it came to fast dashes across gridlocked cities, there was only one person for the job. Emma would kill her, but this was an emergency.

'Hey, Jackie! Over here!'

Lech pulled up in a brand new limousine, beeping the horn and leaning out of the smoked-glass windows.

She hardly recognised him. He wore a suit and tie and a pair of sunglasses. He looked for all the world like a rakish businessman.

'I thought you said he was a pizza delivery guy?' Michelle said. She held a piece of cheesecake in her hand. The sudden burst of pain in the restaurant had turned out to be indigestion, and after it had abated, she'd felt relaxed enough to order dessert.

'Sssh,' said Jackie, as Lech jumped out and came around.

'You want a lift to the hospital?'

'Uh, yes, but . . .' She looked at the gleaming machine in front of her. 'We don't want to ruin your car.'

'It's no problem, please get in.' He threw open the back passenger door.

The smell of new leather hit them full in the face. The interior was cream and unsullied.

'I'll sit on a piece of newspaper,' Michelle assured him. He brushed that aside, but she said, 'No, honestly. I will.'

He was all efficiency and courtesy after that, ushering them into their seats and making sure they were comfortable. Michelle elected to sit on her own in the back. That way she said she could spread out. Jackie got into the front, and Lech sat in beside her.

'Nice wheels, eh? Beats my Ford with the pizza on the side.'

'Lech, I can't tell you how much we appreciate this.'

'Anything for friends. Besides, I was in this part of town anyway.'

He put the car into gear and swung out into the traffic without even looking. Other cars immediately parted to let him through. 'They are intimidated by my success,' he explained to Jackie.

She turned to look over her seat at Michelle. 'Are you OK?'

'I've just found a mini-bar back here,' Michelle told her, delighted. The car was so big that she sounded very far away. 'With peanuts and everything.'

After that she went quiet, except for the sound of packets being ripped open.

'How are you, Lech?' Jackie asked.

'Very well, as you can see.'

'You've obviously not doing deliveries any more.'

'Well, I am. In a fashion,' he said cryptically. 'But not for the pizza place. Pizza, it's a mug's game. And the smell! No matter how many times you shower, you can never get it off. It's a real turn-off for the ladies, I can tell you.' This last bit was said very macho and she wasn't sure she believed him. 'But I make friends there,' he told her, meaning-fully. 'Connections. People who know people. And next thing I know I am moving up in the world and driving this baby!' Showing off, he reached forward and rapidly punched several buttons on the dashboard. Windows eased down, the radio volume went up, and Jackie's head-rest pitched forward with a little *whirr*. 'Is that comfortable for you?' he enquired politely.

'Yes, thanks.' Then she gripped the sides of her seat as he sailed through a red light, shouting something in Polish at a driver who dared to hoot him.

'I'm glad things are working out for you, Lech,' she said.

'And you, Jackie?'

'Me? Oh, everything's great. Terrific! Emma and I have just opened a second branch.'

He gave no indication at all that he was affected by the mention of her name.

'Congratulations. And you cut your hair.' She waited for him to compliment her on her new, streamlined look, but he didn't. Maybe she shouldn't have believed a word that hairdresser had said. Look at what she'd been told about how easy it would be to style at home. An outright lie.

'And Henry?' he enquired. 'How are things on that front?'

'We're still trying to get divorced.' She gave a little laugh. 'But any day now.' Just as soon as she rescheduled her appointment with Velma.

Lech nodded sagely. 'Maybe it is good. To finally end things.'

'Absolutely. That way we can both move on.' She was saying all the right things, the things that made Emma puke, and for a moment they almost made her puke too.

Finally, when there was nobody else left to enquire after, Lech eventually asked, carelessly, 'How is Emma?'

'Emma? Fine. Great!'

'Great?' he asked keenly.

'I mean, not . . . *great*.' She didn't want to give him the impression that Emma didn't give a hoot. 'More, medium.' Was that enough? 'She's put on ten pounds. Comfort eating.' That was really as far as she could go, she felt, without Emma killing her.

He looked straight ahead without comment. It was difficult to know how he felt.

She added, 'We've really missed you, Lech. All of us.' She put the emphasis on 'all'.

'I suppose things change.'

'I suppose.'

Then, just when she was beginning to believe that he really didn't care, he said, 'You'll tell her, yes? That you met me?'

'If you want.'

'Be sure to mention the car. There are only five of them in the whole country. You tell her that. And this suit, it's Armani.'

She duly made admiring noises under her breath.

'She would not be ashamed of me any more,' he declared, with some bitterness.

'Why don't you stop by and tell her yourself, Lech?'

'No.'

'She'll be going on her lunch break soon. Maybe you two could talk.'

He didn't waver. 'Maybe I do not care any more.'

Jackie didn't believe that but needed all her energy to remain upright in her seat as he broke another light and took off up a side street that she was sure was one way only.

He got them to the hospital in record time and parked confidently in a spot directly outside the front doors, below a bright red sign that clearly indicated it was for emergency vehicles only.

Jackie found a hospital porter for Michelle, and there was a bit of a struggle as they tried to squeeze her into a wheelchair.

'I'll never be able to get out again,' she declared as she was borne off.

Jackie put her hand on Lech's arm. 'Thank you so much.'

'You're welcome. Good luck to your sister,' he said.

As she ran up the hospital steps after Michelle, Lech beeped his horn and shouted out the window, 'Don't forget to tell Emma that I am a big hotshot now, OK?'

Chapter Twenty-One

While Jackie was busy in the admissions office filling in forms, Michelle apparently went into full-blown labour at the snack machine on the second floor — she maintained afterwards that it was a king size Twix that had done it — and was immediately carted off to the delivery ward.

What was more, they wouldn't let Jackie in. The nurse at the doors informed her that Michelle was at that moment being examined by a team of doctors, including the master of the hospital, and she would just have to wait.

'But I'm her sister!' Jackie said. 'For God's sake, we look alike.'

'Nobody's looking at her face in there,' the nurse assured her.

'Can you at least tell me if she's all right?'

'I'll let you know what the doctors say,' the nurse said. 'Why don't you join your father over there and wait.'

Mr Ball was here? Surely they hadn't arrived from the golf course already? She'd only phoned them from the car.

She looked around. The only man she could see was skulking by the public telephones in a long overcoat and with a hat pulled down over his ears, even though the place was boiling. He also wore a pair of sunglasses. When he saw Jackie looking at him he quickly raised a newspaper to cover his face.

Jackie marched over and brushed the newspaper aside. 'Justice Gerard Fortune!'

'Ssssh!' he said.

'How dare you pass yourself off as Michelle's father. Even though you're certainly old enough.'

'For God's sake, keep your voice down,' he pleaded. 'Nobody knows I'm here.'

Jackie folded her arms across her chest. 'Well, you've certainly changed your tune. I thought you wanted to stand by Michelle. That you were going to be a proper father to these babies, and to hell with the consequences.'

A passing nurse looked over curiously. He cowered down further under his hat.

'I am,' he hissed. 'In a fashion.'

'What's that supposed to mean?'

'It's just, well, my situation has got a little more complicated. My, um, wife has lowered herself to take me back.'

That explained the disguise. 'And does she know you're here?'

'No,' he admitted.

'You're a filthy, rotten, lying coward,' Jackie declared in the loudest possible voice.

'Absolutely,' he whispered. 'But at least I showed up. With my cheque-book. I've paid for her to go straight into a private room. She'll be more comfortable there.'

'And you can visit without anybody seeing you.'

'That would be a consideration, yes.'

Jackie felt terribly protective of poor Michelle, in there now with a whole load of doctors looking at her while she tried to push out two lumps of babies. And it was this snivelling man's entire fault. She drew herself up and said, 'I think you should leave right now. I don't even know how you found out she was in labour!'

'She rang me,' he said. 'We do keep in touch, you know.'

Jackie had heard Michelle mumbling in the back of the car all right, but thought she was reading the ingredients on a bar of Swiss choco-late she'd discovered. She deflated.

He looked off over her shoulder now, and sighed. 'And here comes the rest of the circus.'

Mrs Ball came hurrying down the corridor towards them, giving nervous little hops as she came. Mr Ball followed along behind, speedily for him, and trailing two sets of golf clubs. Justice Fortune looked resigned at the prospect of another confrontation. But he stood his ground.

'You!' Mrs Ball said. She was wearing spanking white trousers and a visor, even though the sun hadn't shone in over two months.

'Mr and Mrs Ball,' the judge said. 'So! We meet again!'

'Where is she?' Mrs Ball demanded, her forehead crinkled in hundreds of little worry lines.

'In delivery. The last I heard, she was four centimetres dilated,' the judge informed her politely.

Mr Ball glowered. 'Don't you dare refer to my daughter in those terms.'

'What?'

'Have you no respect?'

Then a piercing scream came from the labour ward and sliced through the air. Mrs Ball went pale.

'Was that Michelle?'

'No,' said Justice Fortune decisively.

She turned on him. 'And how would you possibly know what she sounds like when she screams?' Then a possible explanation occurred to her. She reddened. 'You are a filthy lowlife, do you know that?'

'Mrs Ball, just because I had consensual sexual relations with your daughter does not make me a filthy lowlife.'

'Yes, it does,' she said back. 'Oh, my poor Michelle! How will we cope, Jackie, if anything goes wrong?'

'Stop it, Mum. Nothing's going to go wrong.'

'But you never know!'

She seemed to have forgiven Michelle entirely for sleeping with practically everybody she knew, dropping out of her law course, and getting pregnant by a fat, balding, married judge. Once she eventually produced the twins, she would probably be firmly back on her perch as the golden girl, while Jackie languished in the background as the failed divorcée.

She hated herself for having such thoughts, especially at a time like this. Besides, she might be a failed divorcée but she had just opened another branch of Flower Power and Mrs Ball could put that in her pipe and smoke it!

Mrs Ball was rummaging in her handbag now. She took out a travel pack of tissues, then closed the handbag and thrust it at Mr Ball. 'Mind that. I'm going in.'

What use she thought a packet of tissues was going to be to a woman in labour was anybody's guess, but she set off in a confident fashion for the swing doors of the labour ward. Jackie had to move fast to stop her.

'Mum, you can't go in there.'

'I'm her birthing partner. I came back from the golf course specially.'

Not in time to be useful, but anyhow. 'They're doing things to her in there, Mum.'

'What things?' She looked alarmed.

'Oh, just let them get on with it,' Mr Ball said.

Well. She turned to look at him. 'That's my daughter in there, you know. About to give birth.'

'I know. But there are people looking after her. Professionals. Let them do their job.'

'I was just trying to help!'

'How is it going to help, you standing over her, worrying?'

'Oh!' She said to Jackie, 'He's got all cocky since that drill incident. He thinks he knows it all now. Mr Macho all of a sudden! Mr Action Man.'

Mr Ball looked as if he was sorry he'd said anything now. He gave Jackie a look for help. But he'd been let off the hook all his life. She said nothing.

He was forced to rally. 'Well, listen to you! You're already after frightening everybody by worrying that something is going to go wrong!'

'Hear, hear,' the judge murmured.

'It might!' Mrs Ball shouted.

'Or it might not,' Mr Ball countered. 'In fact, there's a far greater chance that everything is going to be fine! As usual, you're getting in a heap about nothing.'

But Mrs Ball hadn't dedicated forty-two years of her life to endless worry and sleepless nights, only for it all to be brushed aside so easily. So callously. By a man who had spent more of his life in the garage than in his own family home.

'And what would you know about worry?' she said, her voice shaking. 'For each of those children, all you've had to do was what the judge here did to our Michelle, and then forget about the whole thing! As if they would raise themselves and neither of their parents need ever concern themselves with the possibility of head lice or damp class-rooms or that . . . habit Dylan developed and that we thought he might have to see a specialist about!'

Mr Ball said, 'He was just doing what boys do at that age. He wasn't disturbed, like you said he was.'

Mrs Ball, in all her white, had the look of a martyr now. 'You'd have to pick the one example, wouldn't you, that made me look like a lunatic!'

'I didn't pick it, *you* picked it—'

'I didn't see you stepping in with your electric drill the day that black spot appeared on Eamon's back, and I had to do the rounds of all those doctors on my own with him, before one of them rubbed it off with a wet wipe? Or when it looked like the whole lot of them would flunk their exams or not be able to hold down stable relation-ships?'

'That happened anyway,' he shot back. 'Worrying about it wouldn't have stopped it.'

'But it would have showed you cared! Do you think they haven't noticed? That you've nothing to say when it really matters? When was the last time you lost a night's sleep over any of them?'

Mr Ball looked a bit stricken.

'Well?' She had her hands on her hips now.

Eventually he challenged, 'Anytime I did get up to any of them during the night, you were always there first! Taking charge and brushing everybody else aside with your fretting and your worry! Imagine if I had started worrying too? We'd have all ended up basket cases!'

'Maybe if you had worried a little more, then I could have worried a little less!' she retorted. 'But you never did! Because life suited you just fine the way it was! It's very easy to turn around now, when it's all done and they're all reared, and protest!' She was really upset now. 'I wish I had the courage of our Jackie here. To decide that I won't put up with second best any more. If I had half her guts and sense of self-preservation, I would have bloody well divorced you years ago!'

It was possibly the nicest thing she had said about Jackie in years. Meanwhile, Mr Ball had gone quite white.

The judge looked at him. 'Any rebuttal?'

'I can't think of anything at the moment,' Mr Ball said miserably.

'In that case perhaps I might call for a summing up,' the judge said to Mrs Ball.

Mrs Ball nodded. She pointed with a shaking hand towards the labour ward. 'Our youngest daughter is in there right now, unmarried and uneducated, and having twins prematurely. If you have an ounce of concern in your body for your children, you will stay here and worry. Because I have done enough and I'm going home.' And she snatched her handbag back and walked stiffly off down the corridor, the fluorescent lights bouncing off her sun visor.

Such was the drama that nobody paid much attention to the swing doors to the labour ward opening. A midwife had to clear her throat pointedly to get their attention.

'Michelle is doing just fine,' she told them all. 'And the good news is that her birth partner can go in now!'

At the far end of the corridor, Mrs Ball took a corner at speed and disappeared from view.

Eventually, Jackie said, 'Her birth partner can't actually make it.'

'Oh. Well, somebody else then?'

It was Mr Ball who stood forward bravely. He swallowed hard before saying, 'I'll do it.' And he began to roll up his sleeves.

'And you are . . . ?' the midwife prompted.

'Her father.'

The midwife looked to the judge, her confusion obvious. He slunk down further into his big overcoat and remained silent.

Jackie glared at him, but he refused to meet her eyes. She said to Mr Ball, 'No offence, Dad, but she might be more comfortable with a woman.'

'Do you think?' He began to roll his sleeves back down again. 'But tell your mother I offered, won't you? And I'll sit right here and wait, I won't go for coffee or anything.'

The midwife led Jackie towards the swing doors. 'She's being very brave in there,' she said. 'It's always a bit more difficult when there's no partner.'

For some reason this seemed to stir the conscience of the judge where everything else had failed: there was a rustle and a sigh, and there he was beside them. He announced, not quite proudly but at least audibly, 'I am the biological father of those twins. I will be the one who goes in!'

And, pulling his hat down a bit more, he did.

Henry was trying to find a word to rhyme with 'Mum'. It wasn't as easy as it sounded. His thesaurus had thrown up only 'glum', 'slum' and 'bum', all of which were totally unsuitable. Perhaps something might come to him if he read it aloud again.

He lifted the page and cleared his throat. '*Happy birthday, dear Mum! You're the tops, you . . .* Make me hum?' he suggested to Shirley. Shirley didn't even bother raising her head. She was used to this carry-on by now: her hitherto peaceful days disturbed by Henry's appalling doggerel. Although in fairness he was actually very good at this greetings card lark. He had already knocked out five children's birthday cards that morning, plus he'd finished off one for an anniversary, and try finding a word to rhyme with *that*.

So he wouldn't win any major poetry prizes with it. But it paid the bills while he got on with writing the real stuff at night.

Actually, it didn't pay the bills. It paid some of the bills. The very minor ones. Meanwhile he was down to beans on toast, whilst a FOR SALE sign stood at that moment in his front garden. Since paying over to Jackie her half of the house, his mortgage had rocketed, right about the same time as his salary abruptly dried up. His bank manager finally became alert to the situation and had called him in for a Very Serious Chat, the upshot of which was that his lovely house had gone on the market and he would have to find somewhere new to live. Probably some tiny studio apartment in an unfashionable part of town where he would get mugged regularly on his way out for a pint of milk. And where they didn't allow pets.

'Don't worry,' he assured Shirely. 'I won't leave you behind.'

The dog looked as though she would rather he did. He was being most unpredictable these days, always humming contentedly under his breath and not scowling all the time. She had grown quite afraid of him.

Henry made himself finish the birthday card to Mum before allowing himself another quick peek at his letter. He was being very self–indulgent, he knew that, but it wasn't every day that he got a positive response. Well, kind of positive.

> I'm not at all sure about the closing poem, Mangled Heart, it seems overly anguished. In fact, overall, the whole collection could do with a dollop less distress. If you would care to resubmit, we might just possibly, maybe, dependent on schedules, and the overall composition of our lists, consider, without obligation, publication.

The phone rang. Oh, fuck off. But he had forgotten to put the answering machine on again and it rang on and on. He decided he would have no phone at all installed in his new studio apartment, and would just keep a couple of homing pigeons for when he wanted to send messages.

He picked it up. 'Hello?'

'Henry? It's Adrienne!'

'Didn't I fire you?' he asked. 'Like, months ago?'

'You know very well that I like to check in with you from time to time. As a concerned friend. Because all that solitary activity can't be good for you. I'm worried that you're going to get depressed.' She sounded hopeful.

'Actually, Adrienne, I'm very happy.' He was desperate to tell her that he was going to be published. Maybe. Dependent on schedules. And a rewrite.

Adrienne said, 'Don't be ridiculous. You're not a man who's going to be content being merely *happy*. That's for lesser people, Henry. Not for someone with your great talent.'

'The world has managed without me.'

'Yes, but we're pining! For your wit. Your knowledge. Your use of the F word. Don't stay away too long, hmmm?

He felt it needed to be pointed out, yet again. 'Adrienne, I'm not your client any more.'

'Darling, you know that I can never let any of you go. You're like children to me.'

He wanted to throw up. In another ten seconds he would say that there was somebody at the door.

She went on, 'All right, so the *Globe* didn't suit you. Didn't appreciate you. I don't blame you in the slightest for giving them the two fingers.' He had actually been fired, but it was no problem to her to rewrite history. 'But don't let your bad experience sour you to all the other options out there. I know for a fact that the *Herald* would snap you up. In fact, I could start some preliminary negotiations—'

'There's my doorbell,' Henry lied.

'Think about it. That's all.'

'I have to go.'

'Yes, all right, we can talk about it more next week.'

Henry wasn't alarmed. Next week was, like, a whole seven days away. These days he didn't usually think past tomorrow. It was a great way to live. But he was mildly curious and so he asked, 'What's on next week?'

'Now, don't pretend you've forgotten,' Adrienne chastised. 'It's the launch, Henry. Of your restaurant guide?'

In the end they had used a file photo of him from the office, and Adrienne had ended up proof-reading the thing for him.

'Look, Adrienne, I probably won't go.' Cut the bullshit. That was another welcome change in his life.

'Three hundred invitations have gone out to celebrate the publication of this book, Henry. Take it from me, it would be very bad form for the author not to show up.' She said bossily, 'I'll pick you up. Try to dress appropriately. Something clean would be nice.' Good thing she hadn't seen him since he'd grown his beard. 'And keep your fingers crossed for the TV thing. They're waiting to see how the book does, I think.'

'What TV thing?'

'Must run, there's my doorbell!' She hung up.

Honestly. The woman was operating on pure fantasy if she thought he was getting back into the media game in any shape or form. No, Henry Hart had finally found his niche and he was happy. Delighted! Couldn't be more content.

Even Dave said that he hardly recognised him any more, and not just because of the beard. Which, if he was honest, didn't really suit him and which he had only grown in an effort to keep the heating bills down. The downside was that it was tricky to wash; did you use shampoo or soap? Did you comb it out afterwards? And even then he kept finding bits of mouldy food in it. Women also found beards unattractive in the extreme, which didn't concern him right at that moment but might at some time in the future. He didn't want to get a reputation as a weirdo or a traditional music player or anything like that. He would shave it off for the launch, he decided. If he decided to go. So what if three hundred people were going to show up? With that kind of crowd, nobody would miss him. He might just conveniently forget and take off into the country for the day with a packed lunch. Take in a few hedges and robins and things. Who knows, maybe he would do a series of poems on nature or something. Why not! The world was his oyster.

Ah yes, the life of a poet was a very satisfying one. And not given nearly enough credit in this age of consumerism and property port-folios, as he had tried to explain to Dave. Dave didn't really get it at all. He hadn't read a poem since his O levels, and had got all flustered when Henry had given him one of his own to read.

'Do I have to memorise it?'

'What? No.'

'What do you want me to do with it then?'

'Just read it. Enjoy it.'

Dave had looked at him like it was some sick joke.

He was quite impressed by the greeting cards thing, though. 'It's amazing! You can actually write this stuff! And it rhymes and every-thing! Do you do rude ones too?'

Henry figured that maybe he could wean Dave onto the heavier stuff in time. It was just a question of broadening his mind, and taking the fear out of it for him. He had never realised before how intimidated people actually were by poetry. They treated it with the same level of suspicion as a subtitled film, or a BBC2 documentary: terribly hard work and completely above their heads anyway.

Henry had discovered poetry in his late teens, but had managed to confine himself to reading it only. The urge to write it had come later, in his thirties, after he'd moved from cooking to reviewing. He would write a poem every now and again, and convince himself that it was enough. By the time he met Jackie, he was indulging in regular, furtive sessions – just one more, he would tell himself feverishly – in the privacy of his own home. But what did she do, only tip him headlong into coupledom, and passion, and the kind of feelings he'd never experienced before. All he wanted to do was giggle and dance about, and write reams of love poetry; turgid, erotic stuff that would make any man embarrassed to read back over.

Especially a hard man like him. The kind of cool, witty, reserved guy that she had married. So he had to do it in secret. In the attic. Without telling her. Even though most of it was about her.

Most of it was still about her, even now. But at least he was able to do it in the open. There wasn't any more hiding, or falseness, and that was a tremendous relief. He had finally come out of the closet

'No, I can honestly say I'm very happy,' he said to Dave that evening as they sat in Henry's back garden with a six-pack.

'Good,' said Dave, who hadn't actually disputed it. 'All you need now is the love of a good woman.'

He would have to lower the tone of the conversation, of course. Couldn't get his head around anything except birds and beer.

'I don't want the love of a good woman right now, thank you,' Henry said haughtily. 'I'm in the most creative phase of my life and I want to enjoy it without being dragged down by domesticity.'

'I suppose,' said Dave, who had come over to escape just such a thing. They sat in silence for a bit, sipping their beers and listening to the birds singing. Bliss, thought Henry.

'How's the divorce coming along anyway?' Dave said.

'Are you trying to ruin the evening altogether?'

'I was just making conversation.'

'You can't just sit here and listen to the birds tweeting?'

'Sorry.'

'It's fucking beautiful! Listen to it!'

'You've got very pretentious since you turned into a poet, do you know that?' Dave complained. 'There was a time when you wouldn't recognise a bird if it came up and crapped on your head.'

But they listened for a bit, and then Dave began to fidget, before bursting out, 'Look, I have to go home in a minute and Dawn will murder me if I don't bring back any juicy details about the divorce.'

'You can tell her it's all going like clockwork,' Henry said carelessly. 'Any day now I'll be a free man.' He lifted his beer bottle. 'Cheers!'

'Cheers,' said Dave, but it was all clunky and wrong, and they lowered their bottles awkwardly. And of course the birds had clammed up just when you'd be looking for a distraction.

'I suppose she'll be getting hitched again straightaway,' said Dave, Mr Fucking Cheerful.

'I suppose she will,' said Henry, with magnificent indifference. He felt obliged to add, 'I might get hitched again myself.'

'You? To who?'

'Well, I don't know. But I'll probably meet someone else. I'm still young, you know. Kind of.'

'Yeah, but you have a beard now. And no job. Or at least not a sexy job, like the one you had. You've no money, and probably no house in a few weeks. And you've put on a few pounds too.'

'Fuck off, mate.'

'I'm just saying. And there's Jackie, a gorgeous-looking woman; she always reminded me of Kate Bush, did I ever tell you that? I used to really fancy Kate Bush. Anyway, there she is, just opened her second branch.'

'What?'

'Of her flower shop. Dawn heard it through her cousin's sister-in-law's best friend who's in the flower trade. Remember, the one who told us about the first branch?'

'Yeah.' The nosiest cow in the whole of Europe.

'Dawn said not to tell you in case it might upset you.'

'But you told me anyway,' Henry said sarcastically. 'Anyway, I don't care. I'm not upset, why would I be upset?' And he looked into the trees again very intensely and poetically, not wanting Dave to see how much he did care.

A second branch! How could she manage to energetically engage in commerce whilst in the middle of a traumatic divorce? Somehow he had imagined that she was going through the same kind of profound life changes as he, involving tons of reassessment and introversion and growing beards. Fat chance. She was too busy peddling cheap sentiment in the form of flowers to the masses. She had changed, all right.

Well, so had he. In fact, he had become more like her. More senti-mental, and lighting scented candles at night. Could it be possible that each of them was mutating into the other? In another year's time would he end up crying at hospital dramas on the television, and wearing strange shoes?

'You look a bit funny,' Dave commented. 'Can you feel a poem coming on?'

'Shut up.'

'Sorry about the new branch thing. I probably shouldn't have said anything.'

'No, no, it's all right.' Henry brushed it off. 'Good luck to her, I say.'

Dave was astonished. 'Even though she falsely accused you of shagging somebody else?'

'That was all a misunderstanding,' Henry said magnanimously. 'The fact is, Dave, I've moved on.'

'Bollocks. I never saw anybody more bitter over a break-up.'

'Yes, all right, but you can't stay bitter for ever. And I've come to the conclusion – reluctantly, mind – that it was all mostly my fault.'

'Really?' Dave's eyes were popping now; wait till he imparted all this to Dawn. She wouldn't believe him. An admission of guilt from Henry! She'd be over herself to hear it from the horse's mouth.

'And are you going to tell her that?'

'Jackie?'

'Yeah.'

'Why?'

'*Why?* Because . . . because . . . Actually, you're right. There's no point at all. I mean, you guys are divorced.'

'Not yet,' Henry said, slightly peeved that Dave hadn't argued with him, or tried to convince him that there was still a chance, or something. Which was ridiculous of course.

'Anyway, she knows how I feel,' he said shortly. Not that she'd given any indication she'd even read his poems to her in the newspaper. Possibly she had scrunched them up and used them to light fires with, or to wipe her feet on or something. Or showed them around to her friends amidst uproarious laughter at what a plonker he was, to be writing her love poems in the middle of a divorce.

Or maybe she hadn't seen them at all. But he knew that she still looked out for him in the newspaper; or at least she did up to six months ago. He'd scraped off the Tippex with a knife from the bottom of that first letter she'd sent. And he saw a chance, however slim. And so he'd anonymously sent her copies of the newspaper. The poems in the personal ads were the only way he could tell her that he didn't hate her, without compromising his position. That he still loved her, despite everything. And that he was the world's biggest idiot for not going after her that night. Although, in fairness, he didn't know she was gone until he had come down from upstairs, his newly written poem in his hand.

He had been going to read it out to her over dinner at the restaurant in a kind of kill-two-birds-with-one-stone way: it would be a very significant romantic gesture on their wedding anniversary after a year that could only be described as rocky, and also a way of letting her know that he wanted to change career. What a plan! It made him want to gag now, of course, but he had thought it was a great idea at the time. Anyhow, it didn't matter, because all that had been left of her was wet footprints all over the house, and a horrendous mess in the bedroom. Then the note in the kitchen, written in eyeliner pencil: 'Goodbye.' It had sounded almost jaunty, or mocking or something, as though she were off to bigger and better things. And then he'd discovered that she'd gone out in all her finery. Another big statement.

His hurt was so great, his shock so big, that he had just thought, let her. It had been wrong from the start anyway. Let her go.

He wondered what would have happened had he gone after her. Still. Too late now.

'You're looking strange again,' Dave said. 'Will I get you a piece of paper?'

'Oh, fuck off.'

Chapter Twenty-Two

Michelle complained that she was so sore that it was doubtful whether she'd ever be able to stand up straight again, and that she would have to walk around for the rest of her life bent over like the Hunchback of Notre Dame, and the twins would be so ashamed of her that they would run off on her when they were about ten, and she'd have nobody to look after her in her old age.

'Don't look at me,' said Mrs Ball. 'I'll be in Spain.'

Michelle had accused Mrs Ball of stealing her thunder entirely with her impulsive purchase of a retirement home, which was presently under construction in Spain. The twins had scarcely been named (Sabrina and Jill, after *Charlie's Angels*) before Mrs Ball announced that she had parted with a hefty deposit on the strength of a brochure depicting a serene elderly woman fast asleep on a sun lounger by a pool. The resort had a beautiful Spanish name that nobody could pronounce, but the literal translation was something along the lines of 'Place To Wither and Die'.

'There's a supermarket and hair salon and swimming pool on site and everything,' Mrs Ball liked to boast. And a cemetery just over the wall, so that when the elderly residents had slept enough by the pool, they could go next door for a more permanent rest. But Mrs Ball wasn't viewing the move in terms of popping off; no, it was more a pre-emptive strike before any more of her children moved back home. Dylan had finally broken up with his married woman – no surprises there – and Eamon was muttering about showing his children their roots.

'Not in my back garden,' Mrs Ball had declared carelessly. She had become worryingly worry-free since Mr Ball had accused her of hogging their children for herself. She seemed to have shed all those lines on her face, too, and looked years younger. In contrast, her clothing had become more grown-up. Gone were the pinafores and dungarees, and she had abandoned pastels and baby pinks in favour of more mature greens and dark reds.

She told Jackie that she was done with fretting over other people. In the Place to Wither and Die, she wouldn't have a worry in the world except beating the rest of them to the pool in the mornings. Obviously she would hang around a bit for the sake of the twins, who were only two weeks old, after all, but thankfully all Michelle's overeating during pregnancy had paid off, and they had both weighed in at a hefty eight pounds each.

As soon as the pair of them could sit up without falling over, Mrs Ball declared, she would be packed and gone to a whole new stress-free life, where she would spend her days snoozing in the sun, and her nights sleeping like the dead.

The only thing was the blessed food. A friend of hers who had holidayed there in the past had informed her that the Spanish had terrible eating habits – tortilla this, and tortilla that, and thrusting olives at you at every opportunity. And the supermarkets were no better. Apparently you'd hardly recognise a thing in them, and there were all kinds of disgusting things hanging from the ceiling in the deli sections, such as giant mouldy sausages, and she had been advised to bring out her own supply of tea bags and rashers or she would starve altogether.

According to the plans, there would be a newly constructed golf course over another wall. Mr Ball would be in his element. But then only last week hadn't he declared that he didn't know if he'd be spending all that much time in Spain what with the twins. That he mightn't move out with Mrs Ball at all!

Of course, that was all put on. No man could be that interested in babies. He was only doing it to get back at her for those things she'd said to him in the hospital. Oh, give him a couple of weeks and the novelty of being 'involved' would soon wear off and he'd be back to those drill parts in a flash.

'I don't know. He really seems to enjoy it,' Jackie said. 'Look at him!'

He had Sabrina up on one shoulder in a very professional manner. 'She's hungry,' he informed Michelle. 'And I think that Jill could do with a feed too. By the way, I've checked those spots you mentioned and I think it's just nappy rash.'

Mrs Ball made a kind of explosive noise under her breath, which Mr Ball ignored.

'Thanks, Dad,' Michelle said. She reached for her feeding pillows. Then she hiked up her top, tucked a baby under each elbow, and breastfed both at the same time. It never ceased to amaze Jackie.

'Fair play to you,' she said.

'I know, but my boobs will never be the same again,' Michelle said happily.

'Well, I think you should go on to bottles,' Mr Ball said firmly. He had been reading up on his baby books. 'That way the rest of us can help out during the night feeds.'

Mrs Ball gave a disbelieving snort.

'Nobody's asking you,' Mr Ball told her piously. 'I meant me.'

'I wouldn't depend on it,' Mrs Ball murmured to Michelle. 'And anyway, at least if you're breastfeeding, it'll keep you off the drink and drugs.' After what she'd been through in the labour ward, there was no need to mention sex.

'I'm not going back on the drink and drugs, Mum.'

'You say that now. Sure you're still high from the epidural. And before they gave you that, I heard you had more than your fair share of gas. It's a slippery slope.'

Michelle ignored her, making little mammy noises to the twins – oohs and aahs and 'There, isn't that better!' The twins themselves were sucking and slurping to beat the band. Mr Ball watched over them, clucking benignly. Then Jill misplaced the nipple assigned to her, and cried, and everybody went, 'Oh dear!' before Michelle popped her back on.

It was like living in a crèche sometimes, Jackie thought. More than once she had got a pang of longing when she looked into the two little Moses baskets side by side in the kitchen. How lucky Michelle was! She was a mother now. She had her own little family. She belonged to someone.

Jackie felt rather weightless these days. As though nothing but her two flower shops were holding her down. Some evenings when she locked up and left, she almost felt like her life wouldn't start again until the following morning.

Which was silly. She had friends, a family, she was a brand new auntie. She had just joined a salsa class, for goodness' sake, even if it was only an excuse to buy a new pair of shoes.

But sometimes she wondered, rather dramatically, who would really miss her if she were gone. If her car inexplicably veered off the road and into a ditch, for example, in the dead of night. (She didn't know why the dead of night; but why mid-morning either?) Or if she touched that thick bunch of exposed wires the builders had left behind in the new branch, and that Emma said were probably harmless but could equally feed into the power supply for the whole city.

Of course people *would* miss her. But not the way they would if she were the centre of their lives.

Jackie wasn't the centre of anybody's life any more.

Maybe she was just too used to having a man, and had turned into one of those women who couldn't bear being single. But when she'd been with Dan, she hadn't really felt the centre of his life either.

And as for Henry, nobody could argue that the centre of his life had been anybody but himself. Jackie hadn't exactly felt treasured twenty-four hours a day. At the same time, no other relationship had ever had the same zing. Wouldn't it sicken you? They were divorced and yet she was thinking about him more than ever before. It was more than sickening. It was bizarre.

Some of her morbidity must have shown because Michelle asked that evening, 'Are you all right?'

'Me? Never better.'

'The babies aren't driving you mad?'

'No, no.' She added with bravado, 'I'll be moving out soon anyway. Finding a place of my own. Now that I'm single again.'

'Single but not yet divorced,' Michelle stated baldly.

'I beg your pardon?'

'Don't act the innocent with me. Velma Murphy rang here yesterday. You never went in to see her after cancelling that appointment.'

Oh! Jackie looked at her. 'And there you were, fooling all of us that you'd gone soft and mushy, and only able to speak in baby talk.'

'Just because I've become a mother doesn't mean I've lost half my brain.' Then she paused. 'I've forgotten what I was going to say. By the way, I highly recommend motherhood, if you ever manage to offload Henry and find someone else. Here, have a go.'

And she thrust Sabrina into Jackie's lap. Jackie had had several goes already, of course, but it was difficult with Mr Ball around as he tended to take over and nobody got a look in.

'She doesn't look a bit like Spanky,' Jackie marvelled.

'I know, isn't it great? I'm starting to think maybe he's not the father at all.'

'Michelle! You'd better tell him.'

'Why?' she said. 'He's quite reconciled to the whole thing now. Not to mention all that cash he's coughing up.' But she grew serious then, stroking Sabrina's soft bald head. 'I kind of like it this way. Just me and them, you know? With Spanky firmly on the sidelines. Do you remember I thought I'd never feel this way about anybody? And now I do. And I've got two of them.'

And I've got nobody, Jackie wanted to bawl. But she just clucked and nodded, and just when she thought Michelle had forgotten all about the divorce, she said, 'So. You and Henry. What's the hold-up, Jackie?'

'Come on, you know how busy I've been with the new shop. I haven't time to make a new appointment.' It was so feeble that her voice trailed off towards the end.

'It's one measly document you've got to sign, that's all.'

'All right,' Jackie admitted. 'Maybe I'm having a mental block. Signing makes it really, totally final. I suppose I just need a bit of time to get used to that.'

'You and Henry have been apart for two years now, Jackie. Don't tell me you've only just noticed.'

Put like that, it did sound a bit ridiculous. What *was* she hanging around for anyway?

'Jackie, do you still love him?'

'No. No!' She gave a little laugh. 'For goodness' sake, Michelle. I left him, remember?'

'Over an affair that didn't actually happen.'

Jackie felt quite cross now, and she said, 'It wasn't just that. There was other stuff. Lots of it.'

'And you can't fix that stuff?'

'I don't think so.'

'Even if you loved each other?'

'We don't. *I* don't. And I'm pretty sure he doesn't.'

'Even though he writes you incredibly mushy poetry? Personally it would make me puke, but I know you're a sucker for all that.'

'If he felt those things, why did he never tell me? Why does he go putting it in a newspaper at the time when we're getting divorced?'

'Maybe he needed to get them off his chest.'

'Sorry, am I supposed to applaud that?'

'No. I just mean, maybe he wanted you to know. Get it off his chest before you two finally said goodbye.'

Jackie declared, 'Anyway, it doesn't matter, because obviously he doesn't feel those things any more.'

'How do you know?'

Because he hadn't written her any more poems, for starters. She had checked every week. He appeared to have left the *Globe* completely. And then, last Sunday, there was a big splashy review of his new restaurant guide in the books section. No wonder he hadn't had time for her. He was too busy furthering his career.

She said, 'Because we're getting divorced, Michelle. And, for all his flowery poetry, he's not doing a single thing to stop me.'

'Yes,' said Michelle. 'That is a bit of a problem, all right.'

'A big problem. You know, for our entire marriage, I was guessing at how he feels. And here I am, doing it again. And I'm tired of it.'

'Would you not go and see him? Try and clarify things.'

'No.'

'Jackie, this is the last chance you'll get.'

It was tempting, God knew. For a number of reasons. And it would settle the thing one way or the other. Finally.

And wasn't she cut out for dashes across seas, dressed in glamorous high heels and recklessly open to dramatic possibilities involving men with dark hair and tortured eyes? And, even better, who wrote romantic poetry? Hadn't she been *born* for it? A headlong sprint into Henry's arms would be just up her street, and she could succumb to the romance of the moment whilst her hair simultaneously broke free from its clip. Oh, yes. She could see it all unfolding before her now as she pitched up outside his front door: a bloody disaster.

He would probably have to strive to put a face on her, for starters – especially with the new haircut. Then he would wonder – reasonably – what the hell she was doing in London instead of diligently applying herself to their divorce.

Worse, he might be amused. Imagine her reading so much into a few throwaway poems that he'd put in the paper for a bit of a lark!

Or, another possibility, the door could be opened not by Henry at all, but some willowy blonde called Penelope. Or Mandy, that old warhorse. Henry could have got himself a new girlfriend. Why not? He was a very attractive man, at least on the surface, and there would be no shortage of women stepping up to take her place. He might be waiting anxiously for the divorce to come through so that he himself could marry again.

But no, Jackie decided with a rush of relief; he was the kind of man who would never get married again. He would just tell put-down jokes about it to his mates in the pub and the like. Mandy, God love her, would wait in vain before he would ever pop the question again.

Or he could have meant the poems, and he might take her back.

And that was where the real problem lay. Because she didn't want to be taken back. She had done enough running after Henry Hart. Had thrown up everything for him. If she went over there now, it would be the same thing all over again. If he wanted her back, he would have to do more than eulogise anonymously in a newspaper. It was his turn now.

But he hadn't come after her the day she left two years ago. And there was no sign of him now, either.

'You know, you're right,' she said to Michelle.

'You'll go over to see him?'

'I mean about me dragging my heels.'

'Jackie, don't go doing anything impulsive now,' Michelle warned. And she after tackling her about it in the first place!

Jackie was suddenly tired of the whole thing. 'I'll do what I have to do,' she declared, in her best recovery programme voice. Emma would be proud of her.

Mrs Ball scuttled in with the news that a car was just pulling in.

'It's probably Gerard,' Michelle said cosily. Things had got civilised on that front altogether. He had taken to popping by a couple of times a week on his way home from sentencing murderers and extortionists, and he would coo over the babies, and change a nappy or two while Michelle made him a cup of tea. Tonight they were due to discuss private schools for the twins, which the judge would be paying for, naturally.

Even his wife had thawed somewhat, and let him put his name on the birth certificate. And there had been hardly any gossip or scandal amongst his legal colleagues at all, once the news got out. Justice West had kindly dropped by one evening to share photos of his own illegitimate toddler, and he must be seventy if he was a day.

There was even talk again of Michelle going back and finishing her law degree. Gerard said that he would spring for an au pair, and Mrs Ball said she just bet he would, but he told her he had only meant he would pay for one.

But Michelle said she didn't want to go back, and certainly not yet. And that she never thought she'd say it, but she wouldn't mind if she never saw a book or a triple vodka again, and that she was going to be a stay-at-home mum.

'It's not Gerard's car,' Mrs Ball worried, looking out the net curtains. Then she said, 'Oh, my goodness!' She turned to Jackie, her whole face lighting up in a beatific smile. 'It's Dan.'

It was like the return of the prodigal son. Mrs Ball took a pear tart out of the freezer specially, even though Dan insisted he wasn't staying long, and then she made Mr Ball go and take the lawnmower out of the garage and park it discreetly near Dan's car, in case he might feel like a turn about the garden before he left.

In the kitchen, she said to Jackie, 'Do something with your hair. And don't forget to mention that you've opened a second branch. That you're a woman of means now. I told Michelle to go in and talk to him about the divorce.'

'What?'

'Just to let him know that it's probably done and dusted. That you're just waiting on the final decree and then you're a free woman.' She was practically quivering with excitement as she hunted about in the fridge. 'Do you think that bottle of champagne would be off? The one we didn't finish after celebrating the birth of the twins?'

'Why would you want champagne?' Jackie said suspiciously.

Mrs Ball said, 'Well, it's obvious what he's here for.'

'And what exactly might that be?' She was curious herself.

'He's called round to give you another chance, Jackie!'

'Oh, *Mum*.'

'And don't give me that tale again about how you were going to finish with him, only he got there first. None of us believes it. Just thank your lucky stars that he came to his senses.'

'Stop. Please. And you've been doing so well lately, too.'

'You can't expect me to stop worrying at this stage of the game,' Mrs Ball said. She peered in at Dan. 'He's got on a very smart suit. And he smells of aftershave.'

Well, that was true, but there was no reason to suppose it was on Jackie's behalf.

'He's probably come round to give me back some of my things. Or to ask for his ring back or something.' She still had it. She had been going to give it to him that night in Le Bistro, but that was before she'd been dumped and humiliated.

'Nonsense,' Mrs Ball said. 'He's nervous. You can tell.'

Well, yes, but Jackie had put that down to the fright of meeting them all again. Could it be because of her?

Mrs Ball handed her the pear tart. 'It's still frozen in places. But I'm sure it'll thaw when the temperature goes up in there.'

'I can't believe you just said that.'

Mrs Ball giggled. 'I know, it's desperate. Oh, look, I don't really care whether you two make it up or not. Doesn't it give us all something to do.' And she pushed Jackie in the direction of the living room, hissing one final instruction: 'And whatever else you do, don't mention Henry.'

In the living room, Michelle was showing off the babies to him.

'Very nice,' Dan was saying. He looked up as Jackie walked in. He was definitely nervous.

'And they're surprisingly low maintenance at this age,' Michelle was going on. Honestly, give her any kind of platform at all. 'They only have three things on their minds: food, sleep and poos.'

Dan said, 'Interesting. Well, you never know. I might go down that route some day myself.' And he looked at Jackie again, searchingly. Sweet Lord. Could her mother be right?

'Michelle!' Mrs Ball chirped from the kitchen. 'Phone!'

The phone happened to be sitting silently on the coffee table in front of them all. It was all very embarrassing, but Michelle sighed, stood and went to the door.

She was back a moment later.

'Sorry. I forgot one of them.' And she scooped up Sabrina and went out again. The door was closed very firmly.

Jackie gave Dan a wry smile, and said, 'My mother thinks that you want to be alone with me. She has this notion in her head that you want us to get back together.'

He smiled back. 'I don't.'

'I know you don't.' Well, she had hoped, a bit. All right, she'd have loved it! She'd have wallowed in him begging her for another chance, just for the satisfaction of telling him no. No, no, no!

She must have let some of this show on her face, and looked a bit tortured, because he burst out, 'God, Jackie, I'm sorry. The last thing I wanted to do was come around here tonight and hurt you more!'

'You haven't. You didn't hurt me the first time, OK? I swear! I'm perfectly OK with us not being together any more.' But now she just sounded in total denial, and so she abandoned her defence altogether and said, 'Pear tart?'

'Yes, please. I love your mother's pear tart.'

Out of spite, she cut him a tiny piece and handed it to him on a saucer.

'So!' she said, now that her mother's hopes had been well and truly quashed. 'How are the Fionas?'

'Very well, thank you.' He offered no platitudes about them sending on their regards. Jackie didn't pretend to send hers back, either.

'And Taig and Big Connell and . . . ?' She couldn't remember any of the rest of their names, and didn't even try. Well, she could hardly be expected to, now that he hadn't come here to prostrate himself at her feet.

'Fine, fine.' He wasn't interested in talking about his brothers either. He finished his pear tart and cleared his throat. 'Jackie, I've a bit of news for you. I wanted you to hear it from me rather than from somebody else.'

Words to strike fear and dread into the heart of any ex-fiancée. Words to heap triumphalism upon humiliation.

He had found someone else.

But she kept smiling serenely – otherwise he would think she was devastated – and said, 'Oh?'

He said, 'I'm getting married.'

A double whammy! Talk about rubbing salt into the triumphalism that had just been heaped upon the humiliation. And she didn't even care about him any more. Imagine if her heart had been truly broken four months ago!

'Well!' she said. Dan waited. 'I suppose congratulations are in order.' Mrs Ball would get to crack open the flat champagne after all, but not for the reason she thought.

'Really?' he said, tentative.

'Really.'

'You don't mind?'

'I don't mind, Dan.'

'Honestly?'

'Honestly,' she said, through gritted teeth.

But, now that she thought about it, he had a right cheek, taking it upon himself to 'do the right thing' and tell her in person. That kind of news was most definitely better heard from somebody else, preferably someone sympathetic who would join in a bitching session about how indecently quick it all was, and that it was doomed to failure from the very start, and that he was a right chump.

But now she was forced to digest such startling news right in front of him, over her mother's pear tart, with no warning at all.

'Who's the lucky lady?' She added a sardonic twist to the lucky lady bit, but he didn't get it, of course.

He beamed and said proudly, 'Yvonne Toomey.'

Plain, thought Jackie bitchily. 'I don't think I've had the pleasure . . . ?'

'You have,' Dan assured her. 'She was the policewoman who came to the house that day about the assault on Henry.' He added hastily, 'Not that we got together back then, of course.'

Jackie was less upset by the revelation that the woman had actually been in her house than by the way Henry's name tripped off his tongue with total carelessness and ease. And to think that the same man had arranged to have him beaten up! Dan was, Jackie decided, superficial.

'I see,' she said. 'Does she dress up in her uniform for you?'

'Well, obviously she would be wearing it when she comes home from work . . .' Then he realised what she had meant, and he looked at her, surprised and hurt. That Jackie, normally so bubbly and nice, would have a nasty go at him like that!

She was sorry then. There was no point in being horrible. Dan was a good guy, and it wasn't his fault that she didn't love him any more. He could have waited a bit before hooking up with someone else, though.

'So when's the big day?' she enquired nicely.

'April,' he said. 'Maybe you might like to come.' He paused. 'Or is that a really stupid thing to say?'

'It's a really stupid thing to say,' she assured him.

'Sorry,' he said humbly.

'Let's stop all this, Dan. I'm pleased for you, OK? It just seems very soon, that's all.'

She shouldn't have given him any encouragement, because he burst out, 'I know! I said that to Yvonne. I said, I don't want to make a balls of this by rushing in, like I did the last time. I said, maybe we should wait a bit. Take things slowly. Make absolutely sure that we're right for each other. But she wasn't having any of it. One night she said that she would arrest me if I didn't propose and, well, that settled it!'

He blushed. Jackie felt a bit queasy

'I hope it all goes well for you,' she said, hoping to bring the conversation to a natural close.

But he leaned forward eagerly. 'We have so much in common, Jackie. Like running, for one. She's very sporty, Yvonne. She trains for her job, obviously – she out-ran a robber last week – and she's a member of the boating club and at weekends we get up early and go for twenty-mile runs in the countryside.'

'Lovely,' Jackie murmured. She looked at her watch.

'We're thinking of training for the London marathon together. But we were worried about it clashing with our wedding plans, obviously. Then Yvonne had this brilliant idea of getting married right after the marathon, so that we would actually be running to our own wedding! She's a trouper.'

His eyes had grown misty during all this. And Jackie realised that he had finally found his soul mate. The woman of his dreams. Someone to get sweaty with, and wear matching sports clothing, and raise a brood of muscular kids in the outdoors.

'Good luck to you, Dan,' she said. 'I really mean that.'

'Thanks, Jackie.' He stood, and patted himself down. 'I'd better go. I'm meeting Yvonne. We're telling her parents tonight.'

'Lovely,' she said. 'Anyway, I'm sure my mother would be delighted to show you out.' While she ran upstairs to rage over the fact that *she* hadn't got engaged again. Life just wasn't fair.

But Dan lingered. 'Would you tell Henry that I'm sorry? You know, for having him beaten up. It's been on my mind.'

She looked at him. 'What makes you think I'm in contact with Henry?'

'Sorry, I just assumed . . .'

'You assumed what? That once you and I broke up, I wouldn't bother divorcing him?' What did he take her for?

'So you *are* divorced then?'

'No, not quite,' she was forced to admit. At the look on his face, she added loudly, 'There's just one final thing to do. To put the seal on it, so to speak.'

He nodded. 'I hope things work out for you, Jackie.'

Why didn't he just pat her sympathetically on the back and assure her that, in time, she would meet some man as sad and lonely and desperate as her?

'Thank you, Dan,' she said, a little tightly.

'Because you deserve it, you know,' he said fervently.

'Shouldn't you be leaving? You don't want to keep Yvonne's parents waiting.'

At this, he blanched a bit, looked at his watch, said, 'God, no,' and jogged out.

Chapter Twenty-Three

For months now, Velma Murphy had found herself at the centre of a conflict of interests. On the one hand, her professional services had been engaged by Jackie Ball to kick Henry Hart's butt. On the other hand, she was having rampant sex every weekend with his solicitor. Despite trawling through her American law course website, she could find no get-out clause or extenuating circumstance. Even her own conscience, when consulted, would give her no relief.

She had to face it: sleeping with the opposition was just plain wrong.

Tom knew it too. 'I could be fired for this,' he had muttered into the folds of her neck only two nights ago, his bony knees digging into hers. Obviously she herself was in no danger of getting fired, and the fact that he was risking everything for her made her feel very warm and full.

He called her Peaches. He said she was like a ripe fruit with the softest skin he had ever known. He said that she smelled like honey, and that her voice made the hairs stand up on the back of his neck. He said he couldn't sleep properly unless she was beside him.

'I'm not a fool, you know,' she had barked at him in the beginning. The extravagance of his statements naturally made her suspicious.

But the idea that he might be spinning her a line seemed preposterous to him. Besides, his hushed, meek voice lent his flowery statements a seriousness that she couldn't dismiss.

At first she consented to let him come over every second weekend. She had enough bitter experience behind her, her own and other people's, to know that such great beginnings often didn't last. Soon he was flying over every weekend. He would stay at the Holiday Inn and they would walk by the canal and go out to dinner where Velma would eat him under the table, and talk about law. She found him very knowledgeable, and sincere and normal, if a little lacking in self-esteem. By and by, she found her belligerence deserting her. It was a relief.

One night she invited him back to her house, and let him take her clothes off. If he were a fat freak she'd be able to tell at once. But there was little evidence of weirdness of any kind. He had just taken her in his long, gangly arms, and she hadn't looked back since.

The only thing stopping them now was Jackie Ball. Velma's client. Who at that moment was sitting on the other side of Velma's desk.

Velma flashed her a guilty smile. 'For a few weeks there I thought you were getting cold feet.' The damned woman had held them up for nearly five weeks longer than necessary.

'Me? Oh, no. I've just been very busy with the new shop, that's all.'

That was an excuse if Velma ever heard one. She had been up half the night agonising over this final step, if the rings under her eyes were anything to go by. But she played along. 'And how's it going for you?'

'Very well. In fact, much better than we thought. After a slow start, we can hardly keep up!'

'Good, good,' Velma said, scarcely listening. She had the necessary form, the D36, ready and waiting. Plus a note of her fees. She never liked to wind things up completely until those were settled in full. In her experience, people with broken hearts were extremely grateful for any help she might give in dispatching their other halves at the time, but that tended to diminish rapidly once the deed was done, and bills were sent out. And often queried. And sometimes not paid.

'So!' she told Jackie. She was dizzy at the thought of getting rid of her. Semi-delirious at the prospect of openly getting it together with Tom. 'Here we are. The final step. The application for the decree absolute.' Then, just in case Jackie might be turned off by gloomy legalisms, she kept her voice nice and chirpy, like the people in Burger King. 'As I've already explained to you, the decree nisi which was issued two months ago is only a provisional licence, so to speak. To let everybody have a bit of a test drive, if I might continue the metaphor! Find out if divorce is really for them.' Damn, she didn't want Jackie to think there was a choice. 'Which of course it is. Why go this far only to change your mind, I say! Now, to make a divorce legally binding, you, the petitioner, must apply to the courts for the decree absolute. Then, and only then, will you and Henry Hart be divorced.'

'OK,' Jackie said calmly.

Velma relaxed even more. This one was going to be easy. Probably Jackie was quite glad to be finally rid of Henry Hart. Who was actually quite a decent chap underneath it all, Tom had told her. But that was strictly pillow talk, of course, and she must not let on that she knew anything more than she should. Oh, the pressure. She was terrified she would let something slip. She couldn't wait to be shot of this case. Then she and Tom could bonk with impunity.

Tom had urged her to tell Jackie. Confess. Tell her she could no longer represent her and that she would have to go to another solicitor.

He could talk! In that big swanky firm of his in London! Velma had been rather chastened when she'd discovered the illustriousness of his employer, and reluctant to confess her own meagre circumstances. The simple fact was that she needed Jackie Ball's money.

'Where do I have to sign?' Jackie asked, calm. Velma admired her.

'Just there. But read it first. I want to be sure that you understand it.' And that she settled her account, of course.

'It seems fine,' Jackie said, without undue hesitation, or a worrying pause.

Velma felt better and better. Tom was arriving in on a flight tonight. She could meet him at arrivals, brazenly, instead of the prearranged dark place on the third floor of parking block B.

'Good,' she confided cosily, as she hunted about for her bill, 'because sometimes people lose the run of themselves. They start getting all sentimental over their ex, remembering all their finer points, all their endearing little quirks. Never mind the fact that they might have smashed the patio doors in a fit of temper, or refused to do an honest day's work in their lives. I've had people sit there, crying, telling me that suddenly they can't stop thinking about how their ex used to make them howl with laughter with his Bruce Forsyth impersonations.' She shook her head in disgust. 'My motto is, once a scumbag, always a scumbag. Divorce them and get them the hell out of your life.'

'He's not a scumbag,' Jackie contradicted her politely. 'Henry.'

Velma saw that she had gone too far. 'Of course not,' she said hastily. 'I was just using an example, that's all.' Hastily, she laid her bill on top of the D36. 'That includes VAT.'

But Jackie didn't really scrutinise it. Not that Velma would have minded; it was a fair bill in her opinion and she hadn't resorted to skilfully inflating her expenses, as suggested by her American online law course.

Jackie just reached for her chequebook. Velma felt she should say something to wrap things up. Something cheerful. 'Well, I suppose I'll see you at the wedding!'

That didn't quite get the response she anticipated.

'Dan and I aren't together any more.'

'Oh! Sorry, I didn't mean to . . .' But then she realised she wasn't a bit surprised. Talk about a lack of chemistry! She'd have given them two years, tops, before Jackie Ball would have been back in her office looking to offload number two.

'It's fine. I probably should have told you.' She gave Velma a little smile. 'I'm not having much luck with men at the moment as you can see.'

Velma found herself blurting out, 'You're the nicest client I've ever had. I mean it. And you deserve someone good. I'm sure he's out there right now just waiting for you.'

It was highly unusual for her to be so ebullient − being in love had softened her brain − but Jackie just looked rather sceptical and reached forward to sign the D36.

'Is that it?' she said.

'That's it.'

She felt very strange walking out of Velma's office and into the street afterwards. A bit dislocated or something. She supposed she *was* dislocated, from Henry to be precise, and it all felt a bit odd even though she hadn't clapped eyes on him in over two years now. The law was all that had bound them together, but now that it was gone too she felt as if a gust of wind would blow her away.

She wondered should she go and get drunk or something. Isn't that what people did? Sit at some bar and drown out the memories. But it was only three o'clock in the afternoon and if she started drinking

306

now she'd be on her ear by teatime. Still, it was obvious that something very momentous had just happened to her. It was the last week in November and she had just got divorced. And she didn't know whether to laugh or cry.

And so she just stood there, on the pavement outside Velma's, lost and forlorn and with her hair blowing in her eyes.

'My God,' Dave chortled. 'Is this yours?'

He held up a nylon T-shirt emblazoned with a picture of the Bay City Rollers.

Henry snatched it from him. 'It was a very long time ago, OK? Look, why don't you go over to the bookshelf there and pack those books, and leave the clothes to me.'

Dave had already sniggered over Henry's collection of Christmas jumpers, and the wetsuit and snorkel he'd bought during his brief flirtation with water sports.

'You have too much stuff,' Dave complained. 'Do you never throw anything out?'

The answer to that was obvious, judging by the piles of bin bags and boxes already stacked up in the hall downstairs. The removal van was due to arrive at ten – an indecently early hour, he'd be barely up, never mind packed. He'd had to resort to an early morning SOS call to Dave and Dawn to come over and help.

Dawn was downstairs tackling the kitchen, and from the look on her face earlier, she had clearly discovered that it hadn't been cleaned in quite some time. But she hadn't complained; just asked Henry a couple of times if he was OK. Like moving house was a big deal or something! All right, so he might have lived there for ten years, but he would be just as happy in his new, white, modern and utterly characterless apartment on the other side of the city. And Shirley would enjoy her time in the kennels until he got something sorted for her; it would, he assured himself, be like a little vacation for her.

'Porn!' Dave exclaimed in delight over by the bookcase. For two pins now Henry would chuck him out. He was like a vulture, picking over the debris of other people's lives. Actually, there might be a poem in that.

'It's erotica,' he said, taking the book from him and putting it in a box.

'Listen, nobody's judging you,' Dave said sympathetically. 'I suppose you had to, after Jackie left.'

'You couldn't resist bringing her up, could you?' As though he hadn't been thinking of her all morning. Every drawer he opened, he found bits of her. Why hadn't he had the wit to pack up her stuff properly after she had gone and send it on? At least five boxes in the hall below were full of her things. What was he supposed to do with them now? Bring them with him? To his new apartment where he was supposed to be starting a whole new life? At the same time he didn't want to throw them into a skip, although some of those outfits certainly deserved it. Not to mention that single earring he'd found under the bed: two miniature dice suspended from a gold chain. It would be a kindness to humanity to throw it onto a bonfire.

'Here, will you take Jackie's stuff?' he implored Dave.

'What? No.'

'Come on. You have heaps of room in your garage.'

'I do not.'

'Your attic then.'

'No! Dawn would kill me. She'll say I shouldn't get involved.'

'Don't tell her.'

'And what if she goes up there and finds bags full of women's clothes? I could get thrown out.'

'She'd know they were Jackie's. Most of it is pretty unforgettable.'

'Does it matter what you do with them?' Dave ventured. 'I mean, she's managed without them for two years now. She probably doesn't want them back any more.' He didn't say, and she's moved on and opened a second branch and she's getting remarried as soon as she divorces you, mate. He didn't need to, Henry thought. And if he made any more fuss over her things, it would look like he hadn't moved on too. Which he had. Yes, sirree. In a couple hours' time he would be ensconced in his new pad, which, handily enough, was on the top floor and so he could call it a writer's garret to all his friends.

It sounded so lonely that he'd be ringing the Samaritans in a matter of days.

'Are you all right?' Dave asked.

'Would everybody stop asking me if I'm all right? I've got a book in the top five nonfiction bestsellers, thanks very much.' It was a smart-arse thing to say, but it covered his feelings nicely. And it was also true. Adrienne was beside herself. 'Number three this week, darling; number one next week!' How she could predict that was anybody's guess. He made a mental note not to give her his new address.

'The *Globe* want you back,' Dave told him now.

'I just bet they do.' Adrienne had already told him. Oh, they come running, now he was hot again. So it was with a great sense of satisfaction that he said, 'Well, you can tell them to bog off. I'm a poet now.'

'And don't we all know it.' Then he said, 'Hey! That rhymes! Maybe I can be a poet too.'

'Just get on with the packing.'

'You could do a guest slot with the paper. I could float it past them.'

'I haven't got time for a guest slot,' Henry sniffed. For one thing, the greetings card company was putting together their Valentine's Day collection and Henry had "Roses Are Red" coming out of his ears. And they didn't pay any more for the schmaltzy stuff, either. He was seriously considering changing greetings card companies. Heck, he was good enough to try out for Hallmark!

And his poetry book was coming along fantastically too. Well, after some spirited discussions with the editor over the tone. That man wanted everything to be funny and light. In the end Henry had had to concede defeat on several of his darker pieces. The editor had buttered him up a bit by saying that he could be one of the freshest voices in poetry today, if he could just keep his self-indulgence in check. Henry knew that was just flattery but had skipped around the kitchen all the same in his socks shouting, 'I'm fresh, I'm fresh.'

'*The Complete Guide To Self-Hypnosis,*' Dave said, looking at another book.

'That's Jackie's.'

'Oh, yeah. Figures. Will I pack it or . . . ?'

'Chuck it out,' Henry said without hesitation. Even if he were still desperately in love with Jackie – which of course he wasn't – he would never keep a book like that.

Dave threw it in the bin. 'I think I'm done here.'

Henry had finished packing his clothes, too. They looked around.

'It looks kind of empty, doesn't it?' Dave said.

'That's because it *is* empty.'

'Here, you know the way they say houses have a memory? You can tell by the air what happened in them? I wonder if the people moving in here today will be able to sense what went on in here.'

'Nobody got murdered, Dave. Me and Jackie, we just split up, that's all. Jesus! If nobody moved into a house where a couple had split up, there would be empty houses all over London! All over the fucking country!'

'All right, calm down.'

Dawn appeared. She said to Dave sternly, 'Are you putting your foot in it again?' She was very protective of Henry today. He basked in it, as Dave squirmed.

'No! I was just saying—'

'The removal van is here,' she cut in. 'Go down and help load it.'

Dave went off, chastened. Dawn turned to Henry.

He said, 'Before you ask, I'm all right.'

She smiled. 'I was just going to say that, contrary to what Dave said, I always thought you and Jackie had some really happy moments in this house.'

'Thanks.' Ridiculously, he felt all choked up. Maybe this moving house thing was more emotional than he had thought.

'And secondly,' she said, 'I think you may have to throw out the fridge. That mould is just not coming off. And you're a qualified chef!'

'Sorry,' he said meekly.

'I'll take care of it,' she promised him.

He looked after her as she went. Caring *and* practical! That idiot Dave didn't know when he had it good.

Neither did Henry. He, too, had had a wonderful woman under his nose all that time and he was too busy trying to 'find himself' to notice. And now that he had actually found himself, she was gone to another man.

Not that she would want him any more anyway. A penniless poet whose glamorous circle of friends had abandoned him so fast that it almost hurt? A guy with no house or car, and who would sometimes cook up the odd batch of lentils when money was tight?

He still had his looks though, he consoled himself. For another year or two anyway. If he didn't drink too much.

'Henry!' Dave shouted up the stairs. 'The removal guys want to know if the mantelpiece is free-standing or whether it's just broken away from the wall.'

'Coming!' Henry shouted back.

He took one last look around the room. The best moments of their marriage had been spent here, right in the middle of that big double bed. He wondered if Dave was right; if houses had such things as a memory, or ghosts, or whatever you liked to call it. If so, then this room would have Jackie's laughter (they had done nearly all their fighting downstairs).

He stood very still, listening. Then the hairs rose on his neck: was that a faint, tinkling noise in the air? High-pitched and squeaky, like Jackie's voice?

Then he realised the noise was coming from his trousers. It was his mobile phone, set on that stupid ring tone that he couldn't get rid of.

'Hello?'

'Henry? It's Tom.' The guy still spoke so low that you had to stop breathing just to hear him. 'I didn't ring the landline in case you'd moved already.'

'Nope! Still here.' Best to sound very jolly in case Tom too asked him whether he was all right. That just might push him over the edge and he would crumple to the floor in floods of tears or something equally embarrassing.

'I won't detain you long if you're trying to pack.' He was quite purposeful on the phone these days, as though somebody had told him to buck up, that he wasn't such a geek after all. Possibly a girlfriend? But no, thought Henry. That would be too far-fetched.

'What's up?' he asked.

'I just wanted to let you know that I've just had a phone call from Jackie's solicitor. That Velma, um, what's her name, it's on the tip of my tongue . . .'

He could never seem to remember her name these days, Henry had noticed. He always suffered from some elaborate forgetfulness.

'Murphy,' Henry said.

'Ah! That's it. Anyway, apparently the application for decree absolute has finally been signed this morning.'

Henry's stomach did a little flip. He didn't know why; he'd known this would happen. But as the weeks went by he had managed to push it to the back of his mind and had almost come to believe that it would never happen. He and Jackie would remain partially divorced, which he found quite comforting, actually. It was like having a little safety net.

Tom was going on, 'About time too, I said, to Miss, um, Murphy. They could have applied for it weeks ago! Anyhow, the courts will take a couple of days to process it once they receive it. But then you'll be free.'

That soon? He had thought the wheels of bureaucracy turned a bit more bloody slowly than that.

'Oh,' he said. Then he rallied. 'Great. Fantastic. Thanks, Tom.'

'I thought you might be pleased all right.'

Henry irrationally thought, how the fuck did he think that? It wasn't like he'd been bugging the guy every second day on the phone looking for his divorce! Or going around with a big smile of anticipation on his face. Jesus, he hadn't seen him in four months and suddenly he was an expert on Henry's feelings?

Tom ventured, 'Are you all—'

'If you ask me whether I'm all right, I'll hang up on you, OK?'

There was a startled pause. 'OK.'

Henry tempered himself. There was no sense in taking things out on Tom. Particularly as his bill would arriving fairly swiftly in the post and Henry had no money to pay it. Oh, why couldn't Valentine's Day be twice a year? 'So, that's it? There's nothing more to do?'

'No. I suppose it's goodbye then. And thanks for being my very first client.'

'No problem.' He hoped he wasn't going to get all sentimental on him.

'And you're absolutely sure about not proceeding with a civil suit against her ex? It's not too late. And I really could do with a bit of litigation practice.'

'No,' Henry said firmly. Then he said, 'Her ex?'

'Yes. Dan Lewis.'

'I know who he is. I just didn't know they weren't engaged any more.'

He waited for Tom to say that he'd made a mistake; that it was a slip of the tongue in the middle of all this divorce talk. But he didn't. 'I just found out myself this morning. Anyway, we'll be sending you out our bill at the end of the month.'

'I look forward to it.'

He stood there, motionless, after hanging up. His brain had gone into some kind of lockdown mode, and if anybody were to ask him afterwards what he had been thinking, he would have had to say, truthfully, hot dogs. But probably something very profound was happening at subconscious level, because the next thing he knew he was gathering his coat and hunting frantically for his wallet.

Dave puffed in. He had a hammer in his hand. 'I can't get that mantelpiece off the wall.'

'Yeah, listen, I'm going to have to leave you in charge here, OK?' Henry said, checking himself in the mirror. He'd let his beard grow back a bit, out of laziness. But there was no time to shave now. And a quick sniff under his armpits told him the situation wasn't great there either.

'What?' said Dave, alarmed.

'Just give the removal guys the address and the keys of the new place. I'm sure they can take it from there.'

'You're going *out?*'

'Yeah. Oh, have you any money?'

'A couple of hundred, but I need that for—'

'Thanks, that'll do.'

'Henry! What the fuck is going on?'

Emotionally, Henry grabbed him in a bear hug. 'You're the best, do you know that, Dave?' he said into his chest. Then he flung him aside and hurried out.

Chapter Twenty-Four

Emma had ironed her most severe brown blouse that morning, and wore it with matching trousers, and a pair of flat, brown, sensible shoes. There wasn't a hair out on place on her freshly washed and ruthlessly blow-dried head. No jewellery or scarf alleviated her severity, or a smile either for that matter. Underneath all that brown, her heart did a calm, sixty-two beats to the minute. Morticia Adams would have been afraid of her.

The shop door *pinged* at exactly eleven o'clock. She lifted her small, brown head from the accounts.

Lech stood there. He wore a flash suit, a tie, and an expression as sombre as hers.

'You're late,' she said.

'I am not. You said eleven.' He consulted his Rolex. Emma noted.

'I said five to. I go on my coffee break at eleven.'

She waited for the implication of this to sink in. It did. He grew more wary and watchful.

'So I've got five minutes?'

'Four now.'

He said, 'You are something else. You ring me up at midnight last night and order me to come to the shop—'

'I asked you to come to the shop. You didn't have to.'

'And then you tell me I've got five minutes?' He gave her a cynical look. 'Well, I am sorry to disappoint, but as you know, I take a bit longer than that.'

Oh! She felt herself redden but didn't change expression.

He said, 'So where do you want to do it? On the counter? The back room? Or maybe go back to your place?'

'Lech, I invited you here this morning to talk.'

'You want to talk? Well, that's a first.'

She ignored that. 'As a concerned friend.'

'And since when have you been my friend?' he burst out. 'Friends stay in contact! They phone each other, they support and help each other. You, Emma, have done none of those things. All you have done is bleed me dry!'

Her heartbeat accelerated a notch. But she couldn't get involved in an ex-lover's tiff. Not when there were serious matters at stake.

'Then that's my fault, Lech,' she said quietly. 'And I apologise. Maybe if I *had* been more of a friend, you wouldn't be in the mess you're in now.'

He looked confused. 'What?'

'Well, look at you!'

'What is wrong with me?' He checked his fly, just in case.

'That car parked outside, the suit, the sunglasses . . . what's happened to you, Lech?'

He squared his shoulders defensively. 'I got a new job, that is all.'

'What sort of a job?'

'A good job.'

She waited for him to go on but he didn't. 'Delivering stuff?'

'Yes.'

'What kind of deliveries do you do where you can afford a car like that?'

'I don't have to tell you that.' Look at him, shifty as anything!

'Stop it, Lech. I know exactly what you're involved in!' Her heartbeat was way up there now, but she scarcely noticed. 'The minute Jackie told me, I guessed. No guy could go from delivering pizzas and flowers to driving a limo in four months flat. Unless they were involved in something shady. You're a drug dealer, aren't you!'

'A drug dealer?' He looked completely incredulous, but she supposed he had perfected the innocent look from having to lie all the time to the Drugs Squad.

'Admit it,' she said.

'I will admit nothing of the sort,' he said lamely.

'Is that it?' she said. 'That's your defence?'

He seemed to shrink a bit under his expensive suit. And she felt any illusions she might have had about him – and there were hardly any, in fairness – shatter.

'Not such a big hotshot now, are you?' she said bitterly. 'What do you do then? The Dublin to Warsaw run? With your boot piled high with . . .' She had to think of a drug quickly. 'Cocaine!' Phew.

'No.'

'Heroin then.' She hoped she wouldn't be forced to list too many more, because after hash, she would be clean out. When he didn't answer, she said, 'For a guy who likes to talk, you're very quiet today, Lech.'

He looked at her and said, 'I am trying to decide which is better. To let you think I'm a drug dealer, or to tell you what I really do.'

So he wasn't a drug dealer. The relief. But she maintained her severe demeanour and said, 'The truth, please.'

'You see, stupidly, I was trying to impress you,' he said. 'By letting Jackie think I was a businessman. That you would see that I wasn't a delivery boy any more and maybe I would have a chance. Because it's very obvious that I am not good enough for you. You want a man of substance. Of means, of class, of refinement. And so I thought this way I could be what you wanted.' He looked her straight in the eye. 'The car, it's not mine. It belongs to someone else. I drive him around.'

Emma went still. 'You're a chauffeur?'

'That's right. So you see, I am still a delivery boy, Emma. I drive a guy who owns twenty-two branches of Pound Universe around his shops. Very classy, eh? But at least my car is better.' He held up his wrist. 'And my Rolex? It's fake, it's from one of his shops. I bet you'll get a kick from that. You will say to Jackie, that is just so Lech!'

'Lech . . .'

'No.' He held a hand up. 'And now that I have explained myself to you, Emma, now that I have humiliated myself in front you for the last time, I am going. Have a nice life. You will not see me again.' He buttoned up his suit jacket dramatically, and gave her a curt nod. Then he turned and walked to the door.

Watching him go, Emma agonised. Engaged in a fierce battle against her reason. Dug her fingernails into the counter, and curled up her toes in anguish.

Then, just as he reached the door, she blurted out, 'I was afraid you were going to be shot!'

Lech stopped.

'Or stabbed. Or have parts of you cut off and stuffed down your throat. I read the papers, you know! I know what can happen to drug dealers when a deal goes sour!'

He turned round. His face was full of wonder.

She was immediately sorry she'd said anything. Talk about making a fool of yourself.

'Anyway. It's immaterial now. You're not a drug dealer. So! Have a nice day.'

'You care,' he said.

'Not really.'

'You were worried about me.'

'All right, so I was! Do we have to make a song and dance about it?'

'My lovely Emma.'

'I knew you'd get like this. All mushy and romantic and . . .'

But then he was putting his arms round her, and she was letting him, and pressing her face tight to the front of his new Armani suit, which she realised was fake too. He still smelled of cheap aftershave, she was glad to find. When Jackie had come back with tales of his riches and importance, she had been sure that he would lose all his rough edges. Successful people often did. And she had feared that he would become smooth and practised, and would stop making appalling style gaffes, and that women would begin falling at his feet. Women much more attractive and exciting than she was, and he would forget all about her in a matter of weeks. Thank God he hadn't changed!

'This is just sex. You know that, don't you?' she said into his chest gruffly.

'It is not,' he said happily.

'We're not getting married or anything.'

'Not yet anyway,' he said. 'You haven't even met my family.'

'What?'

'We will go to Poland straightaway,' he declared. He looked at her.

'I should tell you, they were hoping I would marry a nice Polish girl. So don't be upset if they think you're not good enough. We will talk them around.'

'Oh!' She was sure he was winding her up, just to get back at her. But he looked perfectly serious.

'Will we close the shop for five minutes?' he said.

'Make it ten,' she said.

Henry had got a seat on a Heathrow-to-Dublin flight at an exorbitant rate, and the worst seat too, right on the wing and sandwiched between a guy who reeked of garlic and a woman who kept blessing herself as though the plane would fall out of the sky at any moment. As if he wasn't nervous enough.

'In-flight magazine, sir?' the flight attendant asked him.

'Not unless you sell courage!' he said jovially. He had meant it as an intriguing little joke to lighten the atmosphere, but the flight attendant's face went flat and he could see her thinking, oh Christ, another weirdo.

'No, thank you,' he added primly. He would have buried himself in shame behind a newspaper except that he couldn't afford one after paying for the flight. He still remembered those terrible words at the sales desk: 'Return or single, sir?'

'Sorry?'

'Would you like a return ticket, or a single?'

'Yes, it's just it's kind of complicated, I'm actually sort of . . .' What? Holding out in the wild hopes that his wife – ex-wife now, he had to keep reminding himself – might take his impromptu visit in the spirit in which it was intended and say, 'Stay for ever, darling!' before wrapping her milky thighs around him?

'Return, please.'

'And when will you be coming back?'

'Probably today,' he admitted.

Earlier, adrenaline had borne him all the way across town on the tube and out to Heathrow. There, he had skipped along the polished floors, wild hope beating in his breast. Reality had only begun to bite at the ticket desk, and the conundrum of single or return. Then, the embarrassing search at security, all because he was a lone beardy man,

319

and all those probing questions about the purpose of his journey and why he had no luggage.

'I'm on business,' he lied.

'Where?'

He was going to say IBM or the Central Bank. Then he realised he was wearing sandals. So did they.

'All right. You've got me. The truth is I'm still in love with my ex-wife and I'm going to see if she'll take me back.'

The two big beefy security guys looked at each other, and immediately waved him through, muttering, 'Go on, mate. Good luck.'

Then the agonising wait in departures, when the folly of the entire idea came home to him at last. What kind of madness had possessed him to leave his packing, in pursuit of a woman who had gleefully divorced him that very morning? Well, maybe not gleefully, but surely with a sense of purpose? And satisfaction? In fact, why *not* glee! She could have laughed her way through every minute of it.

By the time his flight was called, he was absolutely positive she was at that very moment throwing a wild, celebratory party where dozens of mad, drunk women were setting fire to an effigy of him, and screaming, 'Down with men!'

And now, here he was, captive on a flight across the skies to a woman who very likely detested his guts.

He would go to a museum or something, he decided. Spend a few hours there before catching his flight back. Or maybe just stay in the airport. Surely he'd find something to eat in one of the bins, and people were always leaving discarded newspapers around. And he would tell Dave and Dawn that he had no memory whatsoever of this day, and that he must have suffered some kind of amnesia due to the trauma of moving house. No one need ever know of his foolishness except for himself.

And he always had poetry, he told himself. He could spend all those long lonely years ahead writing odes to Jackie, and he would eventually have them published in a collection calling them Odes to Tammy or something so as not to raise her suspicions and at the modest launch he would cut a lonely and tragic figure and everybody would wonder who Tammy was.

The captain's voice crackled into the cabin. 'If you could fasten your seatbelts, please.'

Great. The plane was going to crash now. Talk about the worst luck in the world. Jackie needn't have gone to the bother of divorcing him after all; they'd be fishing bits of him out of the sea for the next three weeks.

But no. The captain informed them that they would be landing shortly, and he wished everybody a happy onwards journey.

Fat chance, Henry thought, wondering if he had enough money for a coffee at the airport. He could eke it out for the next seven hours.

He found eighty-seven pence, and Jackie's dice earring he'd discovered under the bed earlier. He must have put it in his pocket instead of the bin.

He turned it over in his hand. An appalling breach of taste, certainly, but then he saw that the little dice had identical numbers facing up at him: two sixes.

Jackie would say it was an omen. Henry knew it was just whatever way they had been lying in his trouser pocket. But he had come this far on fantasy and wishful thinking; what was so wrong with letting fashion accessories lead him the rest of the way?

There was a rerun of a hospital drama on the telly. It was a particularly tragic one, as befitted Jackie's mood that afternoon.

'I'm sorry, but I just don't think she's going to make it.'

'But Dr Raymondo, I thought you said you'd removed all the bullets?'

'Yes, but we couldn't do much about the head injury.'

'She's got to pull through! We've got seven children.'

Just then another doctor rushed in.

'Dr Raymondo. She's flat-lining!'

I know exactly how she feels, Jackie thought, sobbing softly into a tissue. Except for the bullets and the head injury and the seven kids, of course.

It was ten past two in the afternoon and she was sitting with the curtains pulled and a large tub of Ben & Jerry's on her lap. But luckily she had on her massive elasticated tracksuit bottoms and would easily be able to fit in that giant bar of Cadbury's she was saving till later.

She had phoned Emma and told her she couldn't face going back into work after Velma's. But Emma must have been coming down with wreaths, because Jackie's call had gone straight to answerphone and she'd had to leave a message. Or maybe she'd had to go over to the new shop; Daphne, the new florist, hadn't quite found her feet yet.

Jackie lustily blew her nose, and had another spoon of ice cream. Imagine feeling this bad! Really, she should be out painting the town red instead of sitting in a darkened room watching Dr Raymondo give heart massage to some poor creature on a blood-splattered table, and screaming, 'Bag her!' to a nurse.

'Did she pull through?' Michelle enquired a few minutes later.

'No,' Jackie sobbed wildly. 'Sorry about this.'

'It's a common reaction,' Michelle told her kindly. 'You'll identify with other sufferers, outcasts and failures for a while after your divorce.'

'Cheers.'

'And if nobody ever agrees to marry you again, and you end up alone and childless, I'll share the twins with you. You can be kind of their surrogate mother.'

Jackie was quite dry-eyed now, and unenthusiastic. It seemed like the whole house had been taken over by the twins. Babygros hung on every heater, and the whiff of smelly nappies rose from every bin in the place. And the nights! One twin would wake and bawl deliberately to wake the other. Then after they were fed and burped and put back down, which took at least an hour, they would then do a poo and their nappies would have to be changed, after which one of them would decide she was hungry again and the whole cycle would start over.

Michelle said, 'Give me some of that chocolate.'

'No.'

'Come on. The twins are drinking three thousand calories' worth of milk a day. I'm only a shadow of my former self. Have you seen my boobs recently?'

'Aren't we seeing them every two hours?'

'They're like two stones at the end of a couple of socks. I'll never be attractive to any man again.'

'I thought you said you didn't want a man.'

'I don't. Which is more than I can say for you.'

'I don't want one either,' Jackie said limply.

She had only gone and divorced the only one who had ever really mattered. Oh, well. She was sure she'd get over it, in a few years' time. Or at least in a few decades. And she always had his poetry to keep her warm at night. It wasn't all that bad when you thought about it.

Mr Ball bustled in. He was wearing one of Mrs Ball's aprons, and had a tea towel slung over his shoulder. If he just popped on one of her Alice bands, the transformation would be complete.

He had even cut down on his golf outings; he had got two holes-in-one recently, and he felt there was nowhere left to go. But everybody knew he just wanted to get back to the twins. Eamon over in the US had made a crack that Mr Ball had never shown as much interest in any of the rest of his grandchildren. But Mr Ball wasn't put out. Instead, he proudly showed off the new grey hairs that were springing from his temples, the result of worry, pure and simple, and took to reading *The Complete Guide to Terrible Childhood Illnesses*. And to think that Mrs Ball had kept all this to herself for the past forty years! She was a selfish woman, he often thought. Spain was too good for her.

'Sabrina won't settle,' he fretted to Michelle. 'And I think she's after pulling Jill's hair.'

'Dad, she's only five weeks old. She doesn't know yet that she has hands.'

'You can never start discipline too early,' Mr Ball advised, and followed her out of the room.

Mrs Ball was in Spain, on an inspection trip to the Place To Wither and Die. She had phoned last night to say that she had never felt more relaxed in all her life. And the retirement village was beautiful, and she'd be moving in next month just as soon as they installed the cardio resuscitation unit, which the insurance people had apparently insisted upon once they had seen the average age of the purchasers. Then she had fallen asleep in the middle of the phone call.

Everyone had a life plan, it seemed, except for Jackie. Everybody knew where he or she belonged, and with whom. Her family were moving away or staying put, but at least they had a purpose.

She, too, would get a plan, she knew. Because at the end of the day people survived. Monday, she decided. She would get a plan then. In the meantime she was allowed one day of misery and junk food and cheap wine before she had to muster all that energy again.

Thoughts of the cheap wine made her thirsty and she decided she would start drinking, even though it was only about three o'clock.

The doorbell rang. Go away, she thought. It was probably one of the local kids trying to fleece her for some 'sponsored walk'. Michelle had the right idea in making them produce ID, even the very young ones.

It rang again. Didn't they know she was nursing a broken heart?

'Michelle! Door!' she shouted. 'Dad?'

But the twins must be fighting again because nobody came. In the end, Jackie hauled herself up, muttering and cursing under her breath, and hitching up her outsize tracksuit bottoms. She'd get the bottle of wine on the way.

Thus armed, she swung by the front door. She hurled it open, and barked, 'What!'

Henry stood there. On her mother's doorstep. It was as if he had been beamed down from somewhere.

Her heart did a violent flop in her chest. She closed her eyes briefly, wondering whether it was a hallucination brought on by a sugar overload. But when she opened them again, he was still there.

She said, 'Henry?'

'Jackie?' He seemed very surprised to find her there. In fact he hardly seemed to recognise her. And she was suddenly acutely aware of her bad haircut, and her swollen eyes, courtesy of Dr Raymondo, and her outsize clothing, and the bottle of wine in her hand.

'It's me,' she said rather defensively.

'No, I know, it's just I didn't expect to find you here,' he explained. 'I just called by to ask your mother where you lived now.'

'Yes, well, I'm . . .' Then, not wanting to admit that she was temporarily back at home, the failed divorcée, she said, crisply, 'Just visiting.' At least that could explain the wine. But not why she was carrying only one glass.

And anyway, he had disimproved too, she was delighted to note. He had a scrawny beard, and he looked very scruffy, and he appeared to have on a pair of sandals. But he had the same voice. Same intense blue eyes, fixing onto hers. Making her colour rise. And her heart beat faster . . .

'So!' she said, rather breathlessly.

'So,' he said, very throatily.

And then he reached into his trouser pocket and began to root about. To get his phone or something? But no. It went on so long that it began to be a bit unseemly.

'Sorry,' he said, rooting more, and grimacing. Honestly.

'Would you like to visit the bathroom?' she enquired coolly. The drama of the moment was rapidly leaving her, and her heart slowed down. And she was glad. Because that was her great failing: her longing to make everything picture-book perfect, and life just wasn't.

'No, no,' he said.

Finally his hand emerged from his pocket. He held up something. 'This is yours.'

She squinted. 'What is it?'

'An earring.'

And indeed it was. With two dice swinging from it.

'You're . . . giving me back my earring?'

'Yes.'

'You came all the way over from London to give me an *earring*?' Not even one of the good gold ones that she had been missing, but some cheap costume jewellery that had gone beyond even her own boundaries of good taste.

'Yes,' he said. Then, he admitted, 'Well, actually, no. I was only using it as an excuse.'

'Oh!'

'I probably should have come up with something better, but I didn't really have time.'

'That's OK,' she found herself saying. Inside she was singing. He hadn't come just to give her back her crappy earring. He had come for . . . well, she didn't know yet. But *something*.

'Would you like to come in?' she asked, the temperature having warmed up considerably.

He hesitated. 'Is your whole family around?'

'No. Well, Mum's in Spain.'

'Well, in that case I might . . .'

But then a loud wail burst through the air. Sabrina. A second wail joined in. Jill. It sounded like they were being tortured.

'They're not . . . yours?' he asked.

'No,' she said politely. 'They're Michelle's.'

'Ah!' She thought he looked relieved but she couldn't be sure. 'I didn't know she'd got married.'

'She didn't.'

'Ah!' he said again

Then something struck her. He mightn't know yet. It might change things. Whatever he had come for. Which so far he was being very circumspect about. But she'd better tell him anyway.

'Henry, I divorced you this morning.'

'Yes. I know.'

'You know?'

'That's why I'm here.'

'Is there any way you might be more specific? It's just that it's getting a bit chilly, standing here.'

'Yes, sorry, of course.' And he looked away, very uncomfortable. And possibly a bit tortured? Definitely. Look at the way his jaw was tensing and relaxing like that! And his nostrils gave a tormented flare every now and again. He even attractively chewed his bottom lip in anguish. It would melt a stone!

But not Jackie. Not today. Not after everything.

She said, 'I've gone to all this bother of divorcing you, Henry. Which you have fought every step of the way. You've made my life miserable – in between writing me cryptic poems in the newspaper, of course. And now that I've finally managed to do it, finally managed to divorce you, you turn up on my doorstep and you're not even going to tell me why?'

'You're right,' he said, and took a breath.

The babies stopped wailing. A lawnmower in the garden next door stopped. Even the traffic out on the road seemed to slow in anticipation.

And Henry obviously felt the tremendous pressure building on him, because he began, 'Well, I . . .' He stopped, cleared his throat. 'I just wanted to . . .' Then he burst out, 'Oh, fuck it, I love you, Jackie!' Then he hurriedly retracted. 'Sorry. Sorry, I should have put that a bit better, especially me being a writer and everything, and now a poet too. I have to explain all that to you, it's not as romantic as it sounds, especially the money side of things and it's murder to get published. But I can see that right now you're thinking, there he goes, talking about himself again, self-centred prat, and so I'm going to stop now. And regroup.'

He did. And then he went on more slowly. 'You're probably wondering why I'm telling you now. Especially after everything. But then when I heard this morning that you'd split up from that gobshite — I mean from Dan, I thought, well, why not? Why not tell you that I still love you? The worst you can do is spit in my face and send me packing.' He left a little moment, in case she might want to do just that. But when she didn't he went on, 'And I wanted to say sorry. Sorry about the marriage. Sorry about the divorce.' He touched his chin. 'And sorry about the beard, obviously.'

'Oh, Henry.'

'So there you go.' He gave a little nervous laugh. 'I've probably made a total fool of myself here but I've done it. I've told you. And now the only thing I ask is the bus fare back up to the airport, if you could spare it,' he said humbly.

'No,' she said.

'You hate me *that* much?' He looked shocked.

'I don't hate you at all.' And the air was filled with that quivery thing again.

'This time, could you be a bit more specific?' he ventured.

'Stay,' she said. 'A while anyway.'

And she put her arms round him, bottle of wine and all.

Chapter Twenty-Five

In the end they drank it in Jackie's narrow single bed upstairs.

'My God,' Henry said. 'This is possibly the worst bottle of wine you've ever bought. And that's saying something.'

'You see? We're only back together five minutes and you've already slipped back into being a restaurant critic. Even though you *say* you've left it behind.'

'I have! I'm a poet now.'

'Prove it,' she said.

'What?'

'Compose me a poem right now.'

'I can't perform on demand.' Even though he just had. Twice. And very nice it had been too.

'Not even about drowning in the pools of my eyes, or something like that?' She was very disappointed. What was the point in hanging out with a poet unless they wooed you with rhyming couplets during lovemaking?

'You see, I knew you'd find all this desperately romantic,' he complained. 'And it's not really.'

'Oh, it is, it's wonderful! Much better than being a restaurant critic.'

'Really? Do you mean that?'

'Of course I do.'

'I thought you'd be desperately disappointed that I'd changed career.'

'Why?' She was incredulous. Surely he didn't think she missed all that stuff?

'Well, the life of a poet isn't all it's cracked up to be.' And he scratched his beard in a contemplative fashion. The beard would be the first thing to go, Jackie decided. She hadn't looked at it too closely so far in case she saw anything moving in it. The rest of him was pretty OK, though. Delicious, in fact. She kept wanting to rub herself up against him, like a dog. Which reminded her: she must ask him about Shirley once they had finished discussing poetry.

'What *is* it cracked up to be?' she asked. 'Does it involve lots of locking yourself away in the attic?' She didn't know if she could bear any more anguished mumbling through the ceiling. If, on the other hand, it was more a case of sipping white wine in a sunny back garden while he read her out little snippets of his latest poem in an amusing tone, then she would definitely be up for it.

He warned her, 'I've had to give up a lot of things, Jackie. A great job, for starters. My superficial friends. Well, they gave me up, really. And all the freebies and the openings and the parties.'

'I hated all that anyway,' she said, with wonderful carelessness.

'And the house and the money and the car.'

OK, that was slightly more ominous. 'You've lost your car?'

'But I have a bike now. It's quite nice, it's red. And it's got a bell.'

He sounded a bit like Noddy, and she looked at him, wondering was he a little unhinged. But he seemed quite sane. And calm and, well, happy. Not a bit like the old, volatile Henry who would take the head off you as soon as look at you.

'Are you serious about all this?' she asked.

'Yes. I lead a very simple life now, Jackie. No parties or any of that kind of thing. No trips to large shopping complexes.' At that, he looked at her meaningfully. 'Occasionally I go down to the pub for a half lager on a Sunday afternoon but that's about it.'

Obviously he felt it necessary to spell out to her that his life was now strictly non-glam. And she got quite offended. Did he think she lived solely to shop and party? That she was as superficial as that? She'd only gone along with all that stuff because it was part of his career!

She was so cross that she'd have moved away a little from him in the bed except that the damn thing was so small she'd have fallen out. And then he would see how much her bottom had grown since he'd seen her last. Best to stay put.

He picked up on her resentment. 'I told you that being a poet wasn't all that glamorous or romantic.'

'Good!' she said stoutly. 'Because I've *had* the glamour and romance thing with you, and frankly, it wasn't enough!'

'Really?' He looked quite offended now, and she was glad.

'Not nearly enough! I would much rather have a husband who was around for me, who was fully present, rather than a semi-famous one who took me out to parties occasionally.'

He was in a right old huff now. 'I didn't hear you complaining at the time!'

'That's because you never listened to me,' she told him smartly. 'You were too busy hiding things from me, Henry. Going up into the attic and shutting me out.'

He hauled himself up on one elbow, the better to look at her. 'Jackie, we'd just got married. How was I supposed to tell you that I was a big, fat fake?'

'And how was I supposed to know what was eating you unless you told me? I thought it was *me*! That you regretted ever marrying me.'

'I'm sorry, Jackie.'

'I don't want any more secrets between us.'

'All right. Anyway, there aren't any more. Just the poetry thing. I don't secretly make pottery as well.'

'I mean it, Henry.'

'I know. I don't want any more secrets either. Let's be totally open to each other. About everything! Well, to a certain degree. I don't want to know every single thing you get up to in the bathroom, for example.'

They'd talked enough about him, she felt, and anyway, she had been saving the next bit up and dying to announce it. 'I've been making my own changes in the last while too, you know. In fact, I've just opened my second branch!'

'I know,' he said.

That took the wind out of her sails somewhat. Luckily she had something else to fall back on. 'And in one of the local newspapers, Flower Power was described as *the* funeral wreath specialists in the whole of North Dublin!'

'Wow,' said Henry.

'Shut up,' she said.

'Hey, Jackie, come on.'

'Don't laugh at me.' And she poked him sharply in the chest. He was surprised. 'I've worked hard for this, Henry. I would have done it years ago except I trotted over to London after you. And I've made a success of it. So you'd better develop a healthy respect for flowers, OK?'

'OK,' he said meekly.

She wasn't finished there. 'As well as send me a few bunches every now and again, of course. You needn't think you can bury yourself away working, just throwing me the odd poem every now and again to keep me happy. Because that's not enough for me any more.'

'Just so long as you don't expect me to go around brooding all the time,' he complained. 'It gives me migraines.'

Then she thought of something. 'I've just realised! We can get married all over again.'

'I've just been talking to the wall,' Henry commented loudly.

Then she got embarrassed. Perhaps that was being a bit presumptuous. 'That's if you, we, both of us, wanted to, that is.'

He left a very long pause, probably just to rile her, before saying, 'Nothing would make me happier.'

'Oh, Henry!'

'Except if we hadn't got divorced in the first place, of course.'

'Yes, well, that can't be helped.' Already her mind was racing ahead as she mentally planned wedding number three.

'When did you sign that document?' he asked suddenly. 'This morning, wasn't it?'

'Yes.'

'And what time is it now?'

'I don't know. About six . . . Henry, where are you going?'

He was out of bed in a flash and pulling on his clothes.

'Give me a rough idea of where Velma's office is.'

'What? Have you gone mad? Anyway, she'll already have posted it on her way home.'

'Exactly,' he said.

'Henry, please tell me what you're up to.'

'Trust me,' he said. 'I'll be back in an hour.'

★

'I hope he's not leading you up the garden path again, Jackie,' Mrs Ball fretted. She was just back from Spain, and was lightly tanned from eighteen straight hours by the pool. She wore a stylish sundress and looked remarkably relaxed. The taxi driver who had delivered her back had given her such a long look that Mr Ball had stepped forward aggressively in his apron.

'In what way might he be leading me up the garden path?' Jackie enquired sunnily. Nothing could touch her today. She felt she was floating somewhere up around the ceiling, buoyed up by pure happiness. She and Henry were together again. That was all that mattered.

Mrs Ball looked at Mr Ball meaningfully. He cleared his throat hurriedly and said, 'Your mother is right. It's all very well him making a big dramatic flight over here, and the pair of you wrecking that bed up there, but what are your *plans*?'

Going back to bed together, Jackie thought, just as soon as he was back from his errand, whatever it was. And staying there for the whole weekend, talking dirty. Or possibly they should check into a hotel. That way they could get reacquainted properly without the scrutiny of her family.

There they were, watching now, waiting. Even the twins.

'I don't know what our exact plans are right now,' Jackie told them firmly. 'Isn't it enough that we're back together again? I thought you'd all be delighted!'

'We are,' Mrs Ball assured her. She couldn't resist adding, 'But naturally, we're worried.'

'Why, Mum?'

'A month ago you wanted to boil his head.'

'Everything has changed now,' Jackie said grandly. 'It was all a misunderstanding.'

'Yes, but *what* was? At this stage, there have been so many.'

Jackie felt slightly defensive now. 'For starters, he's out of that London scene totally. We're going to have a normal life together, just two regular people.' It sounded so lovely that she wanted to pack her bags right now.

'Where?' Mrs Ball said.

'All that has to be decided,' Jackie told her. 'Naturally, we have a lot of talking to do. But we're not the same people we were two years ago. I'm a businesswoman now. He's a poet.'

Mr Ball, with his newly developed sense of worry, weighed in now. 'I don't like the sound of that at all. I mean, what does being a poet actually mean?'

'It means he writes poetry, Dad.'

'He won't last long,' Mr Ball came back decisively. 'No offence, but we always said he had a giant ego. How is he going to manage without that big job of his?'

'Good, Larry,' Mrs Ball murmured in approval.

'He *is* managing,' said Jackie impatiently. 'He's managed for four months now. He didn't give everything up on a whim to write poetry and ride around on a red bike, and be stony broke.'

A little silence fell over the room.

'He's stony broke?' Mr Ball eventually enquired.

'He rides a red *bike*?' Michelle said.

Jackie tried to keep her frustration down. 'The point is that he's made his decision. And I'm delighted! And I don't care if we're broke!'

'She won't last long either,' Mr Ball commented to Mrs Ball. 'Nothing kills romance quicker than the lack of funds to buy shoes.' He was starting to sound like her now.

'I can buy my own shoes!' Jackie retorted. Why were they all being so cynical? So down on Henry? 'None of you liked him the way he was two years ago,' she said loudly. 'And now he's changed completely and that won't do any of you either!'

'Actually, I think he sounds pretty cool now,' Michelle said. 'And I've always had a thing for beardy guys. Well, for any guy, really.'

'Thank you!' Jackie said, deciding to take it as a compliment.

'And so long as things really have changed, then I say good luck to you,' she finished up.

But Jackie fancied there was a tiny smidgen of doubt in Michelle's voice. As though she couldn't quite believe Henry's transformation.

Well, it was pretty dramatic: from celeb restaurant critic to obscure penniless poet. But he insisted he was happy. That he didn't want to go back to all that. Why couldn't everybody take his word for it?

They seemed to doubt her too; that she really had taken her head out of the clouds and was going at this in a clear-eyed fashion instead of her usual enthusiastic gallop.

Mrs Ball yawned. The stress of the situation was starting to tell on her. 'So long as you're sure you're doing the right thing, Jackie.'

'Your confidence in me is overwhelming,' Jackie said.

'And where's he gone anyway?' Mr Ball demanded.

'I don't know,' Jackie had to admit.

'You don't *know*?'

'No. He had . . . something to do.'

'This is not a good start.' Mr Ball tutted. 'You're only back together a couple of hours and already he's not being upfront with you. I thought you said he had promised that there would be no more secrets from now on.'

Beside him, Mrs Ball nodded vigorously, backing him up.

Why didn't everybody just grab a bucket of cold water and fling it over her right now!

'He mightn't even come back,' Mr Ball added. 'Now that he's got what he wanted.'

That was the final straw. 'I can't believe you just said that.'

Mrs Ball stepped in to rescue him; worry had united them in a way that forty-plus years of marriage never could. She shouted, 'Phone! Phone! There's a phone ringing somewhere!'

There was. But it wasn't the house phone, and then everybody hunted for their mobiles, and finally Mrs Ball pointed to the ceiling.

'It's coming from your bedroom, Jackie.'

She eventually found it under the pink nylon sheets of her bed. It was Henry's phone. He had left it behind in his dash to God knows where.

She answered it before she had time to think about it. Well, they were back together now. And anyway, it might be him, saying that he was lost or something, or had been knocked down by bus. Please God, no, she implored; they'd only just found each other again.

'Hello?' she gulped into the phone.

At the other end, a woman said crisply, 'Henry, is that you?'

'No,' Jackie said. How could anybody mistake her bat-like voice for Henry's? 'He's not available at the moment.'

'Oh.' The caller immediately seemed to lose interest. 'Tell him I rang. This is Adrienne, his agent.'

'And this is Jackie,' she said back. She refused to be treated like a secretary. 'His wife.' There was no sense in mentioning 'ex'. It would only dilute her authority.

But Adrienne said, 'I thought you two got divorced ages ago?'

Jackie retaliated, 'And I thought you were no longer representing him?'

Or so Henry had told her not an hour ago in this very bed. But for someone who had apparently been fired months ago, Adrienne was pretty well up on his private life.

Adrienne obviously sensed there was nothing to be gained by riling the wife, or ex-wife, and so she said chummily, 'I've got very big news for him. The best!' Then, unable to contain herself, and oblivious to client confidentiality, she burst out, 'Tell him the TV deal has finally come through.'

'What TV deal?'

'He probably didn't want to tell you about it himself until we got the green light. But I've been chasing it for weeks and weeks now and they've finally said yes! It's provisionally slotted in for eight half-hour programmes and they're going with *Henry Hart's Square Meal*.'

'What?'

'I know, I know, it's a bit of a mouthful. I'd have preferred something like *Henry Bites* – so much more evil, but Nigella would probably have a fit – but at the same time I suppose it does have a certain tabloid feel. And let's face it, Henry does have the common touch. And so photogenic! I always said he was wasted in that newspaper. Now we'll have him thrashing restaurants on our TV screens!'

'It all sounds very interesting.' Actually, she thought it sounded appalling. 'But I think you'll find he's out of all that now.' She hated the way she sounded: the little wife trying to protect hubby from his own success.

'Don't tell me he's still in his poet phase?' Adrienne gave a sigh. 'I thought that was wearing off. And he had such a marvellous time at his book launch. It's number two this week, tell him, that's what swung the TV people in the end.' She paused. 'I don't think I saw you at the launch.'

'That's because I wasn't there,' Jackie said flatly.

'Anyway, maybe you'd get him to call me. This is all very urgent. He'll have to clear his whole schedule, which shouldn't be difficult, as filming starts next month. They're starting up north and working down through the Midlands and ending up in London, where he'll give some of Britain's most famous restaurants a good kicking.' She finished up breathlessly, 'You must be very proud.'

Jackie was confused. 'Of you?'

'No, no, of Henry. Let's be honest here, he's made some terrible career choices in the last while. But I think he's starting to realise it. Oh, he's going to jump at this one!'

'I really don't think—'

'There's my doorbell, I have to run. I presume you'll come over with him, won't you? See you then!' And she rang off.

Henry skipped along in his sandals, humming a little tune under his breath. He wasn't sure exactly what the tune was for a moment, and then it came to him: 'Love Is All Around', by Wet Wet Wet. He had always thought that it was very possibly the most odious song every written or recorded, the kind of song that was only good to sell chocolates and cheap champagne. It was only now that he fully understood the song's beauty and significance: now that he had got back together with Jackie.

And love *was* all around, he thought dramatically. He had just been too miserable to appreciate it. Too busy looking at his own belly button to think there might actually be a happy ending to all this!

Henry had never really believed in happy endings. Not even as a child; but then again he had been a peculiarly miserable child, always moping around with his long dark hair flopping into his eyes, convinced that the world was out to get him. For him, everything was a flawed compromise; for instance, you either got married to someone you weren't sure you liked, or else you stayed single, which meant spending your life with someone you definitely didn't like. Happiness came in tiny little bursts that you had to snatch very quickly, and it never lasted long anyway.

And look at him now! Fulfilled in every way: his sugary verses on thousands of greetings cards, and an afternoon spent drinking crap wine with the woman of his dreams. Life was good, he thought mistily.

In his jeans pocket was an envelope addressed in Velma Murphy's appalling handwriting to the British Courts Service. He'd had to tear it open to be sure it was the right one. Naturally, he had done that around the corner, when he'd regained his breath after snatching it from the postman and running away at full pelt. Everything had gone to plan, just like the last time, except that the postman had suddenly given chase, which Henry hadn't expected. He had almost caught him too, except that Henry had cunningly wriggled out of his jacket, which the postman had grabbed hold of, and dashed off across the road in his T-shirt in front of a very surprised crowd waiting for a bus.

He was bloody freezing now. And that jacket was his good one. He wondered could he write into the post office's lost property service and ask for it back.

Still, the important thing was that legally, Jackie and he were still husband and wife. When he got back to the house, they would make a little ceremony of tearing her application up, and maybe burning it or something, and then have mad sex.

He couldn't wait to tell Dave and Dawn. They'd be delighted for him – after they had stopped being furious over the way he'd skipped out on them today, of course. He wondered now how the move had gone. Not that he cared, really. He wouldn't be going to live in that sterile new apartment after all. He and Jackie would build a proper home, and Shirley would be delighted to finally be living with someone she liked, and they would all be happy ever after.

He was nearing the house now and he felt for the envelope in his pocket again, just to be sure that it was there. He couldn't wait to see her face when he produced it. And there she was! At the front door, with her hair all in a big, frizzy heap. He probably had something to do with that, he thought bashfully.

Again he thought how lucky he was that things had turned out this way; they had both found each other again after all this time. It only happened in novels, or, sometimes, in his own poetry.

He gave her a big grin and wave. She didn't grin back. Then he saw that she had her arms folded over her chest, combatively. And then her mother (wasn't she supposed to be in Spain?) stepped up behind her. She looked rather aggressive too, though about ten years younger than when he last saw her. He could see Michelle hovering in the background, holding a whole clatter of babies, or at least two, and she gave him a kind of warning look.

But Henry knew conclusively that he was in trouble when Mr Ball appeared on the doorstep too. It would take a great deal to stir Mr Ball to any kind of action. And he had a great big drill in his hand, and he. was pointing it in Henry's direction. Thankfully, Henry heard Jackie say, 'Oh, put it down, Dad.'

'I will not,' he said stoutly.

Henry stopped at a safe distance, and called, 'What is it? What's going on?'

'Well, if it isn't Gordon Ramsay himself!' Mr Ball said.

Henry thought he heard Mrs Ball titter.

'Gordon Ramsay is a chef, Dad,' Jackie told him crossly. 'Not a critic.'

'He's still on the telly, isn't he?' Mr Ball retaliated. 'Using terrible language.' He said to Henry accusingly, 'Which I suppose you'll be doing too. Oh, it'll be effing this and effing that, and your ratings will no doubt go through the roof! I knew the poetry thing was only a ruse. To soft-soap our Jackie into thinking you'd changed.'

'Dad, could you just leave it, please?' Jackie said.

'You hadn't at all! You were just after your own reality TV show!'

At that, Mrs Ball put her arm cosily around Mr Ball. He seemed to grow about six inches.

Henry felt at a distinct disadvantage. He was well used to the Ball family hating him, but usually he knew why. 'Jackie, what is he talking about?'

'Adrienne rang,' she said. Coldly. Accusingly. What was he supposed to have done now?

'So?'

'So?' Jackie spluttered.

'I would just urge you both to think of the money before you make any rash decisions,' Michelle interjected from the back.

'Will someone tell me what's going on?' Henry demanded.

In the end she suggested to him that they go and sit in her car. It was the only way they would get some privacy. To be on the safe side she locked all the doors in case either of her parents decided to join them.

He was still remarkably cool and calm about the whole thing. While she, of course, was all worked up and red in the face. Not a single thing had changed!

Very precisely, she told Henry about Adrienne and the reality TV show, of which he, apparently, would be the star.

'Oh,' he said.

Like he knew all along! For all his talk. 'You don't seem that surprised.'

'I'm not,' he confessed. 'She's been going on about it for a while. I can't believe she's actually pulled it off, though.' And he shook his head in mild wonder.

Jackie grew even more rigid in her seat. 'I'm not going with you, Henry.'

'What?'

'I've made up my mind, OK? Nothing you say is going to change it. Because it would just be a disaster. I'd be doing exactly what I did two years ago, only this time I'd have even more to give up! Do you know how much I owe the bank?' she demanded.

'A lot?' he guessed.

'More than a lot! But, you know, I'm glad, Henry. Delighted that I'm up to my ears in debt. Because every cent interest I pay back to them is a measure of my achievements!' She could see she was losing him. She checked herself, and flicked away a crumb of chocolate – she'd had to finish off the Cadbury's after the shock of Adrienne's phone call. 'And I'm not giving up my two branches to follow you from Manchester down to Sheffield to . . . to . . .'

'Birmingham?'

'Exactly!'

'Although you'd like the curries there. Best in the world.'

'Well, yes . . .' She did like a good curry. 'You see? Already you're trying to persuade me. Thinking that I'll jack it all in for a good curry and a shag, not to put too fine a point on it!'

'Indeed,' Henry agreed.

'Not this time, Henry. I'm not going to orbit round you any more. Those days are over. And anyway, you wouldn't want me to do that. You'd be calling me needy and demanding, and the next thing you know, we'd be breaking up all over again.'

'I agree,' Henry said.

'What?'

'You've laid out the whole thing very precisely.' She hadn't quite expected that he would agree so whole-heartedly with her. She had expected that he might put up a bit of a fight. In fact, after the afternoon they'd just had, all that passionate lovemaking and promises, it was the very least he could do. Instead of just sitting there like it was all over, once again, and he didn't mind a bit!

She reached forward and started the engine.

'What are you doing?'

'Driving you to the airport.' She added automatically, 'Put on your seatbelt.'

'Jackie, I don't want to go to the airport.'

'Tough.' She said it rudely to conceal her upset. She couldn't believe it was turning out this way. The next time she got divorced, she decided grimly, she would do it properly.

'Wait,' he said. 'I've something to give you.'

But she didn't turn off the engine. She left it running and waited impatiently while he rooted in his trouser pocket again. And where had his jacket gone?

'I got this for you. Well, for us.'

It was a torn envelope. When she made no move to fall upon it in delight, which he seemed to be expecting, he took out the contents himself.

'Your application for the decree absolute. I got it back. Don't ask how, but there it is.'

Jackie looked at it, and then looked away. 'Better get a new envelope for it then, and send it off.'

'Jackie!'

'Don't Jackie me! Go home to Adrienne and your career.'

'Don't make me, I can't stand her, I keep firing her and she keeps coming back. It's like a bad dream.'

'Don't joke with me, Henry.'

'I'm not. I'm not doing the TV thing, Jackie. For God's sake. You think I'd be lured by the prospect of millions of viewers and loads of cash?'

'Michelle has urged us both to go for it. Even if it costs us our marriage,' Jackie admitted.

'Yes, but she's always been shallow,' Henry argued. 'Us, we're less shallow. We know what's important.'

'Do we?' Jackie said.

'Yes. And maybe you could turn the engine off before we get carbon monoxide poisoning?'

She did.

'So you don't want to give everything up for me and go to Birmingham?' Henry said.

'No.'

'Good. Because I was actually thinking of giving everything up for *you* and moving here.'

'But you don't *have* anything.' She was smiling now. 'Except Shirley. How is she anyway?'

'Fine.' He sounded cagey.

'Henry, what have you done with her?'

'Nothing! She's safely in the kennels.'

'She hates the kennels. You know that.'

'I'm talking about selflessly moving over here and all you're worried about is the dog.'

'We have to include her in our plans.'

'Why do you always have to talk about her like she's a real person?'

Somehow they had ended up entwined over the gear stick, even though she couldn't be sure who had made the first move.

Probably her, don't you know.

'You think we could end up divorcing each other again?' she asked.

'I don't know,' he admitted. 'But it'll be fun finding out.'